Praise for Draw Blood

"I absolutely love the *Blood* saga – it's gripping, raw, and inventive. *Draw Blood* is a real nail-biter of a zombie novel that will delight die-hard fans and draw legions of new ones to the genre. Thumbs up!"
– Jonathan Maberry, *New York Times* bestselling author of *Rot & Ruin* and *Code Zero*

"*Draw Blood* launches itself at you with relentless terror from the first page to the last. Bovberg, a master of tension, keeps the action taut and breathless, driving the story forward with a combination of excruciating dread and linguistic majesty. In the second book of the series, he reaches new heights and reminds us that we are in the middle of a zombie epic for the new century."
– Alden Bell, author of *The Reapers Are the Angels* and *Exit Kingdom*

"*Draw Blood* is a terrific sequel, propelling the story forward with singular intensity – and a great twist."
– Craig DiLouie, author of *Suffer the Children*

"In *Draw Blood*, Jason Bovberg attains a new level of mastery, guiding us with assurance and control into the finely etched, moment-by-moment travails of his characters without once relaxing the tension. The mutating dangers they face leave us and them in the dark as to when or if a next attack will occur. Their fear and uncertainty become ours. The central father-daughter relationship is nurtured with care through its many changes, anchoring a strong cast of characters vividly portrayed. The story arc is both whole in itself and a natural lead-in to the upcoming final book of the trilogy. *Draw Blood* deserves the widest readership possible and consideration for top awards. This one's a keeper!"
– Robert Devereaux, author of *Deadweight* and *Santa Steps Out*

"Jason Bovberg one-ups himself with *Draw Blood* – this menagerie of grotesqueries is a faster, bloodier, and even more demented thrill ride. The third book of the *Blood* trilogy can't get here fast enough."
– Grant Jerkins, author of *Done in One* and *A Very Simple Crime*

"*Draw Blood* combines the best things about the *Autumn* series, *Invasion of the Body Snatchers*, and *Night of the Living Dead* into one coherent tale. If you liked *Blood Red*, *Draw Blood* will definitely not let you down."
– Robert Beveridge, former Top 50 Amazon reviewer

"*Draw Blood* starts off firing on all cylinders and never lets up. It's a fresh take with all the best elements of the genre."
– David Dunwoody, author of *Empire* and *The Harvest Cycle*

Praise for Blood Red

"An epic addition to the genre, *Blood Red* delivers a nonstop, real-time experience of the End Times – replete with visceral terror, buckets of gore, and, ultimately, a redemptive humanity."
– Alden Bell, author of *The Reapers Are the Angels* and *Exit Kingdom*

"Jason Bovberg proves he's got the goods with a whole new kind of horror novel."
– Tom Piccirilli, author of *The Last Whisper in the Dark* and *The Last Kind Words*

"With *Blood Red*, Jason Bovberg infuses a post-apocalyptic tale with a sustained sense of genuine mystery; of having no idea what's happening to the world and the people around you, or why."
– Brian Hodge, author of *Whom the Gods Would Destroy* and *Dark Advent*

"The *Blood* trilogy is must-read zombie fiction – familiar enough to keep you glued to the action, innovative enough to keep you guessing."
– Craig DiLouie, author of *Suffer the Children*

"Guaranteed to creep you out!"
– Robert Devereaux, author of *Deadweight* and *Santa Steps Out*

"You've been to the end of the world before, but never quite like this."
– Richard Lee Byers, author of *Blind God's Bluff* and *The Reaver: The Sundering Book IV*

"Jason Bovberg's *Blood Red* is unlike anything I've ever experienced. It starts as a slow-burn freak-out and culminates in a series of horror-show set pieces that will forever be etched in my mind. This book made my skin crawl."
– Grant Jerkins, author of *A Very Simple Crime* and *The Ninth Step*

"*Blood Red* is a tour de f***ed-up!"
– Peter Stenson, author of *Fiend*

DRAW BLOOD

BOOK II

JASON BOVBERG

A DARK HIGHWAY PRESS book
published by arrangement with the author

ISBN (trade paperback): 978-0-9662629-2-6
ISBN (eBook): 978-0-9662629-3-3

Edited by Lisa Péré
Cover art and design by Christopher Nowell
Layout by Kirk Whitham

To my mom, Brenda
Moms don't fare so well in these wild, gruesome books,
but you fare exceedingly well in this author's blood-red heart

CHAPTER 1

"Daddy!"

Michael hurtles into consciousness, disoriented. There's a cramping pain in his skull, as if the area above and behind his right eye is gripped in the fist of some sadistic villain. He tries to clutch his hands to his head, only to find that his arms are tucked beneath the starched sheet of a wheeled hospital bed. After a moment of clanging panic, he manages to free his arms and cradles his temple, groaning softly.

"Rachel?" he calls, his voice hoarse.

Where is she? Did she call to him? He's sure that was his daughter's voice, pitched high in anger.

Wait. Anger? Or fear?

He breathes deeply, forcing the anxiety to subside. His exhalations sigh back at him, echoing off white walls in the room's heavy silence.

His next thought is about the money.

I've been caught.

But when? Where? How?

He curses inwardly, wondering whether Susanna and Rachel already know. Of course they know.

He calls out his daughter's name again.

Nothing.

He tries flexing the muscles of his extremities, moving his body under the sheet, searching carefully for injury. He feels no cast or splint, and there are only minor aches here and there. But wait – a bandage has been wrapped around his head. Sweat is seeping from underneath it.

It's hot in here. Why isn't the AC on?

With some investigation, he discovers a sizable knot high on his forehead. Behind that knot, the pain continues, dull but insistent.

Michael can't help but imagine that the knot was caused by a police officer's baton, or the butt of a pistol. Wouldn't that be something? He imagines employees showing up at his office, coffees in hand, to witness his dramatic scuffle with the cops. It's something he's imagined too many times.

It was Michael? they'd whisper, shaken. *You're kidding!*

He tries to recall his most recent memory, but everything in his skull is shrouded in red fog. His thoughts – even these are painful – open out onto an alarming emptiness. He searches back for yesterday, the day before that, the day before that, but there's nothing he can grab on to, only a jumble of fractured imagery and sound.

Rachel calling to him, Susanna in bed, snippets of conversation at his office, driving the early-morning streets ... some kind of blast?

What's that? A suggestion of violence? Something like a – a peal of thunder? It's maddeningly elusive, and when he focuses harder on clarifying the memory, his head clamps down on his efforts.

Fragments of memory jerk through his skull, of Rachel yelling at him, of her tears, her teen rage. The seething détente between her and Susanna. Yes, *there's* a recollection that isn't tough to conjure. It's the sad reality of his life. But this is something else.

Isn't it?

Michael blinks his eyes, trying to clear them, to sharpen his awareness, to rid his mind of this weird sluggishness. He shakes his head a little, instantly regretting the movement. Something feels loose in there, something out of true. After several moments, he's able to focus his eyes from out of the new pain.

"Wait a minute," he whispers. "Where the hell am I?"

Although he's atop some kind of complicated metal hospital bed, he seems to have been wheeled into an administrator's office – not an examination room. There's no medical machinery surrounding him, no computer systems monitoring his health ... not even a blood-pressure cuff. There's a desk with a silent computer and bookshelves crammed with medical texts, and there are pharmaceutical posters all over the walls.

He has the distinct impression that this room was hastily abandoned at some point. The wheeled office chair behind the desk has been flung back against the small, shaded window, and there are papers on the floor beneath it. This is almost certainly a hospital, but it's hot and humid and soured by the smell of something rotting – definitely not the usual cool antiseptic odor – and the cloying scent of smoke.

This isn't about the money at all, he realizes with a dark hope.

Something, somewhere, is burning. He doesn't sense immediate fire danger, but it's close. Too close for comfort.

His gaze moves to the floor on the other side of the room – and locks on the bloody footprints there, leading from his bed to the closed door.

Michael's heart is hammering in his chest.

He attempts to lurch up from the bed and search the area further, but his skull won't allow it. When he half-rises, the lump on his forehead seems to expand and screech. He clutches his temples again, stops moving, but he can't keep his squinting eyes off the blood, and now he sees more of it, in handprints on the sheets. There's blood all around him. Michael feels helpless fear rising through the center of his chest like a cold spike. A droplet of sweat finds his wide-open eye, stinging it, and he swipes at it, blinking hard.

Blood has soaked into the sheets and dried. This isn't his blood, is it? He can't feel a wound. On the floor, the footprints are also mostly dried, but they remain tacky in spots. Whatever happened here happened mere hours ago. Perhaps minutes.

Regardless of its source, why hasn't this been cleaned up?

He considers calling out again, then decides that might be a bad idea. *Not yet.*

He tries to piece things together in his mind, even though he's having trouble concentrating. The very act of concentrating brings on fresh misery. He feels as if the screaming pain in his head wants to yank him back into unconsciousness, but another part of him is flailing for answers and clarity. His body moves restlessly.

At that moment, a clank sounds above him – a metallic clatter, followed by something dragging. Michael flinches and glares upward. The loudness of the prolonged scrape only clarifies the haunting silence of the rest of the hospital. He hears no movement outside his door, no activity in the near distance, no voices. He doesn't even hear any traffic noise outside the window beyond the desk, and yet it's broad daylight. Assuming this is actually a hospital, why is it so deathly quiet?

Is this some kind of revenge?

He feels a sudden cold calm take hold of his veins. Are his employers capable of savagery? Locking him up behind soundproof walls for the purposes of some kind of torture? He laughs nervously for a moment, trying to dismiss the notion.

Is he here to be punished?

He would return the money. He would gladly return it – with interest. Perhaps, afraid of bad publicity, they would even keep the whole thing quiet. Michael was never the ringleader anyway. That was undeniably Steven. He doesn't have a paper trail proving that, but come on. Just look at the guy.

Above him, the dragging stops for a moment, then continues.

"Christ, what is that?" he can't help but whisper.

Michael experiences a difficult moment in which he can't even remember waking up minutes ago. He feels adrift in his own consciousness. Maybe this is some trauma-induced dream. He desperately needs to establish some kind of foundation for whatever reality he's found himself in.

He shuts his eyes and thinks of Susanna. Sees her face, smiling. Beckoning him. He locks onto her, begging his brain to hang on to one thought.

His wife.

She should be here. Where is she? Why isn't she here, next to him? The unanswered questions fill him with dread. But perhaps she *was* here, and she had to leave. For whatever reason.

Perhaps she was forced to leave.

And Rachel, too.

Rachel.

Here, now, are some memories. Last night?

There was another blowout, wasn't there? A blowout culminating with Rachel angrily dropping into the passenger seat of Tony's Subaru and high-tailing it away, her spiteful words still echoing throughout the house. Susanna shrugging, having already given up on her stepdaughter months ago.

Did something happen after that? Could his injury have possibly resulted from a domestic squabble?

God, he hopes not. But it's possible. Tony can be volatile when he's worked up. He's sometimes startlingly defensive about Rachel's positions on matters that should remain private, that should remain between the walls of their home. Michael has never seen him get physically violent, but yes. It's *possible* that this is all the result of something at home and doesn't involve work at all.

Damn it, it's possible.

Rachel and Susanna have never been close – far from it – and that's been a source of frustration for all of them. Michael has felt tension, regret, and sadness in equal measures over time, above all wishing that he'd introduced Susanna into their home in a different way. Now he can't even remember the specific cause of last night's argument – only that his reaction to Rachel's behavior was probably careless. Too many nights, he has skulked off to bed, having missed an opportunity to reconnect with her, to start mending bridges.

He pinches the fingers of his right hand against the bridge of his nose, while using his left hand to cradle his forehead.

Things have changed. Things are different for Rachel. But, damn it, it's time for her to grow up. He loved her mom as much as she did, but she's gone. Has been gone for years. That's not Susanna's fault. Still, he can't deny that ever since he brought Susanna home after the Christmas party at work two years ago, Rachel has drifted. His beautiful girl, with whom he became so close after Cassie's death, is all but gone to him now, on the verge of leaving their home with her born-of-convenience boyfriend to begin her own life. Michael lies awake some nights, Susanna nestled against him, his thoughts locked on the notion that Rachel will hate him forever.

Michael deflates at these memories.

But his breathing has calmed, and his heart has stopped threatening to leap from his chest. His hands fall to the bed.

Nobody knows about the money. He repeats the words in his head, forcefully. *That's not it. Nobody knows about the money.*

Another metallic rattle sounds from above the ceiling, and he flinches again.

Then he hears something like far-off firecrackers.

So much for calm.

"Okay," he says to the empty room, "what the hell is that?" Against his better judgment, he puts some force behind his voice, calling, "Anyone out there?!"

No response.

"Hello?" he tries, before the pain of his injury shuts his mouth down. He grits his teeth, waits for the pain to subside.

I need to get out of here.

Being careful to keep his head steady, he maneuvers the bed sheets off himself, finds that he's still in his work clothes from this morning.

He remembers putting these clothes on. Doesn't he? Is that a real memory or something cobbled from past memories? Can he really pin it to this morning? He doesn't know. But why is he fully clothed in a hospital bed? And why are his shoes still on?

What kind of half-assed operation …?

He edges his legs off the side of the bed, letting gravity take them. He experiences a strong wave of nauseating vertigo until his feet hit the sticky floor, and then he stays planted there for a full minute while his inner ear rebalances and focus returns to his vision.

His eyes catch on the doorknob's lock, which appears to be engaged from the inside. The knob itself is smeared with dried blood. He stares at this conundrum for a full minute without moving. His breath comes in heavy inhalations while his heart thuds. One hand is locked on his forehead again, as if to keep his brain from leaking out of the wound.

Feeling it imperative now that he remain quiet, he begins shuffling toward the window, very carefully, his shoes making loud sticky sounds on the bloody floor. The imbalance doesn't completely go away, and his steps are unsure. He's almost certain he shouldn't be walking. If this were any normal kind of hospital situation, some doctor or nurse would be reprimanding him to get back in bed.

But this is far from a normal situation.

Too many questions are forming themselves in his injured mind, demanding answers, and he's more than a little reluctant to discover those answers.

As he makes his way gingerly past the big desk, he sees a complicated-looking phone next to the dark computer, and so he goes to that first. He doesn't want to sit in the office chair, because he thinks he might end up just staying there, unable to lift himself out of it. He leans against the desk and picks up the receiver, places it against his ear. There's no dial tone. He punches some buttons, but there's nothing. The digital readout is blank. He drops the receiver back into its cradle.

"Great."

He gets past the desk and makes it to the window, despite the fact that his skull feels cleaved. He feels that if he were to take his hand away, the bone would crumble to the floor in shards. He reaches up his other hand to lift the blinds, and the muted brightness is enough to nearly blind him. It's a flare of searing pain right in the center of his brain. After some moments, he can open his eyes again into slits.

The world is on fire.

"Holy ...!" he manages.

For as long as he's lived in northern Colorado, he has never seen a wildfire like this. Above the homes in the immediate foreground, the horizon is choked with thick white and black smoke, urgent and roiling, and there appears to be multiple zones to the fire, dotting the length of the Front Range. But the largest conflagration is the closest, rising over Horsetooth Rock and reaching across the sky to the north. It is a towering, humbling sight, and it has the ominous dread of apocalypse. Michael knows that if he were outside right now, he would have trouble breathing. Tiny particles of ash are floating down like gray snow.

Somewhere in the midst of his shock, he wonders if those fires are the reason everything is so quiet. Has the entire city been evacuated? *Impossible!*

Even an out-of-control blaze wouldn't be able to cross from the mountains and foothills into the city.

Would it?

He brings his gaze lower and scans the immediate vicinity. He recognizes Lemay Avenue, and that tells him that, yes, he's at Poudre

Valley Hospital. He's about two miles from home. But that thought wisps away as he comes to the realization that there are no moving cars, no people, on the street. No activity. He keeps waiting for a vehicle to round the corner, or a bicyclist, or a pedestrian. He peers as far south down Lemay as his head will allow, then does the same to the north.

There's nothing.

Gotta be an evacuation, then. Amazing.

Several parked cars aren't actually parked but rather jammed up against the curb – and, in one case, a fence – as if they crashed gently there and their drivers abandoned them. The driver's-side doors of two of the vehicles are still flung open.

Michael's heart is at a steady throb now, and each beat seems to squeeze the lump on his forehead a little harder. He makes a strangled sound, closing his eyes for a moment even though the scene before him demands investigation.

He needs to get out of this room.

Just as he's pushing away from the window, he opens his eyes into a squint, and his gaze locks onto what appears to be the body of a human being across the street, partially concealed by the limbs of large pine tree. The body is squashed against the tree, and the head appears to be attached savagely to the trunk, the jaw open wide, far too wide, as if cracked open, and there's a repulsive mound of pulp below it on the ground.

It's a woman's body, splayed backward upon itself in an obviously painful position, the arms thrown back and grasping at the tree's trunk and the legs bent so far beneath the body as to appear broken or at least yanked from their hip joints. A bathrobe is hanging from the otherwise naked body. Michael stares at the woman's bluntly exposed genitals with morbid fascination.

The lower branches of the pine have been splintered away from whatever this person has done. And the body is shifting. The movements are slow and deliberate, reminding Michael absurdly of a tree sloth – that oddly sluggish shifting of limbs, that unhurried progress toward some weird inner purpose.

Now the woman is releasing an arm from its grasp of higher branches, and the hand – cramped into a claw – appears to scratch at the tree's bark above her upturned head.

It is one of the strangest, most incomprehensible sights he has ever seen.

Michael only barely returns to the desk without falling unconscious to the floor. He plants his hands on the surface, gritting his teeth in frustration. He desperately wants answers, wants to see up close what the hell is happening out there, but he's hobbled by this injury – whose source he can't even imagine. He's left wondering not only what happened to his head but also what could possibly have happened to empty this hospital and its immediate surroundings, and to cause … whatever is happening out there. The questions are increasing the agony above his eye, and he feels real concern for the injury now.

"Okay, okay …" he breathes, steadying himself, then carefully taking a step toward the door. He's focusing on that bloody doorknob, trying not to let his imagination run wild and yet powerless to prevent it. Whatever is beyond that door, it can't be good.

Clank!

That goddamn rattling sound again, right above him. Metal on metal. Dragging.

"Jesus!"

He can't afford to jerk his head around like that. He lets out a long, shaky sigh, and takes another step. He has never felt uneasy pain in his head like this before.

What in the hell did he do to himself?

Is this some kind of nightmare?

Black spots begin firing across his vision, and he feels his legs go useless.

"No!" he cries helplessly.

He slumps to the floor, instantly pulled down into unconsciousness again.

This time, there is a dream, although its logic is splintered, feverish. There are images of his office colleagues – of Steven's goofy smile deadening on his fleshy face as he turns toward something, and of Carol's voice cut off mid-shout. Of computer screens flickering as hard drives rev up loudly, of windows vibrating. Numbers on the screen – their money – fluttering and going blank.

Are these memories? Did these things happen? He asks himself these questions inside the dream. And there are the faces of his family, again and again, flashes of Susanna's emotion and Rachel's anger, coming as a jangle of sound –

CHAPTER 2

Michael wakes from the shifty, nightmarish imagery, staring at the ceiling.

Bleary-eyed, he glances around again, not recognizing where he is. Then it comes back to him in slivers. He has a sensory memory of the pain he felt upon waking before; that pain has loosened now, thankfully, but his brain still feels splintered.

All he hears now is the dragging noise above him, the dragging and the metallic rattle. It sounds like a caged animal, quietly considering its confinement and then erupting with frustrated anger. After a flurry of loud activity, it goes quiet again.

Very carefully, not wanting to bring on more pain, he pushes himself off the floor, frowning with revulsion at the coagulated blood beneath him. It's syrupy in its worst spots, clinging to him like mucus. He gets to one knee, using the bed for balance, then slowly rises to a standing position – and dizziness threatens to drop him again. He wipes his hand and forearm on his pants, staring at the bloody doorknob. He needs to get to it now, fears be damned, needs to see what is beyond it, needs to get outside, anywhere but here, and at these thoughts, his brain sends black spots into his vision again.

"No, no, no ..." he breathes, holding his chin to his chest, bending over as far as he dares, warding off another dead faint. "Need to rest first."

As the worst of the dizziness passes, he maneuvers himself onto the bed, finally swinging his right leg up and exhaling raggedly. He lets his head fall to the left and stares at that bloody knob, his teeth gritted.

Exploration will have to wait.

Before the thought is even fully formed in his mind, he feels himself falling unconscious again. His first instinct is to fight against it – *Will I never wake up again?* – but then lets it happen, eager for more healing.

He wakes to a blast.

His arms flail, startled. He is disoriented, rudderless. He clutches at the sides of the bed, keeping his head still, not wanting it to explode in chunks across the pillow. His skull seems to squeeze in on his brain.

The blast sounds again – deafening.

That's a weapon. That sounds like a shotgun. Right at the door.

He opens his eyes, his insides seized in alarm.

The veneer around the door handle has splintered, and chunks of wood have scattered everywhere. The metal handle hangs for a moment on a section of veneer, then falls to the bloody floor with a clatter.

Now someone is kicking at the door.

Oh Jesus, this is it!

Michael's injured mind whirls, and he reaches out instinctively for some kind of protection, *any* kind of protection from this threat. There's nothing here!

The door cracks further and finally swings open.

Rachel is standing there.

Michael stares at her. Is his mind playing tricks on him?

No, that's really her.

His daughter looks ashen and exhausted, lines of sweat and tears etched down her face, smears of blood on her arms and clothes. She looks as if she's been through a war zone. He opens his mouth to speak, but nothing comes out. Despite her appearance, he realizes that it is relief that is flooding him.

Rachel's eyes fill with tears as she comes fully into the room.

A flood of recent memory crashes through Michael's injured brain. Tears in those same eyes last night, her expression of teen indignation and disappointment and rebellion directed straight at him, the shouted words, Susanna quiet in the doorway. And for the life of him, he still can't remember the source of all that emotion. Just the same old arguments.

"Hi Daddy," Rachel says now, her face looking like a prelude to shock.

Michael stares at her, squinting. He can't find words for a moment. He can't process her. Then, finally:

"What on Earth are you – ? What happened? Where are we?"

"We're at the hospital." She just stands there, seeming about to fall down. "I'll explain everything."

Michael takes several deep breaths, watching her.

"Did I fall?" Michael reaches up to the wound at his forehead, touching the dressing there. "I remember – "

There's something more in his memory now, teasing him even as he speaks, but it remains elusive, foggy under pain. Something happened at his office. Some kind of violence?

Rachel is shaking her head. "Better not mess with that."

Michael drops his hand and watches Rachel standing there. She looks so far removed from the Rachel he knows – older, tougher, more rugged – that she might as well be a different person.

He takes another slow breath, lets it out. He's immensely glad to see her, but the questions remain. For the moment, he lets the questions go and simply lets the words come out.

"Listen, Rachel, I'm sorry about last night. I didn't mean to take all that out on you." He doesn't fully know what he's apologizing for, but he's sure it's necessary.

And then Rachel says something remarkable.

"No, I'm sorry, Dad."

It's at that moment when Michael understands that something has happened that is bigger than he can easily grasp. He feels a surge of trepidation, and he scans his surroundings again. The hospital's atmosphere still feels all wrong, feels bloated with bitter energy, like stress or anger. Just as you can sense the aftermath of a bad argument or a fight, like a foul vibe, he feels it here. He looks at his daughter again and sees that she's not merely smeared with blood but injured herself. There are superficial wounds on her arms.

"Hey, you're all scraped up – you're bloody! What happened? What's going on?"

Emotion blooms across Rachel's features.

A different kind of emotion than Michael has seen her exhibit since her mother's death.

Rachel has been through something, and whatever it is, he can see in her expression that somehow, some way, for some reason, it has brought her closer to him. After the upheaval of their home over the past three years – some of it Michael's own fault, he admits, but some of it Rachel's fault, and most of it no one's fault at all – he can't help but feel a wave of relief even as a precursor to the knowledge of this horrible thing that has happened outside.

Rachel leans over his supine body, and he feels the feverish heat of her, the exhausted tremble. He feels a tear drop into his hair.

She says, "I saved you."

Confused by the words, Michael lets them hang in the air. She saved him? From what? The police? An accident? Where's Susanna?

He lies there bewildered, with his aching head, with his blurry confusion and fractured memory. What terrible thing has Rachel endured to cause this complete reversal in attitude and emotion? What in heaven's name has he missed?

"What do you mean? How long was I out?"

But Rachel only burrows into him, and he bears her exhausted weight, holding her. He lets her cling to him more and more tightly, and he feels her sobs against his chest. Questions are reverberating against the walls of his skull – *Why are fires raging out of control above the town? Why is this humid hospital desolate and silent? Why is that woman outside bent back upon herself, crammed against a tree? Where is everybody?!* – but the needs of his child outweigh his own, and he holds her silently.

The world itself is silent around them, and as he embraces his daughter, feeling the emotion pour out of her, Michael knows that everything in his world is terribly wrong. Everything except this embrace.

CHAPTER 3

Michael wakes violently again, cursing himself. Apparently the concussion has done its work again, squashing him down into unconsciousness. He has to get up; he has to be able to rise.

He still feels the phantom weight of Rachel embracing him. He supposes he should feel grateful that he has been able to retain new memories.

He blinks his eyes, staring around at the room. The light is still bright in the window. How much time has passed? Where did she go?

Holy shit, that wasn't a dream, was it? She was really here, right?

And then he finds her, slightly behind and to the left of the bed, curled up on a starchy blanket against the wall. Her position is fetal. The shotgun is lying next to her, within her reach, and several shells are scattered out around it. Her backpack is next to her, partially spilling its contents on the floor: Michael sees a browning banana, a bottle of water, some kind of large syringe, and what appears to be – of all things – a unit of blood.

Rachel is clutching her ratty old bear, a stuffed animal she's had since he bought it for her seventeen years ago. The bear's matted fur peeks through the gaps in her arms, which are pulled in tight. He can't see her closed eyes, but he can see her dirty brown hair and dried sweat on her forehead.

He can only stare at this young woman whom he barely recognizes. Even in slumber, fiercely clutching that ratty bear, she's a different human being. He thinks again of his wife, Susanna, at home, and he's filled with even more anxiety. He feels restless and yet cautious. He has to catch up with what Rachel obviously knows – even though he almost certainly doesn't crave that knowledge. Whatever has happened, it can't be good.

The metallic clank sounds again from above, and he flinches. He glances up warily. Whatever is up there is in the same spot, repeating the same mindless motion, but it's random enough to convince him that it's either human or animal. And though his imagination might be getting the better of him, whatever it is sounds angry.

He has to find out what it is. In an apparently empty hospital, it might be his only way to find out what happened.

With effort, testing his limits, Michael maneuvers himself to a sitting position, stops, takes a long breath. He gingerly touches his forehead.

He notices that his daughter hasn't moved at all, not even the tiniest shift, but he can see her deep, even suspiration.

After long minutes, he eases himself off the bed. Steadying himself, he walks flat-footed to the door. He grasps the door by its splintered veneer and eases it open.

His breath catches in his throat.

The hallway is caked with blood. He has never seen so much blood in his life. It's spattered on the walls and even the ceiling. It's printed in frantic hand prints on the wall across from him, sprayed toward what he judges to be the hospital's emergency entrance. Mostly, it's spilled across the floor in great chaotic puddles, tacky and crusted and putrid.

He peers around the doorframe to take it all in.

Something has happened here, something violent – there's much more tacky blood in splotches across the floor, practically a muddy lake of it toward the double doors leading to the reception area.

"Jesus Christ!" he cries. "Hello? Anyone?"

Many of the gurneys are overturned and even broken. It's a nightmarish scene, made even more so by the faintly buzzing emergency lighting. Michael finds it impossible to make sense of what lies before him, or place it into context with whatever is happening outside. The hospital looks like a slaughterhouse. The air is humid and smoky and *wrong*, as if the entire world has descended into some kind of apocalyptic nightmare.

At the thought, Michael's breath catches, and he turns consciously away from the scene, back into his room. Immediately he feels cowardly.

"Okay, okay, okay ..." he breathes, staring in at the bed and at Rachel beyond it.

He doesn't want to fall back onto that bed. He doesn't crave further unconsciousness. He paces restlessly, nearly slips on a moist patch of blood. He anchors himself at the foot of the bed and closes his eyes, willing himself calm. There are words tumbling through his consciousness, serene words, mumbled words that he sometimes uses during the more stressful moments at home, when Rachel screams at him with all the venom of her late-teen youth, or when his new wife adds her own fuel to the domestic fire, or when he feels the hot trill of paranoia about the money in his closet.

He looks down at his sleeping daughter now, curled up with her bear, then moves back to the door and peers out again.

The smell is dreadful – rotting and stagnant.

Michael steps out into the hallway, feels the stickiness and slipperiness of the blood patches under his feet. Guiding himself along the edges of gurneys, careful not to touch any blood with his hands, he trudges through the hallway that runs along the west side of the hospital.

He finds a room with a half-closed door, into which innumerable bloody footprints lead. He stares for a moment at the floor, trying to imagine the scene. Everything is quiet and dim beyond the door. He reaches out and pushes the door. It swings inward.

This is the source of the sour stench.

Swallowing, Michael steps into the large, open room, squinting to make out details. When he sees the bodies stacked against the far wall, he lets out an involuntary cry. One hand at his mouth, he edges closer to the corpses. There are at least fifty bodies there. Most are wrapped carefully, tightly, in white hospital sheets, but the bodies at the periphery are wrapped more haphazardly, their pale flesh showing through gaps in the cloth. He comes within ten feet of the closest corpses, examining them even though every instinct is screaming at him to get the hell out of this room.

The bodies appear to have suffered in horrific ways – great patches of twisted, mottled flesh on the exposed skin. Some of their facial expressions are equally ghastly. One of the bodies is a young girl, so badly injured that her eyes are white with cataracts and her skin is sloughing from her bloated face.

Michael backs hurriedly from the sight, bumping into a metal table and then dashing out.

His heart is thudding. A terrible event occurred here – very probably while he was asleep – and he's now convinced that his daughter witnessed it. She might have even been at the center of it.

He's finding it difficult to breathe. He stumbles forward through the hallway, needing fresh air.

Scuffed and bloodied double metal doors give way to the admissions area. Michael pushes through one of them and stands before a scene of further stinking atrocity. The floor is so caked with blood that it's more dirty reddish brown than its original gray tile. The admissions desk is in utter disarray, papers and computer hardware flung everywhere, torn and broken. The stench of putrefaction is overlaid by smoke and, Michael believes, the cordite reek of gunpowder.

On the far side of the large waiting room, a makeshift barricade has been assembled out of chairs and tables and other items. There's even a large framed print – some generic mountain scene – leaning askew in the teetering assemblage. It appears as if the barricade was built and then destroyed. Many of the items are broken and flung helter-skelter. There are bullet holes all over the wall behind the barricade.

Oh Jesus, Michael keeps repeating in his head. *Oh Jesus.*

It's the silence that fills him with the deepest disquiet. The sense that this place was the scene of unspeakable violence and is now abandoned. A sensation of failure, that a tremendous fight was lost. And the overriding feeling that he was powerless for the duration of it.

"Hello?" he calls again, but his voice falters and trails away.

He steps into the large area.

"Hello!" he calls, louder.

He hears a distant clamor upstairs, as if in response to him – it's the same sound he heard above him in his room. A metallic clatter. He peers up the open stairwell beyond the fallen barricade. There's no one at the landing that looks down on the lobby. He swallows hard.

He makes his way toward the front windows, stepping over the larger puddles and blood swipes and smeared footprints. He can feel his heartbeat at his scalp wound. He tries to take long, slow breaths to keep it under control.

The glass sliding doors there are wrenched halfway open and skewed slightly as if off the tracks. He steps up next to them and feels a waft of warm air. The day is bright out there. What might have been a beautiful day in northern Colorado, if not for the horror, the death. To the south, below a bruised veil of smoke, blue sky is dotted with other disastrous plumes in the far distance. Still no people or animals of any kind. No aircraft. No movement. Nothing. Just empty streets and about a dozen abandoned cars, at skewed angles down Lemay Avenue. Ash drifts from the sky. It's warm out there, and inside the hospital it's humid and foul.

Worst of all, just beyond the small parking lot are two more human beings crammed beneath a pine tree, whose needled limbs have been splintered out of the way to make room for the bodies. The bodies – both of them doughy, nearly naked men – are painfully bent backward, the limbs wrenched out of their sockets, so severely that the position almost seems natural – as if these people have been, under the force of some cruel god, remade into an entirely new monstrous species.

Their mouths are locked against the bark. Michael sees movement at the throat, and a slow drip of splinters and saliva and sap has created mushy stalagmites of mulch below their inverted, sap-caked faces. Michael feels a gag forming at the back of his throat and has to force his gaze away.

He's breathing very quickly, and he feels a knot of emotion building at his chest.

He's summoning the courage to try the stairs when he catches movement out of the corner of his eye. South on Lemay, a police cruiser is heading north, toward the hospital, winding its way around two wrecks in the middle of the street.

"Oh shit," he breathes, feeling as if his worst fear has come true. It has come down to the money after all. Even as the thought slashes through his brain, he understands its irrationality, and yet it's potent enough to fill his veins with acid.

He braces himself to bolt, his thoughts immediately turning to Rachel.

He can't leave her. No way will he leave her.

And then he sees, following in the wake of the police cruiser, a large blue Chevy truck. A civilian vehicle. Both are headed this way.

Michael is frozen to the spot, caught between impulses to run outside and wave them down or to get back to Rachel and gather her up and get the hell out of here. Can he even trust that the police car is occupied by an actual policeman? Why is a civilian truck following it?

He moves to the edge of the window and watches the vehicles approach, straight north along an otherwise deserted street. In a moment, he sees that the man driving the cruiser is indeed wearing a police uniform. The sight fills him with despair.

The cop's passenger is a woman, in her forties maybe. She looks exhausted, her head lolling against the window. He can't tell if anyone is in the back seats. The driver of the truck is a large man with a determined expression on his face. Next to him is a young blond woman. And now Michael notices several people in the back of that truck. They also appear exhausted, sprawled out and heads bowed.

The vehicles pull into the emergency parking lot. Michael decides to fall back to the double doors leading toward Rachel, see what these people decide to do. He walks purposefully across the destroyed lobby, nearly slipping and falling in front of the registration desk but finally making it. He maneuvers behind the door. He touches his head wound carefully, relieved to find that the pain there has subsided by several orders of magnitude. He still feels a bit blurry and thick, but the dizziness is gone for the moment. He watches the entrance.

The vehicles rumble straight up to the door, and their engines shut off. Car doors clank shut.

Voices just outside the wrenched-open outer doors.

" – not something I ever thought I'd say seriously." This voice is pitched authoritatively. It's the voice of someone in charge. It must be the cop. "I mean, in real life."

"Me neither." A female voice.

"It's ridiculous," comes another male voice – the driver of the truck? "But I keep trying to think of a less batshit idea, and I can't. And then I start arguing with myself, and I sound like Scott."

Michael watches through a gap in the doors, and now the men appear at the entrance. Yes, the cop is leading the way in, wrenching the doors back further. Michael is amazed by his haggard appearance: His uniform is extremely unkempt, covered with stains, ripped in places, and his cheeks are starkly unshaven below his military crewcut. He's laughing humorlessly at what the large man has just said. The big man steps in behind him, and he's similarly splashed with blood. His massive forearms are smeared with it. His hair is greasy, thinning.

"I mean, bodies struck down and … and … inhabited by something," the cop says as he comes further into the lobby. "And that light, that's the weirdest thing, right? This red … thing. Like a possession. I'll probably never understand that."

"We all saw it. Believe me, you're not alone."

Michael is listening hard but is thrown into confusion by what this man saying. Squinting under a persistent dull throb, he watches the middle-aged woman make her way through the doorway. She's dirty blond, just on the verge of heavy, but still attractive – at least she would probably be on a better day. She's red-eyed, on the brink of collapse. As she steps into the lobby, she says:

"I need food. And sleep."

The large man says, "We should start organizing trips to Safeway, grab whatever food we can find. The cafeteria is already almost wiped out of water."

The cop doesn't appear to hear them.

"But what about the way they move? Suppose that's how they move wherever they're from? On their planet, or whatever? Like their original bodies are used to."

What in the hell? Michael thinks as he watches three younger women – all of them exhausted, leaning against one another – follow in behind the more matronly woman. *Is this some kind of joke?*

"But that's their mistake, maybe. They aren't familiar with our bodies, they don't know how to work them. And something is keeping them from using them right."

"Like what?" one of the younger women says tiredly.

The three younger women appear to be the same age, and in fact two of them seem to be twins. They're young; perhaps younger than Rachel. The twins are tall, gangly, and athletic – basketball players at CSU, perhaps. They both have shoulder-length brown hair, moistened by perspiration and then dried in tangles. The other is smaller, meek, blond. She looks wrecked.

"Well, I don't know, but it's probably the same thing that prevented them from knowing that a certain kind of blood would make some of us immune to them."

One of the twins says something unintelligible, and the cops shoots back:

"No, it's not! Come on. That's not *all* it is, anyway. I mean, *look* at it. *Look at that.*"

The cop has about-faced in the lobby, at the window, and gestured out toward the two bodies at the pine tree at the edge of the parking lot.

Silence, followed by the shuffling noise of the small group coming to a stop in front of the admissions desk.

"And you heard it. You can *still* hear it. I've never heard anything like that in my life."

Michael catches only a few words of what the older woman says. " – is it – when – "

"I think they're communicating," the cop says. "I think that's what that is. You remember – Bonnie, you remember – when that happened before. When all those bodies were up there, right up there." He gestures up the stairwell. "Just scowling down at us, ready to jump down and attack, or whatever they had in mind. And then this – this sound happened, and every one of those things stopped. The mood changed. Right? I'm telling you, they're communicating."

The big guy says, "I feel like Scott again when I say that, yeah, if these things are alien, well, *of course* they're communicating. I doubt they'd try to take over the world without a plan."

The woman named Bonnie says, after an exhausted pause, "If they're communicating, what are they saying?"

"Yeah, that's the question. And I have no clue."

Bonnie lets out a shaky sigh, and she says, "Where's Rachel?"

Michael feels a rush of relief at the mention of his daughter's name, and yet something is keeping him from revealing himself. For a long moment, he can only hold his breath, trying to make sense of the strange conversation he just overheard. He shakes his head, unable to process. And then the imagery conjured by their words brings back the image of Rachel blasting through the door to find him. Did that really happen? He still has the sensory memory of the shattered door handle; he can still see the shredded veneer. The tacky blood smeared across the floor, starting to stink.

And now these words.

He almost feels that, if he could only slink back to Rachel undetected, he could steal her away from this crazy place, and go home. Go back to where things might still make sense.

Finally he clears his throat and calls out, "Hello?" The word comes out raspy and not loud enough to be heard in the lobby. He tries again. "Hello! I'm unarmed!"

The group is startled, each person wearily frozen in his or her tracks, watching him emerge from the hallway. The cop has some kind of large weapon at his side, loosely at the ready. It appears to be a police-issue patrol rifle. As Michael makes his way fully into view, the cop relaxes into an odd expression of resigned satisfaction. He's a clean-cut young man, former military, Michael is sure.

"Oh my God, look who it is!" Bonnie has a look of glad surprise on her dirty, lined face. Michael sees relief, surprise, and also melancholy in this stranger's expression.

Patches of the woman's skin and great swaths of her clothing have been splattered and even drenched with blood. The same is true of all of these people.

"Rachel's dad!" the large man says, stepping forward. He brings up a meaty hand holding a red ball cap, secures it on his head, then reaches for a handshake. Michael tentatively lifts his own hand and returns the gesture. His hand is engulfed. "Name's Kevin. It's good to see you alive, brother." The man is sweaty and filthy, obviously fatigued, and after only a brief moment of gladness, his features bend toward a stark solemnity.

And then Bonnie is embracing Michael, hard. He grimaces not only at the jarring clinch, and the way it seems to clang his loose skull like a bell, but also at the smell of her. He detects the sharp tang of sweat, but also a coating of blood – wiped at but still evident in the creases of her flesh – and what he imagines to be the stink of an awful experience. Perhaps the same experience that Rachel went through.

"I'm Bonnie," she says into his chest. "I was afraid I'd never see you conscious."

"My name is Michael," he says to the group over her shoulder. "Do I – do I know any of you?"

"Oh, we know who you are!" Kevin says.

Bonnie murmurs quiet laughter and pulls away. There are

actually tears in her eyes. She glances back at the cop, as if searching for what to say.

"You have no idea what happened, do you?" the cop says. It's his turn to step forward, switch the rifle to his left hand, and shake hands with Michael. The man has that confident way of carrying himself that speaks of good upbringing and strong training, and he has a powerful handshake. Michael has never met this man, and yet the cop greets him as if he has known him for years and is relieved to see him alive.

Michael can only shake his head in response to the cop's question.

"I'm Joel." A small smile takes hold of his lips. "Michael, huh?"

"Yeah."

"All this time, you've been 'Rachel's dad'."

Kevin murmurs a laugh. "True."

Joel gestures behind him, toward the three young women. "That's Chrissy there – she and Rachel are pretty tight – and the twins, Chloe and Zoe."

The young women nod to him, too tired to do anything more. Chrissy, the petite one, is in gray shorts and a blue tee shirt that is spattered with dried blood. She looks to be in her early twenties and has a dark, haunted quality to her face. Her eyes and face are red as if she's been crying uncontrollably for days. The twins, about the same age as Chrissy, are wearing what Michael might consider nightclothes: cotton pants and white blouses, all of it filthy with blood and grime. Michael stares at the young women with increasing confusion.

There are three others just now entering through the main entrance, a man in a business suit and a woman in a drab pantsuit, both of them perhaps in their fifties. Also exhausted.

"That's Jerry and ... Karen, right?" Kevin says.

The woman acknowledges Michael with a half-hearted smile.

Michael doesn't know what to say for a long moment. The enormity of everything leaves him speechless. Kevin lays a hand briefly on his shoulder, offers a weary smile, and then pushes away and through the double doors. The young women settle to the floor in a heap, utterly spent from whatever they were doing outside.

"I don't remember anything, no," he says, belatedly answering Joel's question. He feels a tinge in his skull as the words escape him. "I'm pretty sure I've got a concussion."

"I'd say that's a safe assumption." Bonnie reaches up to touch his bandage, begins to expertly remove it.

"I keep falling asleep," he says.

She's blinking exaggeratingly as if to keep her own eyes open. "Your body is trying to recover. How does your head feel?"

"Like a truck ran over it."

"Nausea?"

"A while ago, but not now."

"How about your vision?"

"Fine, actually."

"I think you did suffer a concussion, but it's healing. Just gotta take it easy. I'll get you some Tylenol."

He nods gratefully.

"Where's Rachel?" Joel asks.

Michael looks at Joel curiously. "She's back there, in the room where – where I was sleeping."

"At least she found her way back," the cop says.

Bonnie's expression holds a mixture of relief and a haunted kind of emptiness – almost a hopelessness.

"Are you hungry?" Joel asks.

Michael pauses to think about that, and at the suggestion, he realizes that he's ravenous. "Yes."

"We have a little bit of food rounded up from the cafeteria, stuff that's gonna start going bad pretty soon, so we might as well eat it while we can."

Food that will go bad soon?

"Okay."

"I'll get that, and I'll leave you to Bonnie."

Michael feels that his agitation is palpable in the air around them. He needs answers to the riddles he's hearing, but at the same time, he feels as if those answers are the last thing he wants to hear.

As these people start losing interest in him, he finally turns to Bonnie and whispers, "What the hell is going on?"

Bonnie seems to brace herself for an explanation.

Michael swallows heavily and tries, again, to focus on specific moments in the past: rising from bed, his breakfast, his rituals before going to work. Susanna murmuring from bed. The early morning drive. His work.

"I – I can't remember *anything*. I mean, there are fragments, but … not much. How did I get here?"

"I'm not surprised some of your memory is gone." She squeezes his forearm. "But it'll come. Maybe best not to force it."

"All I know is I have a hell of a knot on my forehead. Maybe I fell, but I have no idea why or where I could've fallen."

She touches the skin around the wound again, feels for warmth. "Did you talk to Rachel about this?"

He's shaking his head. "I'm afraid we both fell asleep."

Bonnie's hands are moving expertly.

He watches her face, coming to a realization.

"You treated me?" Michael says.

"After Rachel brought you in, yes. I just took care of you once you got here. Rachel's the one who saved your life. Did she tell you?"

Michael can't help but let out a murmur of surprise. "She said … I don't – "

"Quite a young lady you've got there." Her smile looks incongruous beneath dark-ringed eyes. "Rachel thinks you might have fallen down a stairwell at your office. That's where she found you."

"This morning?"

"I wish. No, that was two days ago."

Michael gapes at her. "You aren't serious. I've been out for two days?"

"Yeah," Bonnie breathes. She looks at him with a kind of longing. "Wow. Part of me wishes I could be waking up only now, like this. To not have been through the past two days at all. You're lucky, in a way. But then … to wake up to a world that – that – " She casts her eyes downward.

"What?"

When she lifts her head, her eyes are glistening. She appears to give up on restraint. "Everything has changed. Everything is … horrible."

Emotion twists her features, and she slowly recovers. He doesn't know how to respond. He opens his mouth, closes it, then opens it again.

"What is it?"

She's shaking her head miserably. "I don't even know where to begin." She glances around, as if for help.

The dead-eyed middle-aged couple, now huddled at the abandoned admissions desk, peer at Michael as if they feel sorry for him. The man nods vaguely at him, but the woman looks away, down at her feet. Michael turns to stare out the big front windows again. There's no movement out there.

"Where is everybody?" he whispers.

Bonnie can only stare at him.

Then, "Let's check on Rachel, okay? I need to clean up a little bit first, and then let's see if she's okay. I'm worried about her. She went through so much. So much." She offers a sad smile. "And then we can both fill you in on everything."

At that moment, Joel comes striding back through the double doors, hefting his rifle. He's all business. He looks straight at Michael, accusatory.

"I think we got a live one."

CHAPTER 4

He knows, Michael thinks again, irrationally.

"What do you mean?" Bonnie asks Joel, her voice descending into near-petulance.

"I found Rachel. One of those things is moving around right above her, second level. Did you hear it in there?" he asks Michael.

"I did."

"You checked every room, right? Before we left?" Joel asks Kevin as the big man hurries back into the lobby.

"Far as I know, it's cleared out, yeah. There were a few locked or closed doors that I didn't have time to check. But I guess anyone could have wandered in here from the street while we were gone."

"It's been clanging around up there for hours," Michael offers. "I think it's what woke me up."

"What else did you hear?" Joel asks.

"Just something dragging around, like metal on metal. Frantic. Sounds almost angry."

"Those things wouldn't have come back in, right …?" Bonnie says, a near-whine.

"Not saying I understand anything about those fuckers," Kevin says, "but I'd guess not. Why would they?" He considers something. "When they left, they left in a goddamn hurry, so …"

Joel slants his gaze up the stairs, tries to get a geographic lock on the area above Michael's room. "Let's check it out. Bonnie, will you go ahead and look in on Rachel? We've got this."

"Of course." Bonnie turns to Michael. "You feel okay to go up?"

Michael nods. His head still aches, but not with urgency of before, not with that feeling of alarming looseness, as if his brain matter were sloshing around. His heart is still thumping hard, but he can focus now. He takes deep breaths, trying to keep everything in place.

"Yeah, I want to see this."

"C'mon," Joel says, checking his rifle and handing it over to Kevin. "Here, you take this." He pulls his sidearm from his hip and checks the magazine.

Michael watches the weapons with a new anxiety, thinking of the money again, thinking of the crime. Is it possible that all of it means nothing now?

The cop leads the way across the sticky floor and to the stairs. The three men navigate their way through a gaping hole in the barricade. Large swaths of carpet on the stairs are soaked with brown blood, but the way is relatively clear, save for occasional knocked-over furniture and toppled IV stands. Michael, aghast, can't take his eyes off the chaos of chairs and tables in shambles all around him. Some of it has been splattered with blood. There's an obvious shotgun blast in the wall to his right, and what he believes to be brain matter has dried in pieces around and below it.

"Will someone please tell me what the hell happened here?"

Joel and Kevin exchange a glance. "I guess you'd call it a last stand," the cop says.

"Against what?"

"Those things. Those corpses. All those bodies upstairs? They all flowed down through here. Angry as hell. At least, that's what we thought."

Corpses? A last stand against corpses? What?

A bark of laughter escapes Michael's mouth, and all he gets in return from his companions are sober reactions. Kevin and Joel glance at him for only a moment, then continue ahead. Michael flashes on the human beings he saw outside, their bodies compressed against those trees. They were like nothing he'd ever seen before, but he can't get past the disconnect between that behavior and whatever it is that these people are talking about.

He tries to visualize this horrific scene, and fails. It's as if these people he's never met are asking him to accept that his life has become some insane horror film. It can't be real. It *can't*. Yes, the skies are filled with smoke and ash is blanketing the city, and yes, everyone but a small fraction of humanity has simply disappeared, and there are a thousand other pieces of evidence backing up the crazed words of these sweaty people, but it *can't* be real.

Kevin gives voice to his thoughts.

"Gotta be weird, waking up to this."

"You missed all the fun," Joel says as they reach the landing and proceed cautiously west along the carpeted hallway. The three men step past fallen IV stands and assorted tubes and cables. "The only bodies left in this hospital are the corpses we managed to kill for good. Or the people those things killed from the start."

The image of the stacked corpses downstairs flashes through Michael's head. Those were victims of ... reanimated bodies?

"We tried to give those people as much ... dignity ... as possible." Joel peeks inside an open door, then moves on. "But the really active ones? They're all out there now." He gestures up and away from himself. "Outside. Doing God knows what. And the one exception appears to be the one we're about to – "

Michael comes to a halt, hands out, wincing under new pain in his head.

"Okay, wait – wait – stop – !"

The other two men slow to a stop, turning toward him expectantly but almost reluctantly. Michael waits for a wave of dizziness to pass, then considers these two relative strangers. There's no denying the horror in their expressions, and evident in the blood and filth on their clothes, caked in swaths on their exposed skin. The lack of sleep in their eyes. The fatigue. These men are near collapse, and yet they keep going.

But Michael can't hold it in.

"The 'corpses you managed to kill for good'? Look, guys ... Joel, Kevin ... just be honest with me here. We can't be talking about ..." He eyes them carefully, waiting – hoping – for grins to crack broadly across their faces. "... I mean, you don't expect me to believe that – "

The two men watch Michael for a moment, then Kevin is nodding slowly.

"Did ... uh, didn't Rachel tell you anything?" Joel asks.

Michael brings a hand to the bridge of his nose and squeezes. "No. No, unfortunately, no, this is all new to me."

There's a moment of quiet indecision, broken only by distant movement and voices downstairs and then – serendipitously – the sound of metallic dragging, coming from somewhere ahead. All three men turn abruptly in that direction, trying to locate it.

"Well," Kevin says, "I think you're about to get a crash course in what you missed while you were knocked out."

"Yeah, let's just take a look, huh? A lot of shit is about to get real clear."

Michael just looks at him, feeling a chaos of emotions.

"Let's go," the cop says. "Trust me, okay?"

Not waiting for Michael, Joel starts moving again, firearm at ready position.

Kevin follows, and Michael takes a deep breath, taking up the rear.

They approach a new hallway to the right and pause. The sound has stopped, but now a brief clamor informs them that the sound is coming from down the new hall. Joel urges them forward. It's close.

"You don't remember *anything*, huh?" Kevin whispers next to Michael. "You don't remember what you were doing when – "

"I remember just flashes ... nothing concrete. I don't even remember driving to work. Nothing about that morning."

"Maybe not a bad memory to lose, I guess," Kevin says. "... when the end of the world happened."

"The end of – " Michael starts.

Joel slows abruptly and gestures Michael and Kevin forward with his pistol. "It's that room there."

Michael sees a closed door. To the right of the door, directly below a small metal rectangle designating the room as Room 278, a chair sits empty and crooked. Joel moves quietly to the door and takes hold of the handle. He glances at Michael and gestures for him to position himself behind him. Michael takes his place.

"I think I know what's happened here," Joel whispers.

"What?" Kevin says.

Joel quietly moves to the door and tries the handle. It's unlocked. It opens soundlessly inward. He takes in the scene, nods quickly.

Michael feels his veins pulsing. A low gasp comes from within the room, raising the hair on the back of his neck.

"Yep, we got one," Joel says, grimacing. "Come take a look."

Michael steels himself, then steps forward with Kevin.

The room appears to be a typical ICU recovery room, with hulking machinery dark and silent in the background. There are whiteboards everywhere, scrawled with barely legible notes and incomprehensible numbers. But Michael's eyes go immediately to the bed, which has been dragged to the far edge of the room, and the body on the floor right at the foot of that bed.

The body is that of a heavy, tattooed bald man. He's half covered by a hospital gown, and much of his exposed skin is loosely swathed by bandages. The man is bent over backward, straining, on all fours. Cords in his neck are standing out in stark relief, and the expression on the upside-down face is one of pure torment – red, furious, eyes bulging. Michael, appalled, notices something right away about the eyes: The pupils are wide and black. The effect is like a shark's eyes. There's malevolence there.

"Oh my god!" Michael can't help but blurt. "What's wrong with him?"

The man locks dead eyes on Michael, then on Joel, and unleashes a dry, throaty gasp. He thrashes once, mightily, and drags the bed's metal legs a few inches across the floor.

"Same thing that's wrong with mostly everyone," Kevin says.

Michael can't take his eyes off the man. He can't comprehend what he's seeing. The bodies at the trees were one thing, but this is something entirely different: malevolent and almost completely alien despite the humanity underneath the features.

"He's locked to the bed," Joel says. "See?"

A pair of handcuffs secures the man's left hand to the bed railing. The wrist is obviously broken, and the flesh is mangled, twisted. In fact, Michael realizes, the man is on the verge of dismembering his own hand to escape. The skin is taut and torn, and the bones appear to be nearly separated. Soon, the only thing keeping this man tethered will be tendons and skin.

"He's a prisoner," Kevin whispers.

The room stinks of the man's sweat, a heavy scent that mingles with the smell of shit and piss, which have stained the bed and his clothes.

"Fuuuuuck, that's rank," Kevin says. His rifle is pointed down and away, but Joel is on high alert.

"Goddamn," Michael says, still trying to make sense of the scene before him. "What's he doing?"

"He's got that thing inside him – that light."

Michael wrenches his gaze from the impossible sight of this human being, and looks straight at Joel, then at Kevin.

"Uh," Michael says. "What?"

"That's the thing," Joel says. "Whatever is happening to these corpses, it's all because of this insane ... presence ... inside their heads. It's like a ... an illumination. A radiation. Inhabiting them." He murmurs a dark laugh. "I know that sounds crazy as hell, and that was our first reaction, trust me. That was everyone's reaction. But it's true."

Michael doesn't see anything like an illumination.

And he still can't get Joel's word out of his head.

Corpses.

But this man isn't dead. Far from it.

Except for the eyes.

At that moment, the man lunges for Michael, and Michael nearly falls while scrambling backward out of the way.

"Whoa, whoa, yeah, watch out," Kevin says. "You don't want that thing to touch you. That light can fuck you up."

"I don't see any light," Michael says, composing himself.

"Oh, it's there."

Michael considers that silently, just watching the bald man – the bald man's corpse? – flail about, seething.

"Show it to me," he says.

"Show you what?"

"Show me this light you're talking about." He clutches his throbbing forehead, feeling the need for that Tylenol that Bonnie spoke of.

Joel takes a look around the room.

The man is on the floor to the left of the bed. His upturned face is still contorted in an animal fury, and as Joel steps to the other side of the bed, the man watches him warily, upside down, snapping out at him once, teeth clacking. The man's blunt chin has become his most prominent feature, like the end of a proboscis.

Joel reaches the window and draws the shades. The room falls into relative darkness, and now Michael sees the crimson glow coming from the man's face – or, rather, *behind* the man's face. His breath catches. It's an unwavering luminescence coming from the area behind the nose, visible from the nostrils and open mouth, and just barely beneath the skin of the cheeks.

"What – " he whispers. "What's happened to him? Why is he – "

"Not just him," Kevin says soberly behind him. "Everyone."

"*Everyone?* I mean, are we talking – "

Joel sees where he's going. "We've had no interaction with anyone for hundreds of miles, no communication, no glimpses of flights, no evidence of life anywhere," he says in a low voice. "Nothing. We think it's worldwide."

Mike swallows thickly, doesn't know how to digest that. Finally, he decides not to. He turns back to the man's body.

"This same thing is in – "

"Every damn one of them." Joel opens the blinds again and goes back to the doorway, keeping his pistol trained on the bald man. "We were able to see inside one of them the other day. A motorcyclist whose head had been broken open. Not a pretty sight. But this thing inside him, it was like a – a sphere. A bright ball of light. A ball of energy." He curls the fingers of his left hand as if he's holding a baseball. "About that big, in the middle of the head. Strangest shit I've ever seen."

Michael feels himself shaking his own head slowly back and forth.

"And the weirdest part?" Joel says, coming to Michael's side. "These bodies are dead. They don't breathe, there's no heartbeat. Look at the eyes. The pupils are dilated. They really are walking corpses. These bodies were just lying around dead for a whole day before that thing in there started bringing them back."

Those words hang in the humid air for a moment, and the thing on the floor continues to watch them warily.

It is a profoundly alien sight, Michael has to admit.

"How did this *happen?*" he asks. "What *happened?* I mean, my *God!*"

Both men are shaking their heads, but it's Kevin who responds. "No one knows, man."

"I keep wondering what they're seeing through those eyes," Joel whispers. "Look at that."

The thing just stares with its flat eyes, obviously seeing them, regarding them ... somehow ... but there's no denying the feeling that no actual human awareness remains.

"*How* are they seeing out of those eyes?" Joel continues.

"And it looks like it wants to tear your face off, right?" Kevin says. "Yeah, that's what we thought. But I bet if we unlocked him and got out of his way, and we left that door open ... he'd run right past us and search for a way out of this place."

Michael looks at Kevin. "What do you mean?"

"I think this thing is more scared than angry. It just wants out of here."

"He looks like he wants to murder me."

"I know. But Kevin's right. I think it's scared out of its mind," Joel says. "The question is, who's in control of that mind?"

Michael flashes on the bodies he has seen attached to pine trees outside. The incomprehensible sight of those bodies. Just like those bodies, this man's limbs are hyper-extended into what must be an extraordinarily painful position. The skin covering the shoulders is enflamed, speaking of damage to the sockets. And yet the one arm not fastened into handcuffs still works, scrambling for purchase on the slippery vinyl tiles.

"Jesus, why is he – bent over backward like that?"

"All right, so here's what I've figured," Joel says, keeping an eye on the prisoner. "I think what we're dealing with is an alien invasion. I'm not kidding. And I'm not talking about little green men in flying saucers. I'm talking about something atmospheric. A presence coming down and taking us over. Something has inhabited these bodies, and it's not from here. I don't know if you've seen what's going on in the sky, but that's what's clinching it for me. These are aliens. Aliens that have taken over our bodies. And wherever they're from? This is how they get around. This is how they walk."

The three men watch the bald man squirm angrily, occasionally gasping.

Finally, Michael turns back to Kevin. "Please tell me this is a joke."

"Heh," Kevin says. "I'm not sure I'm on board with the alien-invasion theory." He eyes Joel with eyebrows raised. "But this thing is no joke ... and I know it's not exactly the greatest thing to wake up to at a destroyed hospital, either."

Michael doesn't really know what to think. Or how to respond. He stands there staring, finally bracing himself against the doorjamb, his eyes moving from the bald man to these two survivors. These two survivors, with whom his daughter apparently endured an honest-to-God apocalyptic event.

He can't think of anything to say.

Then Joel is raising his pistol arm – the weapon is some kind of semi-automatic – for a kill shot. Michael starts from his daze.

"Hey, *hey hey!*" He reaches out toward the policeman. "What are you doing?!"

Joel is still aiming. "You don't understand, Mike."

"What are you talking about? What the hell is going *on around here?!*"

He moves forward to somehow prevent the shot, and then –

Wait," comes a voice behind them. "Don't shoot."

The men turn to see Rachel behind them. Her face is pale and streaked with dirt and sweat. Several days' worth of grief are evident in her expression.

"Rachel!" Michael says.

Behind her, Bonnie is heading in their direction from the end of the hall.

Michael takes his daughter's shoulders, automatically turning her away from the horror in the room, as if to protect her. Immediately he understands that she has already seen far worse. But she falls into the embrace, almost eagerly, as she keeps an eye on Joel and his firearm.

"Are you all right?" Michael breathes into Rachel's hair.

A pause. "I'm far from all right."

"I'm here now," he whispers into her hair. "I'm sorry I wasn't before."

There's a pause, and her voice breaks when she says, "Me too."

Michael glances over at Joel, who is keeping an eye on the room's frightful occupant. His pistol is raised, barrel pointing at the ceiling.

Rachel pulls away from Michael, shaking her head.

She turns to Joel.

"Don't kill him," she says, her voice wavering. "We can save him."

CHAPTER 5

"He was alive," Rachel insists. "When I put that blood in him, he turned back. I swear it's the truth." She begins melting into further tears. "He spoke to me. And I killed him. I killed my Tony. But he was alive." Shaking her head, in utter misery. "He was human."

"Are you serious?" Bonnie says, her hand all fluttery at her throat.

"That can't be right ..." murmurs a young woman – one of the twins, Chloe or Zoe – to Michael's left. She appears stunned, her eyes glassy beneath her mop of unkempt brown hair. "We've killed so many of them ..."

The rest of the survivors are silent for a long, tense moment.

They're in a large open space at the north end of the hospital, a broad vestibule that leads to various types of specialized examination areas. Through one open doorway, Michael glimpses a hulking CT scanner, and he has a fleeting thought that the machine – once a marvel of 21st century medical science and now just a dark, useless conglomeration of metal and plastic – might never be used again.

Michael silently considers the assembled survivors, and he feels a shockwave wash over him at the fact that there are fewer than a dozen of them.

This is what's left?

He feels the urge to go back to his room, get back into the bed, and dive into unconsciousness, in the hope that he might find his way out of the nightmare.

But no.

Each person appears numb, as if a collective rug has been pulled from underneath them. There's Joel, Rachel, Bonnie, and Kevin, and then there's middle-aged Karen and Jerry, who would appear to be a couple. Michael wonders fleetingly if they are – and whether they were before this thing happened. What would the odds of that be?

There's also the trio of girls leaning against one another on a bench at the far wall, off to the left. Michael has to remind himself of their names – meek Chrissy and the taller twins. Given the concussion, he's surprised – and privately relieved – that he can remember all their names, even though he can't yet tell the twins apart.

But that's it! Ten people!

Michael is afraid to extrapolate from this motley crew any kind of figure estimating how many people have actually survived this event.

Even at that thought, he's literally shaking his head out of his ruminations, in fervent denial.

Rachel's words have indeed thrown the exhausted band of survivors into a muted, collective confusion. After Joel reluctantly shut the door on the handcuffed prisoner, he began questioning her and then stopped, preferring instead to bring the larger group together. Joel whisked her downstairs and called on the entire group to meet here at the humid epicenter of the hospital. He described the locked-up corpse, then called on Rachel to explain what she meant when she prevented him from killing it for good.

Now Joel looks angrily expectant, pacing around, ready to receive the full weight of Rachel's information but holding himself back from exploding. Rachel herself looks miserable, having just dropped a figurative bomb about her final encounter with her boyfriend Tony.

"I'm totally serious," she says, her voice monotone. "He spoke to me."

"Are you sure he was infected in the first place?" Joel asks.

She gives him a tearful glare. "His goddamn face was wrapped around a tree trunk, and his mouth was full of sap and splinters. Does that sound like human behavior?"

Joel watches her out of the corner of his eye. "Calm yourself, girl."

"He had that light in him like all the rest."

Michael watches his daughter from his bench adjacent to the door of a restroom. She's commanding the attention of this diverse band, even in the grip of a firestorm of her own emotion. He can hear her voice cracking. He knows she's carrying something inside her that's toxic. She's just told the terrible truth about her boyfriend Tony. About his death and apparent rebirth – and his second death, by her hand. Even Michael feels a sudden, sharp remorse – he knows Tony well. Too well. It's true he never completely warmed to the boy, thinking his daughter too good for the likes of him. But he feels the weight of the loss, and its effect on his daughter, who loved the boy.

Rachel is despondent.

"After I put the blood into him, he said – he said – my name." She wipes a frantic tear from her cheek. "He looked at me. He recognized me. But I was too late to hold back the trigger. I couldn't stop it. One half second, and – and – and – it would have been different. He'd be alive." Her chin falls to her chest. "He'd be here."

These words are met with about thirty seconds of silence. The faces of the other survivors betray some kind of worried pain. They're glancing around at one another, their expressions almost pleading. Pleading for understanding, or seeking kinship in despair.

Michael feels alone on the outskirts of the room, knowing that his time in unconsciousness has cost him any sense of that kinship, for better or for worse. Over the past couple days, these people shared an experience that would bind them together for the rest of their lives – however long those lives lasted.

He's also further flummoxed by some of the revelations escaping these survivors' mouths, including his daughter's. This is the second mention of blood, and he has no idea what it means. He can only flash on the unit of blood he spied in Rachel's open backpack, and, of course, the horrendous presence of the stuff on almost every surface he has seen.

"But what does that mean?" Bonnie says. "Does it mean – "

"I don't know what the hell it means," Joel says. "Could be some kind of … some kind of vestigial memory of what he was before he – I don't know. Maybe even a trick. We have no idea what these fuckers want. What they're up to. Hell, it could be that she just heard something she wanted to hear."

"It wasn't like that." Rachel stares laser beams at the cop. "I pumped the blood into him, and he changed. *He changed back!"*

The group is silent.

"Don't you look at me like that!" she shouts. "I know what I saw. I know what happened."

Kevin says, "But how – I mean, look, Rachel, I'd trust you with my life, you know that, right? I've known you for all of two days, but that's something I'm sure of. But listen … those goddamn things are eating trees, okay? Their throats are filled with chewed wood. Their bones are all broken – look at the way they move. Everything dislocated. Everything wrong. How could they still be … alive?"

"Don't forget," Bonnie puts in as gently as she can while barely maintaining a sense of sweaty calm, "those things had no pulse for over a full day. Their eyes were dead. No respiration. We talked about it, right here. We were dealing with corpses."

"I know, I know," Rachel says, looking up. "So – look, I'm not saying I have the answers … far from it – but maybe … maybe while that thing is inside them, it's keeping them alive in a different way? I don't know! What I *do* know is that despite all that – no pulse, no respiration, all that – those things felt alive the whole time. Their skin was warm." She turns to Bonnie. "You remember – I told you that." There's a pause that no one jumps in to fill. "And Kevin, I have no idea what it would feel like to wake up like that. They'd be dealing with broken bones for sure, and a hell of a sore throat." She looks at Joel. "You're the science-fiction guy, you have any ideas?"

"Let's say it's true," Joel says evenly, darkly. "That we can inject those things with O-negative blood and essentially cure them. That's what you're saying, right?" He involuntarily swallows. "You realize those goddamn Thompson brothers are burning thousands of human beings in the foothills, right? You understand how many of them we killed ourselves?"

"You don't think I've considered that?"

"And yet you decided not to tell us till now?" His voice turns into a shout. "You've been sleeping while people are being murdered?"

Michael rises. "Hey, hey!"

"What?" Joel demands.

"Take it easy."

"It's all right, Dad," Rachel says miserably. "I deserve it."

"But Rach ..." he begins. "You didn't know – "

Joel has yanked his radio from his belt and is thumbing its face. He brings it to his ear, glaring at Rachel as he walks into an adjacent hall.

"Jeff Thompson, come in, you read? This is Officer Joel Reynolds. Come in, over."

"I don't know what to say," Rachel says, and Michael sees in her gaze something he's never seen before, even in the crush of grief following her mother's death. "I didn't know what to – "

Bonnie strides across the room and takes Rachel into her arms. The affection takes Michael by surprise – another suggestion of something he missed while he was unconscious. The moment brings strong memories of Rachel's mother to his mind, and of course his own private guilt. He falls back onto the bench.

"Jeff or Pete, goddammit, put your ears on! Over!"

The entire group watches Joel stalk out of the room, his voice trailing off as he moves down the corridor toward Admissions.

"We should test it," Kevin speaks up. "I mean, like ... now."

"Yes," Rachel says, gently extricating herself from Bonnie's embrace. "And we have the perfect way to test it."

"I thought they all rushed out of here ..." Chrissy says, miserable.

"... unless they were locked up," Kevin finishes the thought.

"It was the first thing I heard when I woke up," Michael says to her. "In fact, that might have been what woke me. Just dragging around above me. Scared the shit out of me."

"So how is it trapped?" one of the twins says. Michael thinks she's Chloe. Closer to her, he notices her slightly darker, more haunted eyes. Also distinguishing from her twin is the fact that she's covered in more dried blood than her sister Zoe. "Is it just barricaded in the room somehow? I mean, we know that these things can open doors. They're obviously escaping from the cars, and from their homes – "

"Handcuffed to the bed," Michael says. "A prisoner. There's a chair outside the door. Joel thinks he had a guard positioned there."

"How secure is he?"

"Flopping around on the ground, just one arm secured. And actually that hand is just about severed."

"How do we get close to it?" Chrissy asks, glancing around the room. "This thing isn't exactly gonna be cooperative."

Bonnie speaks up. "We haven't tried knocking one out with drugs. What about a barbiturate? Chloroform? Nitrous?"

"We'd still have to get close to it to administer those, right?" Kevin says. "I'm not getting within ten feet of that thing."

Bonnie slaps her forehead with her palm. "You're right."

"Knocking it out is a fine idea, but we'd need to do it from afar – how?"

"Tranquilizer dart?" Zoe says from across the room.

Everyone looks her way, and she shrugs modestly, then continues.

"My mom works at ... I mean, she *worked* at the CSU vet hospital." Zoe pauses as emotion touches her features and makes her voice husky. "They partnered with the Colorado Division of Wildlife sometimes. Last year, there was a bear they had to tranquilize and kill because it came into town. For the gun, they would fill and reuse these things, basically like syringes, so I'd think you could fill them with blood."

Kevin says, "No shit? I mean, not about the bear, but about the tranquilizers. Would you know where they're kept?"

"Ummm."

"And sorry, I don't mean to be a dick, but which one are you? Chloe or – "

"That's okay." She sniffs. "She's Chloe. I'm Zoe. Our mom was the same person."

"I figured," Kevin says, laughing a little. "And I'm sorry."

"I never saw them, but I'm sure there are darts and guns at the vet hospital, and the Wildlife office too. I think that's on Prospect near that big hotel."

"Do you think a tranquilizer will work, though?" asks Rachel. "I mean, like I said, there's no heartbeat. Does that mean there's no circulation, or is something else moving blood through them? Any kind of drug would need a bloodstream, right?"

Michael listens to his daughter. He feels as if he hasn't been asleep for days but rather months. Years. However long it might take for Rachel to grow into this take-charge, no-nonsense persona.

"Blood is obviously important to these things," Bonnie says, "so I'd imagine that – whatever's in their heads is moving that blood around? In something approximating circulation?"

It takes this latest mention of blood for Michael to glance over at Rachel thoughtfully. Of course, one of the things the two of them have in common is their blood type. The rarest blood type. It was a fun connection between them when she was a kid, a goofy talking point. O-negative blood. The universal donor. The universal healer.

"Look, this is a conversation we need to have, for sure," Kevin says. "What makes these things tick and all that. But we don't have time to go to the Division of Wildlife or whatever. We have to test this thing now. I say we all get in there and hold it down like we did before, get it done."

Bonnie murmurs, "Oh no."

"I agree," Rachel says. "We know how to handle them. For chrissakes, we held off a whole hospital full of them. We can handle *one*."

"Exactly," Kevin says.

"How much blood do we have left?" Rachel asks the room.

"Alan took about half of it out of storage last night, right before he – " Bonnie says softly. "We probably have thirty units."

"And not to be morbid," Kevin says, "But we're all carrying quite a lot of that O-negative stuff in our own bodies."

The other twin, Chloe, calls out, "We're like weapons. Our bodies are weapons."

All the survivors pause to consider that.

"She's right," Kevin says.

The girl says, "Fuck yeah," and Kevin manages another laugh.

"If this thing works," he says, "I say we start drawing blood from everyone."

"Yep." Rachel's voice sounds more confident now. "Okay, let's do it."

The group springs into motion, Rachel and Kevin taking charge of the operation. Rachel instructs the trio of young women to gather blankets and sheets, perhaps pillows, and for a moment Michael is baffled as to the reason, but then he understands that the cloth will help keep the light, that strange radiation, from affecting the survivors' exposed flesh. Bonnie is sent to collect a unit of O-negative plasma and two high-capacity syringes. She knows exactly where to go, and though she begins her journey with a plaintive sigh, she takes to the mission and is out of the room in a flash. The remaining survivors return to their posts at the hospital entrances, helping to clean up and keep an eye on things.

In the middle of the commotion, Joel reenters the room and finds Rachel buried in her father's chest.

"I got Buck on the horn, anyway."

"Yeah?"

"Told him to get over to the Harmony hospital and secure that blood."

"What about the Thompson brothers?"

"No answer." And then, loudly enough to reverberate down the hallways, "*Fuck!*" After a moment, Joel gives Rachel a look. "Those dudes are survivors. More so than the rest of us."

Rachel removes herself from Michael's embrace and moves toward Joel. She grasps his forearm with both hands.

"Joel, I'm sorry, okay? I didn't – "

"Now, no – " He tries to shrug her off, but she holds fast.

" – I was in shock, all right? I still am, probably. I couldn't – process. So I fucked up. But I'm trying to make it right."

Joel visibly softens and manages to remove her hands. Michael knows that there's still a lot beneath this cop's surface, and it's directed at Rachel.

Kevin walks up. "We're ready."

"Ready for what?"

"We're gonna test that motherfucker upstairs, inject it, see what happens."

Joel looks from Rachel to Michael to Kevin.

"To wake him up?"

"To bring him back to life," Rachel says.

"Now hold on, just wait a goddamn second." He raises one hand authoritatively. "The man in that room is a felon."

Rachel looks stunned. "He's a human being."

Joel steels himself. "Not what I was getting at – but Jesus, couldn't you have a picked a better specimen for your test?"

"Hey, we might be really lucky that there was a prisoner here at all."

He looks at her for a long moment. "Point taken, but *shit*."

"All right, then, let's go."

CHAPTER 6

In moments, the group has reassembled, and everything is ready. The loose team walks up the stairs purposefully, quiet as they tread the barren hallway and approach the closed door. Arriving, they exchange glances. Rachel and Bonnie have blood-filled syringes at the ready – they look huge, perhaps 100 milliliters. Kevin and Michael are holding big wads of starchy hospital blankets in front of them as if they're looking to capture some kind of wild game, and Joel is to the side. The cop now holds a tactical shotgun, loaded, aimed low and tight. The three girls remain behind them, ready to jump in if they're needed.

There are only subtle movements coming from inside the room, sounding like halfhearted attempts to escape the handcuffs.

"Ready to get this done?" Kevin says.

Nods all around.

He takes hold of the handle and swings the door in.

The inverted corpse whips its head around to face them, hissing an unearthly gasp. On top of the odors of human waste and filth, Michael smells something like dry rot coming from the open mouth – the smell of poor teeth, poor health. The odors have filled the room. The survivors around him frown with disgust.

"That hand is close to coming off." Joel edges his way in, his weapon trained on the thing's head. "Get on in here."

Kevin leads Michael in, cautiously, and they step around the corpse, surrounding it but not getting too close. It watches them, one at a time, back and forth, its eyes wide and red and dry. Michael takes a look at the hand, and yes, it's connected to the arm by mere tendons now, the flesh hanging in strands, veins dripping sluggishly. There's a Rorschach pattern of swiped blood beneath the corpse, and its skin is pale, almost gray. He wonders if, given time, the thing might just expire from blood loss.

But the blood dripping from the nearly severed hand is more akin to thickened oil than blood.

"Remember – don't let that head get near you," Bonnie reminds them for the third time. "We should probably get some vests from an x-ray room." Her voice is filled with uncertainty, and Michael knows she's directing her words at him.

"I got it."

Just as he speaks, the corpse furiously thrashes its whole body. There's a sickeningly loud snap as the final tendon is severed and the dismembered hand falls to the floor. The thing is abruptly a whirling dervish of chaotic anger, screaming through its ragged throat, its bent-backward limbs swiping at the floor, its arm stump painting broad red strokes on the tiles, and it's rushing toward them, hobbled but quick. The entire group rears back, and Joel brings up the shotgun as the corpse prepares to lunge.

"No! Don't kill it!" Kevin shouts at the cop. "We got it! We need it!"

Joel swears loudly, swinging his weapon up, and Kevin leaps at the thing that's scrabbling across the floor.

"Kevin!" shouts Bonnie.

Michael, against all sound judgment, rushes forward to help the large man, pressing the cloth into whatever gap he can find, trying to secure flailing limbs and use his weight to collapse the body onto the floor. The corpse is all elbows and knees beneath him, battering him, and squawking at him in horrid barks. Michael gets within a foot of the thing's peeled-wide eyes, sees immense anger or fear there, and he arches away from it as it attempts to thrust its head at him like a stinger.

At that moment, Michael understands that the thing *knows* it can inflict harm with whatever is inside it. There's an intelligence behind that awful face.

And something else.

Michael freezes for an instant as the thing glares at him, screeches at him. The eyes, those terrible eyes – they burn into him. He stares into them, glimpses something behind them –

"Daddy!" Rachel screams.

Her voice knocks him from his momentary paralysis, and then Kevin's weight finally brings the thing to the floor. Michael uses all his strength to help him pin the body down, his skin protected by hospital cloth.

"We got it! We got it! Do it!" Kevin is yelling.

But Rachel is already pressing into the gap, expertly wielding her fat syringe. She thrusts it forward, toward the bulging carotid artery at the strained neck. But the thing thrashes its head toward Rachel and the tip of the needle accidentally plunges deep into its cheek, beneath the enraged eye. Rachel flinches more than the corpse does.

She cries out, repulsed, and yanks the syringe from the flesh. "You've got to secure the head! Use the blankets."

Bonnie dives into the fray and blinds the thing with the sheets from the bed, leaving the neck free. Rachel inserts the needle and begins to push the O-negative blood into the vein.

The reaction is instantaneous. The body goes rigid, and the wild flailing energy becomes more of a nervous thrum beneath Michael's hands.

"Okay!" Rachel calls. "Done!"

The survivors scramble backward as one, leaving the corpse straining and vibrating on the floor. It's coughing and sputtering, and in the weak light, the red glow inside the head is sparking and strobing.

"What in the hell?" Michael gasps, backing into the wall next to the door. He sees that Rachel has emptied only about a quarter of the large syringe into the corpse's neck.

The corpse is no longer paying them any attention; instead, it is consumed by what is happening inside itself. The glow finally pops out, audibly – sounding like an electric crack – and the body slumps to the floor, lifeless.

Blood is still pumping weakly from the wrist stump.

"We need to get a tourniquet on that," Rachel says, pointing. "He won't be any use to us if he bleeds out."

Behind Michael comes the sound of tearing fabric. Kevin is ripping a thin length of cloth from a blue bedsheet.

"I don't think he can hurt you now," she says. "Go ahead."

Kevin visibly swallows, staring at the bald man. After a moment of trembling indecision, he quickly wraps the stump with the cloth and yanks it tight, tying a messy knot while avoiding the blood still flowing from the devastated wrist.

"I think he's lost a lot of blood, can you give him the rest of the syringe?"

"I doubt this is how a transfusion works, but what the hell, right?" Rachel reinserts the syringe and gives it steady pressure, emptying the contents.

"Check for a pulse!" Bonnie calls from behind them.

Kevin shoves his finger beneath the man's jaw. He concentrates, searching.

"I don't – wait!" The big man tentatively touches the man's chest, then dives in full force, beginning a frantic series of chest compressions, counting audibly with the effort. Sweat is standing out on his head in big droplets, some of them raining down on the prisoner. Abruptly he drops and fastens his mouth to that of the unconscious man, blowing air inside his lungs. He returns to the chest compressions.

In moments, the bald man coughs. Breathing has resumed. But the eyes remain closed.

"You *have* to be kidding," Joel whispers. "He's alive?"

"There's a pulse?" one of the girls cries from the hall.

"I don't fucking believe it," Kevin breathes.

Both of the man's shoulders appear nearly dislocated, but perhaps not; the body seems to be subtly deflating and attaining at least a measure of its former shape and contour. There don't appear to be any badly broken bones, but the body still looks to have been through the ringer.

As if reading his mind, Kevin says, "Let's put those arms back while he's out. Mike, hold him down at the shoulder, will ya?"

Michael moves quickly to put his weight against the bald man's upper body, and Kevin wastes no time popping both arms back into place. Even so, the body is in terrible shape, and Michael feels a wave of dark pity wash over him. He stands and regards the body silently. It's a mess. All of the limbs, all the fingers and toes, remain wrenched out of shape, some subtly, some unmistakably. He certainly wouldn't want to wake to such an existence. If this man were awake right now, he would be screaming his head off.

Rachel bends down carefully toward the man's head and, using a blanket, manipulates the jaw so that she can see inside the mouth.

"It's gone. There's nothing in there." She tosses the blanket aside and places her hand above his mouth. "And he's breathing. This guy's *alive*."

Just as she says it, the man lets out a ragged snore, and repeats it, as if he's having trouble breathing in unconsciousness.

"Let's get him up on the bed," Bonnie says, coming forward. She takes charge effortlessly, although she can't hide the grimace on her mouth.

Michael grasps the left side of the body, opposite Rachel. They share a glance as Bonnie positions herself next to Michael, directing Kevin next to Rachel with a gesture. The four of them lift the body up and back to the bed, all of them straining under the body's crumpled deadweight. They settle the body to the half-stripped mattress with something approaching dignity, and Joel immediately uses his own cuffs to attach the man's good hand to the metal bar at the bedside.

Rachel gives him a look. "Fair enough."

All of the gathered survivors are crowded around the body, waiting for something to happen. But nothing does, save for the throaty suspiration of the prisoner and the expectant breathing of the group.

"Imagine if we'd done this to one of those outside, with all that wood and sap and splinters and shit all down their throat," Kevin says, shaking his shaggy head. "Even if this dude survives, I think it'll be a very different thing to turn the ones outside. Hell, I can't imagine most of those fuckers *wanting* to live after this shit. Not to mention that there's hundreds of thousands of them out there, and we're dealing with just one here. You know, a controlled situation."

Bonnie touches the man's forehead. "Maybe a fever there."

They all stand there expectantly for long minutes, listening to him breathe.

Michael notices Rachel glancing around impatiently, and he's reminded of the teen daughter that he's seen all too much of over the past few years – that glare, that thrust-forward jaw. Before he can give it too much thought, Rachel is shoving at the man on the table.

"Wake up!"

Bonnie grabs at Rachel's arms. "Rachel! What are you doing?"

But the man is abruptly convulsing and coughing. Everyone takes a step back, wary. The man is writhing atop the bed, trying to find his voice. He opens his eyes and stares straight up, blearily. He blinks exaggeratedly, tries to lift his hands up to rub at them, but he finds one hand secured and the other ending at a stump. He can't seem to process either fact, though, and the hands fall back. Finally he finds his voice, hoarse and loud. A stream of sound issues from his mouth, just a groan at first, and then attempts at words.

"*Nnnnnn – nn – hnnnn – hunnnnnn – *"

There's an expression of suffering across his features, and Bonnie appears desperate about it.

"Oh my God," she cries. "Such pain!"

"*Huuunnnnnnnnn – *"

"Why didn't we bring morphine?"

The man's sounds dissolve into some kind of squeal, foamy saliva rimming his lips. " *– rrreeeeeee – *"

Now Bonnie is hustling from the room, pushing past Michael and between the twins. The man on the bed inhales a choking breath, then starts again, bellowing sound, his mouth working. He's trying to say something.

"*Neeeee – *"

He twists across the bed, helplessly. With each movement, it's clear that the hyper-extensions and sprains from before are now excruciating. Michael hears a muffled grinding sound coming from the man's hips, and he instinctively reaches forward to brace the man against the bed to stop him from flailing.

"Help me!" Michael calls. "Keep him still."

The man reacts only vaguely to the hands pressing against him.

"Uh – uhhh – uhhhh – neeeeeeeeeeeeee – "

"Needs?" one of the twins shouts, translating. "Needs what? What does he need?"

Joel is glaring over everything. "I can put him out of his misery right now." He's holding his shotgun at the ready.

"No!" Rachel calls, but there are tears in her eyes. "We need him! We have to learn! We have to see if we can bring him back."

The man's throat bulges with veins, and his face is red with struggle, and just as he's about to let go with another burst of shouts, he goes mercifully unconscious, deflating to the table. Simultaneously, blood bursts from both nostrils in a fine mist and then in thin streams, down his cheeks to the sheets.

"I got it on me, I got it on me," Kevin is saying, stumbling back and away. With a big forearm splattered with fresh blood, he's reaching for one of the white towels. *"Jesus!"*

Bonnie arrives with morphine, out of breath, and stares down at the body.

"What happened?"

Numb, Joel says, "Passed out." He's got his weapon aimed at the ceiling now. He won't need it anymore.

The group is left considering one another, and considering what has happened on a lone bed in the middle of this decimated hospital.

CHAPTER 7

Michael wakes gummy-eyed to the sight of a tray table next to him. There's a packaged turkey sandwich, a banana, and two bottles of water there. He feels an almost violent urge to grab all these items and clutch them to his body. Instead, he reaches over carefully and takes one of the bottles. He twists it open and drinks, gulping down the water.

He is weak with hunger and still terribly thirsty.

And here in the deep dark, his first real waking thought is –

Susanna.

He's still in this godforsaken hospital, in a state of horrified confusion, the world crumbling around him, and he still has no idea what happened to his wife. He feels a lump of emotion in his throat, knowing that he's back to square one in this awful new reality, having fallen unconscious again, alone once more in the dark. He needs to find her; he needs to know what happened to her.

"You passed out again," Bonnie says from the doorway.

Michael jerks, startled.

"Sorry." She gestures toward the water. "I knew you'd be thirsty. You're probably dehydrated. I should have realized that earlier. I'm sorry. Take it easy, though. The body can reject it if you go too fast."

Michael brings the bottle down, savors what's inside him. It's like a blast of healing balm. He takes hold of the sandwich and forces himself to slowly unwrap it.

"They're a little stale, but we're not exactly in the business of making fresh sandwiches these days. We found them in the cafeteria. At least they're not spoiled yet. That's almost the last of the water, but we'll get more at Safeway."

He takes the first bite of the sandwich, feels an almost comical surge of energy come from it, then takes another. He nods his appreciation.

"Thank you," he says. He smiles weakly at her, embarrassed. "I passed out?"

"Kevin caught you before you hit the floor." She gives him a slight smile.

He drinks again, swallows. The hospital is silent and dark behind her. "Where's Rachel?"

"She's next door, sleeping hard." Her brow trembles, and her gaze drifts. "Poor girl is hugging an old teddy bear."

Michael imagines Rachel in her own hospital bed, curled fetal with her bear, and he feels a new tug of emotion.

He tries to recall the last thing he did before falling unconscious.

After the incident with the body upstairs – directly above him – Bonnie took charge of the situation medically, and she determined that the man had suffered hyper-extension in all the major joints. She used several braces to support the healing of the hyperextension. She found cold compresses to help, too. He remembers Bonnie saying, "I'm stunned his back isn't broken. You saw the way he was bent backward. My spine hurts just thinking about it."

After that, the survivors started in on the task of cleaning up the battle zone that the hospital had become. Michael probably took on more than he should have; he has a strong recollection of cleaning major portions of the floor in the lobby.

He doesn't remember anything after that.

"You tried to brace yourself with your mop," Bonnie says, "but you started slipping right down to the ground. Luckily Kevin was right there next to you."

"So how's it going out there?" Michael asks, motioning toward the hospital's inner rooms and hallways.

"The man … the prisoner … he's still asleep," she says haltingly. "Everything else is coming along." She gives in to a weary sigh. "I feel like – like what happened before, that the worst is over and now it's time to recover. You know what I mean? I guess I need that. To feel like things can get better."

"Sure, I get that."

"We're cleaning the place up as best we can … moving bodies to the morgue. For a sense of decorum as much as to isolate them." She walks farther in, a frown crossing her face. "They're starting to decompose in this heat. But I – I feel like, at least I can get my head around this. Dead bodies coming back to life and eating trees, not so much. But put me in charge of cleaning up a hospital? That I can do."

"Makes sense to me." He finishes a half-sandwich, resisting a strong instinct to plow right into the second half. "What time is it, anyway?"

She automatically brings up her wrist, but there's no watch there. "It's late, around midnight, I think. I was about to try to get some rest before my shift at the door."

"So I've been out for how long?"

"Oh ... five hours?"

"Jesus. Sorry."

"Don't knock unconsciousness, it's your best medicine right now."

"I need to be helping, but I keep falling asleep!"

"No one holds it against you. They just want you healthy."

"I should be – "

"You helped a lot! All you missed was a bunch of indecisive people trying to plan what to do next."

A long beat of silence inflates the distance between them. Bonnie appears about to come closer, perhaps settle into the plastic chair that has been pulled up next to the bed, but then she turns toward the door.

"I need to find my wife," Michael whispers, not wanting Bonnie to leave.

She offers a sad smile, and now she moves to the chair. The chair is new to him, and he realizes that Rachel was probably sitting there at some point, watching him.

"Michael," Bonnie says. "If I were you ... I would start preparing for the worst."

He doesn't know how to respond to that. He takes a bite of the sandwich's second half and chews slowly.

"I just need ... I just need to make sure, I guess."

"I understand."

He swallows, drinks more water.

"So ... what happened to you?" he asks. "I feel like I've been learning about all this piecemeal. It would be nice to know what you saw. What happened that morning?"

"It must be strange," Bonnie says, introspection in her voice, "to only see the aftermath ... to not have lived through that ... hell."

"It's frustrating, actually."

"No, I know, just that ... it must feel like some kind of blank spot, between what life was like before and what it is now."

"Something like that, yeah." He touches the small bandage at his forehead.

Michael considers Bonnie – this woman who is unutterably exhausted and yet continues to check up on him, probably more than he realizes, even when he's been asleep. Obviously a natural-born caregiver. She's still walking around in the spongy white shoes of a nurse.

"Did you work here at the hospital, before – ?" he starts.

Bonnie offers a slight smile, as if the gesture is difficult to summon. There's mirth somewhere in this woman's face, buried deep underneath a lingering haze of psychological trauma. It's a glimpse of this woman's life before this one. Whatever has happened over the past couple days has taken its toll on Bonnie both inwardly and outwardly.

It takes her long moments to find words, but she finally says:

"I worked at a pediatrician's office down the street. I was on my way to work when it happened. It was the – it was the craziest, creepiest thing I'd ever seen." She stands and moves to the counter that runs along the north wall of the room. The counter has become some kind of haphazard medical-supply area. "I was driving up Lemay, it was right around 6 a.m. and I was coming in early for some admin work. I was a physician's assistant, and Saturdays were the best opportunity for some catch-up work."

She turns back to face him, and he notices she's holding a penlight.

"Anyway, there were just a few cars on the road," she continues as she approaches close and shines the light into his eyes, one by one. "I was listening to the radio and probably singing along or something, and – some of the people I've talked to mention some kind of, I don't know, a pulse or something, but all I remember is that all of a sudden every other car on the road, ahead of me and behind me, started drifting. Well, first I noticed just the car right in front of me – I thought, *Hey, wake up, wake up! Get off your damn phone!* – because the car faded out of the lane, more and more. Finally, I was honking like hell at her, but nothing. No response at all. And that's when I saw that other cars were doing it, too. Everywhere." She shakes her head. "Just bumping against each other, and crashing into the trees, skidding against the gutters ... crazy. Just right outside there!" She gestures out the window. "I was one of the first people here."

She finishes up with the light, apparently satisfied.

For the next twenty minutes, Bonnie tells Michael what she experienced after walking through the front doors of the hospital. How no one was here at first, except for slumped-over bodies here and there. How people began arriving, desperately seeking help for loved ones who had been mutilated by family members overcome by some kind of foreign inhabitation. How the situation grew increasingly more chaotic and horrific, as what they first deemed to be corpses started twitching to new life and new purpose. And how Rachel took charge, desperate to find not only Michael but also some kind of answer to the mystery that had descended upon the world.

Michael listens with a kind of detached disbelief. At times, he has to keep from laughing at the absurdity of Bonnie's story. But even as she speaks – with her hoarse, ravaged whisper – he can't deny the evidence that he's witnessed ... the blood-soaked floors and the dried arterial sprays on the walls ... the eerie emptiness of not only the hospital but the streets outside ... the putrid, humid stench of smoke and death ... the bodies ...

"What about you?" she asks as she finishes her story. "How's your memory? Do you remember anything about that morning yet?"

"I keep getting flashes of it," he tells her. "Like, I remember – I think I remember – walking into the building. It was all dark because it was Saturday." He experiences an odd moment in which he is about to tell her exactly why he was at the office – just lay it out bare. It doesn't matter anymore, anyway. Then he shakes himself from that potential mistake. "I remember the janitor arrived a few minutes after I did. I just get patches of that memory. The sound of his vacuum. I also have this flash of ... running? It's frustrating, because I know that whole memory is there – I just can't get to it."

"That sounds about right. At least you're getting those flashes now. I bet you'll get a full recovery of all those memories."

"Something tells me I'd rather not."

She smiles in a way that reminds him of Cassie, and even Rachel a little bit, back when she was his little girl. At the thought, he sits up straighter and looks at Bonnie carefully. He touches her hand.

"You need to sleep, I know. But can you do me one more favor? Tell me about Rachel."

"What do you mean?"

"I mean ... I'm kind of amazed by what she's done. And I'm ashamed to say that I'm not sure I would have expected it from her."

Bonnie is looking increasingly sleepy in her chair, but her eyes go all deep-watery, and she says, "Your daughter ... Rachel ..."

"Tell me."

"Just that ... she took charge when we needed it most."

Michael already feels his head shaking minutely.

"She's a resourceful girl," Bonnie goes on. "She discovered things that the rest of us just – missed. You know it was Rachel who discovered the link with the blood, right? The O-negative blood? She figured that out."

Michael has learned almost through osmosis that the one key trait setting the survivors apart from the possessed corpses is the fact that they all have type O-negative blood flowing in their veins. Meaning, probably, that their blood type saved them. He didn't know his daughter made that discovery. His Rachel!

How on Earth did she figure that out?

"I'm O-negative," Michael whispers.

"That's what Rachel told us."

"When she was a kid, that was our thing, the cool thing we had in common. I made sort of a big deal about it back then, but I'm surprised she remembered it."

"Her quick thinking ... it saved us."

Not only did their blood save them, it also proved a potent weapon, thanks to the stores of O-negative plasma in hospital storage. That's mostly what Michael saw smeared over the floors and walls. He was right that there was a great battle right outside his door, but it was not at all what he initially thought. They had sprayed the scrabbling, crab-like bodies with blood, and the things had reacted violently, retreating out the front doors and leaving the survivors stunned and blood-soaked, but alive.

The picture Bonnie is painting of Rachel is of a gritty survivor who has figured everything out ... a resourceful girl who, in the heat of the mortal chaos, kept her cool. Everyone else was making mistakes, jumping to conclusions – everyone but her. But that's not the Rachel he has seen since waking up.

"If all this is true," he whispers, "why is she curled up in a ball next door? You heard what happened with Tony."

Bonnie sighs. "That was later. None of us saw how this would end."

"End?"

"They don't even care about us, you know. Those bodies just – they just disappeared into the night." She shakes her head with some kind of regret. "Oh, that poor girl. She didn't deserve what happened to her."

Michael listens to her breathe.

"Where did they go?" he says after a moment. "Those things."

"They've – most of them have massed in the foothills, where most of the trees are. I don't know what they're doing. You saw them, right? Out front? At the trees? We live in a world where everyone is dead, doing this thing that's – that's – that's just incomprehensible."

According to Bonnie, there are groups of armed survivors burning the forests, torching the bodies, denying whatever force is inside them from achieving its strange goal. And now the forests of the foothills are on fire, thousands of corpses going up in flames alongside the trees.

"We aren't all that's left, I hope you didn't think that," Bonnie says. "We ran into some men, and they were hell-bent to burn every last one of them. In a bid to survive. They had live grenades, flame throwers. They were armed to the teeth. Just destroying them."

Now Michael can grasp the moral weight of the situation – particularly as it falls on Rachel's shoulders.

"My God, just the thought of what to do next!" Bonnie closes her eyes, and when she reopens them, there are tears there. "That girl – Rachel – your daughter is going to need you." She's staring down at the floor. "Yeah, she needs you. I'm so glad you're awake."

"Have you been in to see her tonight?"

"I have." Bonnie looks troubled as she stands up.

"Is she all right?"

"She was awake, yes, but – she's not very responsive. She's just lying there, on her side."

"I'll go see her."

"She needs to stop blaming herself." She's brushing the front of her blouse, straightening up, looking ready to leave. She goes to the counter and opens a packet of Tylenol, brings the two tablets back to him. He swallows the pain relievers dutifully. "Anyway, you need your rest. You'll need a lot more. I know you want to jump right in to help, but you should be careful with that concussion. Don't overdo anything."

He smiles his thanks at her. "What about you? Going to sleep?"

"I realized last night that I haven't slept in about 72 hours. Is that even possible?"

"Seems we've had opposite experiences."

"Yes."

After a moment, Bonnie turns to leave.

"One more thing," Michael says, a thought occurring to him. "What about animals? Is this happening to them? Have you seen any dogs? Birds?" Ever since he woke, he can't recall seeing or hearing evidence of any kind of animal – either outside his window or out the front doors.

Bonnie considers him, her eyes still moist. "I'm actually not sure that's occurred to anyone." One hand on the door, she yawns terrifically. "There was a lot going on."

After Bonnie excuses herself, Michael sits with his head in his hands, waiting for the Tylenol to work.

Michael knows his skull is healing, thanks to Bonnie. When he first woke, he was in a state of confusion. But now he feels more and more grounded, even though it's inside a reality that he'd rather not be a part of.

He's beginning to think he has Bonnie as much as his daughter to thank for his survival. She has been incredibly attentive, treating his wound when Rachel brought him in, and later treating him for the resulting concussion. Bonnie reminds Michael of Cassie, strongly now, and so submitting to her care was easier than it perhaps might have been.

Bonnie ... Cassie ... Susanna ... Rachel ...

If Bonnie is to be believed – as well as the evidence all around him – his daughter is a broken, exhausted shell of herself; the sky is filled with the stinking smoke of an uncontrolled pyre of cremated human beings; and most of the world is dead – including Susanna.

He stares at the ceiling, listening to the silence.

CHAPTER 8

Michael pushes himself out of bed, past a wave of dizziness, and goes to the already open window. He stares out toward the burning foothills. Along the western horizon, licks of flame brush the dark orange underbellies of smoke clouds drifting northeast, and behind everything are weird flashes of purple and red, atmospheric and alien. He can't quite see the mountains to the south – Longs Peak and the neighboring summits, so familiar, so reliable. They're blocked by the homes and businesses down Lemay. But he doesn't *want* to see them in the context of this new reality.

Michael is startled by a noise that he has never heard before. It's a deep, rumbling roar, vibrating the walls – throaty and yet almost … electronic. As soon as it begins, it starts to fade away.

Bonnie is back at the door, new alertness in her eyes. Right behind her is Joel, still up, still on alert.

" – what I was talking about," Joel is saying. "Hey Mike."

They join him at the window.

"This has happened a few times," Bonnie explains to Michael. "Joel thinks it's how they're communicating. This is the quietest one we've heard."

"It doesn't seem to have any rhyme or reason," Joel says. "The volume of it, or the frequency. At least, to us, it doesn't. But I think it makes sense to *them.*"

"I think you might be right," Bonnie says. "I know it happened right as all the bodies raced out toward the foothills."

Michael watches the horizon carefully. Did the smoke react to the low roar, shivering in the sound wave seemingly originating from above it? He voices the question, and Bonnie and Joel agree silently.

After perhaps ten minutes, as nothing further has come of the comparatively quiet phenomenon, Michael is left alone at the window, both Bonnie and Joel giving him separate pats on his shoulder.

"Try to sleep, okay"? Bonnie says.

He continues to stare at the foothills, mesmerized. The longer he watches, the more apparent it is that there's a great red fog rising into the night. And there's a relentlessness to it, paired with the columns of smoke rising from the burning hills. It's a constant pulse. And it's all too clear that the two forces – the red fog and the roar – are somehow related. Michael tries to understand it, to connect these phenomena with what has happened to humanity.

He comes up with nothing. Only more questions.

At just past 1 a.m., Michael pulls open his door and peers up and down the empty hallway. A contingent of survivors has spent some time cleaning up the blood on the floor, but there's just no way they could erase all trace of it – and the proof is in the stench. It still smells rotten, and he knows it's only going to get worse with those bodies in the basement.

He steps into the dimly lit hall, makes his way to Rachel's door, and pushes into the room, which is softly illuminated by a night light. He looks at his baby girl.

Baby girl.

It's odd to think in those terms now, he knows, in light of everything that has happened. But seeing her there, curled into a protective ball, holding that old bear – it's apt. And he can't blame her. Can't blame her for going fetal, escaping within herself to heal. He would probably be this way, too.

He steps over to the complicated metal bed and sits on one of the three chairs next to it. At the sound of the chair squeaking on the floor, Rachel snaps awake with a momentary look of absolute fear on her face. Michael calms her, and she closes her eyes, sighing.

"Daddy," she whispers.

"Hey Rach."

She brings her hand to her brow, closes her eyes hard for a moment.

"How are you doing?" Michael asks.

She squints her eyes open. "Can't shake this headache."

"I know the feeling."

She manages a weak smile, and crinkles her nose. "You stink."

Michael glances down at the clothes he's been wearing for three straight days. He's sure they're more odiferous that he even realizes. The tan polo shirt has sweat stains at the armpits, and even dried blood splotches that probably came from him, but he's not entirely sure.

"I imagine showers are tough to come by," he says.

"Almost as tough as ice water."

"What I'd give for a tall glass." He reaches over and touches her sweaty hair, the side of her face.

She stays silent, stares straight ahead as he curls her hair behind her ear. In the humid silence, her eyes begin to fill with tears. She lifts an arm toward him, beckoning for an embrace, and he stands and bends over her, holding her. She begins sobbing into his chest, shaking, her muscles clenched. Both of her arms are now around his shoulders; she's not about to let go.

He lets her cry.

Finally her embrace slackens a bit, and he gradually draws himself away. Her arms fall, and she wipes at her wet cheeks, refocusing her eyes. She looks at him with a rueful smile.

"Sorry Daddy."

"You don't have anything to be sorry about."

"But I do! I do!" And the tears threaten again as she shakes her head savagely. "You don't know – " Her voice hitches loudly. " – you don't know what it was like, you don't know – you – "

He doesn't know how to help her. In the silence that falls between them, he simply touches her hand and watches her.

When Rachel's mother died five years ago, Rachel and Michael became very close. They weathered the pain together, and they recovered together. He was so in tune with what she needed emotionally then! Maybe the reason he focused so intently on Rachel in that horrible aftermath was to deflect his own reaction to his wife's death, but the upshot was that it was his proudest moment as Rachel's father. It's a terrible notion, perhaps, but it's true: His best moments as a father came in the wake of his wife's death.

For a year, he and Rachel were closer than they ever were. When she retreated from her friends at school and was in real danger of becoming a melancholy loner, he didn't let it happen. He became Ultra Dad, arranging sleepovers and chaperoning trips to the mall and hosting impromptu parties and simply keeping Rachel's friends close to her. He wanted to make sure that his 14-year-old enjoyed – at least, for the most part – the teen years she deserved to experience.

Often his efforts were in vain. Maybe too often. Sometimes, despite all the energy he could muster, Rachel folded inward upon herself, disappearing into her bedroom for long hours, collapsing onto her bed, sleeping or reading or staring at the wall. Michael didn't deny her those periods, knowing that she had to endure what she needed to, but he would always quietly suffer on the other side of the house, wanting to help but powerless to do so.

One day, after another six or seven hours spent in solitude in her silent room, she emerged a bit dazed and found Michael in the kitchen nursing a beer. It was his fourth of the evening, and he was in his own daze, but he remembers watching her shuffle into the room to stare at him. They just looked at each other for a long moment. Then she said:

"I miss Mom."

Michael felt a familiar stab straight in the gut. "I do too, Rach."

"No, I mean – I mean, I miss her, but ... but I – I don't know – I don't want to cry about it anymore."

"Okay," he said.

"I mean, not for a while."

"All right."

He didn't want to say more for fear that it would be the wrong thing to say.

She stood there some more. Then she meandered over to the refrigerator for a Coke. She popped the tab and fell into the chair across from him. He can still remember that moment clearly, despite his beer haze at the time. The way her shorts and tee-shirt were twisted and frumpy from bed, the way her acne reminded him that he should feed her better, the way her eyes looked blasted from crying but clearer somehow.

"So ... let's do something," she said.

"What do you want to do?"

"Can we go to a movie?"

It didn't happen that easily. It's not as if one day she shook off all her sadness and became the same bright-eyed girl she was before the death of her mother. In fact, further tears came from her room later that night, after their movie, after their laughter. Maybe she felt bad for allowing herself to be happy again. But that night was a turning point for both of them. And getting to that place together – that's what made all the difference.

They had two strong years, on their own, father and daughter. The best years of his relationship with Rachel.

He tried to introduce Susanna carefully into that father/daughter dynamic. He really did.

He waited longer than he might otherwise have, in deference to Rachel's healing. But life happens. For a year, their courtship favored Susanna's apartment and local hotels, but at a certain point everything felt deceptive, and so he casually hosted Susanna for a pizza dinner that included Rachel, and –

– perhaps that was the mistake. The key mistake.

Since that fateful evening, Michael remains convinced that Rachel would have had the same reaction regardless of how many years had passed since her mother's death. For him, two years of mourning was sufficient. Yes, his wife's death was a body blow to his soul; it was wrenching. But he felt that he had earned the right to carry on. For Rachel, it might've seemed more reasonable that he married for life, that he be content with later years marked by emotional and physical celibacy.

So maybe he was doomed from the start.

Michael loved his daughter, but he needed his own life, too. He just wasn't sure when Rachel would have been ready for that. He thought the best tactic was to confront the thing head on, but in retrospect, that was the worst tactic.

Rachel considered it a breach of trust. In what seemed a single night, she turned from a healing, increasingly happy girl to a brooding, distrustful teen. He remembers now that it started the day after she got her driver's license: His sweet-sixteen daughter from the day earlier, all grown-up and ebullient – but still so little behind the wheel of his Acura – collapsed into moody instability, and she never really recovered.

Until yesterday – here at the end of the world – when Rachel burst into his locked, disheveled hospital room, brandishing a smoking shotgun, and said, "Hi Daddy." His miserable teenager transformed into some kind of action-movie heroine – and not only that, she embraced him as if the past two years had never happened – or had happened in an entirely different way.

His daughter has returned to him, and in dramatic fashion.

And Susanna is apparently gone.

Dead?

But now, Rachel is threatening to become that angry, insecure teen again, the demon that possessed Rachel that night he brought Susanna home. He knows this tone all too well – and for the first time, it occurs to him that perhaps he, Michael, is the key differentiator. In his absence, she took on an apocalyptic threat, bravely, heroically. Now that he has returned, she has regressed to what she was before.

She sniffs, exhales loudly now.

"You were *unconscious*, Dad, you don't know how – how – how *terrible* it was! The things that happened, the decisions we made! The decisions I made! I *fucked up*, Dad, I mean I really – " She draws in a high-pitched gasp and stops talking, the muscles of her face clenching. "And I'm *still* making shitty decisions! I just –

Michael sits there helplessly, quiet, just stroking her hair while she cries. In his peripheral vision, he's aware of someone peeking into the room briefly. He turns, sees Bonnie's face in the shadows. Her eyes meet his very briefly – he thinks he catches a sad, understanding smile – and then she's gone, down the humid hallway. Why is she still awake?

"Rachel," he says, "I'm sorry I wasn't here with you, to help you through – whatever the hell this is. But whatever has happened … no one has the answers. No one knows anything. You were incredible – that's what everyone is telling me. And the one thing I know for *sure* is that you were there for me. I'm only here right now because of you. That's about the bravest thing I've ever heard."

Rachel can only stare straight ahead, subtly shaking her head left and right. Silence swallows up the room, and Michael can hear only his daughter's breathing. Finally, he can no longer hold his next question inside.

"Rachel …" He swallows. "Do you know what happened to Susanna?"

The muscles of her face flinch. Her wet eyes meet his, and something flickers there, maybe the usual resentment, maybe something new.

"When I woke up, she … she had that thing inside her."

Michael waits for more, but Rachel goes quiet.

"You don't know what – ?"

"No, I don't know what happened to her." Her voice is quiet, seething. "I got out of there. Everything was going to hell, okay? I saw that thing inside her, and I tried to wake her up – " She holds up her hand to show him a palm that appears as if it has been splashed with bleach. " – but that didn't work. I got out of there to look for you."

"It's all right, it's okay."

"And then Tony was the same. And his mom. And almost everyone."

"Shhhh …"

Her voice goes softer. "She's gone, Daddy. I'm sorry."

"But you saw what happened upstairs. If it's possible – "

"She's gone."

"Do you mean she's – "

"I just – she's gone, okay?" Her voice is a desperate whisper.

Michael looks at his daughter curiously, a sudden ache of foreboding clutching at his chest.

"Is there anything else? Rachel, anything you're not telling me?"

She turns to him, beseeching. "I don't know what you want me to say, Daddy – I watched her die. I don't want to talk about it anymore."

Rachel turns away from him and won't say anything else. Michael stays with her for another half hour, right next to her, considering her, until her eyelids grow heavy once more and she succumbs to sleep. Her features finally relax, and part of him – that part of him that helped his little girl weather the grief of her mother's death – feels grateful that she has that escape. He places his hand on her brow, feels the warmth there. Ripples of emotion cross her face.

Susanna.

Is she still there, in their bed, where he probably left her that morning? Is she burning in the foothills? What happened to her? His brain still suffering from the effects of a concussion, he finds it difficult to contemplate so many questions at once. He needs to take them one at a time. The first question is lying right in front of him, and yet no answers are forthcoming. Not yet.

Then he kisses Rachel's forehead and makes his way out of the room.

Beyond the walls, off on the western horizon, the foothills continued to burn.

CHAPTER 9

Michael can't sleep.

He glances around in the dimness. The window is still dark. It must be around 3 or 4 a.m. now.

An itch has grabbed hold of his innards, and it's growing increasingly difficult to ignore. He knows it's wrapped up with that feeling he had earlier – the notion that these survivors have lived through something together, have battled together, and have formed a bond that Michael doesn't understand.

That's what happens when you nap through the entire thing, he thinks in a burst of self-loathing.

Even in this bed, he feels like an outsider.

But there's more to it than that.

It's Susanna. His wife. What happened to her? Where is she? When he closes his eyes, he sees her ghostly, beseeching him. Lonely. Lost. Scared. He imagines her out there somewhere, and he feels a crushing hopelessness. He misses her. The feeling is like something heavy yet empty at his core.

I can't lose a second wife.

The whole situation is playing out like some bizarre wish fulfilment for Rachel. He wishes he could banish that thought from his head, but there it is. It's part of why this all seems so unreal. He knows how much his daughter has come to resent Susanna. She might even hate her. That festering wound isn't going to heal instantly – even now, when everything is different. It's too easy to see Rachel as the angry, moody teen … rather than the bold survivalist who burst through that door.

Michael can't help but think about the trajectory of his life *before* this nightmare. The sensual Susanna, alive to his touch. The life they were building together. More important, perhaps, was the life *he* was building for *her* – and for Rachel, too! Neither woman ever knew about the life that was in store for them, that he was accumulating at the back of his closet. Their lives were about to change. Because of him. Was it naïve of Michael to believe that healing was about to begin? That he was taking charge of the deteriorating home situation and on the verge of being the hero?

He sighs.

Maybe.

But now everything has abruptly shifted in a very different, horrific way. *Not fair!*

He finds that he's still staring at the window on the other side of the room. After days of near-narcolepsy and exhaustion, he seems to have turned a corner: Now he has insomnia. Great.

Quite suddenly, a thought occurs to him.

He is going to disappoint Bonnie.

He can still hear her voice, reminding him in that way of hers – so like Cassie's – to get his rest, to let his head heal, to sleep. He knows he needs that sleep. Bonnie would probably scold him for being awake right now. His head is still aching, and his mouth is very dry, and any movement makes him a little dizzy, but yes, he is going to disappoint her.

Just as he would disappoint Rachel if she knew the whole story of her mother's death and his courtship with Susanna. That is a truth that even the end of the world can't wrench from him. No, that will go with him to his grave.

My grave.

He edges his way out of his bed, feeling his feet softly hit the floor. In the eerie silence, he moves quietly to the counter and finds a half-empty bottle of water. He twists open the top, drains it down, and places the empty bottle into the trash can below the counter.

How can he even think of leaving Rachel? She risked her life for him – repeatedly. He can't abandon her now, can he?

Resting in the corner is the shotgun that Rachel used to blast her way to him yesterday. He goes to it, hefts it, gets accustomed to its grip. He knows weapons fairly well – has ancient memories of target practice with his dad behind the family farm outside of St. Louis – and this one is easy to figure out. He ensures that it's loaded and takes up the box of shells that's situated immediately above it on the counter. Then he finds a Tylenol sample kit filled with packets, and on a whim, he grabs a few of those, too. All of this goes into Rachel's backpack, which is tucked in the same corner. Already inside it are some bruised pieces of fruit and some medical supplies – probably from his own refrigerator and bathroom.

He glances at the large administrative desk beneath the window. He walks over to it and gives it a quick search, turning up a pen and some paper. He sits down in the expansive leather chair and gives careful thought to his note. He'll be honest about his essential plan. Although he intends to leave this hospital alone, without alerting anyone, he's not stupid. So he lays out what he has to do, omitting certain information, and details his precise route. On the off chance that he's held up and can't return before dawn, he knows Rachel and perhaps the others will come looking for him. He's confident, given what he's learned, that he'll finish what he has to do before that time.

The bottom line is that he has to find Susanna. To discover some kind of truth for himself. To start the process of digging up some memories.

That's really what this is about, isn't it?

He folds up the note and leaves it in plain sight on the bed.

Well, that and the money.

Then he takes the backpack and shotgun and enters the dim hallway. He makes his way into the admissions area and faces the double doors leading to the outside.

To the left, slouched on a blue vinyl waiting-room couch, is Kevin. A rifle is balanced atop the worn cushions, and three empty Mountain Dew cans are crumpled at his feet. When he sees Michael enter, the large man sits up straight.

"Hey," he says, clearing his throat. "I wasn't sleeping."

Michael takes a look around. The stairwell has been emptied of furniture, and the way is clear. The seating has been replaced in the waiting area, and the whole area looks clean and orderly, except for the residue of blood.

"How are you feeling?" Kevin asks, blinking his eyes exaggeratedly to wake himself up.

Michael's hand automatically rises to his forehead. "Like I've been down for the count. For too long."

"Well, like I said before, you're probably lucky you were out for the worst of it."

Michael is already shaking his head. "I would've given anything to be awake. I'm getting the feeling I was just a burden – deadweight."

As Kevin stands, his expression turns contemplative. "I'm not saying we couldn't have used your help, but you know what? You became a sort of – what's the word – a talisman? A good luck charm? Something to fight for? Especially for Rachel."

"I'd rather have been a conscious good luck charm."

"I mean, just the thought of finding you and rescuing you – I think that gave her what she needed to keep going. You know what I'm saying?"

Michael looks at Kevin.

"Yeah," he says.

For the first time, Kevin notices the backpack and the weapon that Michael is carrying. "Uh, Mike, I – I wouldn't go out there."

"I have to."

"Look, I know you just woke up, but – " He glances past Michael toward the doors that lead to the hospital's innards.

"But I've been awake long enough to see how things work now. I need to see my home. I need to see if my wife is there."

"I'm almost positive she's – she's – "

"I need to see for myself, I'm sure you understand."

Kevin watches him warily for a long moment. The two men are surrounded by silence and the subtle stench of rot.

"Mike, I'm not gonna keep you here. You're free to do whatever you want. But it might still be dangerous out there. I'm sitting here to guard these doors from whatever might come *in*, not to keep people from going *out*." He pauses, pitches his voice lower. "Rachel is gonna go bugfuck when she hears you've left."

"I just need to go home, check the house, gather a few things, and come right back. You know? It won't even take an hour."

Kevin is shaking his head.

"We really only have the barest sense of those things. If there's one thing we *do* know, it's that they're unpredictable."

"An hour," Michael repeats.

"Sure, that's what you say *now*. Nothing has worked out the way we thought it would."

Michael gives the big man a small smile. "Who did you lose, Kevin?"

"My folks. Probably all my other friends and family. No big deal." He stares at Michael, almost defiantly.

Michael nods. "I'm sorry."

"I suppose you don't want me to tell anybody about this, at least right away."

"Give me an hour."

Michael turns to the front glass doors, which now look out onto a burgeoning dawn. He walks over to them, stares out into the pitch black, and sighs. He feels Kevin walk up beside him.

Even by predawn light, they can see that the world is on fire. Thick smoke is curdling over the horizon to the west, milky white occasionally stained by black, signaling yet another structure lost to the flames. The blaze is towering, world-crushing, and too close, and apparently with only the puniest firefighting force to face it. He can only hope that the blaze is confined to the areas outside the city.

Michael stares into those ominous and silent scuds of smoke and feels a crush of despair. If he is to believe the weary, soot-smeared people that he has met in this strangely desolate hospital, there are human beings burning in that blaze. Thousands upon thousands of human beings. It's too sickening to comprehend, and yet judging from the emotion on the survivors' faces, it's true. It's no joke.

The smoke is thick and oppressive, even right at this window. The hospital is under generator power, and air conditioning is an obvious first casualty of that fact. Michael can hear fans whirring somewhere, though, bringing some relief from the heat outside but also giving no respite from the smoke. Michael can feel it sharply in his lungs.

He is beginning to grasp the import of what has happened, and it feels like a hollow blackness at his core. He aches for Susanna, for news of her fate, and he needs Rachel to be healthy, to be okay. He needs that connection to those close to him.

He turns his head and regards Kevin, who hasn't said another word.

"I'll be back."

As he steps forward, Kevin says, "Dude?"

"Yeah?"

"Need a car?"

"I guess that wouldn't hurt."

"There's quite a few in the parking lot that are unaccounted for, but honestly any car out there is just waiting for a driver. Find one you like."

In any other situation, this information would be humorous, but Kevin says it with a sobriety that gives Michael pause.

"Just don't take my truck. It's the blue one."

"You got it."

"Be careful."

"Thanks."

Then Michael makes his way out the double doors.

CHAPTER 10

Dawn is breaking ugly and acrid.

And empty.

Fort Collins is deserted.

He's not entirely sure what he was expecting – the emptiness, yes, and that awful sense of desolation he glimpsed from his window – but what strikes him now about the world outside is its muted sense of menacing *wrongness*.

Even as the east brightens under a sickly orange sun, the western foothills are alive with strobing colors, quiet now but deeply alien. Above and beyond the great clouds of gray and black smoke, whatever's up there is alive and active, pulsing as if eager. He catches glimpses of columnar light, mostly drifting heavenward.

Wrong.

In a sort of private denial, Michael looks away from the phenomenon, focusing on his path. He holds Rachel's shotgun tightly in his fist, and he wears her backpack on his back.

North of the hospital, the streets are dim and dry. Kevin's right: Several vehicles lay ahead of him, empty, neglected against curbs, their doors hanging open. He peers down a quiet neighborhood street and sees more: a black Volkswagen Beetle crushed up against a crooked mailbox, a white Ford Escape sitting almost serenely in the middle of a weed-infested yard, and – way down the street – a milk-delivery truck on its side.

Michael doesn't search immediately for a viable car, preferring to walk for now. He heads north toward Mulberry, wanting to get a feel for this new world before insulating himself in a vehicle.

He sees only one body, perhaps a hundred yards down the street, what appears to be an old man, naked, wrapped around the base of a small pine, right near the curb of what was probably his own home. Just before Michael passes beyond that street, he catches a quick glimpse of a forgotten blue bicycle in a gutter.

Just as that thought whispers through his consciousness, movement to the far north causes his heart to flip in his chest. A vehicle is moving slowly along Mulberry, at the Wal-Mart intersection, and continuing east.

So there are other survivors.

He needs to be careful. If there's one thing he's sure of, it's that people in desperate situations can revert with astonishing swiftness to their basest instincts. They can become human monsters, making the most of dire circumstances. He hurries his pace, sticks to the shadows.

He reaches the intersection of Lemay and Riverside and pauses. Is he okay? He touches his bandage tentatively, makes sure it's secure. He concentrates on his headache, makes sure his eyes are focusing correctly. The concussion seems to be healing. What was once a cramping pain in his skull is now a mostly tolerable ache, and he aims to maintain that pain-reduction trajectory. Just as an extra precaution, he reaches into his pocket, roots around for a Tylenol packet. He rips it open and pops the tablets into his mouth, crunching them dry.

According to Rachel, he sustained his wound in the concrete stairwell at work, but he still has no memory of falling there, or of anything at work that morning – and that makes him nervous. There's only one reason he might have been at work on a Saturday, and to have no memory of it? It's too much to just leave to apocalyptic chance. And yet, he's not sure at all what he would do with the information if he had it. The world is totally different now, and that fills him with guilt-ridden loss, but he just has to achieve a sense of finality.

He has to know. To just *know*.

Everything is an alarming red blur, underneath which flit shards of memory that he can't grab on to. When he tries, his head warns him with searing pain. One of the things he feels might happen at home is an ability to begin retracing his steps, see if he can encourage the reconstruction of his memory.

He begins walking again, keeping his eyes wide open. There's zero activity now on the street. Zero! Typically this intersection is one of the busier in the city, but there's nothing, and it gives the entire area a haunted vibe. The business center to his left – the Wendy's, the Walgreens and the Albertsons, a branch of the bank where he and Cassie secured the mortgage for their home – appears ghostly, already part of a distant past. It is utterly forsaken, empty of any life. There's no electricity anywhere. All intersections are powered down, all windows are dark, and there's nothing buzzing or ticking or thrumming or moving.

He pauses under the dawn shadows of the corner bank as the noiseless morning creeps into day. Directly in front of him, a late-model Cadillac is partially crumpled against the base of a street lamp, its broad hood flapped upward at the impact site. The left blinker is still strobing weakly.

Michael is deeply creeped out, but strangely, he feels little overt fear. He feels as if he *should*, given everything that has happened, but ever since he first saw with his own eyes that twisted body cramped up against that tree across from his hospital window, feeding in such an alien way … he hasn't felt threatened by the new reality. All he feels – as he looks out on this usually bustling but now uncannily silent section of north Fort Collins – is that hollow sense of loss and unreality.

He takes Riverside northwest, hurrying along the sidewalk of the exposed street, then ducks west on Myrtle, into a deathly still neighborhood. He sees more abandoned cars, and he sees front doors of homes standing open. Empty.

Michael stops abruptly.

He's just caught sight of what he's sure are the tail and hindquarters of a dead dog. The animal is deep into the yard to his left, immediately to the right of another human being wrapped around the base of a pine tree. The upper half of the dog is out of sight, but the tail suggests a larger dog, perhaps a German shepherd or a Collie.

For some reason, the fact of that dog lying there dead disturbs Michael more than the thought of ninety-six percent of the human population taken over by some tree-hungry alien thing. Even now, outside beneath a rising sun, he sees no evidence of animal life. The early day should be filled with birdsong, and yet there's nothing in the air but smoke and ash. There are no wandering dogs or cats, not even any insects that he can see. He wonders if the same thing that happened to humanity has happened to the animal kingdom.

He finds himself mumbling mindless prayers. He's never been a particularly religious man, but something inside him is pleading with whatever invisible force gives rhythm to the world to just please knock it off, just please stop. Let there be room for hope. If his daughter has really found some kind of solution, please let it be the beginning of something positive.

And yet he knows he's praying into a maelstrom of chaos, in the face of this gigantic thing that is beyond his understanding, perhaps beyond human understanding altogether.

He's about to continue forward along the sidewalk, but then he pauses again. He exhales sharply through his teeth, deciding to get a closer look at the human form. He can't deny his dark curiosity. He reassures himself with the heft of the shotgun, then creeps up quietly on the body, which is moving in weird ululations, wrapped backward around the tree. It shifts very slightly as if sensing him, but its face is hidden beneath heavy branches. It doesn't make any other movement.

It's such a strange sight – what appears to be a businessman, decked out in a now-tattered, haphazardly arranged suit, bereft of any human purpose. Michael approaches stealthily, finally feeling a spurt of fear in his chest, despite the fact that the body really does appear to have no interest in him – until he gets too close, within a few feet, and he sees the body's muscles tense minutely. For what? To spring away from the tree and attack? What threat could it be with its mouth full of splinters and sap?

He decides not to tempt fate any further.

Michael takes a quick look around the neighborhood again, then turns to the dog. He carefully takes hold of one of its paws and slides it out from the shadows onto the lawn. Yes, it's a German shepherd, and yes, it is dead. There is no life, not even any strange otherworldly light emanating from it.

Michael grits his teeth hard.

"Oh fuck."

He remembers high school science, of course. All that stuff about the earth being a complicated system of interconnected species, each one shaped and defined by its relationship to those around it. The thought of eliminating species after species? Well, that's an extinction-level event in itself. At that point, who cares about bringing those infected human beings back to life? Because in a world without other life forms, it wouldn't be long before humanity collapsed anyway.

He rises and has a moment of dizzy imbalance. He stops and gathers himself. He has to be careful. A concussion is not something you just bounce back from. It's almost as if he can hear Bonnie's voice.

Time to find a vehicle.

He scans the street. There are abandoned cars here and there along the street, and if what Kevin said was true, the vast majority of them are ripe for the taking. Keys in the ignition, very little damage from their collisions. Most of them apparently just drifted to the sides of the roads in the immediate aftermath of the event. And then later, as the bodies in those cars began to reanimate, they abandoned the vehicles in search of a strange, common destination.

Michael spots a silver Honda Pilot with two doors flung open. He approaches it warily.

It sits crookedly on a grassy embankment, one rear tire in the gutter. He peers inside, notices that the dome light is emitting a weak glow. He checks the rear seats – nothing. He hops in, shuts his door, then reaches over to close the passenger door. He drops his weapon and backpack into the seat next to him.

The key is right there in the ignition. From what he has gathered from the other survivors, some kind of electromagnetic pulse must have wreaked technological havoc at the instant the world changed, some kind of temporary blast that rendered almost everything useless. Cars drifted to gutters, phones sputtered dead, personal electronics became bricks. But vehicles almost immediately became viable again.

No one knows why.

He cranks the ignition, and the engine does a slow churn, then begins to click uselessly. He sits there for two minutes and tries again. This time, the engine sounds a bit livelier, and finally it catches. The Pilot rumbles to life.

He backs off the curb, straightens out into the street.

"Okay, here we go," he whispers.

There's a part of him that hoped against hope that everything he'd been told was a fiction. Some kind of elaborate practical joke. But the evidence of it is all around him now, and his insides go increasingly colder.

Beneath a bruised sky, everything beyond the windshield is silent and gray. Fort Collins, Colorado is ruined. When Michael gazes in the direction of his home, off to the west, all he sees is smoke – not just the white-mottled wildfires across the horizon but thick black plumes rising from Old Town. It appears as if the entire length of north College Avenue, even Old Town Square – where he once walked with his little girl, enjoyed the free evening concerts, bought her ice cream, watched her play near the fountain – has been reduced to timbers and ash.

Michael navigates the streets in a state of numbness. Nothing is moving except his appropriated Pilot. He feels all too alone beneath the fat clouds of smoke drifting across the atmosphere.

As he approaches Mulberry, he begins catching sight of more bodies. There are probably many more along these streets that he's not seeing, simply because they've managed to cram themselves so completely against their trees and effectively hide beneath the branches. Their bodies appear mangled, bent back upon themselves and, in many cases, seemingly broken and splintered. Those arms and legs *must* be fractured. The stress would simply be too much at those angles. The bodies resemble great, straining beetles with their bulging abdomens and thoraxes and their sharply slanting limbs.

In one yard to his left, he sees one of the things in full view under a sparsely branched evergreen. He slows down and pulls to the curb, brings down his window. The face is mashed against a section of chewed pine bark, and the mouth is slowly working, like a turtle, maybe, or a cow chewing its cud. But even slower than that. Most disturbing is the almost rhythmical movement of the throat as it takes in whatever the mouth is letting pass. And even as Michael makes that observation, he sees that a large portion of whatever the thing is chewing is sliding down the top of its upturned face, filling and piling at its nostrils, forming a chunky wood paste over the eyes, turning its hair into ragged columns of wet mulch. There's a sizable mound of bark and pine splinters on the ground beneath the head.

Michael stares at this sight for long minutes, trying and failing to understand what this thing might be ferreting out of the tree in the midst of these constant efforts. Something in the chemistry, something cellular? There's a desperation to the thing's clutch, a hunger, and Michael is reminded of an addict satisfying a need.

That thought jibes with what the survivors heard the prisoner say last night. Was he really voicing his need for – something?

"Nneeeeeee – "

The ragged voice nags at him. He doubts any of these bodies out here, outside the hospital, would be able to so quickly find an approximation of their voice, considering their mouths are bloated with wood and sap. He can't imagine the physical state of their mouths, throats, and stomachs – hell, their entire digestive systems.

Michael moves on.

After ten minutes of careful driving, winding his way around and through collisions, he is crossing the main thoroughfare, College Avenue. A glance to the right, up the street and into the heart of Old Town, shows him a scene of blackened devastation, of ash and drifting smoke, of broken glass and stalactites of splintered building foundations upheaved like claws. The tail end of a jet is plainly visible, blackened by fire. There's an abandoned fire truck, its hose snaked out and forgotten.

He consciously looks away, instead locking on the street ahead of him. He can't fathom a world in which buildings would be left to just burn until there was nothing left to burn.

The gray sky is filled with ash, drifting like snow, and the smoke is on the edge of oppressive. With the Pilot's vents closed, he continues forward along the deserted street.

A pulse of adrenaline hits his bloodstream when he realizes how close he is to home now. He has to force himself to slow down and not go barreling through the occasional wreckage.

He is not under the illusion that Susanna might be alive, or that he might even find her body at their home – but a part of him feels a trill of urgency, as if he might save her if he would only rush, now, to her aid. Too many days have passed. But there is knowledge to be had, and for that he feels an almost tangible pull.

Michael takes the turn onto Jackson and is facing a scene that is at once intimately familiar and completely alien. This is the beginning and ending of every journey he has ever taken from his home. It is his route to work; it was the beginning of his mad dash with Cassie to the hospital to give birth to Rachel, and the start of every trip to that same hospital to attend oncology appointments and chemo treatments for his wife. It was the address from which he drove to meet Susanna at local hotels or her cramped, messy apartment near the old Holiday Twin drive-in.

There's the home of the Powells, longtime over-the-fence friends and occasional drinking companions; the house is now dark and creepy in the slouch of its lumber. His mind doesn't want to imagine the fate of those good people, but he knows they've been no luckier than the multitudes. Over there at the edge of Olive is the Kaufman home; Daniel was an accomplished artist, and now his skill has no doubt been obliterated under this incomprehensible intelligence.

There's a body at nearly every conifer tree – sometimes two or three at the same tree. As he turns onto Magnolia, he catches sight of poor Mrs. Carmichael, the stunningly obese woman from down the street, a woman he has never actually seen beyond her porch until this moment. Her corpulent body is twisted around an Australian pine, her blue patterned muumuu hanging off her, revealing great doughy expanses of white flesh. Michael looks away.

He pulls into his driveway and twists the ignition off.

He sits there for several moments, watching the neighborhood. He can't see any movement anywhere. He's paranoid all of a sudden, feeling as if every darkened window is hiding someone – or some*thing* – surreptitiously watching him. In particular, he is eyeing the Sanders home next door to his own. The living room curtains there are hanging askew, and as he parked, he could have sworn they moved – but probably not. More likely, that was his mind playing tricks on him. He's darkly curious about what might have happened to Darin and Sally, casual friends for over ten years but now, more than likely, somewhere out there doing something ungodly to a fucking tree.

Finally, he eases the Pilot's door open and steps onto his driveway. He pulls Rachel's backpack over his shoulder and takes hold of the shotgun. He's watching every direction, but there's nothing out there. He doesn't think he's ever heard this measure of silence in his life. The city is empty of all noise. He can practically hear bits of ash striking the pavement at his feet.

He hurries now to his porch, climbs the steps, and grasps the door handle. Taking a breath, he tries the door, and it opens into a humid house. The door handle knocks against the interior wall, echoing.

"Susanna?" he calls, hoping against hope. *"Suze!"*

Nothing.

He stands in the foyer surveying the room – tense, shaking. Everything seems in its place, but his eyes land on a browned, mostly dried apple core sitting on the living room table to his left. He frowns at it for a moment, then moves forward.

He stops.

On the air is the scent of death.

Something plummets inside him.

His eyes close involuntarily, and he feels emotion at his throat. He becomes aware of his heartbeat, his breathing. He focuses on keeping them calm.

He opens his eyes, carefully turns around, and clicks the door shut. He finds that he is unable to move toward the bedroom. He is afraid. Afraid of what he will find. Afraid of what he will not find.

He sets the backpack on the couch and stares into the hallway's early-morning blackness. He can just see the edge of his own bedroom doorway, a dim maw leading to an unthinkable mystery. The house around him seems to press in on his ears, throbbing. His mouth is acrid, his teeth close to chattering.

Shotgun at the ready, he begins creeping into the dark hallway.

As he approaches his bedroom, he can see muted sunlight slanting across the floor from the window. He arrives at the doorjamb, supporting himself against it, and stares in.

For a moment, he doesn't see her – or perhaps he just doesn't want to. He sees bedsheets in disarray, and white pillows, their pillows, thrown aside.

Then he sees the flesh of her bare thigh.

No.

A sound escapes his mouth, something caught between a cry and a cough.

No, this can't be.

Susanna is sprawled across the bed. Naked. Dead.

He can't move farther in, and yet he can't look away.

He's shaking uncontrollably now. Frozen between impulses to rush to her and flee this place, he can only stand there staring at anything but her. His gaze locks on a flaw in the wood at the jamb, a scuff mark where the vacuum cleaner has scraped repeatedly over the years. After long moments he's breathing evenly and deeply.

He turns from the door and goes numbly to the kitchen. He sets the shotgun on the kitchen table – location of so many drowsy breakfasts, the beginning of so many days – and numbly opens the refrigerator. The innards are just about room temperature, and the contents are on the verge of spoilage. A subtle odor of food decay touches his nostrils. Nevertheless, he roots around and comes up with a can of Coke, pops it open, and downs it. The sweetness seems to help the ever-present throb in his temples, and the carbonation helps with the undercurrent of nausea. Or maybe it's just the sense of comfort that comes from drinking this soda after the end of the world.

Susanna is dead.

He can't process it.

He tosses the empty can across the room, and it clatters against the wall, wide left of the trash can. He barely notices.

"*Suze, Suze, Suze ...*" he's muttering.

She can't be dead, can she? She can't be sprawled across their bed. It's impossible. Not his Susanna.

He closes his eyes and listens. The house is utterly silent, and that silence seems to extend out from him in waves, out into the neighborhood, the town, the state, the nation ... how far?

Wait, but there is a sound, a steady hum under all that silence, a low bass note that's almost too low to hear. It might even be his imagination. He moves his jaw, pops his ears. No, it's there. Something is there.

For some reason, there are no tears springing from his eyes. He feels as if he should have tears for Susanna, but they won't come. Perhaps it was because he half-expected to find her like this. He expected the worst. Some variety of worst.

No, you did not expect this. You didn't expect to find her here. You expected her to be gone, to be lost in the wilderness somewhere, engaged in some unspeakable act, among a hundred thousand other ruined human beings ...

He takes deep breaths, then steels himself to return to the room. He moves past the doorjamb and inside. Everything is gray and hollow. He reaches his wife's side, looks down on her, and now emotion comes erupting from his throat, raw, hitching.

He lets a shaking hand descend to Susanna's shoulder, her face, lets his fingers trace the contours of her lips.

Cold.

Tears fall from his eyes to the sheets, darkening them.

Susanna's body is fully exposed to him, as if in cruel spite, her breasts deflated, her taut belly sunken, her labia dry and cold. She's pale, lifeless, bruised. He grabs at the sheets, then, quickly covering her stony nakedness. He doesn't want to see her like this. He tucks the cloth around her stiff limbs, providing as much dignity as he can muster.

He stands back and regards her.

For a long moment, he's perfectly still.

Then more tears come. They leak out of his squinting eyes.

In the crushing quiet of a bleak morning, he stands in the middle of his bedroom and weeps.

He feels as if nothing has been real until this moment. His angst-ridden teen daughter has transformed overnight into a leader, a survivor, and the entire world has shrunken to the space of a barren hospital. And the event that caused everything is lost beneath this ridiculous concussion. And everything else, every hobby and desire and routine, it's all gone, all meaningless. But now …

Susanna is dead.

He turns away from her but catches a glimpse of Susanna's purse, splayed open on the floor. It looks as if it has been rifled through. Her cell phone is on top of the bed, near Susanna's feet, having fallen from the sheets when he wrapped her up. What happened here? His hands are still shaking, and he feels faint. He steps slowly backward, finally falling into the chair next to their dresser.

Wait, wait, wait …

His blurred gaze lands on Susanna's purse once more, then shifts to Susanna's covered corpse. As he wipes his eyes, he tries to imagine what happened to her. What her final moments were like. Was this a struggle? Why is she dead and not … turned? Why *isn't* she among the multitudes in the foothills?

It's only after long moments of considering several insane scenarios that he can look away from the scene and focus on the closet on the other side of the room. Synapses are firing in his skull even as he glances at its closed doors. He wipes at his eyes, composing himself.

In the throbbing silence, he makes his way past the bed to the closet, opens the door. Near the back, in the corner, there's a section of wall that is removable. It's hidden seamlessly behind a false section of laminate. He slides the loose drywall away, and stares dully at the combination lock that is revealed. He twists the combination and opens the small, heavy door. Then he lets his weight fall to the floor and just sits there, half-inside the warm closet, the hidden safe blatantly displaying its contents. At last count, he had one hundred thirteen thousand, four hundred dollars sitting there, in neat stacks.

It all means nothing now.

But now his memory of the end of the world has returned.

CHAPTER 11

When Michael woke the morning of the apocalypse, he made love to his wife. He always felt a surge of friskiness on these Saturday mornings when he knew he would be making money.

Even as Susanna moved languidly beneath him, he cast occasional glances toward the closet, feeling a perverse thrill about the cash stacking up in there, savoring the itch of paranoia surrounding it – paranoia that he might be caught at any moment, this gradually building dream dashed by carelessness. It felt good to tempt fate.

And it felt delicious to be flesh-to-flesh with this amazing woman, drowsy at the start of a new day, the sun already warming their skin through the curtains.

He thought of the money again and smiled.

Michael had all kinds of plans for the cash, despite Steven's ribbing, accusing him of inaction in the face of good fortune. It's just that Michael's plans were more about the future than about the now. Steven, the building's morbidly obese IT guy who had started all this nonsense, was quietly and quickly building a world-class home theater in his basement, filled with obscure, ludicrously expensive audio/visual components. He probably had a hundred thousand invested in that man cave already. With his share, Steven was hell-for-leather. He also talked about a certain massage parlor over on Lemay that offered happy endings, if you asked the right way. Maybe Steven was kidding, but Michael always shuddered at the image.

Michael hadn't spent a dime of the pilfered money. Perhaps it was because some part of him believed – silly! – that if the three of them were caught or even suspected, he could just quietly insert the money back into the hundreds of accounts they had unobtrusively slipped it from. Once, he had whispered this rationalization to Carol, the third leg of their little embezzlement tripod, on the elevator at work, carelessly, and she had just stared at him, slim hip cocked, then left without a word when the doors opened, off to the parking lot.

The money gave him a sense of stability – a sense of calm power – that nicely counterbalanced the paranoia of the theft.

Before long, Susanna was more participatory, less drowsy from sleep, and she had flipped him over and mounted him. The position always reminded Michael of their first time, in his office chair at work – that forbidden night, before Steven's game-changing idea, before Cassie's downward spiral, and long before the end of the world. It was that night, maybe, when Michael had started down a path from which there would be no easy return. He often wondered whether he would have found himself wrapped up in Steven's scheme had he not wrapped himself up with Susanna that night.

She'd started as an intern, doing the busywork of filing the promissory notes in the firm's vault. She'd worked her way up to legal secretary, getting closer and closer to actual client relationships until she was a bona fide paralegal, landing contracts that veteran lawyers had failed to secure. Everyone attributed it to her demeanor – spunky, a little flirty, clear-eyed, and of course naturally attractive in a Boulder kind of way. That wasn't where she was from, but she might as well have been.

Michael, on the other hand, attributed her success solely to her body. Right on the edge of voluptuous, it was tight and plump in all the right places, and toned in a way that Cassie had never been. A pang of regret always tweaked him deep inside when he thought that way, but he couldn't deny its truth. After Rachel was born, Cassie never regained her shape and never seemed really motivated to do so.

"You okay, baby?" Susanna breathed languidly. It was barely light out, and he knew this was just a dreamy interlude for her, that she would eventually slip off him and go back to sleep once he was gone.

Michael opened his eyes. "Uh huh." He gave her a look as she moved atop him: *Why do you ask?*

"You had a funny look on your face," she murmured, "like it hurt or something."

He shook his head and focused on the sensation. He banished thoughts of Cassie from his mind.

"I'm gonna go in to work for a while," he whispered. "Not long. A couple hours."

Susanna shook her head in mild exasperation, her hair tickling his nose. "Overachiever." She leaned further, kissed his forehead.

"Best time to get work done," he said, his Saturday morning mantra.

"Don't forget we planned to get to Denver early, before the game …

mmmm." She took up a rotating motion at her hips, nearly setting him off.

He took the opportunity to think of the money again, warding off the inevitable.

"I won't be long," he whispered, relishing the double entendre. "Want me to grab donuts?"

She frowned, eyes closed. "Eww."

In twenty minutes, he was in the shower, mentally preparing for the morning. His cell phone had received no warning text, and brief pings from both Steven and Carol had greenlit the morning. They would meet at the office at 6 a.m. and then head off to the three separate banks when they opened.

He stepped out of the shower and dried off while admiring Susanna's naked body on the bed, partially concealed by the sheets. She was already drifting off to sleep again, a satisfied smile ghosting her lips. It was going to be a warm day, for sure, and she looked sultry as hell.

On his way out, he gave her a peck on the cheek, then closed the door to a crack. At the other end of the hallway was the door to Rachel's room. It was closed. He approached it and carefully eased it open. Setting his jaw, he watched his daughter breathe steadily in deep slumber. No telling when Tony had brought her home. Her jeans were in a wad on the floor, panties still inside them. She'd essentially fallen into bed – at some obscene hour, no doubt. He let loose an inner sigh and eased the door shut.

Then something odd happened on the way to work.

Halfway there, just past Whole Foods, something flashed in the sky. At first he thought it was sunlight arcing off his rearview mirror, but whatever the light was, its source wasn't the sun. It was a ripple of red light in the atmosphere, reminding him of the Northern Lights, and it was intermittent, he noticed as he drove.

"Huh," he said in the confines of his Acura.

The lights in the sky recurred twice before he entered his parking lot, where the edge of the building blocked out most of the western horizon. Michael tuned them out to focus on the other cars. There were two besides his. Carol had arrived, but Steven was late. Typical. The other vehicle was the van belonging to the janitor. Michael entered the building casually, just a dedicated employee in for some extra time on the weekend. He took the stairs up, jogged them while humming a favorite tune, and entered Accounting.

"Carol, good morning," he said, as if this was just a regular day at work.

"Mike."

She was already at her desk, studiously avoiding eye contact. He could see only the back of her head, the dirty blond hair tied in a loose pony tail, an earthy-hued headband holding it up.

"Everything okay?"

"Why wouldn't it be?"

The office was preternaturally quiet, as always on these mornings. The landscape of silent, darkened cubicles never failed to strike Michael as jarring, despite the knowledge that these early Saturdays had become fairly regular.

"Did you see the sky out there?" He walked over to the water cooler and filled his cup. "Weird."

She was shaking her head, staring intently at her screen.

"No word from Steven?" he asked.

As the name escaped his lips, they could both hear the elevator begin to groan.

"Ah," Michael said, and powered on his docked laptop.

Just as Steven's devious chunk of software revved up from the encrypted thumb drive, the man himself made his appearance.

"Jesus God," he wheezed. "It's way too early for embezzlement."

"Good grief, man," Michael said, unconsciously looking about the room.

"No one else here, boss."

"It's not embezzlement, anyway," Carol said.

"Right." Michael nodded.

"It's just skimming off the top."

"Sure, no court in the world would bat an eye," the large man said.

Carol finally looked up from her system. "Shut up and do your stuff, will ya? I have to get back home and get Sophia ready for a soccer game."

"Hey, it's your own fault you decided to go the suburban mom route." Carol sent him a withering gaze in response. "Mike, you got Intrepid up?"

"Yes." Gritting his teeth at the name Steven had given his little program.

"Okay, let me get the screen sharing working through the encrypted tunnel."

Steven sat his massive bulk at the desk of the latest intern. The chair audibly complained. His pudgy fingers danced across the keyboard, and as Michael watched, several windows opened onscreen, one full of nearly *Matrix*-like code, the other the company accounting UI, and one more showing Michael's desktop. Michael looked away then, preferring not to understand any of Steven's methods and thereby further incriminate himself. Michael entertained an elaborate fantasy that, were they ever caught, he could maintain a comparative innocence in this whole sordid endeavor.

Network security required that they gather during off hours to initiate these little transfers, and they'd watched the building for months on the weekends to determine the best time to come in for "overtime." Steven demanded that all three of them actually be onsite for the transfers – no way would he take on the entirety of the risk. All three of them working off hours might raise suspicion, but no other employees ever came in at 6 a.m. on Saturdays. Ever. That made it easy for Steven to cover their tracks in the system.

There was only the janitor cleaning up the lobby, his first of seven jobs on the weekend. No getting around that, but he didn't care about anything involving the actual businesses upstairs. Michael always greeted him openly, innocently.

In his mind, Michael had somehow convinced himself that he really was here for some extra work, doing good by the company. What kind of labyrinthine thought processes could possibly lead to that kind of self-delusion? He shook his head.

"What do you got planned for the weekend, Mike?" Steven said, as if he sensed Michael's wandering attention.

"Headed to Denver for the Rockies game," he said. "Playing the Dodgers. Should be good. We'll grab some lunch down there, too. Make a day of it."

"Rachel tagging along?"

"I don't think so."

Michael hesitated to talk about Rachel with Steven. He felt that the huge man had developed an unhealthy fascination with her ever since their meeting at the company Christmas party, when Rachel was just freshly 19 years old.

"Just you and Suze?"

Steven was just the kind of person to use a casual nickname for someone whom he really didn't know at all – and even waggle his eyebrows a little. Of course, the whole office knew about Michael's involvement with and eventual marriage to the former intern, but no one knew how long ago it had begun. At least, he thought so – Steven's eyebrows notwithstanding.

He changed the subject.

"How about you? Encasing yourself in that basement again?"

"Ah, spoken from a place of deep envy." Steven shifted his bulk in the chair, still typing. "But yeah, on hot days like this, I like to relax with some cold ones down there and take in a triple feature."

"Sorry I'm gonna miss that," Carol said from her desk. "And by 'cold ones,' I'm assuming you mean ice cream sandwiches?"

Jason Bovberg

"All right, Miss High and Mighty, what are *you* up to this weekend? And no, my cold ones are frozen daiquiris. If you weren't already married, I'd ask you to join me."

Carol barely glanced at him. "Let's just get this over with, okay?"

The coworkers made up a motley crew, that was for sure. The fellowship began spontaneously one afternoon, when all three of them happened upon each other on the patio – on the heels of an offhand remark muttered by eternally pessimistic Carol. Something about a white-collar crime film she'd seen that weekend. And Steven had cocked his jowly head, a thought occurring to him. "Shit, I actually know a way that could work," he'd said. And then things had started happening.

Michael left the details to them: the brains of the operation and the IT guy who secured the process. Michael just provided the keystrokes. The cover. The prestige, you might say.

It was easy. Far too easy. It just added up and up and up.

The Saturday before, Michael had brought up the notion of stopping. Quitting while they were ahead. Not tempting the fates.

"Are you fucking kidding me?" Steven had been flabbergasted.

"We don't want to be greedy."

"He's probably right," Carol had said.

"Screw you guys, *I* want to be greedy."

Michael had hoped to come away from that conversation with a hard stop date, but instead they'd floated the possibility out to an undetermined horizon. He wanted to bring it up again. He just needed to find the right opportunity.

Steven was quiet, waiting for something onscreen.

"Just five more minutes, then you can pull the plug."

Michael sighed and pushed himself out of his chair. He went over to the window and looked outside. The memory of that ribbon of crimson light came back to him. It wasn't there anymore, at least from this vantage point. The town was waking up. A few vehicles were inching up College Avenue, crossing Harmony.

The large window strobed with red flickers. Michael backed away from it, but he got the distinct impression that something was falling from the sky.

Falling light?

"Whoa, whoa, what the hell is that?" Carol was rising from her seat.

And then the sound reached them. Like thunder but deeper, more resonant, more all-encompassing. The building vibrated sharply for a moment.

Light was flowing down, perceptibly, in waves, in columns. It was everywhere, like a drifting rain made of illumination.

"What is it?" Steven asked from his chair, merely curious.

Their computer desktops zagged with digital artifacts, and all three working hard drives seemed to go into overdrive simultaneously.

"*The fuck?!*" Steven said, his pudgy hands flying up, palms out.

"I mean, holy shit, what the hell is it?!" Carol cried. "*What is th – ?*"

Michael, watching this strange atmospheric phenomenon with a kind of muffled dread, heard Carol's words slice away. He only half-registered the sound of her body slumping to the floor, because he was focused on the vehicles out on College that had suddenly veered in their paths, drifting to the sides of the road, some gently, others somewhat violently. He watched these things with a stunned detachment. He felt his eyes go closed, expecting something – the end, perhaps? Was his body going limp?

No, it wasn't.

He finally turned to face his coworkers. Carol was on the ground, and Steven was slumped backward in the chair, his massive head flung back, mouth wide open. And then Michael was in motion. Swallowing, he rushed to Carol, knelt, felt for a pulse, listened for respiration.

Nothing.

"Carol! *Carol!* Wake up! Steven!"

The memory begins to fracture, his screams breaking into aural shards –

– *racing to Steven, shaking his large body in his chair –*

– *attempting chest compression on Carol, supine on the floor –*

– *bending toward mouth-to-mouth –*

– *something about Carol's mouth … what was it about her mouth?*

– *the memory of recoiling –*

– *glimpses outside the red-rimmed windows again –*

– *the light continuing to fall –*

Everything abruptly motionless, like a jittery pause of a recorded picture. Some kind of tremor at the edge of everything. Or was that just his own delayed reaction, finally spurting him forward into who knew what direction.

– *running –*

– *shouting –*

That's where the memory really breaks up.

CHAPTER 12

Staring at the money in the safe, in the dusty, claustrophobic silence of his bedroom closet, he wonders about Steven's and Carol's fates. Steven, who had ribbed Michael constantly about his too-conservative plans for his share of the cash, who had teased him about the way Michael always said, "I'm tucking it away, man, just tucking it away for the future." Carol had smirked at him too, in her quiet way.

Are they gone, along with nearly everyone else?

Michael had never uttered a word about his financial misadventures to his wife, let alone Rachel. The very idea had always seemed ridiculous; he would not be deemed a criminal. His family knew nothing, and yet they were the primary benefactors of all his activities.

Those dreams are even more fanciful now, aren't they?

Michael takes a long last look at the cash. His eyes fall on the holstered .38 Colt that his dad handed down to him before he died. It's positioned in there next to all the cash, and even in the confines of the safe, it seems to have gathered dust. He remembers when he removed it from its box, higher up in the closet, last year, as if placing it with the money added any real security … as if he anticipated that some kind of Bonnie and Clyde shootout would someday mark the end of this financial misadventure. A stupid, dangerous idea.

He pulls out the Colt now, along with the single box of cartridges, handling it all delicately. After some thought, he unholsters the weapon. All while staring at the useless piles of cash.

All that money is just paper now.

He stands up, securing the .38 in his waistband.

Gazing upon Susanna's wrapped corpse, he can't help but feel that her death was his fault. He wasn't here when it happened. Could he have saved her, given the chance? He's still not sure what to make of the scene. All evidence points to the notion that she might have survived the initial event but died in the aftermath. Had he not been stealing from his company, for whatever insane purpose, might he have saved her?

"Oh god, Suze, I'm sorry," he whispers.

He's rooted to the center of the room, just looking at her.

After a moment, he curses loudly, knowing the entire world is deaf to him.

He has lost a second wife.

Photographs of both wives adorn their dresser. Susanna never really minded them there, and Rachel insisted they remain. He walks over now and studies them. Alive in memory.

The photos of Cassie look old. Antique, almost. Before the cancer came.

She discovered the lump in their shower one morning – the shower just beyond the bed on the other side of the room. The shower that he has since shared Susanna.

Cassie asked him to feel her lump, watching his reaction with a mixture of fear and laughing disbelief. Swallowing heavily, he came upon the swelling instantly, and it felt as if a dark abyss had opened beneath their bare feet.

But that's the past. So long ago now.

The truth is, they weathered the oncological storms of chemotherapy for so long that it became their new normal, and his first wife was never the same. She was never again the woman he had married out of college, seemingly before they'd even flung off their caps and gowns. He hardly remembers that Cassie now. That Cassie is far more present in these fading photographs than in the decaying human being that bore her name in those final years.

Were he forced to admit his deepest truths, he would have to say that his first wife's physical deterioration at the hands of her disease disgusted and embarrassed him. He bristled under the outpourings of sympathy that he received at work and from distant family. He couldn't take it.

He needed to project a façade of health, not only for his own well-being but also for work, where appearances meant quite a lot.

Susanna was young and vital, and she never got sentimental. Could he be entirely blamed for responding to her flirtations? He acknowledges that, yes, he *could* be blamed for that. He had a duty as a husband to remain at Cassie's side – in good times and bad – and he was adamant with himself and even with Susanna that he abide by that contract. And he did. He held Cassie's hand through the bitter, soul-rending end, even as he watched her blood pressure plummet and her pulse plunge. And he did the best he possibly could for Rachel, standing by her side for every moment of her mourning. No one could say otherwise.

But just as he did the morning the world ended, he had been fucking Susanna for a year before his wife's death.

He flinches at the blunt way the memory slams through his head.

He pockets the extra ammo, then takes long minutes to consider how he will carry Susanna's body and transport her to the hospital, where he can properly – at least, as close to *properly* as he can manage now – deal with her remains. He'll do his best, anyway. Out of habit, Michael checks his wristwatch. It is 7:49 a.m. That doesn't tell him much, except that he's already a bit later than he promised Kevin.

He'll understand.

Just as he's beginning to tuck Susanna's arms more tightly at her sides and get the fabric wrapped more securely around her, the sky lets loose with another roar. It goes on and on, seemingly ripping at the fabric of reality. He settles Susanna's left shoulder gently to the bed, covers his ears with his hands, and races through the house to the front door. He steps out onto the porch, then down to his lawn.

Above him, the sky is throbbing. He tries to discern other phenomena in the smoky red haze, searching the horizon, past the smoke, past the sunlight. There's a distinctive, rhythmic pulse. As in the office that morning, something is cascading downward, but something else is flowing up. The former sight is reminiscent of distant thunderheads shedding rain, gushing clouds spewing across the plains. The latter is not unlike rays of sunlight through clouds, except for the color and the steady upward movement. This is the more subtle of the phenomena; he has to strain his smoke-stung eyes to see it.

It is the downward-flowing pulse that is making the sound.

Here in the outdoors, it is a gargantuan, earth-shattering noise.

It fills Michael with horror.

He feels himself stumbling backward, back up to his raised porch, slamming against the door. He shuts his eyes and feels as if he is drowning in red noise.

It seems to last for minutes, and by the time it ends, more tears are streaming down Michael's face. Shouting his relief, he falls to his butt and crumples onto his side.

"Jesus!" he screams. "Jesus *Christ!*"

When he finally reopens his eyes, the street is as motionless and hazy, just as when he arrived, and the morning heat is already making the scene swelter. As ever, a fine miasma of ash is drifting over everything. His cheek is cool on the weathered boards of the shaded porch. He takes a few moments to catch his breath.

And that's when he sees it.

The movement startles him – just to the east. It is the body of a young man, twisted back on itself like a crab but moving almost confidently on its back-turned hands and feet. Michael raises himself slowly, not wanting to attract its attention. He maneuvers himself to his knees as the thing approaches, its limbs angled, its upside-down head darting left and right.

Michael feels his limbs go cold.

Far different from the handcuffed man in the hospital, this is a thing fully realized. In the wild. Michael remains mystified about its purpose, but here it is, in front of him, in this reality, in his own sights. Whatever it is doing, it is doing it with focus and clarity. And it is utterly alien, despite its human flesh.

It's closer now, and Michael judges that it's the body of an early teen, perhaps a middle-schooler from this neighborhood. The boy was wearing white workout shorts and a blue Nike tee when he was – what? – taken over? The shirt is torn at the shoulders, allowing for freer movement of the bent-back limbs. Even from this distance, Michael can see the evidence of sap at the mouth, and bloody teeth, and now he can hear the thing coughing erratically, hacking out splinters.

This is behavior he hasn't seen yet – a body once attached to a tree and now disengaged from it, ostensibly for a new purpose.

"What are you up to?" he breathes, staying still.

According to Rachel and the others, two days ago the survivors ventured from the hospital in search of answers, only then discovering the full extent of these things' purpose, one that was surprisingly non-threatening to the remaining humans.

So he was safe.

Right?

Michael feels the first real twitch of uncertainty.

He watches the middle-schooler, suddenly feeling very exposed on his porch.

It's searching. It's looking for something.

A tree? Is it looking for a particular kind of –

Three houses away, and it's still wandering in Michael's direction. He shuffles backward, positioning himself low and concealed behind a post, keeping a wary eye. He withdraws the pistol from his pocket, and its solid grip reassures him, although he wishes he had the shotgun in his fist.

What is that goddamn thing looking for?

The boy-thing pauses in its nightmarish, loping crabwalk and stares to its right. Michael follows its weird gaze but sees nothing but a silent, defeated neighborhood. The houses already seem abandoned. The scene does not merely resemble a quiet morning, everybody still peaceful in their beds, but rather a glimpse of the end, the homes' occupants yanked violently from within. The neighborhood appears bruised, ashen and gray. Sickly.

The boy-thing cocks its head, its mouth stretched open crookedly, like an afterthought. The eyes move in their sockets, but even from this distance, Michael can sense the deadness there. And now a sound emerges from the thing's throat – a gaspy, broken call.

Oh no, Michael thinks, even before he sees the second corpse.

It comes from straight down Scott Street, from just beyond the Nowells' corner yard. As it comes closer, Michael recognizes it as the young Whitham boy from a few houses up that street. The boy is perhaps seven years old, a once-happy and formerly mischievous blond kid now caught in this peculiar, bone-cracking alien grip. Michael feels a deep snap of horror at the sight of the boy in his bright blue pajamas and can't help but rip his gaze away to stare down at the weathered planks of his porch, trying to ground himself. He begins breathing more quickly.

For the first time, it occurs to him that these things might be searching for *him*.

He risks another glance, just as the two figures come together in the middle of the street. They stare at each other, necks straining. Neither is looking in his direction, though. Still, he can't process the notion of that little boy – Michael thinks his name is Jack – suddenly becoming an inhuman monster, hunting him.

"Good god," he whispers, and a bark of desperate laughter escapes his throat.

When Michael edges to his right for another look into the street, he sees two more crab-like bodies moving onto the scene. One of them is Mrs. Carmichael, whom he saw attached to the pine at the corner of Jackson and Magnolia. Her body is a huge, lumbering thing, the torn and dirty muumuu fluttering behind it, great expanses of fatty flesh undulating with the movement.

He moves his gaze back to the original two, and now they're definitely staring in his direction.

He pushes up from the porch, stands, and makes a break for the door, leaping into the vestibule. Just as he enters, he sees that all four of the bodies are heading his way with greater purpose. They're snarling. They're actually snarling.

"Harmless, they said!" Michael breathes harshly through his teeth in the center of his humid living room. "They said those goddamn things were harmless! Not interested in people!"

Well, he saw that harmlessness himself, right? Just outside the hospital. And not just there but in every body he passed that morning.

What has changed? Why are they after me? What did I do?

He engages both locks on the front door and moves quickly through the house, locking all the other windows and doors. He returns to the front window just in time to see the first crab-thing, the teen boy, disappear around the north side of the house. A fifth thing is approaching from between two homes to the south, struggling in its odd gait, one arm broken and useless. But it's determined, moving straight toward him across the sidewalk, and now out onto the warming asphalt. As it gets closer, Michael sees what was once a pretty young woman, her startlingly naked body – clothed only in a gray sports bra – now splayed back upon itself, the flesh straining and sunburned, the monstrous eyes dead but peeled wide. She's got a mostly shredded cast hanging off that broken arm, flopping roughly against the ground.

She catches his eye through the window, locks her gaze on him, and hisses like a feral cat.

"Holy shit," he whispers. "I'm in trouble."

CHAPTER 13

Michael takes a stutter-step toward the kitchen phone, stops, remembers that phone service is still knocked out everywhere, then goes ahead into the kitchen and yanks the receiver out of its cradle anyway.

Gotta try.

Nothing.

He sets it gently back, then stands there, weighing his options, chewing the insides of his cheeks. Sweat beads on his forehead. He swipes it away angrily.

Michael left the hospital under a certain assumption – that whatever had happened to these poor people didn't constitute an overt threat to the survivors – and now that assumption is being seriously challenged. Worse, when he left the hospital, the only person he told about his destination was Kevin, and he might not have told anyone where Michael was going, out of a sense of some kind of confidentiality. Yes, Michael left a note in his room, but now he's worrying that he didn't put the note in a place where it would be immediately found.

Michael moves back to the front window, peers outside. On the otherwise barren street, three more of the things are crab-hobbling toward the house.

Christ.

He shoots his gaze toward the Honda, which is parked diagonally across the driveway. Can he get to it? Can he just walk out there, unharmed? Maybe those things aren't so dangerous after all. But if they *are* dangerous – if they're all as aggressive as that cornered prisoner was at the hospital – then would Michael even be safe inside a vehicle?

Safer than outside, that's for sure.

If he wants to make a run for the Honda, he knows it has to be soon, before more of them come.

Even as that thought moves through his consciousness, he remains rooted to the spot.

Are they really coming for me?

Maybe they're not, maybe they're just streaming around the house in search of something else. In search of whatever the hell they're here for in the first place? He doesn't have any pine trees in the back yard, just a couple of ash trees and a barbecue and some junk. A vegetable garden that Susanna was tending half-heartedly. But there's that big pine hanging over the fence, near the back.

At the thought, he turns from the window, barks his shin on the edge of the coffee table, and sends the lonely apple core tumbling to the ground. He curses and proceeds through the room, limping gingerly at first, through the hall and into Rachel's bedroom, where the window looks out onto the back yard. At her dresser, he pushes aside some old trophies – from one of which a white bra dangles, inexplicably – then edges the blinds aside. Three of the things are back there, angling past one another, all of them glaring at the house with their dead eyes, as if searching for a way in. None of them is paying any attention to the pine tree.

"Goddamn!" he whisper-shouts against gritted teeth. "How did they get *back* there?"

Michael feels absurd and stupid, having abandoned the relative safety of the hospital for this dangerous seclusion. He checks to ensure that his firearm is loaded, and as he does so, his head snaps up.

Garage! he thinks.

His Acura is at the office, of course, but Susanna's Civic should be parked in there – unless Rachel took it. And he has an extra box of ammunition in the locked toolbox. Even if the car isn't there, he needs to bulk up his defenses. He's got the shotgun with its half box of shells, and he's got the Colt, with perhaps a box and a half – seventy-five rounds?

He sprints for the kitchen, and abruptly his vision goes blurry. He braces himself on the edge of the sofa at the entrance to the living room, steadying himself. It's the concussion, he's sure.

There's an abrupt thud against the back door, then another.

With eyes squeezed nearly shut, he forces a look in that direction, toward that recessed hallway, sees shadows playing there.

And now the front door rattles in its hinges underneath what sounds like a full body blow.

Michael staggers over and peers out the side window. The naked girl has crashed into the door and is now on her back, scrabbling around like an overturned snapping turtle. Her face is full of fury, beneath its glaze of woodsap and injury. There are superficial wounds all over it, and blood is caked in her hair. The head juts forward rhythmically at the air, the mouth clacking so hard that the teeth must be breaking. Michael shrinks back from the sight, but not quickly enough. The dead eyes lock onto his.

The head goes still at the visual contact, and a cold horror fills Michael.

They're after me.

He's sure of it now.

Another crash into the back door, and this time Michael hears something splinter deep in the jamb.

"What do you want?!" he calls out to them uselessly.

And why now? What did he do to cause this? No sooner did he return home and dig up his now-useless pile of pilfered cash, than this happened. As he stands there gripping the bridge of his nose, trying desperately to calm the blurry pain, he can't help but think that the two phenomena are connected. Mere moments after he recalled the crime he was committing that morning, and held the stolen money in his hands, this horror came down upon him.

Coincidence?

He blurts out a constricted laugh – and feels wetness on his palm and wrist. He brings his hand away from his nose, looks at it.

"Shit!"

On top of everything, he's got a bloody nose.

He winds his way to the kitchen and rips a paper towel from its roll, blots at his nose. He crumples a small bit of another sheet into a tiny ball, and stuffs it up the nostril. Then he uses the rest of the sheet to wipe the blood off his hand.

He makes it to the door to the garage, pulls it open. The Civic is gone.

"Dammit!"

Think, think.

"Okay," he breathes.

He steps down into the darkness of the garage anyway, on instinct flipping the switch repeatedly. He pauses briefly in the humidity, letting his eyes adjust. There's just enough light to get to where he needs to go. He steps over to the yellow DeWalt tool chest and roots into his pocket for the keys, pulls them out. He finds the key and quickly turns the lock. The lid opens, unlocking the lower drawers. In the third large drawer is the second box of .38 rounds. He removes it and sets it on the ledge next to the doorway to the kitchen. Then he grabs the hammer and an old box of 16-penny nails left over from the shed he built out back three years ago.

A wave of dizziness passes over him, and he nearly falls. He clutches the edge of the tool chest for balance. At that moment, something slams into the garage door, and Michael's heart nearly leaps out of his ribcage. He's sure it's a body. He can hear its raspy gasp now. The damn thing has sensed him inside the garage. Michael coughs, shakes his head.

With trembling hands, he gathers up his stuff and steps back up into the kitchen. His legs are weak and unsteady. His eyes keep wanting to cross, so he opens them wide to make them cooperate.

Spots begin appearing in his vision.

"No!"

He will *not* fall unconscious now.

He has no choice but to stop at one of the kitchen chairs, letting his load of items clatter across the table top. He needs to wait out whatever is happening in his head. He feels on the verge of nausea. He clutches his skull between his forearms and drops it between his knees and whimpers curses at the floor.

Under his voice, he half-hears another splintering thud at the back door.

He deserves this, of course. He knows that. He deserves whatever is coming to him. He probably deserves worse.

He sets his jaw and wills himself still and quiet, forcing out the racket of the continued assaults. He lets his mind go to Rachel, in her better moments, Rachel before her late teens. Her smiling innocence and her bravery in the face of her mother's suffering. And then there's Cassie herself; warm thoughts about her are difficult to separate from what she became in her final year, but they're there. And Susanna, enticing and young, spirited and saucy. He lets the better memories of these women wash over him, as if they could heal.

But then his secrets and betrayals get the better of him.

He has failed all of them, in turn, and – yes – he deserves what he's got coming.

That thought brings a kind of blank calm.

After long moments he opens his eyes. He blinks repeatedly, focusing and refocusing. The pain and blurriness have eased slightly. Enough for him to get up, to get moving. He grabs the hammer and nails.

He drags himself to the hallway leading to the back door, steadying himself along the wood-paneled walls. At the door, he moves the curtain aside and stares at the collection of human monsters that have collected on his back porch. There are nine of them now, including two middle-aged women and a rail-thin teenaged boy, an elderly woman Michael recognizes but can't place, and a tiny blond girl, maybe four years old.

It's the girl that freezes his blood.

This was someone's daughter. She could be Rachel fifteen years ago.

The poor child is staring at him, her blue eyes wide and angry but flat in their sockets, her little mouth formed into a permanent sticky snarl. He can see the inner workings of her mouth and throat, the dry, wounded tongue roiling. The throat is red and convulsing. Her blond hair is muddy with mulch and her own blood. She's rigid, tense, like a single-minded predator, her tiny body trembling with the effort of targeting him.

They're all enraged and hobbling around, their hair hanging in thick strands. Through the door he can hear their heavy gasping. The sound intensifies as, one by one, they notice him there in the window. They glare up at him with their inverted faces, their ruined mouths twitching.

Where are they coming from?

As this question occurs to Michael, the teen tenses and leaps over the girl, throwing himself at the door, his already distended shoulder making hard contact with its lower half. Michael jumps back but keeps watching. The boy falls briefly to the cement, then scurries back into the moving crowd, apparently unhurt. His feral eyes remain on Michael's.

"What do you want?!" Michael shouts at him.

Another of the monstrosities comes spidering into view – a naked black man, his genitals enflamed and erect but useless between his raised hips, waggling like a dark finger. The thing's eyes are instantly on Michael, as if judging.

Michael turns away.

Why are they naked, for chrissakes?

Given the timing, many of them were probably showering when this thing hit. It was a Saturday, so many of them were just getting ready for the day. That, or they were still in bed.

He sets the box of nails on the low table to his right, fishes out a few, and begins hammering them into the door, at an angle into the jamb. He winces at each blow, feeling his head throb in time. Just as he's beginning the third nail, one of the things delivers a vicious blow to the door, and the nail goes pinging to the floor. Michael pauses, trembling furiously. He steadies himself, then starts a new nail. He gets ten or twelve nails hammered in along the door's perimeter, mostly on the non-hinged side, and then he stops, breathing heavily, bowing his head toward the floor.

The goddamn things are growling out there now, scrabbling at the door, their limbs thrashing at it. He watches them from under a furrowed brow, sweat streaming from his scalp into his eyes. He blinks away the saltiness, wipes at it.

A body is scaling the back fence, about to hop down into Michael's yard. He eyes it with dark curiosity. The bent-backward pose of the thing – and the others, too – at first seemed ridiculously strange to Michael, but now it's beginning to make a bit of sense. Somehow, they're actually nimble this way. It's as if they're learning, or maybe more appropriately *relearning*, according to what they know, wherever they're from.

What did Rachel say? Something about their flesh being too soft, too malleable. Something about the bodies reforming themselves for a new purpose?

He's seeing the evidence of it right now. Whatever it is that has inhabited these human bodies, it's doing something to the flesh, probably even the bones and the joints, the ligaments and the muscles. Softening the tissue, softening the bones, making it all more malleable to the instincts and preferences of the new inhabitant.

This new thing, scaling the back fence … it's the body of a muscular young man, in his early twenties, and it's moving deftly and assuredly over the fence. Michael hasn't seen this yet, this level of confidence, among these weirdly animated bodies. Most of the bodies he's seen have seemed clumsy, as if their new minds are struggling, frustrated even, with their uncooperative limbs. This is different, and it frightens him as much as anything he's seen since he woke to this new world.

The body jumps down from the fence and lands efficiently, then scurries toward the back door. Its dead eyes find Michael. The face is slathered with blood and sap like all the others. The mouth opens raggedly. Michael can just make out the wet gasp that issues forth. And then the body leaps at him, launching from the limbs of the other bodies, and it crashes into the window, crunching the glass but not quite sending shards flying.

"Jesus!" Michael yells, his whole body flinching away from the door.

The young man's body falls to the porch, re-establishes its balance, and begins ramming itself against the door.

Michael turns and hobbles back to the front room.

He scans the front window, sees more shadows at play there. There are bumping noises on the wooden porch – more than just the girl now. A heavy, lumbering plod tells him that it's probably the body of Mrs. Carmichael out there.

He's facing the prospect of nailing shut his front door and effectively barricading himself inside the humid dungeon that his home has become. He stands there with the hammer and box of nails, indecisive. What's his best chance of escape? He's already nailed shut one of the doors, because for whatever reason, the back is where the things have focused –

Why? Why?

– and the two remaining exits are the front door and the garage. He can't imagine leaving by way of the garage, waiting poised as the door creaks upward, letting whatever's out there crawl its way underneath. It would be like giving them a head start.

Is the front door his only option for escape? What about the attic? Is there access to the roof? And if he got to the roof, what would he do? Wait there for some potential rescue by helicopter while those things figure out a way to scale the walls? Not likely. He has a vision of himself standing on the roof while thousands of these bodies surround the house, gasping his name.

"Michael! Come down, Michael!"

He shudders, clutches his head, tries to focus.

Michael feels new blood from his nose draining down his throat. With contempt, he blows out the little paper-towel plug from his nostril, throwing a fine red mist across the floor. Goddamn bloody nose!

He's particularly susceptible to them – thanks to Colorado's dry climate and thin air – and he typically takes vitamin supplements to combat them. But he hasn't taken them for days now.

He hocks back the blood, feels its coppery warmth at the back of his throat. He needs to spit it out.

And then his eyes go wide.

Blood.

"Holy shit," his whispers, careful not to swallow.

He lets the bloody mucus, syrupy and viscous, swirl around his tongue.

He goes to the front window and peers between the curtains again. The naked girl has paused to the left, right on top of the welcome mat, hobbled by her broken forearm. Her head is stabbing at the limb, as if trying to make it cooperate. The blunt splay of her meticulously groomed genitals fills Michael with sadness for some reason. It all means nothing now, just like the money in the back of Michael's closet. Just like his marriage to Susanna.

He looks away from her with something akin to shame.

He encourages more blood into his mouth from his nasal passages.

Closer to the door is indeed the massive Mrs. Carmichael, like a fat tarantula. Doughy flesh sways with her movements, the flowery muumuu shredded and inconsequential. Also on the porch is a woman in casual business attire – Michael imagines that she was struck in the act of climbing into her car, heading to Starbucks and then work. This woman is the first on the porch to notice him between the curtains:

Her upside-down head goes still, studying him. Michael hears her gasp through the window. The sound is choppy and rough, hissing from a ravaged throat. Before he steps back away from the window, he scans the lawn and the street, sees one more body angling toward the house, from about half a block away.

Just as he rears back, the businesswoman stabs her head at the window, her mouth wide open. Michael can just barely make out the red glow emanating from her upper palate, from her flared nostrils ...

Time to go.

He turns away, snuffling more blood, letting it collect in his mouth. He almost gags. It feels as if he already has a few tablespoons in there, swirling around with the slippery tendrils of mucus.

Surging through the pain from his head, he grabs Rachel's backpack from the couch and hustles to the kitchen. He yanks open the fridge and grabs the two bottles of water he finds in the door, tosses them into the pack. He also takes the loaf of wheat bread and Susanna's jar of organic peanut butter. He's ravenous, but he can eat later. As he turns, he squeezes his nose with clenched fingers almost brutally, encouraging more blood flow. Then he snatches up the shotgun from the table.

Back out in the living room, he throws in the new box of .38 ammunition, then zips up the pack. He secures the shotgun against the side of the pack; for now, he prefers the heft and size of the handgun. If he needs the raw power and spray of the shotgun, he can easily yank it away. He pulls on the pack, cinching the nylon tight.

He feels the keys to the Pilot in his front left pocket. He removes the Colt from his waistband and ensures again, compulsively, that it's loaded, taking deep, even breaths through his nose, feeling the hot sluice of blood sliding forward into his mouth. The gun will be his last resort – probably best not to make a lot of racket.

He goes to the doorway and readies himself.

If he were a religious man, he'd kneel down and cross himself or something, but he does find himself conjuring a kind of prayer to the heavens. Through eyes half-shut with cramping pain, he looks ceiling-ward and nods fervently.

Just let me make it to the car, just give me that, okay, and then we'll see where we stand, just let me make it to the goddamned car, will you, you fucking silent bastard?

His mouth full of O-negative blood, he pulls the door open and storms out of the house.

The naked young woman swivels at him, surprised, but doesn't have time to react to Michael's foot, which makes solid contact with the side of her head. She goes tumbling down the steps, squawking like an animal. Mrs. Carmichael is turning her bulk to face him, but Michael's eyes are on the businesswoman beyond her. The reversed face glares at him, inhuman, and the body tenses for its leap, then launches. It uses Mrs. Carmichael's body to extend its leap, and abruptly the businesswoman is dropping directly in front of Michael, her chin tensing to stab.

Michael leans forward and sprays blood from his mouth in a rushing red mist. It coats the woman's enraged face, and she shrieks loudly, losing control of her limbs, tumbling to a stop at the welcome mat. But Michael is already leaping down the steps.

The naked girl has made it back to her broken-limbed crabwalk and is waiting for him. She appears to do a nimble dance on the grass, repositioning herself, and she too prepares to leap. As he hits the ground running, Michael spit-sprays what's left of the blood at her, and mostly misses. A mist lands on her shoulder and upper chest, and even that is enough to induce a gasp from deep in the girl's throat. She trips up and slides into his legs, nearly making him fall.

He jumps past her reaching arm and sprints across the lawn, an agonized wail coming from the porch. In his peripheral vision, he now sees three more bodies spidering toward him, clearly attracted by the noise. At the Pilot, he flings open the door and jumps in – but the naked girl has squeezed into the gap. Her upper body slides up against his left leg, on its back, too fluidly, like an awful parody of some erotic gesture. He's kicking at her furiously, and it's not working, she's too strong, too single-minded, so he steadies the firearm and fires a bullet into her brain.

There's a spark of red in the confines of the car, and the dirty, pink body goes tumbling out. He tosses the Colt onto the passenger seat, then slams the door shut just as another body leaps against it, rocking the Pilot on its wheels. Keeping an eye on the body, he maneuvers the backpack off of his shoulders, also dropping it on the seat next to him.

He twists the key in the ignition, and the engine roars to life.

Bodies are pouring out of the back yard.

Michael wipes his mouth with the back of his hand, tries to control his breathing. Blood is still trickling from his nostrils, into his open mouth, and he wipes at it with his arm, smearing himself vividly. He shifts into drive and punches it, two screeching bodies crumpling beneath him.

The Honda careens down Scott Avenue, which still lies silent and smoky under the midmorning sun. Michael presses his battered head to the soft headrest, his left eye nearly closed under a throb of pain there. He can barely see.

He tries to dispel the sensory memory of that damn woman, slinking up his leg, her eyes alien and frenzied, her gasp rotten, her body a horrible bastardization of human eroticism. A full-body tremor passes over him at the memory.

In the rearview mirror, he sees the bodies swarm onto the street in front of his house, all their heads facing him. They're like giant, absurd insects. There must be twenty of them now. They're all moving inexorably toward him as they fade into the background. His trembling lip curls with loathing.

Flooring it, he takes the wide turn out onto Mulberry, and then he jerks backward at the abrupt sight of a police car moving directly in front of him. He jams the brakes hard, and the tires scream.

The collision crushes the Pilot's left front end and deploys the airbag, knocking the breath out of him. The Colt, shotgun, and backpack launch forward from the passenger seat to the floorboards, and Michael sees a bright chaos of colors and piercing sun. The Pilot stutters heavily to a sideways stop, not quite turning over. There's nothing but the sound of the ticking motor and air whistling out of a tire.

"*Holy –* " he manages to breathe out after a moment.

The rapidly deflating airbag gives way to a scene of new smoke rising from the Pilot's hood. In the background, smoke from the foothills chugs skyward in massive columns. Michael tries to focus on something and can't; it's just blurry black and gray and white smoke. He doesn't know if this inability to focus is a symptom of his concussion or this collision.

Does it matter?

He feels consciousness swirling away into a dark gloom. He squeezes his eyes shut and tries to hold on, but the dizziness takes firm hold and swallows him, and then there's nothing.

CHAPTER 14

D-d-d-d-d ...!

A strobe of light, a ratcheting crescendo of sound.

Michael feels himself being yanked.

"D-d-d-d-aaaadddy!"

He jolts awake to the sight of Rachel's blurry face large in his vision.

"Daddy, wake up, *wake up, WAKE UP,* I am *NOT* dragging you to the fucking hospital again!"

Rachel is pulling roughly at his arm, and he's halfway out of the Pilot's passenger side.

"Wait, wait – " he hears himself repeating, because something's wrong, what is it? "Wait, wait – "

He can't clear his vision, but there's someone else, a man, it's the cop, Joel, he's there yanking at him too, and now Michael feels himself being lifted from the vehicle, and he wants to plummet back into unconsciousness again – the feeling is as strong as the pull of slumber after a string of sleepless nights.

But something's wrong.

"Daddy!"

"Calm down, girl, he's hurt. Look at his mouth."

"But they're coming!"

"I know they are," comes Joel's calm voice. "I'll take care of him, and you better hope that Toyota over there has keys, now go get it, pull it right over here. This cruiser is shot, goddammit."

With Herculean effort, Michael opens his eyes to a squint.

Rachel is running toward a green sedan that has bumped against the curb fifty yards to the east. She's carrying something that Michael can't focus on. A weapon?

Joel has pulled Michael completely from the wreckage and is leaning him up against the crumpled left fender. Michael tries repeatedly to open his eyes, but they just want to stay closed.

"You all right? Come on, big guy." He's snapping his fingers in front of him.

The police car looks similarly crushed, its right front end like a broken mouth. Steam is escaping something, and a loud ticking noise is coming from the grill. And there's another sound. Michael turns his head.

Bodies are approaching from all directions.

Adrenaline trills inside Michael, making him stand up straight and get his bearings.

"Okay, I'm okay," he says, "I think," feeling blood in his mouth, dried on his lips and cheeks, and forgetting for a moment where it came from.

"Good – here," Joel says, handing him a child's plastic Super Soaker rifle. It has a cold, dark, unbalanced heft to it. Michael is momentarily flummoxed, but then he understands. "Bonnie rigged these up – good ol' O-negative, complete with anticoagulant. Get ready!"

Joel turns quickly away, ducks into the passenger seat of his car, and pulls another Super Soaker out. He scans the area, locks on Rachel.

In the distance, Rachel arrives at the Toyota, but there's a body closing in on her. Michael tries to focus. From here, he can't determine the size or gender, just a purple, spidery blob, and it's close to her. Rachel hops into the vehicle, and the door slams shut. The body buffets off the vehicle, snarling.

The engine comes to life.

Michael feels a bewildered relief.

"Here they come!" Joel calls out.

Michael swivels, sees three of the things within ten yards of the collision – all men, all three of them heavyset. One is bearded, looking all the more alien for its furry proboscis jutting forward above the shadowed face. They're all seemingly infuriated, with their hyper-extended limbs and jerking movements and wide flat glares. Beyond them, more. Naked old women and pajama-tattered kids and frumpy housewives and athletic teens and businessmen in hanging ties – there must be forty of them here.

"Fire! Fire!" Joel is shouting, letting loose a barrage of blood streams.

The liquid ammunition is ludicrously silent in its launch from the weapons, arcing away in thin red lines, but the effect is one of instant cacophony. The closest three bodies, beefy men, stagger back as one, screeching from their ragged throats. Two of them collapse, their limbs wiping awkwardly at their faces.

And Michael discovers that he, himself, has been squeezing the trigger of his Super Soaker, almost unconsciously, into the rushing crowd.

The air is filled with the noise of anguished animals.

One of the things is suddenly flying at him from over the car, and Michael ducks, firing a staccato red burst at its head. It gasps loud as it passes, its legs crashing into Michael's shoulder, spinning him. The Super Soaker nearly flies from his wet grasp, but he holds on. The thing tumbles to the hard asphalt, caterwauling. Michael aims dark jets straight into its dead eyes, and the whole body goes spastic.

Michael chances a look toward Rachel, sees the Toyota lurch forward and stall.

"It's a manual!" he cries, trying to surge his way through the constant pain in his head.

"What?!"

"The car! Manual transmission! Rachel can't drive that!"

"Aw, fuck! Let's go!"

Joel's strong arm grasps Michael's bicep, and he practically drags Michael, whose limbs remain obstinate. He feels drunk and uncoordinated.

"Come on!"

"I'm trying."

He forces himself to move and gathers some speed.

"Don't look back!" Joel yells. *"Just go go go!"*

Michael doesn't need the extra encouragement. As he runs, he has an image of snapping dogs at his heels – there's a fleshy patter against the hot street, and an urgent gasping, that fills his limbs with energy.

The Toyota looms ahead. It's coasting forward, and Rachel is frantic at the wheel, trying to make it work. The body poking viciously at its door is that of a woman, her long black hair whipping spastically as she seeks an opening, jabbing her head relentlessly at the side mirror, at the window, the tire. The locked-open mouth is emitting an endless huffing gasp, and the skin of the forehead and cheeks is streaked with blood from Rachel's Super Soaker. The car lurches again, stalls.

"I can't do it, I can't do it!" Michael can hear his daughter screaming now.

Joel begins firing at the thing from ten feet away, and the body goes scrambling backward, hissing.

"Get in the back!" he yells at Michael.

Rachel sees them coming and is already heaving herself over to the passenger seat. Her eyes are wide, watching whatever is behind them. And then Joel and Michael hit the side of the car simultaneously, twirling to face their pursuers.

They're all there, spidering at them, maybe fifty of them, counting the bodies racing out of yards, flowing in from neighboring streets. Michael recognizes the crowd from his house arriving on Mulberry now, all the angry upturned faces turned his way. It's like a swarm – an impossible swarm of human bodies, moving with liquid agility despite their injuries, despite their hyper-extended limbs and dislocations.

Blood is pumping from his Super Soaker, but even in his frenzy, he can feel that it's approaching empty. Just in time, in his peripheral vision, he sees Joel duck down into the car and slam the door shut. Michael feeds a final arcing spray to the monsters in his midst – sending them skidding to the asphalt – then opens the rear door, tumbles in, and slams it shut –

– directly on one of the things' probing heads.

It's a kid, just a kid, an eight-year-old kid, the face smeared with blood and sap, the teeth in the jaw broken and bloody, the expression furious. Michael rears back his leg and kicks savagely at the face, breaking the jaw – he hears it snap like a branch. The kid, undeterred, lunges at him, the chin sliding and scraping upon itself but making contact with Michael's leg. Michael feels an abrupt tingling sensation along his shin. He fires the last of his blood madly into the kid's eyes, and finally the body reels back, out of the car, enough for Michael to shut it.

They're all breathing heavily in the cramped interior, and now the bodies are overwhelming the car, crashing against it on all sides.

"*God!*" Rachel screams, then follows that with an expulsion of childlike sound that's somewhere between fear and revulsion. "Why can't it just *stop!*"

"Let's get the hell out of here, huh?" Joel says, impossibly calm.

He cranks the Toyota's engine and guns forward, trampling three scrambling bodies. Michael nearly gasps himself when he feels the sickening crunch of bones breaking beneath the tires. The vehicle bucks and bounces.

"Joel!" Rachel cries, desperate tears in her eyes.

"What?"

"Just – "

"*What?!*"

"They're *human beings!*"

"Not anymore they're not!"

As if purposefully, Joel twists the wheel into the loose crowd, crushing several more, which screech beneath them. Rachel grasps at the wheel, moaning now.

"Joel! Knock it off!" Michael shouts. "Just … just get us out of here."

Rachel turns on him. "We wouldn't even be here right now if it wasn't for you!"

Michael is speechless.

"How could you leave? I can't believe you left!"

"I – "

"I saved you, and you … you – "

"That's just – " Michael can't even finish the sentence.

The car meets asphalt again, bouncing, and Joel floors it, straightening out, heading east on Mulberry. The bodies thin out, but Joel manages to steer directly into a teenager's body, sending it spinning to the curb, screeching. Rachel buries her face in her hands.

"I thought I could get back before – " Michael says.

"Didn't quite work out that way, huh?" Joel says, tight-lipped.

"I didn't ask anyone to come after me."

"No, you left that decision to your daughter."

"Joel!" Rachel says, miserably. "Don't be a dick."

Michael twists around to watch the scene behind them – the wreckage of the cars in the distant background, and the foreground a chaos of crab-like movement. Several of the things remain motionless on the asphalt, observing the retreating humans with alien calm, but the majority are scrambling after them in tireless pursuit.

"Why are they after *me?*" he says, almost philosophically.

"After you?" Joel says.

"They just started attacking the house, coming from all directions."

"Dad, they're attacking everyone."

Michael stares at Rachel blankly. "But – " He tries to get his head around this information. He nearly lets loose a scoffing sound, directed right at himself. He thought they were after him, as some kind of comeuppance. Ego or divine expectation? Who knows?

Rachel returns his gaze, still irritated.

"It was right after one of those – that thunder," she says. "Didn't you hear it? It broke a few windows at the hospital. We all went to the windows to see what was going on. That's when these things just started creeping out of the neighborhoods."

As they drive, they catch glimpses of other bodies scurrying in the streets. A few blocks east, near College, they see a dozen of them swarming toward a home west of the thoroughfare.

Michael finds a wadded-up gray shirt at his feet, and he grabs it, uses it to wipe at his bloody nose and mouth and his stained arm. The blood has stopped flowing from his nostrils, but when he pulls the shirt away, it's filthy. He spits into the cloth and wipes some more.

"They sure seemed to get more certain of themselves," Joel says, his voice monotone, seething with his own brand of fear. "They know we're here now."

Michael remembers the teen at the back door, the way it seemed only too comfortable with the back-breaking transformation its human host had endured. But then Michael latches on to Joel's other words.

They know we're here now.

The words speak of an evolving mindset on the part of the animated bodies – perhaps even a series of events that Michael missed while he was unconscious. Joel is suggesting that whatever is possessing these bodies has an intelligence. Michael himself has seen evidence of this in their eyes – a strategizing, animal cunning – but he thinks Joel is also referring to a more collective consciousness. A hive mentality?

After swerving around a series of abandoned automobiles, Joel shifts into third and gathers some speed, passing the Safeway and the 7-Eleven where Michael took Rachel for countless Slurpees in her youth. He watches it flit past with a painful ache – or maybe that's still his concussion.

"So, what, are they sensing us? Smelling us? What?"

"Something we need to figure out," Joel says. "Hey, here's a question you haven't answered yet: Why'd you leave the hospital? In the middle of the night?"

Michael feels the urge to match Joel's venom, but he backs down, looks away. "Look, I'm sorry, Joel. Okay? I needed to – I needed to find my wife. And I needed to do it alone."

The interior of the car is silent as Joel navigates the dead street. Michael lets his gaze move to Rachel in the front seat. Her entire body is clenched, expectant. He tries to read something there, but her angst could have any number of causes.

What do you know? he wonders.

"All right, Mike, I'm just a little pissed off about the way it went down. I lost my cruiser, goddammit."

"Yeah, well, I lost my wife."

Michael regrets the words immediately.

"Did you find her?" Joel asks.

"Yes, I did."

"Was she – "

"Dead."

"Like – not like one of those things?"

"Not like one of those things," Michael repeats. "Just – dead."

Rachel interrupts. "Look!"

Racing toward them, south on Mathews, is a boy, about nine years old. A still-human boy. His eyes are nearly popping out of his head with fear. Behind him is a group of perhaps eight scrambling bodies, two of them riding the boy's shadow.

"Stop, stop!" Michael shouts.

Joel is juddering to a stop and furiously stabbing at buttons to roll down his window. He finds the right one, and the window squeaks down. Immediately they can hear the boy's frightened squeals and the bodies' throaty exhalations. He's twenty feet away and closing fast.

"Mike, it's up to you," Joel calls back. "I'll be ready to soak those bastards."

Rachel is already handing Joel her half-full Soaker. Michael lets his empty weapon fall to the floorboards.

He opens his door and gets ready to receive the boy. He holds out his arms.

"Come on, little man!"

Joel lets loose an arcing spray of blood, aiming for the two bodies directly behind the boy. He's a sharp aim, nails them in the eyes, sends them tumbling away, squalling. In one fluid motion, the boy dives into the car, Michael flings the door shut, Joel hits the gas, and the two bodies collide clumsily with the rear bumper as the Toyota shoots forward. The other bodies in the near distance react with a frenzy of gasping grunts, and then they recede behind the car.

Michael gets the boy settled next to him. He's wearing a soiled white tank top and gym shorts and smells foul.

"You all right?"

The boy is nearly hyperventilating. "Thank you," he says breathlessly, then to Joel and Rachel, "Hi." His chest is heaving. He appears to be bravely holding back tears.

"Catch your breath, son," comes Joel's voice, sounding like the cop he is – or was.

"Okay." He's gulping for air.

Michael locks eyes expectantly with his daughter, and there's some kind of spark there, something passes between them, but Michael catches only the ghost of it. It feels significant, though. He's certain about it now: She's not telling him something.

"What's your name?" Rachel asks the boy, breaking the eye contact.

"Danny." His breathing is slowing but still ragged. "I live over there." He points back toward where he came from. "My sister is one of those …."

Michael can tell the kid is in shock and running on fumes. "It's all right, Danny, you're safe with us."

"Do you have any water?" The boy's eyes are still wide as saucers.

Michael thinks of the backpack sitting on the floorboards of the Pilot and feels suddenly very thirsty himself.

"I've got some," Rachel offers. "There was one in the car, half empty."

She takes it from a compartment next to her and hands it back to him. "Here you go."

Danny twists open the cap and drinks greedily.

Rachel is watching him carefully. "Have you been hurt at all?"

Danny just looks at her, drinking.

"I mean, have those bodies hurt you? Your family, maybe?"

The bottle comes away from his lips. "I still don't know where my mom is, she was supposed to come right home after work. She works the night shift. My dad is – "

Silence finishes that thought.

Rachel is still looking him over. Michael knows what she's searching for: the pale spots on the skin. To Michael, Danny appears unblemished.

"Are your dad or sister still back there?"

Danny prefers not to acknowledge that question. He looks away, takes another drink, then lets the empty bottle fall to the floor. He finishes swallowing.

"I'm sorry, Danny, I didn't mean to – "

"Dee Dee was chasing me." Danny is flattened against the cloth seat, legs akimbo, palms up, exhausted. "But I don't know where Daddy went. I sure wish I did."

Joel makes the turn onto Riverside. Michael keeps searching all vantage points, watching for movement. There's nothing for a quarter mile.

"He went to work in the morning, and he usually calls me on my phone. I have a phone that he calls me on to make sure I'm up. But he didn't call me. He didn't call. But I thought that was because my phone was broken."

"Danny, we're gonna take you somewhere safe, okay?" Rachel says. "There's more people there, and there's plenty of food and water and places to sleep. I don't know what happened to your folks either, but we'll make sure you're okay."

All he does is nod.

Rachel is watching him over the back of her seat. "So you've been in your house all this time? Waiting for your parents?"

He nods again.

"What have you been doing?"

"I played Nintendo for a long time until the battery wore out, and then I found Momma's old phone with Temple Run on it and I got six million points. And then ..."

Michael listens to the boy talk, lets his head fall back against his headrest. He swallows dryly, craving water. He can wait until he's back at the hospital, where Bonnie can tend to his head. He dreads her admonishments, but he deserves them. He doesn't regret going home to find Susanna, but at the same time … he does. His head is just a thick dull throb now; it has gone beyond sharp warning pains and into some kind of hushed panic mode.

"… I have a lot of books, too, and I'm the best reader in my grade, and I mean all three classes at the school …"

Rachel, propped there in her seat, listening almost raptly to this boy, is like a stranger to him. Without her makeup, without the trappings of her old teenage life, she has emerged as if from a chrysalis into a new being. Hair slicked back, jaw set, she exudes purpose and initiative and confidence. Michael feels a weird resentment that it took the end of the world to bring out these qualities.

"Were you scared?" Rachel asks now, pulling Michael from his thoughts.

"No," Danny says, as if not appreciating the question.

"Well, I would have been."

"I wasn't *scared*. But – why are they all mad now? Why are they running around like that? They didn't chase me before. I even went to other houses, I went to Jake's house next door, and the people next to him, and I found food, and they didn't bother me at all, they just kept on chewing those trees. Now it's like they want to chew on *me*."

He's playing with his empty water bottle, letting it twirl between his fingers.

"I don't know, little dude, but we're trying to figure that out."

Joel takes the turn onto Lemay, and the road begins its rise toward the hospital. Michael watches Culver's pass by and thinks he has never felt hunger for a cheeseburger quite as poignantly as in this moment. As the road levels out near the hospital parking garage, the emergency entrance comes into view.

"Shit!" Joel shouts.

The car comes to a quick stop.

Scores of bodies are flowing toward the hospital entrance, and there's no telling how many are already there. The urgency of their movement fills the car with held-breath horror.

CHAPTER 15

"We're out of blood!" Rachel reminds them loudly, clutching the edge of her seat, her empty, blood-stained Super Soaker impotent in her lap.

Danny has leaned forward to gawk at the hospital entrance.

"The bags are in the cruiser." Joel checks his own weapon, tosses it in front of Rachel. "And so is the portable."

"The portable?" Michael says.

"The radio. Kevin's got one, but – "

"My pack is back in that Pilot. So is your shotgun, Rachel. And my Colt."

"Grandpa's gun?"

"Yeah."

The car idles as they watch the frenetic activity at the entrance.

"Think everybody's still inside?"

"I'm thinking these bastards wouldn't be in such a frenzy if they weren't," Joel says. He's staring at the mass of former humanity, his jaw working, thinking, thinking.

Michael realizes that he's clutching the side of his head with his palm. Now that everything has effectively paused inside the car, he realizes that his skull is throbbing like a drumbeat and his eyes are watering as if he's been sobbing.

With a strange sense of detachment, he flashes on Susanna's corpse and feels more tears pulse at his eyes. Through blurred vision, he glances at his daughter, who hasn't looked at him for the bulk of this entire insane journey.

"We need a better vehicle," Joel announces.

He reverses the Toyota in a rush for twenty yards, then makes a tight left onto Doctors Lane, behind the hospital.

"Do you think any of those things saw us?" Danny says, falling back into the seat.

"I don't think it's a matter of seeing us, Danny," Joel says. "I think they sense us some other way."

"Like they smell us?"

"Maybe."

"I know I stink. Our shower isn't working anymore."

"I think it's something else," Joel says. "Something inside. Just the fact that we're different."

He circles around the north side of the hospital, hoping for a view of the emergency exit from the east. Michael is leaning forward anxiously, still clutching his forehead, and Danny is right there with him.

In the expectant silence, Joel says, "I just want to see if we can spot Kevin's truck. If it's still there, they're in trouble. If not, maybe they got out."

"But those things are targeting something, right?" Michael asks, under a prolonged wince. "Someone's in there."

"Yeah. Shit. Well, I still want to see if some of them got out."

They make it to the east parking lot, winding through parked and silent cars, only a few minor collisions, and then they see the relentless activity at the emergency exit. Kevin's truck is gone.

Joel brings the Toyota to a stop and drapes his arms over the steering wheel.

"Okay, so I'm gonna assume that most of them got out. Where would they go?"

"The college?" Rachel asks. "You and Kevin were talking with Ron over there."

"Would they have gone looking for me, too?" Michael asks reluctantly.

"I don't think they know where you lived."

Joel's casual use of past tense hits Michael hard. He lets his hand drift down from his brow and cover his clamped-shut eyes, and he grits his teeth. He really has awakened into a dark new existence, and there's no way he's ever going to return to his previous one. A few days ago, he had firm hold of his destiny. His marriage was strong in all the right ways. He had managed to work through not only his own grief but his daughter's profound grief over the death of Cassie, and sure, even though Rachel had her own complications and rebelliousness, she was a good kid, so much better than her father. Hell, you could see her basic goodness right now, in the way she had responded to this madness. And he was amassing cash toward – what, something better? He had so much going for him, and was on the verge of so much more, and now it's all gone, replaced by this new and brutal truth.

Everything, like the money at the back of his closet, is worthless now.

When he opens his eyes again, Rachel is staring back at him. Father and daughter finally share a meaningful look, and then she breaks it, returns her gaze to the bodies swarming at the emergency entrance.

"Looks like one of them is on to us," she announces.

Sure enough, one of the bodies has sensed them in the car, and is advancing across a knoll to the asphalt a hundred feet away. It's an old man, scrawny, in long johns. His face, hanging from a straining neck, is full of craggy, red anger. And now a second and third body have joined the first.

"Interesting," Joel breathes, leaning back and preparing to leave.

"What?" Rachel asks.

"It's like they're keying in on us when we're stopped or when they're right on top of us. If we're in motion, maybe they don't sense us?"

"Well, I wish you'd get in motion right now. Those things freak me out."

"Just a sec."

There are now five or six of the bodies approaching. Fifty yards, forty. Michael can see the exaggerated fury in their eyes, the rivulets of sap stuck to their foreheads, plugging up their nostrils, and sticky in their hair.

"They're swarming," Joel says. "Like they're – like they're all of one mind."

"You're right," Michael says.

"What does that mean?" Danny asks. "Like bees or something?"

"Except a bit more aggressive." Joel spits out the words.

He hits the gas and pulls a U-turn, heading out of the parking lot. Michael and Danny crane their necks to watch the scrabbling mass give futile chase.

"Okay," says Joel, "last thing Kevin talked to me about was getting over to the Wildlife office off Prospect, seeing if we could get our hands on some tranq guns and darts. I figure, even if they're not there, we can round up the supplies and head elsewhere. Maybe join Ron at the school. Sound like a plan?"

"You think those tranquilizers could work?" Michael asks.

"What, cure them?"

"Yeah."

"Well, especially the way those things are now, no way do I want to get close to them. Tranq rifles will let us pump in the blood from a distance. Rachel is right, blood is our greatest weapon against these things. I'm just not sure ..."

Rachel pipes in: "Not sure of what?"

"Look, girl, I'm all for saving lives, but I'm just not sure these lives are worth saving. You saw that body at the hospital. Once the blood was pumped into it, it was screaming in pain. Broken bones, hyperextended everything, who knows what kind of tissue damage."

"Bodies heal," says Rachel.

"And that was a body that never went outside, never attached itself to one of those trees. It didn't have woodchips and splinters tearing up its entire digestive works."

"Are you suggesting we don't bother?" Rachel's voice is confrontational. "That we just sit on this cure and let them suffer? You don't think it means anything that the blood flowing through our veins can reverse all of this?"

"I'm just wondering what I would want if that had happened to me, that's all. Don't take it personally."

Rachel doesn't respond, just stares forward.

"I'm the one championing the tranq darts, remember," Joel says. "And anyway, we might not have any choice in the matter. Things are changing every minute around here, and right now those goddamn things are monsters. *Monsters!* Let's just see what happens, huh?"

The car is silent as they make the turn back onto Lemay, heading south toward Prospect – and back toward the emergency entrance.

"Uh ..." Michael says. "I can't help but notice that you're – "

"They're distracted on the other side now. Should be clear."

Sure enough, only a few stragglers are out in front of the emergency entrance. Joel slows the Toyota to a crawl, and the survivors search the area for any evidence of struggle or escape. Everything looks fairly calm. Michael sees no bodies lying dead on the ground and feels a distinct relief. But who knows what lies farther in? He does see movement in there, but it's the crooked crab movements of the infected.

The infected.

It's the first time that word has passed through his mind in any natural kind of way. He can't recall it being uttered by any of the survivors, but his concussion is probably to blame for that. He quietly considers the word, its implications, but the line of thought dwindles away into pain-threatening contradictions. His mind refuses to even acknowledge the notion of some otherworldly infection.

Or perhaps *possession* is a better term.

The thought makes him shudder.

The whole scene in front of the hospital has the feel of an area attacked and then hastily abandoned.

"I think everyone got out," Joel says.

"We can only hope they had time to grab blood and medicine,"

Rachel adds.

"Right."

"I hope they're okay."

As Joel picks up speed, Danny speaks up.

"Is there any … any food?" The words comes out quietly, meekly.

"Oh, I'm sorry, Danny," Rachel says, twisting her body to look him in the eyes. "You're hungry? When's the last time you ate?"

"I've been making peanut butter sandwiches every day, and I never ran out, but I got a little tired of those. There's cereal, but the milk went bad. So did all the turkey."

"Meat's gonna be tough to come by, little dude," Joel says. "But right now everything in the supermarket is free, so I'm sure we can find you something. Can it wait an hour or two till we get a better idea what we're up against?"

Danny bows his head and seems to dig himself in for a wait.

Michael's right hand is aching in its clutch of his forehead, and now he realizes that the pain has eased enough to let go. He brings the hand down and blinks hard. Perhaps it's the relative rest his body has received, sitting here in this seat, or perhaps it's just being reunited with his daughter, but either way, he feels a gratitude to … to whatever small benevolent force seems to be on their side, letting them escape the awful fate of the bulk of humanity.

"So let's say we get the tranquilizers and build up some blood supplies …" Michael says. "And Bonnie gets everything in order with the anticoagulant, and we can reliably weaponize ourselves. What about after that? Are we gonna – "

At that moment, another vehicle, a large late-model BMW, comes careening out onto Lemay from Pitkin, a residential street to their left. Joel curses loudly, stamping on the brakes. The BMW swerves, missing them by inches. Michael can see the sweaty red face of a middle-aged man, for a split second, and then the car rights itself just as two scrambling bodies come surging out of the neighborhood in pursuit. But as the BMW roars south, wildly twisting around the wrecks that dot the street, the bodies immediately sense the four survivors in the Toyota and come leaping toward them instead.

"Jesus Christ, man," Joel whispers, and Michael can hear a helplessness there that doesn't exactly fill him with optimism.

He jerks the car forward as two of the bodies hit the side panels, almost in unison. Michael is staring right into the wide, dry, dead eyes of a woman who might as well have been the BMW driver's wife – a hideous mockery of a suburban housewife. She gasps at him, her jaw poking at the window, and then she's gone, receding into the background.

"Just keep moving," Rachel says, obviously shaken.

"Ri – " Joel starts, then pauses, reacting to something ahead of them. "Hey, hey! That's what I'm talkin' about."

"What?"

He nods his head forward.

About three hundred yards ahead, crooked against the curb next to the flower shop, is a bright yellow Hummer.

"Oh brother," says Michael. "Seriously?"

"Fuckin' A – sorry kid."

Danny doesn't seem fazed by the language.

Michael lets out a humorless laugh. "And environmentalism was rendered pointless in the blink of an eye."

"Goddamn liberals." Joel's laugh is more vocal. "Okay, I'm gonna stop quick right next to it, and Rachel, you're gonna jump out and check that thing for keys, see if it starts up. Got it?"

Rachel releases a whiny sigh. "You sure we need that?"

"Yes. I am sure."

"Wait a second," Michael interrupts, "I should do that, I can jump out and get it started."

"No you can't, man, not yet." Joel scans the area and hones in on the Hummer, then checks the rearview mirror. "We're clear. No shame in it, Mike. You're still recovering. Just be ready to climb in."

"I can do it, Dad."

Michael flashes back four years to when he tried to teach Rachel how to handle a stick shift in his old beat-up Volkswagen Rabbit, that clunker he hung on to just for her, knowing it would be her first car, and believing that it was essential to teach a first-time driver how to handle a manual transmission. Her heart had never been in it, though. She'd never really wanted to learn it, and had sold that car to save up for a dreamed-of newer VW that never happened. Michael feels a deep twinge of something like loss when he realizes that here, right now, is when that stick-shift lesson would have paid off.

"Here we go."

The Toyota lurches to a stop next to the Hummer, whose door is barely clicked shut. Rachel jumps fluidly from her side and leaps up onto the huge vehicle's sideboards, pulling at the heavy door. It swings open and she slides in. She quickly gives a thumbs up, and the ignition turns. She knows enough to start up a manual transmission and idle in in neutral. The battery is a little sleepy, but the engine fires.

"Okay, out," Joel calls.

The three remaining doors fling open, and the survivors make a run for it. Danny is inside the Hummer before Michael can barely edge past the Toyota's rear bumper, and even Joel is already climbing in to replace Rachel at the wheel.

Michael's heart is at his throat, his pulse rushing at his ears. His eyes twitch in all directions, anticipating any attack. The area is wide open, and he feels like the largest, most lumbering target in all of Fort Collins.

But no bodies rush him. The ones behind them, in the distance, have veered off into a neighborhood.

Rachel rolls down the window on the rear passenger side. "Take the front, Dad."

He pulls himself up into shotgun and lets out a grunt as the door slams.

The Hummer rumbles forward confidently, like a tank. Under his headache, Michael rolls his eyes but even he recognizes the vehicle's value in the current situation.

"Little over half a tank of gas," Joel says, scanning the dash.

"Good, that should give us a few miles anyway." Michael can't help it. "Okay, I'm done."

"This is a nice car," Danny says, smiling.

Joel tosses Michael a smirk, then takes the immediate right onto Prospect, heading west toward the Wildlife office. Between here and there lies about a mile of residential streets leading into quiet neighborhoods. But now every street appears poised to let loose with scurrying bodies. All eyes are on alert, watching for movement – and they soon find that most of the streets appear deserted. Danny even spots a few bodies still wrapped painfully around the bases of evergreens, as if they simply haven't awoken to the "scent" of nearby survivors. That, in fact, becomes the working theory: that the bodies are only becoming active and aggressive when they sense that they have an opportunity, nearby, to take out a surviving human being.

The most haunting image reveals itself as they pass a church just west of Robertson, where a group of the things is swarming beyond a small parking lot, at the building's curved front entrance.

"There's people in there." Rachel's voice is hard and sad. "Survivors. Or there were."

"Can we go get 'em?" Danny asks.

Joel brings the Hummer to a stop, considering. He glances over at Michael.

"I think the boy's got a point. Let's see what this bastard can do."

He lurches the heavy vehicle toward the parking lot, and as if they've passed over a kind of psychic barrier, all the turned-over heads of the scurrying bodies swivel to face them.

"Wait!" Rachel says, understanding dawning.

"I wanna see what those things are capable of, too," Joel adds.

"Joel ..." she says warily.

"Don't worry."

As he enters the parking lot, Joel mashes down on the horn, jolting everyone in the car. The blatting sound is surprisingly weak for a suburban tank, but it does its job of causing a stir. All of the bodies in front of the church position themselves as if to pounce, their limbs jittering. Michael's breath has stopped in his throat.

"You're gonna attract a thousand of those things!" Rachel cries.

"What are you doing?" Michael calls loudly, grabbing for his *oh-shit* handle.

"Watch the doors, see if you can spot anyone in there. I'm gonna try to attract a bunch of these assholes, lure 'em away from the entrance."

Joel rips through the parking lot, which is empty of vehicles, and the bodies follow the Hummer diligently. Michael avoids meeting their snapping gazes, instead focusing on the windows of the church. At first glance, he sees nothing but dim emptiness beyond them, and then Danny shouts, "There!"

"Where?" Rachel says.

"Next to the – to the right of the front doors."

That window is already fading behind them, but yes, there is a face there, in shadow, and hands pressed to the glass.

"He's right," Rachel says. "One person."

"Okay, I'll head back around, maybe we can grab him. Or her."

Just as Joel blats the horn again, a small crab-like body, a female, scurries from the sidewalk off Ellis, directly in front of them. Joel makes a token effort to swerve, but immediately the body – a bright yellow tattered nightgown trailing at its naked limbs – goes under the Hummer's huge tires, and Michael can't help but look away, back at Rachel, in time to see her curl up into a ball on her seat, slapping her hands to her ears, shutting her eyes.

They all feel a hideous bump and lurch as the body is crushed beneath them.

"That was a little girl!" Danny shouts.

"That was no little girl," Joel responds, revving it at the top end of second gear and bouncing onto Ellis. A quick, arcing turn gets them back onto Prospect, where Joel brings the vehicle to a shuddering stop.

"Oh God, that's terrible," Rachel squeals. "Joel, we can save these people, you can't just crush them like bugs!"

"The hell I can't!"

One of the bodies broadsides the Hummer, making the heavy vehicle jerk on its treads. There's a shrieking gasp outside.

And then the rest of the bodies are on them. And coordinated. Three or four of the bodies position themselves against the Hummer to provide the next wave leverage to jump higher. Two inverted male heads hit the left windows simultaneously – *hard* – the one next to Michael cracking into two long lightning-shaped fractures.

"Jesus – !" Joel shouts.

He floors the gas, and the Hummer leaps forward. Two bodies go under the tires, and this time Rachel moans in frustration, twisting to peer through the bleary rear window. The two bodies are squashed like giant bugs, trying furiously to manipulate their broken limbs.

Joel rumbles back into the church parking lot and pulls up close to the door, honking his horn. All eyes go to the window next to the church's front door. There, peering out miserably, is a face that both Rachel and Joel react to with identical gasps.

CHAPTER 16

"I don't believe it," Rachel says.

"Believe it," Joel manages, wrestling the steering wheel and coming to a heavy stop directly adjacent to the front doors. "It's him."

"Him who?" Michael says.

"A grade-A asshole," Joel says. "Rachel, open the door quick. We've got ten seconds."

"His name is Scott. Caused all sorts of problems at the hospital. He was an administrator there." Rachel pushes the door open. "What if he doesn't want to come with us?"

"Then that's his problem."

The Hummer's occupants stare at the face behind the glass. Scott's red hair is matted, and he appears gaunt, troubled. He looks desperate.

Joel waves him forward impatiently.

"Get your ass in here if you want to live!"

Michael turns to judge the distance of the bodies scrambling toward the vehicle. Thirty feet ... twenty-five.

"Joel," he warns.

But Scott is now scurrying out the door, leaving it wide open and racing to the car. He's hobbled, favoring one leg, and he appears slightly hunched over. Rachel has scooted into the middle, next to Danny, and her face scrunches with distaste as the man hauls himself inside and heaves the door shut.

The Hummer roars forward, gasping bodies tumbling in its wake.

Scott's face is pale and sweaty, and Michael can already smell his sour breath.

No one has said anything.

Michael breaks the silence.

"Were you in there all alone?"

Scott raises his head, looks at him miserably, doesn't answer.

Joel bounces down onto Prospect again and heads west, shifting into third. He casts one glance through the rear-view mirror, then returns his eyes to the road.

"We're not going to the hospital?" Scott finally says.

"Are you all right?" Rachel asks.

"Oh, peachy."

"What do you need?"

"What I need, frankly, is at the hospital."

"Well," says Joel, "we're not going there."

"Why not?"

"I don't know if you noticed, but things have changed in the past couple hours." Joel swerves around a Jeep that is crumpled against the median. "Hospital is overrun."

Scott is silent.

Michael can sense that he wants to say something else, but the tension in the air is tamping it down. Rachel is still sneering at Scott, but she asks, "What is it you need?"

"Forget it." He clutches his stomach.

"I think a detox is what you need."

"Oh, for fu – " Scott stops himself, possibly for Danny's benefit, and just stares out the window. "I just need pain meds. Did it ever occur to you that some people might be SOL because of preexisting conditions? Pharmacies are kind of a free-for-all now, that's just the way it is."

"Hey, you want to watch the tone, pal?" Michael says.

"Who the hell are you?"

"That's my dad," Rachel replies, hard.

Joel slows down and maneuvers the large vehicle through another collection of stray cars, inching through one collision and simply shoving the smaller vehicles aside.

Michael watches the desolate streets to the left and right. A few of them aren't so empty anymore. North on Whedbee, he catches a glimpse of a young man sprinting across the street, from one home to another, three bodies scurrying after him, their heads stretching toward him, one woman's hair whipping at the ground. Michael points, urgently, and Joel is in the act of making the turn when the young man disappears in the opposite direction, between houses, racing into some kind of shadowed greenbelt. Just like that, he's gone from view, and the animated bodies disappear in his wake.

Joel pauses, glances back at Rachel. She continues to watch the street. Joel continues on.

"We can't save everyone."

"But – " Rachel starts, then deflates.

There is a long moment of guilty silence. Danny is glancing around, searching their faces expectantly. Finally, he looks away, back outside.

"I'm glad you stopped for me," he says.

The kid has a quality about him that is quite endearing: an innocence that can't be torn away, even by the end of everything he's known all his life.

As they pass Peterson, Rachel notices a body on the asphalt that is clearly the corpse of a former survivor. "Oh no."

"What?"

"Wait, wait, slow down, look."

The Hummer rumbles to a slower pace, and Rachel looks past Danny, out his window, at the body. It's a dark-haired woman, heavyset, unfortunately face-up. Her features are hollowed out, bleached, desolate, as if every ounce of life has been sucked away from her. Michael takes one look and has to turn away.

"What happened to her?" he says.

"Those things," Joel says. "Those bodies happened to her."

"*How?*"

"That's what they do, isn't it?" Rachel breathes. "Even from the start. Whatever it is that's inside them, it's a weapon. Or at least, they can use it as a weapon. It's what happened to a lot of people we saw coming in to the hospital that first day. It happened to my hand," she says, lifting her palm to show the skin there: off-color, pale ... subtly damaged. "And this was just a little bit. That – " She pauses, settling back. " – that's what happens when they really want to hurt you."

"That light inside them?" Michael says, his eyes still on the destroyed body.

"It's more than just light."

At that moment, a large body slams into the passenger side of the Hummer, rocking it on its wheels.

"Fuck!" Scott screeches through gritted teeth. "Why did I get in here?"

When Michael jerks his head around to see what has collided with them, he finds a round face glaring up at him, its mulch-crusted mouth a jowly oval of rage beneath the sap-smeared chin. It's the body of a gigantic man in a tattered flannel shirt. As Joel punches the Hummer forward, the huge body recedes into the distance, still lumbering toward them.

Michael settles back into his seat, bringing one hand up to clutch at his forehead. During moments of relative calm, the ever-present ache reminds him that it's still there, waiting to be dealt with. Behind closed eyes, images clank and clatter, his too-recent memories of this day already splintering and scattering. It takes him a full minute to recall the circumstances that led him from the hospital to home to here, and when he opens his eyes again, the awesome sight of the burning foothills at least brings back the awful, solid truth of the immediate present.

"... hell are we going anyway?" Scott's loud voice filters into his consciousness, but he lets it drift away, as well as Joel's steely-edged response.

Michael is simply staring forward, losing himself in the monstrousness of the blaze before them, and the atmospheric phenomenon above it. Great columns of white smoke, streaked with black, drift northeast, and above it all, there's that almost purple sky-throb.

The tendrils of pulsing light that reach down into the smoke remind him of the morning it began, when Steven and Carol dropped to the floor behind him, and vehicles along College veered out of their lanes and coasted to stops, their drivers slumped over the wheels. And the appearance of the sky, when it happened ... the shards of light raining down on the earth, defying reason, defying his very grasp of the meaning of the world. Even now, the sight fills him with a dread that reaches beyond bewilderment and into a kind of numb disconnect. It seems to have that effect on everyone in the car: They all cast occasional bleak glances skyward, and then look away, their faces reflecting a kind of futility.

But the sight also sparks something deep within ... more pieces of memory –

– *at his window at work, mesmerized despite his fallen colleagues –*

– *the dark red pulse within the columns of light –*

– *the huge atmospheric phenomenon above everything –*

– *something shifting there, at the zenith of it all, something roiling above the blue Colorado heavens, casting cosmic shadows, something larger than his comprehension, something searching and ... watching –*

– *and his mad dash toward the stairwell, crashing into desks, stumbling –*

– *his only thoughts of Susanna and Rachel ...*

The memory of that ... whatever it was ... something mind-boggling shifting above the sky ... fills him with new dread, and he leans forward to search the heavens, but he sees nothing but blue sky streaked with smoke. The jagged memory leaves him feeling infinitesimal beneath the sway of a malevolent presence that can only pound and bellow.

Joel and Scott are sparring again.

"... gonna make me wish I'd just driven on by, dude."

"Yeah, I'm wishing the same thing, Officer."

Laughter. "Good ol' Scott."

"I mean, did you guys have any sort of plan, or are you just out for a leisurely drive?"

"We just saved your life, asshole!"

Rachel's voice shakes Michael fully out of his spell, and he glances back at her. She returns his gaze, gestures with her head toward Scott with exasperation. Michael maintains the eye contact with his daughter, trying to communicate something but unsure what that is.

Her expression darkens, and her mouth opens slightly, and he realizes that a tear has spilled from his eye. He wipes it hastily away, turns forward to face the windshield.

"I didn't ask for any rescue," Scott says. "I was safe in there!"

"Coulda fooled me," Joel says, "the way you were pressed up against the window, like some hungry puppy."

For some reason, this image tickles Danny, and he bursts out with helpless giggles. Michael supposes it's the boy's way of releasing some pent-up emotion, finding some small measure of catharsis.

"He's right," the boy snickers, "you were just like that!"

And then he dissolves into mirth again.

The adults glance around at each other, smiles on their faces. Scott appears ready to explode but finally sighs out of his anger and just watches the kid. In a moment, Michael and Rachel are laughing, and even Scott cracks a lopsided grin before facing away, toward the window.

"You were just like Molly!" Danny says, the giggles starting to subside. "Just like Molly. That was our dog."

"Glad to hear it," Scott says, giving Danny an almost reluctant but friendly shove against his bony shoulder.

The laughter feels good to Michael, and he savors the sensation in his chest. He hasn't laughed in days. Then he responds to Danny's comment about his dog.

"So what happened to Molly, Danny?"

Danny comes all the way out of his laughter, then, and just starts nodding.

"Molly didn't wake up either."

Silence.

"I'm sorry, Danny."

"That's okay, she was old."

Michael pats the boy's knee and is trying to think of something more to say when –

"Hey!" Joel blurts.

Directly ahead, coming toward them, is a familiar truck.

"It's Kevin!" Rachel says.

"Wait," Joel says, trepidation in his voice, "something's up."

The blue truck is jerking left and right as it barrels forward. Joel slows the Hummer and they all watch as Kevin skids the truck north onto College Avenue. Michael can just make out the large man's face contorted in alarm.

Rachel lets out a gasp.

There are several survivors hunkered down in the flatbed, and three bodies are clutched to the rear gate like spiders poised to strike. Raised voices are coming from the vehicle, echoing along the barren street, and then they fade abruptly as the truck careens out of sight.

"Holy shit!" Rachel cries. "That was Chrissy in there! And the twins!"

The Hummer lurches forward, its motor roaring.

"I take it they weren't able to grab weapons," Joel says. "Or any blood."

"Or they ran out."

"Like we did."

"Oh, the blood again!" Scott cuts in.

Rachel throws a glare at him.

Joel clips the bumper of a Volkswagen Beetle, sending it spinning, and then they're turning onto College.

The truck is a hundred yards ahead. Joel starts jabbing at the horn, sending staccato blasts to catch Kevin's attention. The rear of the truck is fishtailing, but the bodies' ability to remain attached to the tailgate is inhuman. None of them falls.

The truck is flailing around stalled cars and wrecks, and the things grasping for purchase at its tailgate keep lunging forward at the flatbed's occupants, who seem to be cautiously warding them off with their arms and feet.

"How are those things not falling?!" Rachel cries.

"Maybe we can give them a little help," Joel says, goosing the Hummer still more.

"Careful!"

They close the distance rapidly after Kevin hears their horn, following in the wake of the zigzagging truck, weaving between abandoned vehicles. Michael holds on for dear life, feeling as if he might crash right through the window and fall into the street. The rear of Kevin's truck looms suddenly before them, and the three things holding on to the tailgate glare at Joel and Michael, then back at their female prey cowering in the back of the truck. The bodies' heads swivel jerkily, insect-like. The upside-down faces are caricatures of fury.

And yet their basic underlying humanity is undeniable. One of them is an athletic teen sporting a blond buzz cut; Michael can't help but imagine the boy's trip to the barber, his after-school workouts, his celebrations with whatever team he belonged to. The other is a woman around fifty, her hair long and gray, all her clothes gone, her otherwise toned body splayed wide, the joints inflamed; and yet there's kindness hiding in her features, beneath the alien rage. These observations – occurring within the space of mere seconds – cause Michael's breath to catch. He sees what Joel intends, and there is a part of him that is compelled almost beyond restraint to reach over, grab the wheel, and veer them off course.

Somehow he resists the urge.

Ten feet, five, and –

"Hold on!" Joel shouts.

The impact jars Michael forward, and Joel and Rachel let loose with emphatic *ooomphs*.

The lower extremities and pelvises of the teen and the older woman are crushed between the vehicles, and a terrible, tormented gasping fills the air. The third body – that of an older businessman in a torn suit, his tie flapping uselessly – slides across the Hummer's massive hood and comes to rest against the windshield, flat on its back. Its head is right there, the flat eyes darting from Joel to Michael as if to gauge which of the two men is the greater threat – or the more vulnerable target. Its hands and bare feet clamber across the slick hood, quick and sure, the fingers grasping the barrier between the hood and the windshield, the bare toes finding the grill in the center of the Hummer's ridiculous expanse of hood.

Michael rears back, shielding his face, despite the safety-glass barrier.

Both bodies at the truck's tailgate go down to the asphalt, falling out of sight, and then the Hummer is bouncing roughly over them. Rachel makes a kind of mewling noise.

Kevin's truck goes swerving to the right, free of its attackers, and Michael has a glimpse of the three girls in the back, exhausted but safe, holding on tight, watching the drama on the Hummer's hood – or perhaps still trying to determine who has come to save them.

Joel continues straight north, and as they slow to swerve through a collision immediately adjacent to the CSU track, the body on the hood takes the opportunity to jab its head straight at the windshield. There's a horrid thump, and the head stays riveted there as if attached.

Joel rounds the wheel in a vicious swerve, but the thing stays anchored right where it is. "Damn!"

There's a vibration now at the dash, and a throbbing heat, and impossibly the glass begins to fog.

"Holy shit!" Scott cries from the back. "It's melting the glass!"

"Can it do that?" Joel says, and there's a dark awe in his voice.

The face of the thing is a human parody, its mouth a mocking slash. Michael can definitely sense intelligence there.

"Get that thing off of there!" Scott cries.

"Hold on!" Joel shouts, and plants both feet on the brakes.

The Hummer shudders violently, and the former businessman's face snarls as the limbs struggle to maintain their backwards grip. Finally, the body goes sliding across the hood, stopping at the front grill, half of it hanging down toward the bumper.

Michael sees only the head and thrashing limbs.

"Die, you bastard!" Joel shouts, then punches the Hummer forward again.

Right in the center of the windshield is a plate-sized blob of bruised glass, not shattered or broken, but partially sagging, as if molten. Even as he's thrown back against his seat, Michael can't help but stare at it with frank curiosity.

Joel swerves the Hummer mightily, left and right, trying to dislodge their unwelcome parasite.

"Crush it against a tree or something!" Scott yells.

"I don't want to wreck this thing!"

The body manages to gain a sturdy foothold and leaps onto the hood again, sliding directly toward Michael.

"Truck!" Rachel calls. "Here it comes!"

The Chevy surges in from the right, revving hard. Michael risks a glance, sees Kevin's sweaty face, and Bonnie next to him, hysterical.

The body scrabbles for a grip on the slippery surface, continuing its awkward slide. It reaches for the edge of the hood, misses. It clutches at Michael's side mirror, does a heavy flip, and lodges itself on the side rail directly next to him. The thing's head is bent over in a neck-cracking position, the eyes staring into the vehicle with dead, red-rimmed ire, and the body is bowed so severely backward that it hardly seems human at all. Michael leans as far from the door as possible, frantically gesturing Kevin closer.

The head lunges at Michael, thumping mercilessly on the nearly shattered window, and Michael somewhat pointlessly reaches over and locks the door. The dead eyes react to the proximity of his hand, darting at it, rapping the glass loudly. Michael sees mottled, bruised skin where it comes into contact with the window, but the thing seems to be suffering no pain.

"Hold on!" Joel cries, and Kevin's truck comes heaving at them broadside.

But the thing is aware, leaping up and above the window just as the truck clanks hard against the Hummer's side panels. Joel maintains his hold on the wheel, and the thing clangs and batters the roof above them. Michael remembers seeing a luggage rack up there and knows it's got just what it needs now to hang on.

"Watch the windows on all sides!" Joel yells. "Lock your doors!"

He swings the Hummer wide, left and right, but the body on top of them hangs tight. Joel straightens out to maneuver between two substantial collisions, and the body swings over the opposite side of the vehicle – effortlessly, as if it has learned from what happened at Michael's window – and positions itself at Danny's window.

"Look out!" Michael calls. "Rachel, watch it!"

Anchored tightly on the luggage rack, the thing has the leverage to swing its head down against the window, savagely, and the glass spiderwebs in a quick *thwack!*

"Danny!" Rachel cries, reaching over the boy protectively.

What happens next occurs too quickly for Michael – or any of them – to comprehend.

The head comes swinging at the window again, with a dexterity that fills Michael with outright terror. Elbows angled and framing the shattered window, the head pokes through, gasping. Its flat, dry eyes swivel madly in their sockets, regarding all of them in an instant and landing on its closest target.

Rachel is already yanking Danny backward. *"Noooo! Get the f – "*

Danny's seatbelt locks, and Rachel loses half her grip.

The gasping head jabs at Danny, at his face and his desperately stretched-back neck, and the boy makes a terrible wet squelch in his throat.

Everyone is yelling.

"GET OFF HIM, YOU BASTARD!" Rachel is screaming, angling her hips to kick at the inhuman face, but the head receives the blows with the merest of flinches, then dives back at Danny, lunging, lunging, and Rachel is shrieking.

Without even realizing it, Michael is shouting and angling his body to kick at the head, too, but the thing is relentless, and now he can feel the tips of his toes going numb as his foot makes repeated contact.

"Don't touch it!" he cries, yanking his leg back. "Rachel, don't touch it, it'll hurt you!"

"I don't care!"

Joel has tried everything with the Hummer, jerking it violently, and now he comes to a sudden halt, heaving his passengers forward. Rachel, unbuckled, goes flailing against the large center console, screeching in fear and anger. Scott thumps the back of Michael's seat, cursing. Some part of Michael is aware of Kevin's truck sailing past them.

Danny is now fully in the thing's grasp. The boy's eyes have rolled back in his head, and Michael gets an awful glimpse of melted skin across his face. Just as Michael is reaching out to grab the boy with one final desperate grab, the thing yanks Danny's small body through the destroyed window – glass scraping the boy's flesh cruelly – and flings him to the asphalt. The body of the businessman then drops nimbly to the ground like some obscene crab and falls on Danny, the stabbing head working frenetically.

Rachel squawks raggedly in despair.

"He's gone!" Michael cries, appalled.

"No no no no no!" Rachel is repeating hoarsely.

"For fuck's sake!" Scott says, his voice trembling and pitched high. "Get us out of here!"

The Hummer is already moving, and Kevin's truck is fifty feet to the north, idling. Kevin's head is down on his chest, and Bonnie has her hands over her face. The girls in the back are all perched at the tailgate, staring at them with horror.

Joel clears his throat, doesn't say anything.

Rachel is mewling on the floorboards.

The Hummer closes the distance and pulls up next to Kevin. Michael's window slides down in damaged fits and starts, the glass falling away in webbed chunks.

"Who was – ?" Bonnie manages.

Michael shakes his head, unsure what to say.

He acknowledges the girls in the back of the truck. They are splattered and streaked with a terrible amount of blood. Their eyes are full of exhaustion and fear, their mouths hanging open. Scattered in the flatbed are several empty Super Soakers, and there are deflated blood bags everywhere. There's also a large cardboard box full of something that Michael can't make out.

For a long moment, there's just the sound of heavy breathing. Michael can clearly make out the look of shock on Kevin's face.

"What the fuck, man?" the big man says. "I mean ... what the fuck?"

His expression is full of not only horror but worry. Michael can relate.

"We can't stay here," Joel says, his voice sounding hollowed out.

Kevin is nodding his head slowly, distracted by the horror.

Neither man cares to directly address what has just happened.

"Have you heard from anyone?" Joel asks. With shaking hands, he reaches into his pocket, finds a cigarette back. It takes him a moment to realize that it's empty, and he lets it drop to the asphalt.

Rachel lets out a sob.

"Ron at the school," Kevin says. "They were driven out of there.

They weren't prepared. There were maybe a dozen of them there, a dozen survivors. Lost a few of them, like we did."

"Who did you lose?" Michael cuts in.

"Karen, for one, and I'm embarrassed to say I don't remember the other one's name. The dude."

"We gotta get out of here," Joel says. "We need a place to go, we can't just keep driving around. We need a location."

"The library," says Kevin.

Joel stares at him.

"That's where Ron went. He'd been thinking about it for a while, I guess. Easily defendable. Two stories. Good views out of thick windows, upstairs and down. And a generator on the roof."

"How's he know that?"

"Someone in his crew did janitorial there a while back."

"Well, let's check it out."

Kevin pauses, eyeing Scott. "I guess you found someone."

Joel glances into that back seat. "Oh. Yeah."

Kevin sighs raggedly, firing up the Chevy. "All right."

No one says anything then, and the only sounds are weeping and tires on asphalt.

CHAPTER 17

The downtown Fort Collins library, southeast of Old Town on Peterson, is the oldest and largest library in town, and right now its mass of accumulated knowledge means almost nothing. Its books sit forlorn on the shelves. Instead, the library is the focal point of two groups of rattled survivors at the end of the world.

Joel rumbles the Hummer effortlessly over a curb and tears up the recently manicured grass, heading toward the front entrance. Kevin's truck bounces onto the lawn behind them. Two vehicles are already parked next to the entrance, and there are faces in the dark glass of the library's front sliding door. There's no activity on the expansive lawns surrounding the library, but Michael knows it won't be long before those damn things sense them and begin approaching.

The Hummer lurches to a stop, and Joel twists off the ignition. Just as he does so, the sky lets loose with another atmospheric roar, and everyone flinches, craning their necks to stare out their windows, up into the mottled sky, until the sound rumbles out into a strange crackling. Through his window, Michael notices a subtle red brightening in the sky to the west, above the smoke, above the blocky corner of the library roof. For a fleeting moment, it looks like great sheets of blood cascading down from the heavens. And then it's only dark clouds and smoke.

Michael shakes his head, hoping against hope that these things he's seeing are merely products of his imagination.

Then everyone is moving again.

"Let's go," Joel says.

Rachel is still curled up, crying over the loss of Danny. She can't seem to stop the sobs. Michael touches her shoulder, briefly, and she flinches, lifting her wet-eyed gaze.

"Those goddamn fucking things!" she screeches. Her face is filled with red-streaked anger. *"Why? Why are they doing this?"*

Michael opens his door, jumps down from the Hummer to the ground, and goes straight to the rear passenger door. Scott is already out of the vehicle, pushing roughly past Michael, and jog-limping toward the library's front sliding doors.

"Come on, Rach," Michael says as gently as he can, taking her by the upper arm and urging her out. She comes as if reluctant, shrugging him off, embarrassed of her tears.

Michael's eyes dart everywhere as he leads Rachel toward the library. Kevin, carrying the large cardboard box in his arms, shuffles in their direction. Bonnie is right ahead of him, along with the girls; they're all carrying empty, blood-smeared Super Soakers, and – to Michael's surprise – several units of plasma.

"Do you need help?" he calls to the women.

"We got it," Bonnie says miserably. "This is the lot of it."

"Come on, come on!" Joel calls from the doors. "Before they see us!"

They're a ragged crew, slogging the short distance across the concrete sidewalk. Michael nods to Kevin as they come abreast of each other, and the big man gives Rachel a double-take, no doubt never having seen the young woman so vulnerable. He glances at Michael, then moves ahead and through the open doorway. When Bonnie catches sight of Rachel in distress, a new energy quickens her step.

"Rachel, dear!" Bonnie cries. "What – "

"It's the boy," Michael breathes, urging the kind woman forward.

"Oh my," Bonnie whispers, ducking her head and continuing on.

They reach the doors and hurry inside. Immediately, Michael feels relief as the relative cool of the indoors wafts against his face. And there's the somehow extremely clean, welcome scent of books – quite a contrast to the intensifying summer heat and smoke outside.

The library's lobby is dotted with people watching them enter – in all, there are only six new people in addition to the hospital crew, about fifteen in all. Two unfamiliar men – one heavyset and middle-aged, the other hale and hearty, in his thirties – are poised on either side of the sliding doors, ready to shove them closed.

Joel is talking wearily but alertly with a young man near one of the check-out kiosks, and Michael knows this must be Ron, whom Joel has been in touch with over the radio. Ron is a lanky, tall man with poor posture. Bookish. Steel-rimmed glasses over a narrow nose. He has a certain low-key intensity to him, like a first-year teacher, maybe. Michael automatically associates him with the college, although he probably just ended up there by chance.

Michael helps Rachel to one of the vinyl benches lining the room. His daughter's breathing com in sharp hitches, but her sobs are gradually subsiding, giving way to a trembling anger. She appears on the verge of lashing out.

Suddenly Bonnie, minus her burden, is sitting next to Rachel, petting her forearm.

"Poor girl."

"Crazy out there," Michael murmurs.

Bonnie just shakes her head, watching Rachel.

For the first time, Michael notices that Bonnie is also covered with patches of both tacky and dried blood. He finds the three young women across the room – Chrissy, looking small and fragile, and the athletic twins, breathing heavily still. They're hanging off each other, still trembling, tears and dark astonishment in their eyes. Their limbs, particularly their forearms, are painted with blood.

"Hard to know what might happen next," Bonnie whispers, tears threatening her voice.

Michael turns to the older woman, finds her eyes shiny, and then she's leaning toward him and pulling him into a trembling embrace. He lets one arm return the gesture, leaving the other reassuringly on Rachel's thigh. And Michael is stunned to feel a cough of emotion coming up out of his throat and hot tears of his own stinging his eyes. His chest convulses helplessly. He lets his eyes close, and –

– she feels just like Cassie, long before disease claimed her, long before their daughter morphed from angelic child to surly teen, long before his career turned from professional to criminal, and for a moment all the ensuing years dissolve, and this ridiculous, horrific reality is just a strange nightmare, and they're a family again –

– he clears his throat, shakes his head, pushes away from the embrace.

Because flashing behind his closed lids is the image of Susanna, urgent, as if shouting at him, and as he returns to the present, the recollection of her corpse on their bed is vivid, too vivid, and wrong, and yet all his questions about that, all his stunned grief – it all feels like it's on hold while he deals with this preposterous reality he's found himself in.

He realizes that Joel is speaking.

"Obviously things have gotten out of hand, so we need to establish a stronghold here in a hurry – that is, unless anyone can think of a better location. I'm open to ideas, but they better be goddamn quick. And good. Because I'm not exactly thrilled by the prospect of going out there again."

"I'm not going out there again," Scott calls from the corner, where he appears to be hugging himself in an odd clutch.

"Figured," Joel says. "Anyone else?"

"I'm with that guy," says a young Asian woman near the checkout counter. She's got her hip thrust forward jauntily, and she's rubbing one eye with her knuckle as if to remove an eyelash.

Michael glances back at the front doors. The two men are still poised there, watching the immediate grounds. But Michael isn't considering them; he's focused on the glass of the doors and remembering the way the body on the Hummer pressed its head to the glass and distorted it ...

"Uh," Michael speaks up, "I don't have an alternative in mind, but I'll just point out that the perimeter of this library is dominated by glass. Big windows."

"Right, I was just talking to Ron about that." He gives the lanky fellow a nod. "These are very thick windows, even at the entrance. Heavy, reinforced double-pane panels. They look an inch thick to me. I know what you saw out there, in the Hummer, I saw it too. But windshields are more like an eighth of an inch. I'm willing to bet we're safe behind these panels, but like I said, I'm open to ideas."

"Wait," Ron speaks up. "What did you see?"

"Those things, whatever is in their heads?" Michael says. "It basically melted that glass and was eventually able to punch through."

Bonnie stares at him in anguish.

"Jesus." Ron says.

"Yeah."

"What is it? Heat?"

"No, not heat," Joel answers. "More like ... radiation."

The cop scans the room, and everyone stares back at him almost sullenly. It's a scared, jumpy bunch, and they're exhausted. These people are unwashed and grimy, their eyes sunken from stress and lack of sleep. And Michael would bet that most of them are suffering from shock.

"Okay," Joel continues, "obviously those bodies out there have become much, *much* more aggressive than before. Everything is different now. We have to defend ourselves, and that means barricading this library – especially any entrances but also possibly these windows. Before we do anything else, I want to do a sweep of this whole damn place, check for open doors, check for any way inside those things might have. Seems to me we have a lot of opportunities as far as heavy shit for blocking entrances."

He's gesturing at the bookcases that surround them on all sides.

"So let's spread out and make sure we're okay – how about Ron's team to the south end, upstairs and down, and the hospital crew can split up and take the north side? Most of all, check for bodies that are still in here. We found one unlocked employee door in the back, so who knows? Some employee probably came in early to do a little work. Check all offices and stock rooms, whatever, *every room.*"

He pauses, glances around, making sure everyone understands.

"Now, I'm told this building has a generator – "

"That's right," says a stocky man leaning against a large display of mystery novels. His face holds a naturally pinched expression beneath jet-black hair. "It's on the roof."

"We'll get that in working order after we're done, but barricading happens first. So let's get to it, and then we'll meet back here and get to know each other. Sound okay?"

There's a general murmur of fatigued consent throughout the lobby.

"Good, let's do it. I think we can make this work." He points at the door guards. "See anything out there?"

"Surprisingly, no," says the younger one on the right.

Joel thinks about that for a moment, then shakes out of it. "You two stay right there, keep an eye out. Do those doors lock?"

"There's a key lock," says the bigger, sweatier guy on the right. "Obviously we don't have the key, but there's also a security bar that I already dropped in place. That oughta do it."

"All right, shout if you have a problem."

"You got it."

No one has moved out of the general area. They all still seem to be catching their breath. Michael has been so laser-focused on his daughter's tears – she's still snuffling, buried now against his shoulder – that he's failed to recognize that two other women and a young man are also weeping. The young man, possibly a late teen, is part of Ron's crew; the other two are Chrissy and Chloe. Michael sees hopelessness in their sodden gazes. And he catches sight of Scott again; he's now squatting in that far corner, head down, cracking his knuckles.

Joel appears on the verge of blowing up, but he grits his teeth and releases a frustrated breath.

"Look," he says, easing up but still intense, "if we don't do this *right now*, chances are good we're all going to die. *You* are going to die. Pretty horribly. Now come on, let's pair up, right now. On your feet."

Kevin stands up from his bench. He appears to have a moment of light-headedness and sways to his left, enough for a look of concern to make its way to Chrissy's blood-streaked face, but he rights himself.

"Okay, who's with me?"

Bonnie gives Rachel a squeeze, then Michael an encouraging glance, and wearily gets to her feet.

"We'll take the south end over here," Kevin says, and they walk off,

Bonnie placing a hand on Kevin's broad back.

"That's the spirit," Joel says. "Watch the windows, but don't get too close. If you see anything threatening, give a shout."

The rest of them get moving, with at least a modicum of purpose, and begin scattering through the building. Even Scott pairs off with someone – that young Asian woman from Ron's group. As he leaves the room, he locks eyes with Michael, as if to communicate something, but then he's gone. Michael frowns.

Then he nods at Joel, as if to say *Gimme a minute,* and Joel heads upstairs with Chrissy and the twins.

Rachel is breathing more evenly. Michael looks down on her, watches her face, which is still trembling as if with the effort of holding back emotion. Indeed, her grimy cheeks are striped with the paths of tears.

"You all right?" he asks softly.

"No." The word comes out monotone, quick.

"Stupid question."

Rachel tries a deep breath, but it falters and turns into a quavering exhale. "Let's go, I need to stand up."

"Okay."

He gets to his feet and helps her up. She stands up straight, gives a sad, apologetic smile to the two men at the door who have been half-watching her, then finally manages the deep breath she wanted moments ago. Superfluously, she straightens the fabric of her bloodied shirt at her waist.

"All right," she says. "Let's go."

Beyond the main checkout counter is the darkened multimedia area, but it's wide open and obviously clear. Father and daughter move quickly beyond the racks of discs and tapes, entering the large children's section.

An arm grabs his bicep. Rachel glances back, and at the sight of Scott, she can't prevent a grimace from snarling her lip. She continues forward.

"Nice to see you, too," Scott says out of the side of his mouth, letting go of Michael's arm.

"What's up?" Michael says, noting that the Asian woman is waiting behind him. She's watching the back of his head curiously. Michael nods at her, and she returns the gesture and glances away.

Scott moves his gaze from Rachel to Michael. There's something shifty there, and Michael curses inwardly, recognizing it.

Assholes even at the end of the world.

"See anything?" Michael asks.

"So you're Rachel's dad."

"Name's Michael." Impulsively, he reaches out to shake Scott's hand, and Scott – seemingly stunned – finally accepts it in a sweaty grip. Like Michael always told Rachel (and Michael's mom told him), it's best to meet assholes with kindness; they're the ones who need it most.

Scott takes a breath, seems to shake himself out of something. "Yeah, I'm Scott. Glad you woke up. I know your daughter went through hell to find you."

"Okay, Scott, thanks." He lets Scott's clammy hand go. "It's good to be alive. I think."

Scott makes an effort to give that an appreciative murmur of laughter. "Look, I didn't mean to be a dick back there. I don't even know how that happened. I'm not the bad guy here." He combs his fingers – minutely trembling – through his unkempt red hair. "It's just that cop, man. All I'm saying is don't just fall in line behind Joel, okay? Watch that guy."

"Glad we found you, too, looked like you were in some trouble there."

"God, that was a mess." He scratches behind his ear – another nervous gesture. "I lived not far from there. I ended up there when one of those fuckers unclamped from this giant tree near the street and started racing toward me. Goddamn thing. Like an animal. And once it saw me, it was all over. Suddenly a bunch of them were surrounding me. I'm just lucky that door was unlocked."

"So you weren't at the church long," Michael says, keeping an eye on Rachel, who is just about to turn a corner.

"Not long at all. I felt a little guilty – "

"Listen, we gotta check this place out, right? But let's talk later, okay?"

Scott looks at him, and Michael can see some kind of pain in his eyes. "Sure. Yeah."

Michael watches him go.

Huh.

Then he jogs to join Rachel. She's walking one long aisle, letting her fingers pass gently along the books' spines.

Broad windows surround them.

The bright daylight dazzles him. Not only that – the expanses of manicured green lawn, the rare glimpses of blue sky between gray scuds of smoke, the faces of familiar suburban homes directly north … the sight jars Michael into a weird reality shift, as if all the horrible shit that has happened in the past few days – the past few minutes! – has been a fever dream, and this quiet glimpse of near-normalcy is like a broken fever. Michael feels his breath catch with false relief.

He also notices with very real relief that his head is not gripped in a vice. He blinks exaggeratedly, at once relishing the sensation of apparent healing within his skull and taking in this brief peaceful moment with his daughter.

Rachel glances at him, sees that he's alone.

He doesn't think he's ever seen her so devastated.

"Can I just curl up in here with these books?" she says. In any other situation, a mischievous smile might be lifting the corner of her mouth at this small joke, but right now, she just looks deadened.

Michael walks past two large tables of bright children's books and stops at one of the windows. After his close call in the Hummer, he knows he won't feel truly safe next to a piece of glass any time soon. He lets his gaze wander east and west, paying particular attention to the areas beneath the gigantic pines that dot the library lawns. The bark of several trees has clearly been assaulted; on one close tree, lines of blood mar the trunk from the damaged area all the way to the ground. He supposes the blood came from the injured mouth of whatever poor soul was attached there.

At least in the immediate vicinity, there are no reanimated bodies scurrying madly like mad spiders.

He shakes his head at the conjured image, bringing up one hand to rap softly on the window. The sound is deep and resonant. Joel was right – it's very different from a windshield. Thick. Reassuring.

"Probably shouldn't get so close there," Rachel says. "They're tinted, but – " She shrugs. "Hell, maybe we pulled one over on them. Maybe they lost sight of us."

"It's weird, isn't it?" he says, stepping away. "Why haven't they surrounded us here?"

Rachel's voice is tired. "They don't like books?"

Michael manages a difficult smile. "But books are made of trees."

Rachel lets out a stunned giggle, then stops it short, sniffling. "That's my dad."

The open room is expansive, and although they can hear several survivors stamping about above them, on the second floor, and several more shouting all-clears to one another farther south on the main floor, there's a welcome ration of relative silence in the air.

Michael follows Rachel through the room at a measured pace, listening to her breathe.

"Listen, Rachel ...."

In front of him, her shoulders hunch almost imperceptibly.

"I know, Daddy."

She turns to face him, as if to stage one of her typical acts of teenaged defiance, but then she immediately crumples, and her hands come up to her face, covering her mouth. She moans miserably, emotion filling her eyes. She begins to shake her head back and forth, and now she turns back around. She's shaking.

"... I'm sorry about Danny," Michael finishes his thought.

"It's not fair."

"You're right."

"Just a kid ... a perfect little boy." Her eyes are darting around helplessly. "How can something like that happen?"

She's not looking at him. She's quiet for a long moment.

"Rachel ...?"

"I didn't mean to ..." comes her querulous voice.

"Mean to what?"

She takes a long, shuddering breath, stays quiet, choked up, as if she can't go on.

"Mean to what?" Michael says as gently as he can.

"Did you go home?" She turns back around to face him, letting her hands drop. "Did you make it? Were you at the house?"

"I made it."

"Then ...."

"She was – she was there."

"Oh Daddy."

"What happened?"

Rachel makes an attempt to answer that question, but it's clear she's been dreading it. She can only whimper, tortured. Finally she buries herself against his chest. She clutches at him fiercely, sobs taking hold of her entire body.

Michael swallows heavily, tentatively returning the embrace. He strokes her back, doing his best to calm her. He only wants the answers to come.

Joel peeks in at one point, sees them, and Michael offers a cautious thumbs up. Joel nods and returns their privacy to them.

And Rachel tells him her story. Her words are labored at first, but then they release themselves from her in a torrent, and as they rush out, she won't let him go, she won't release her desperate grip.

She tells him how she woke to find Susanna afflicted, like everyone else, how she tried to help her, how she tried like hell to help her, but she was –

" – scared, Daddy, I was fucking *scared!* There was that thing inside her, and it didn't make any goddamn sense, and I tried like hell to get rid of it, whatever it was, and I tried! *I tried!* But I tried too hard, or something ... because the light sparked out, just popped out of her, and she was gone, she was dead, she was just – *gone!* – and I didn't know what to do, and I'm sorry, I'm sorry, I'm so sorry!"

Michael listens mutely, calming her. Over her shoulder, the library remains serene, save for distant voices calling out, establishing order. The windows look out on a changed but oddly peaceful world.

And when she begins repeating herself, her words start trailing off, and finally she's just breathing raggedly against him, her face pressed almost violently into his chest.

Michael is gazing outside, but in his vision, images of Susanna are flashing again, images of her both dead and very much alive, and he shuts his eyes tightly and grinds his teeth to control the flow of emotion. His head pulses with a sensation that threatens pain but doesn't quite get there.

He feels as if he's detached from himself, watching Rachel embracing him, sensing her need for him at that moment. He has failed her so many times, in ways that she'll never know, and he realizes with a sense of black resignation that those failures have colored his perception of her now. A part of him is still suspicious of her, yes. He can't so easily let the angry memories drop away – the many times Rachel screamed at him, screamed at Susanna. And he's attributing dark motives to her, his own flesh and blood!

He *wants* to understand her, *wants* to grasp what has happened. He feels a need to simply appreciate that his daughter has survived.

But the truth is, Susanna is right where Rachel might have wished her. He shakes that thought away, but it keeps coming back.

"Shhh," he whispers. "It's okay."

The words feel wrong in his throat.

After a long moment of quiet, she pulls her head back, regards him hopefully, and then pushes away, wiping her eyes. "It is?"

He nods slowly.

Silence.

He's not sure how to feel. And he realizes that he himself is close to tears, because of this emotional morass. Whatever happened at his house, on the morning the world ended … perhaps it was *nobody's* fault. Perhaps it was inevitable. Or maybe something else happened that's too horrible to imagine, something that Rachel would never admit to him.

And that makes the situation hurt even more.

Can he possibly ever get beyond that kind of internal question?

Finally, he steels himself and lets the words flow.

"Rachel, I wouldn't blame you for anything," he says softly into her ear. "You haven't done anything wrong. I know that. I really – I really just needed to know the truth. I needed to know if Susanna was alive … if there was any chance I could have saved her. If I could have helped her."

Long minutes pass before Rachel composes herself, and Michael is hyper-attuned to her reaction to his words. He feels her trembling. He feels her quickened pulse. But he can attribute these things to any of the awful phenomena his daughter has suffered over the past few days.

He sighs into her neck.

She rears back and studies him. Her eyes are reddened, and her mouth is drawn, making her appear far older than her 19 years. She seems to read a lot in his sigh.

"She was infected. She would have been out there. One of them."

Her lip trembles.

"I didn't mean to hurt her, Daddy," she whispers. "I promise."

Something breaks inside Michael.

"I tried to help her."

As she melts into further tears, a wave of memories washes over him, of he and Rachel weathering the storm of Cassie's disease and passing, of the two of them finding meaning after devastation. As a new reality stretches before him now, he imagines the impossible task of doing it again.

"Rachel," he says, "you've done better than anyone in the world would expect you to do." He pets her head.

"No." She's shaking her head again. "No, I could've done more."

"I doubt it, I really do."

"No! I could have saved Tony!"

Michael continues the embrace, searching for words, and in the few seconds of silence, he feels her tension increasing again. Words begin once more to tumble out –

" – I was *wrong, wrong, wrong,* if I'd just – I mean, by *half a second,* Daddy, I shot him, I *killed* him. He said my name! He called out to me, but I *pulled the trigger,* Daddy, why did I do that? I could've saved him! I couldn't save Sarah, that poor little girl, and now Danny, that fucking thing pulled him right away from me! Right out of my arms! I couldn't save anyone!"

"Shhhh ..." he tries, feeling his heart beating hard. "You saved *me,* right?"

She just sniffles, her head burrowed. "That doesn't – "

"Now wait a minute, you remember what Joel said. Maybe Tony wouldn't have wanted to be saved."

"What do you mean?"

"You're a smart kid. You know what's going on. You saw what happened at the hospital, with that prisoner. There was a lot of pain. Maybe a lot of it irreversible. And that man hadn't even been outside. He still came out of it screaming."

He can feel Rachel considering that, as she rocks against him.

"There's a good chance that you ... well, that you *helped* him. That you actually *did* save him."

Rachel releases a massive sigh against him, then pulls back. She moves away from him, walking the aisles as she wipes at her face with her forearms. She does a half-hearted sweep, then about-faces, comes back his way, continues east in the dimness.

"Look," he calls to her, "all I'm saying is that it's not as simple as you're thinking. As we're *all* thinking. Whatever has happened to those bodies is deeper and more devastating than we know. I'm sure of it. You can't punish yourself for this, when you did what anyone else would have done, and when there are so many unanswered questions."

Michael keeps an eye on her body language. He thinks he's said the right words, but it has been so long since he's been able to find them that he's not sure what they sound like. It's been years since she embraced him like that, and equally long since they've had a conversation like that. A conversation that matters.

But the way she's bounded away from him, avoiding eye contact, makes him think he should do more, say more ... that everything he said was wrong.

Then she stops between two towering tables of kids' books and appears to consider something. She turns back, walks back to him, and embraces him anew.

Then she lets go and returns to her search.

Michael feels his spirits lift like the release of an almost physical weight. He falls in step behind her, and he can tell by the way that she's holding herself that he has – in some small way – helped her. He's stunned to realize it, but right here, right now, in the midst of the bleakest horror, this is his finest moment with his daughter in years. It's all wrapped up in death and misery, and yet there it is.

He wants to reach out to her, touch her shoulder, hold her back, and sit with her among these books, savor the moment.

But he doesn't lift his hand.

"Let's finish this up and get back, huh?" she says.

He feels his head nodding.

There are two small private rooms off the library floor, and Rachel pokes her head into the dim one with the open door. "Clear."

The other door is closed. Michael tries the knob.

"Locked."

"Let's tell Joel. Probably just files in there or som – "

Then something clanks beyond the door, and Michael jumps. Rachel goes reeling backward, nearly colliding with a computer kiosk.

CHAPTER 18

"Holy – !" Rachel cries.

"Shhh! Wait."

"What if …?"

"Hold on."

"What?!"

Michael moves back closer to the door and raps on it softly. "Hello?" Rachel is wide-eyed, ready to bolt.

"Is someone in there?"

Silence.

"We won't hurt you, we just want to help."

Rachel covers her mouth with a white-knuckled hand, and they stand there listening, but there's nothing. Finally, her hand drops.

"I'll get Joel," she whispers. "And blood."

Michael extends a hand, as if to say *Wait …*

"Whoever's in there, you have the chance right now to come out and talk to us, and we'll help you." He pauses, listens. "But in a few seconds, there will be weapons here, and it won't be as nice."

An immediate scuffling sounds behind the door, and there's a fiddling with the knob.

"Daddy!" Rachel is batting at his arm, ready to run.

"Don't worry."

The knob is still jerking around.

"Wait!" comes a small voice from behind the door. "I'll come out!"

Michael swallows with relief as Rachel's jaw drops. She stares at him, mouthing, *How did you know?*

The lock gives, the knob turns, and the door is opening inward. The room is dark, and a waft of humidity finds Michael's face, along with a slightly tart, slightly sweet odor of sweat. His gaze darts downward to find a preteen child staring fearfully up at him. She's a young African American girl, and she's attached to the door, her lip quivering, but determined to show strength. It's taking a lot of energy to hold back tears.

"Hey," he says, automatically dropping to a crouch. "You okay in there?"

She doesn't respond, just looks over at Rachel, who has also kneeled down.

"I'm Kayla," she says, barely audible.

"I'm Michael, this is my daughter Rachel."

The girl's deep-brown eyes move back and forth between them. She opens the door a little farther, revealing herself and the darkened room behind her. Michael sees stacks of books, empty food wrappers, water bottles, and three flashlights. Kayla herself is thin and athletic, with shoulder-length hair, thick and unkempt, and a slightly upturned nose over a full-lipped, expressive mouth.

"Have you been staying here?" Rachel asks gently.

Kayla nods. "Is that okay?"

Rachel tentatively touches the side of Kayla's head.

"Of course it's okay, sweetie," she says. "How long have you been here?"

Kayla swallows. "I don't know."

"Since all this started?"

"Since after my mom – after she woke up."

"Where do you live?"

"Across the street." She points vaguely out the window.

"How old are you, Kayla?" Rachel asks.

"I'm twelve."

The girl is warming to them already, venturing out, inch by inch, hanging onto the knob, swaying a little.

"But I'm okay."

Michael knows she's certainly not okay, but he smiles despite himself, admiring her pluck.

Rachel says, "Well, it's been very *hard* for me, and I know I could use a hug from a pretty girl."

Michael is startled by how quickly Kayla lunges for Rachel. The poor girl practically plows into her, eager for human contact. As Michael stands from his crouch, he touches the girl's head, and then Kayla is sobbing into Rachel's shoulder, strangely mirroring the moment he shared with Rachel moments ago. The emotional synchronicity strikes him sharply, briefly, pricking him with a feeling of loss for what he's missed out on with Rachel over the past few messy years – and then he moves away to check the rest of the room while Rachel and Kayla embrace, talking softly.

Michael makes his way to the edge of the room, peers down the corridor, sees Bonnie sitting on one of the benches, her posture beaten down.

"Bonnie!" he calls softly.

She turns.

"We found someone."

"One of *them?*" she whispers, alarmed.

"No, no, a girl. Where's Joel?"

"I'll get him."

Michael knows Bonnie will keep it quiet for now. He doesn't want to overwhelm the poor girl with a throng of sweaty survivors. As Bonnie hurries off in the opposite direction, Michael watches from afar as his daughter soothes this unlikely newcomer. There's something immediately ... almost sacred ... about the contact. He lets them have their moment.

"What's up?" says Joel, arriving with Bonnie, as well as Chrissy and the twins.

"Found a girl," Michael says, gesturing.

"Really?" Chrissy says, excited but utterly wiped out. She cranes her neck to see beyond the small clutch of survivors. For the first time, Michael notices that she has a tiny nose ring, glinting in the semi-darkness.

"Yeah, looks like she holed up in a storage room there."

Now Rachel is looking at them from Kayla's doorway, and she waves her arm for everyone to come over. Kayla is smiling, wiping her eyes.

Michael leads them over to Rachel, and it turns out he needn't have worried about bombarding Kayla with survivors. Now that she's had her moment with Rachel and found herself embraced by humanity again, she's remarkably poised at the center of attention. She's gesturing into the room where she's been hiding.

" – had plenty to read!" she's saying.

Her voice sounds almost enthusiastic now, and Michael can detect an edge of overcompensation: He's sure she's still scared out of her mind, he can see it in her eyes and in the twitch of her mouth, but she's already trying hard to be the girl she was before.

Bonnie asks Kayla where she found food and water, and Kayla answers with a politeness that sounds almost nostalgic.

"That's actually how I – how I ended up in there. See that little refrigerator there?" She gestures behind her. "It was full of bottled water, and people had left their lunches in there, I guess. I ate those. There's still water, though, if you want some."

As the group murmurs, Michael cranes his neck to read the titles of the books Kayla has been accumulating. There are several teen fiction titles in there – unsurprising. But one of the titles does startle him: *Deciduous and Coniferous Trees of the Rocky Mountains*.

Michael breaks away from the group, moves past Kayla into the room, and picks up the book. He takes the opportunity to scan the small space, sees the fridge, notes the small sleeping area that Kayla has fashioned out of towels, both cloth and paper. He brings the book out.

"Oh, yeah, that one," Kayla says.

The small group exchanges glances, and then everyone is focusing on this twelve-year-old kid.

"You're really reading that book?" Rachel asks.

"Kind of," Kayla says, her gaze flicking from one survivor to the next. "You've seen what those people are doing, right? They're eating the – "

"No, yeah, we've seen it."

"I still don't get it, but they want something in those trees. And they're only interested in the pine trees – the coniferous ones."

She pronounces *coniferous* a bit oddly, too carefully, as if she's never said the word aloud before.

Rachel can't help but laugh at the things coming out of Kayla's mouth.

Michael is flipping through the book's pages.

Joel says, "Kid, you've just appointed yourself head researcher. Nice to have you with us. You up for telling us what you've learned?"

"I guess so." Kayla has a wide-eyed look of innocence about her, but there's also a flintiness there that's unusual for a preteen. The kid is sharp.

"Okay, we're gonna have a little Town Hall meeting right now out there in the lobby. We're gonna lay everything out, see where we stand. We've got two groups coming together here – we're from the hospital, and Ron's group in there came from CSU. We learned some things at the hospital just as you learned here, so we're all gonna start sharing things with each other."

Ron's group has started filtering in toward Kayla, but Joel directs them back out to the lobby.

There's a cool cleanliness and order to the library, thankfully, but Michael can tell that's going to be a brief pleasure. Perhaps a day or two. The group – now sixteen people strong – has a sweaty, animal humidity to it that is already spreading, and Michael knows that these books are soon destined for the floor as their heavy shelves are shoved against the windows. It's only a matter of time.

Joel's group – as Michael thinks of it – heads for the lobby in a loose, nervous cluster, and Rachel falls in next to him, her arm around Kayla. The two are already close pals. Rachel looks up at him, then briefly places her head against his shoulder – a reminder of the moment they had before the discovery of Kayla.

Michael allows himself an uncertain smile, and then Joel calls out to the two men at the front doorway.

"What are you seeing out there?"

The sweaty guy speaks up. "A whole lotta nothin'. There are a few clamped to trees, way off over there. But they don't seem to be interested in detaching."

"I don't get it," Joel says.

"They had no trouble sniffing us out at the hospital," Bonnie says.

"Okay everyone, let's settle in, grab a quick seat."

The groups come together amiably, finally nodding to one another in tentative companionship, and there's an eerie quiet over everything. Michael likes to think it's the communal remembrance of being at a library, but he knows it's merely the shared exhaustion, the common grief for the lost friends and family that every single person here is feeling, the dark uncertainty of the future. Heavy things like that – they can't have surmounted them during the time he was unconscious. In fact, they're probably only now just coming to terms with them. Or will in the near future.

At this moment, Michael would rather feel the soft pressure of his daughter's head against his shoulder than deal with the fact that every other aspect of his life and identity has been devastated.

CHAPTER 19

Most of the assembled crew has collapsed to the floor, looking as if they might at any moment crash into slumber. The young women, in particular, look useless in their exhaustion: Chrissy and Chloe have slumped against each other like a couple of drunken sorority sisters.

Except that their clothes and skin are blotched and swiped with dried blood.

"All right, folks," Joel calls from the foot of an open stairwell leading up to the second floor, "we have a fairly secure perimeter, as long as those things can't break through the heavy glass of these windows. I'm pretty sure they can't, but then again, they've surprised me more than a few times already."

There's a murmur of dismal consent across the lobby.

"We've completely blocked the three smaller entrances to this building – a smaller door to the south and two employee doors to the west. Ain't nothing getting through those. Thanks guys." He nods to two men to his left – the young man he noticed earlier, as well as the black-haired man, who looks like a heart-attack candidate, sweaty and heavy. "I guess the biggest news is we found another survivor, this scrappy youngster over here. Her name is Kayla, she's – how old?"

Kayla says, "I'm twelve," in a voice that contains far more enthusiasm than it probably should, given the circumstances.

A ripple of laughter flows through the room.

"Glad you're okay, Kayla," Bonnie says, over on the far side of Rachel.

"Me too."

"As you can imagine," Joel goes on, "Kayla's been doing some reading in here. Apparently she's even been reading about the types of trees that these goddam things seem most interested in. So maybe she can help us get a handle on what we're dealing with out there. Turns out we've got several young ladies who are pretty smart cookies. Kayla, I'm glad you found Rachel first. You two are the ones who are probably gonna figure a way out of this mess."

Joel is striving for a tone of hope in his ragged voice, but Michael can hear the cracks. On a kind of instinct, Michael searches the room for Scott, finds him leaning against the wall over by the book-return slot. His mouth is closed tight, and there's the slightest twitch at the corners, a grimace. Then again, Michael is looking for it, so it might just be imagination.

"For some reason, those things are leaving us alone at the moment," Joel goes on. "Now, we can debate all we want about the reason for that – and we should – but we can't just assume we're safe here. That's what we started to do at the hospital, and that was overrun."

He nods to Kevin, who is standing side by side with Chrissy and the twins.

"We had the sliding doors open, like morons, just to let in some fresh air," the big man says. "That place got incredibly rank, with all the spilled blood and the bodies – Jesus! But yeah, while we were cleaning up, they creeped right in, four of the motherfuckers. Sorry. We lost two people, and Bonnie was hurt."

Michael, surprised, turns to Bonnie. Rachel does, too. Bonnie doesn't appear to want the attention. Timidly, she shows her hands and forearms, which appear as if they have been splattered with bleach.

"They just … rammed into me, with their heads. I shoved at them, but they were stronger." She drops her arms, hiding them behind her as if ashamed. "They're a little numb. Those monsters would've killed me if it hadn't been for Kevin."

"Monsters?" comes Rachel's voice, hardened. "Is that – " She composes herself. " – is that how we're talking about them?"

"Yes," Scott says from the edge of the group. "Yes it is!"

"Well, you haven't seen what we've found."

Kevin and Bonnie exchange an uncomfortable glance.

"Because they're still – well, they're still *people*, right?" Rachel is looking around sharply for support. "Underneath it all? We know that."

A few survivors start talking at once, but it's Joel's voice that's most forceful.

"Rachel, I can't see how you can go through something like what we just saw in that Hummer, and think there's any humanity left in those things!"

"But you saw it yourself, at the hospital." Rachel is defiant, and her pose suggests a protective shielding of Kayla. "The man in that bed came back. The blood turned him back."

Kevin steps back in. "Rachel, that dude is dead. He's dead."

"How?"

"He was in pain," Bonnie says. "The worst pain I've ever seen, even worse than Jenny."

Michael doesn't know who Jenny is, but the words have a stinging effect on Rachel, who closes her eyes and brings her head down.

"Whatever is inside them …" Joel says, "… it has changed them irreversibly."

Rachel shakes her head.

"I have to believe," she seethes, "that we can cure them. That we can fix this." Her eyes come up blazing. "Otherwise, we're doomed, aren't we? As a race! I mean, we've found this solution, and it's a solution inside all of us. We've found what it can do. We can't just ignore it! I don't believe that it's … that it's irreversible! It can't be. How did he die?"

Kevin takes a moment before answering. "Those things got him – "

Michael is suddenly aware that Chrissy is crying. "He was – he was screaming."

"All ri – " Joel tries to cut in.

"So you're not even sure?" Rachel says. "You left him to die? I know none of us knew him, but … you left him in that room and they just swarmed him?"

"He was the only reason we were able to get away," Bonnie says, and Kevin gives her a reproachful look.

"That's terrible," Rachel murmurs.

"He was gone, Rachel," Kevin insists. "Too far gone."

"Well, Rachel has a point," Joel says. "If nothing else, the blood – injecting the blood – has the effect of destroying what's inside them." He turns to Ron. "I think we're getting ahead of ourselves, though. I'd like to fill in Ron's group about what we've discovered, and vice versa. So now seems as good a time as any to share some names. I'll start with the hospital crew …"

Joel introduces Rachel, Kevin, and Bonnie, even gives an inclusive nod to Scott. He points to Michael, and makes special mention of Rachel's desperate search and successful retrieval of him south of Harmony. He finishes off the introductions with Chrissy, Chloe, and Zoe, and Kevin mentions the two other survivors at the hospital – Karen and Jerry – both of whom were injured and took off in their own vehicles for other locations.

Mostly, Joel summarizes Rachel's discoveries about the blood, and as he does so, Michael feels a weird pride for his daughter. He's learned that she was the first person to discover the temporary solution of smothering out the strange luminescence from those bodies' heads, in addition to being the first to find the common link between all survivors – O-negative blood. She's proven herself to be an honest-to-goodness survivor, seeking answers in the face of outright horror. Yes, she made mistakes, but she's capable of thinking in a way that Michael doubted even he would have been able to in the same circumstances.

Joel finishes with an account of their blood test on the prisoner in the upstairs room. The story has Ron's crew riveted, and they ask a few questions in disbelief, not daring to hope that the fate of these bodies everywhere might actually be open to reversal.

"Holy shit," says the small, wiry Asian girl.

Joel gives her a glance, then goes on. "You've probably gathered by now, but this is Ron here," Joel says.

"Hey."

"Ron and his group were at the college, holed up in the student center. Do you want to ..."

"Sure, yeah, I'm Ron, but you guys from the hospital know me as the voice on Joel's radio."

A murmur of quiet laughter among the survivors.

"I don't have any affiliation with the school, just ended up there through circumstance. Started with Mai over there." The young Asian woman gives a pert salute from her perch atop one of the checkout counters. "We ran into each other on Drake, near the Walgreens, just, you know, bowled over by everything. And then we just started gathering people. We saw Old Town in flames, and we started in that direction to see if we could help, but then we met this other guy, Randy – he's dead now – but after we met him near the Chuck E Cheese, we saw another big fire west of there, so we headed that way. That was at the Varsity Apartments – where we found Bill and Rick, trying to stop the fire." Ron nods toward the door. "See anything yet, guys?"

"Quiet," says the younger man on the left. He's a good-looking fellow with bright blue eyes, an easy smile, and crooked teeth. "Hey, I'm Rick."

"Joel, Rick was the one who picked you up on the portable CB that first time. Anyway, it was a small private aircraft, a Cessna, embedded in one of the apartments. Scariest thing I'd ever seen – at the time, anyway. Man, I wish now that's *all* I'd seen. But that whole place was full of bodies. All of them dead ... glowing out of their heads. We thought we were gonna get that fire under control, with the four of us throwing buckets of water on it, but it was just too far out of hand. That whole thing went up ... all those people."

"You tried, at least," Bonnie says. "That's all you could do."

"Wait, wait, wait – I'm sorry, can I say something?" Scott says from the edge of the group. "I mean, yeah, ordinarily you'd want to save people from a fire – of course! – but considering what they've become … isn't it more like, I don't know, good luck that they burned?"

Next to Michael, Rachel stiffens. "Didn't you hear what I just said? We have a way to save these people – "

"Okay, okay, you two, you'll get your turn," Joel says, and Scott just shakes his head. "Go ahead, Ron."

"Right," Ron says, eyeing both Rachel and Scott curiously. "Well, after that, Mai led us through the college, and we found …" He cranes his neck around to locate two more survivors. " … Brian and Liam there." The two men are on a bench by the stairs. Brian is the stocky heart-attack candidate, but he's calmed down how. Looks to be in his forties, appears devastated, haunted; he very probably lost his whole family. Liam is younger, with angular features and a sharp gaze; might have been a student. "Brian had the keys to the student center, so that's how we managed to dig in there."

The two men give unenthusiastic nods to the rest of the group.

"At its largest, our group had about thirty people, but a few of them left to try to find family, or they were just restless, and at one point we had a group venture out to Old Town to try to help out, but it was too far gone, and those things were starting to come back. We got your word about smothering them to kill them, and we did that to a few of them in the building, to clear it out."

Rachel appears to hang her head in private shame.

"We were all prepared for some zombie-like attack." He offers a mirthless laugh. "But they just crawled away."

"Never saw that coming," Rick grumbles from the door.

"Yeah, well, now they're definitely after us, and here's where we might have something to add to the discussion. Those huge goddamn roars coming from the sky? They're communications."

"I knew it," Joel said, "but tell them what you saw."

"We had windows that looked straight out onto a big mass of those things west of the Lory Student Center, in a park. Every time that roar happened, it was like the sky opened up, and all this red light came rushing downward. Immediately after that, there would be some kind of change in behavior in the bodies, whether it was as small as a twitch or an angle of the head, or a movement from tree to tree or from area to area. Something synchronized. The biggest roar was this morning, and that's when a bunch of the bodies broke away from the trees and started targeting us."

"And there was another one when we got here," Chrissy says in a small voice.

"Which is about when, if you noticed, they suddenly stopped targeting us. At least for the moment."

"Why would they stop?" Michael asks. "They had us on our heels."

"That's the question." Ron lets that sink in. "But the communication goes both ways. Whatever those things are getting out of those trees, we think it's being sent – " He jerks his thumb skyward. " – up."

"I'm sorry, I've gotta jump in here," Scott says. "Are we really talking about aliens here? I mean, yes, things are fucking weird – all those people are doing things that I don't understand at all, and yes, there's something going on in the sky, but we're not seriously saying that the obvious conclusion is little green men … right?"

Ron pauses, glances around. "I actually don't think there's any question about it at this point."

For a long moment, the band of survivors react mutely to Ron's certainty. A sort of dumbfounded acceptance. Then Scott releases a scoffing laugh, shaking his head.

Liam says, "If you'd seen everything from the perspective we had, you'd get it."

"Oh, *then* I'd get it?" Scott says.

The young man just eyes him coolly.

"Because as far as I can see," Scott says, "no matter what those things are doing, they're still people. Just because we don't understand it, well … maybe that doesn't automatically mean they're from outer space."

"Scott," Rachel says, "I think you're forgetting that a lot of the time we were learning about these things, you decided to make yourself scarce."

"Gotta say," Mai says, "I'm kinda siding with Scott on this one."

"Little Miss Contrary," Rick mumbles from the door, looking away, and Michael can sense a little history there.

"Fuck you, limp dick," Mai says, hopping off her little table and glaring lasers Rick's way.

Rick consciously looks away, preferring the view outside to staring Mai down.

"Guys, guys!" Ron says. "Come on, now. Whole new place, whole new start, right? Let's be nice."

Mai is still glaring at Rick.

"Mai, it was you who suggested some kind of invasion at the school!" Brian challenges her.

"A girl can change her mind." She twirls back toward the checkout desks. "Maybe it's the government. Maybe a *foreign* government. Hey, maybe it's some whacko religion." Michael hears glee in her voice.

Scott fidgets, as if he can sense the conversation getting away from him.

"It could be anything. Anything on *Earth*. Occam's razor."

"What's that?" Mai says over her shoulder.

"Forget all the wild theories. The simplest explanation is probably true."

"What's your simple explanation, Scott?" Rachel asks.

"We did this! Man-made! Yes, maybe a government somewhere fucked up. Foreign astronauts in the ISS let an experiment get away from them. Hell, I don't know."

"Exactly," Rachel says.

"God, you're – " Scott starts, then his eyes land on Michael and he shuts up.

Rachel is gearing up for an attack, but Joel cuts her off before she can start.

"Rachel," Joel gives her a look, "take it easy."

Michael wonders what might have caused such a rift between Scott and his daughter, but he supposes that's a discussion for another day. But he speaks up:

"It doesn't really matter where they're from or what's driving them, does it? All that's important is that they're a threat. A very weird threat."

"It would be nice to understand it even a little bit," Bonnie whispers gloomily. "To get some kind of … I don't know … starting point."

Bill speaks up uncomfortably from his bench. "Has anybody considered …?"

"What?" Joel says.

"Well, the Rapture."

One of the twins – it's Chloe – giggles, and Chrissy gives her a sharp glare.

"He's right, how come no one has talked about that?" the unassuming young woman asks the room quietly.

"I don't know," Mai says, "how about because it's a fairy tale?"

There's a cough and a gasp.

"And last I checked," Scott says, "everyone is still, you know, on the planet. They haven't been whisked away to paradise. Just the opposite, I'd say. Hell on Earth."

"Who says it has to be that literal?" Bill says. "What if it's just the souls that have been snatched away?"

"Jesus, we're not gonna get far if we start bringing the Bible into this mess," Scott says.

"See, I think you're perfectly wrong with that statement," Bill says, his face pinched again. "It might be *exactly* the thing we need to be talking about. And stop being an asshole about it, huh?"

"He's right," Chrissy says, more confident than Michael has seen her before. "No one here has spoken a word about God except to curse."

"And what about all those tree chompers out there?" Scott says. "Leftover sinners partaking of the Trees of Life?"

"Okay, I see this isn't quite the right crew for this kind of talk," Bill says, looking at his hands. "But when I hear all this nonsense about aliens and evil governments and scientists, I'm thinking your Occam's razor might just be pointing at the wrath of God."

"End of Days," Chrissy says solemnly. "It could be."

Michael finds himself tuning out of this conversation. His has never been a God-fearing soul; he has always found the notion vaguely unpleasant. He determined long ago to spend his life searching for meaning rather than succumbing to predigested answers based on a Golden Age text written by ignorant farmers. He put a certain amount of pride in the fact that he raised Rachel unhindered by predisposition.

It's her voice that pulls him from his thoughts.

"My dad's right, it doesn't matter. It doesn't even matter if it's the Rapture or whatever. All we have is what's left. Right now, we need to come up with a plan to survive, and that plan would be the same no matter what caused this. As far as God, well ... here's what I think." She glances around at all of them. "When I think of God, I think of helping my fellow man. Or woman. Right? And it can't be just a fluke that we've found a way to bring our fellow men and women back – "

"Rachel – " Joel starts.

"I'm serious!"

"Your point is well taken."

The lobby is buzzing with a kind of indecision. Is more going to be made of this, or have Rachel's words mollified them?

"Scott did bring up the trees," Joel says, obviously eager to steer the conversation back down to Earth. "They're still a mystery."

"What could they possibly want from trees?" Bonnie says, almost a whine. "Has anybody figured that out?"

All eyes seem to land on Kayla now.

"Did you learn anything about that?" Rachel says quietly.

Kayla locks eyes with Rachel for a moment, waiting for a nod of encouragement, which she gets. Then she turns her gaze outward.

"Well, they're all doing something really ... strange ... to the pine trees," Kayla says, her voice starting a little shyly. "And they're not just eating the bark. They're, like, really getting in there deep, into those inside layers, and – " Her mouth curls with revulsion. " – they're wrecking their own mouths. I was watching four of them outside the windows. It's gross. I don't even like to look at them."

"I don't either," Rachel says. "Did you find anything in the book?"

"I don't know, it's kind of hard to read. I didn't know a lot of the words."

Michael senses the girl's shyness overtaking her.

"It's okay, honey," Rachel encourages her again. "I know you found something, you told me a few minutes ago. All these people here are friends." Her eyes fall on Scott. "Even that guy."

"Nice," Scott says.

Kayla laughs a little. "Well, I was just curious why they only wanted the pine trees. That's why I looked for that book. You know, what makes them different from regular trees." She stops talking, shy again.

Rachel is smiling, urging her to go on.

"Well, so one thing I found is that those evergreen trees ... what makes them what they are is that they don't lose their leaves in the winter. You know? So that made me think of survival. Like, why do they need it? Maybe just to survive, I guess. To live longer."

Joel looks impressed. "Told you she was a smart cookie."

"Oh," Kayla says, her voice rising slightly with confidence, "and most regular trees – those are the deciduous trees, I mean – they're hardwood trees. Evergreen trees are soft wood. I thought that was interesting. Easier to eat." She makes a disgusted face.

The group considers that, but Michael's thoughts are still focused on the notion of evergreen trees being some kind of source for longevity. Survival. He thinks there actually might be something to that – until Kayla delivers another possible revelation.

She sounds very self-assured now.

"Oh, oh! There's another way evergreens are different, too." She's actually smiling, like a confident student presenting a book report to her class. "It might be the most interesting thing, at least *I* think so. Evergreens have seeds. You know, in the cones. They're called coniferous. That's how they reproduce. So now I'm thinking – "

"They need it to reproduce," Rachel finishes. "To continue."

"Okay, okay," Scott can't help but jump in. "Look, this is all terrific – and you're a sharp kid, no question, good for you – but again ... and okay, I'll say this as nicely as I can ... we can't just jump to conclusions like this. You have to – "

"Do you have ideas?" Rachel asks him. "Have you come up with *anything* as useful as anything Kayla just said?"

Scott purses his lips. "Ah, young lady, you make it hard to be nice."

"No, I'm *serious.*"

"Well, the immediate conclusion I *didn't* come to is that those human beings out there – those people who are our friends and our family – are actually ... desperate aliens? That they've traveled through space to find some chemical in our trees?"

Kayla doesn't detect the sarcasm. "Just the coniferous ones."

At least three people in the room snicker.

Scott rolls his eyes. "Do we have any reasonable theories yet? Anything in the real world? I'm serious. Anybody?"

Kayla backs down, sits meekly next to Rachel.

"Scott, can you *try* not to be a dick?" Rachel says.

Michael still has Kayla's book with him and has been paging through it. "I noticed something that might be pertinent," he says, eager to cut Scott off at the knees. "It's about *phloem*. I'm not sure how to pronounce that either." He smiles at Kayla. "It's a sap. Sugars, proteins, hormones, minerals, and so on. The interesting thing is ... and this could support what Kayla said ... is that phloem is thought to also send informational signals through the tree. It says, 'Recent evidence indicates that mobile proteins and RNA are part of the plant's long-distance communication signaling system.' And there's this picture of leafhoppers and ants feeding on the phloem. So, I don't know, we could be looking at a situation where these things – whatever they are – are using human bodies to collect something not only tangible like food or whatever ... but also ... something intangible ... something I can't even imagine, but something in the cellular memory of the tree?"

"Well, I'll tell you," Brian says, "one of the first things I thought of when I saw those things bending back like that was some kind of insect."

"Sure, *that* sounds reasonable," Scott says. "Giant insects."

"I'll ask you again, Scott," Rachel says, not bothering to look at him, "what are your theories?"

"And are you being serious?" Joel adds. "You were out on the streets, you've seen what's happening to these bodies, right? You *were* at the hospital, right? You saw the light glowing from the center of their goddam heads? The way they crawl around? You've seen the atmospheric disturbances? The sound they make? Are you being willfully ignorant here, or should we start trying to find out if a good psychologist survived?"

Scott pushes away from the wall. His eyes are edged with red, and his cheeks are flushed, showing faint freckles.

"I'm a little tired of being talked to like that, *Joel*. Look, no offense to the kid, okay? I'm just not sold on the 'little green men' card."

A look passes between Ron and Joel. Ron is the one who speaks up.

"At this point, we're just sharing observations. Anyone can do that. Like I said, we could look directly up into the center of that thing, and it was clear that something was happening up there. Something coming down, and something going up. After all these observations, you're still thinking it's something else? Something manmade? Terrestrial?"

Scott lets his gaze flit from one survivor to the next. "Of *course* I'm thinking terrestrial. Has everyone gone nuts? Something horrible happens, and the first instinct is to blame space aliens?"

"That wasn't our 'first instinct,' man," Joel says.

"One of the reasons I left the hospital in the first place was this kind of thinking."

"What?" Rachel asks. "Observing things? Testing things? You mean like 'scientific method' kind of thinking?"

"Yeah, and attitudes like that – all high and mighty about the 'answers' you're coming up with, at least until those theories turn out to be totally wrong."

Michael listens to the conversation devolve from there, and although he finds himself – remarkably – siding with Scott on some of his arguments, he's had enough of the tone. He knows that if these two combined groups are going to accomplish anything, it's going to require a sense of harmony.

"Enough!" he yells, and abruptly everyone is staring at him.

He lets the word echo out among the books, and he stands up on wobbly legs.

"It doesn't matter! Do you get that? No matter what anyone's theories are – and Scott, I get where you're coming from, I really do – but it doesn't matter. I'll tell you what matters. Regardless of what is happening to these bodies, they're after us, and they can hurt us. We have to deal with that. And the way we deal with that would be no different whether they're from down here or up there. It doesn't matter. So knock it off!"

Scott doesn't say anything for a moment, just shakes his head, eternally frustrated by everything and everyone around him. Michael finds it an annoying trait.

"It's a good point," Joel says. "We're not gonna get far biting each other's heads off."

"What's important right now is protecting ourselves," Michael says. "Once we're reasonably sure we can hold off a wave of those bodies, then we need to talk about how we can solve this thing. We have this new information from Kayla, and we need to look at that some more." Next to Rachel, Kayla smiles shyly, looking down. "But for now, I want to know where we stand with the blood. We might differ on why our blood type matters in all this, but the fact remains that it does."

Michael pauses, looking around. Everyone is quiet, listening to him.

"Zoe said something last night that really made an impact on me," he goes on, and Zoe blinks, watching him. "Remember, you said that we have the answer to this inside us. We are the weapons. We all are. We are the solution. There's a lot more of that to explore, too. But for right now, we need to focus on the 'weapon' part. Those bodies out there have a way to hurt us, yes, but inside every one of us is something that can kill them." He turns to Joel. "Am I right in assuming we have no other weapons? Guns?"

"Well, obviously I have access to them, but the weapons I *did* have were in the cruiser."

"And most of the firearms we had at the hospital are still there," Kevin adds. "I have a shotgun in the cab of my truck, but no more shells."

"I don't think we're getting outside anytime soon, so I think it's reasonable to say that we need to make the most of this weapon we do have. Our blood. Hell, maybe we're wasting time right now when we *should* be stockpiling *blood*."

Michael glances down to find Rachel staring up at him with a half-smile. Perhaps even an expression of pride. He hasn't seen an expression like that on her face in years.

"We did manage to bring in a box of tranquilizer guns and a crapload of reusable darts," Kevin says, glancing over at Zoe, who speaks up.

"Yeah, we got to the wildlife office before here, and we gathered up everything we could find, which was – how many?" She twists toward Chloe.

"I don't know the number, but a fucking lot of them," her sister says. "We grabbed everything we could. And we still have the Super Soakers."

"Wait, you grabbed a fucking lot of what?" Scott asks.

"Tranq darts," Zoe clarifies. "We got a shit ton of them, and we got six rifles. Those darts are reusable. I'm not exactly sure how to use them, but I don't think they'll be too hard to figure it out. They're 5cc darts. I'm pretty sure we grabbed everything we need – stabilizers, pressurizing syringes, everything."

For the benefit of the college team, Joel says, "I told Ron about the effect blood has on these things, even on their skin, but it's really injection that turns them back. The Super Soakers are great for annoying the shit out of them, especially if you get it in their eyes, but you really have to get the blood inside them. That's what extinguishes that light. Problem is, we can't get too close to 'em. So … tranq darts. Worth a try, anyway."

Liam says, "You guys were busy over at the hospital." The young man has a nervous energy to him that looks like sickness but could just be anxiety.

"Sure helped that we had a bunch of O-neg plasma bags in the next room," Joel says.

"We need to figure out how much blood we need in each dart," Rachel says. "I mean, is a drop enough to change them back, or do we need to inject a large amount?"

"Exactly!" Kevin says. "*This* is the conversation we need to be having."

Scott rolls his eyes.

"So how much blood do we have, anyway?" Michael asks the room.

Bonnie says, "I managed to take twelve units, which was basically all we had left, but when we were attacked in the truck, we used a lot of them. We only have a few left."

"How many is a few?" Scott says.

Bonnie looks disconsolate. "Three?"

"Well, like I said, let's not forget that our bodies are filled with the stuff," Michael says.

"And I did grab some equipment for drawing blood," Bonnie says. "As long as we can find a way to sterilize it. I didn't grab any alcohol from the hospital, but I'm hoping there's some around here. I *did* grab a lot of liquid Heparin – that's an anticoagulant. It doesn't work long-term – things will still get gummy after a while – but as long as we keep everything refrigerated, the blood should be pretty effective for – "

It's at that moment that another thundering roar rips the sky and vibrates the entire library. In the middle of her sentence, Bonnie goes to one knee, her hands going to her ears. Several people cry out. Cringing under the onslaught, Michael sees Rachel protectively covering Kayla's ears and squeezing her eyes shut. The room itself seems to cower under the weight of the sound, the walls shrinking beneath it, books shivering atop tables and falling to the floor.

The roar lasts approximately fifteen seconds but seems longer. It seems to go on forever, until the survivors simply give in, helpless to the advance of the possessed bodies outside. But it finally ends on a sharp note, and only in awful retrospect can Michael process it: It wasn't quite as long as the aural assault that preceded the recent aggression from the bodies, but it was a major event. The quiet that descends in its wake feels malevolent.

All of the survivors are gasping and glancing around warily.

"Oh no!" says Bonnie, the first to form a coherent thought. "What are they doing now?"

CHAPTER 20

Chrissy and the twins immediately rush to the windows by the doors, peering out, searching for activity. Liam and Brian hustle up behind them. Michael is there too, fearing the worst. Joel and Ron are at his side, angling for a view.

"Look there," says Rick, to the left of the door. He's pointing.

At a coniferous tree directly across Peterson, in the lawn of a nicely restored Dutch colonial home, a body is attached to the bark.

"That's one of the two we've had our eye on," says Rick, to the left of the door. "It hasn't really moved at all, just the usual chewing – "

" – but it's moving now," Michael finishes.

"Yes."

Bonnie starts emitting a series of moans.

Although the body is roughly fifty yards distant, its movements are visible: Formerly attached organically, almost seamlessly, to the pine, the body – that of a young, shirtless man with longish hair – has paused in its splintery mastication. Even from here, the survivors can see blood, bright at the thing's mouth, flowing in slow rivulets down into its eyes and stiffened hair. The mouth has stopped chewing, but the jaw is still working as the face detaches from the trunk with sticky effort. Then the upturned face seems to consider something – an almost human expression, except for the sealed-shut eyes and the streaming sap and mulch.

"What's it doing?" Kayla whispers.

"I – I think – " Rachel starts, "I think it's . . . is it thinking? Considering?"

"Or just following orders," Joel says.

"God," Ron says quietly, "I almost feel sorry for it – "

"I do, for sure," Rachel says.

Behind them, Scott lets loose with a derisive noise. "Yeah, they're just pitiful, aren't they? Poor things."

Mai laughs briefly behind them, but all of Michael's attention is focused on the body at the tree. It's shaking its head with seeming frustration, as if trying to fling pulpy mucus from its eyes. It's rising a little from its cramped, bent-backward pose, extending its limbs just slightly. Something has been communicated, Michael is sure of it. Or is it merely reacting to the thundering sound from the heavens?

"That one over there is doing the same thing," Kayla says.

She's gesturing southeast, but Bonnie says, "Where?"

All heads turn.

Michael can't spot it for a moment, but then there it is, partially obscured by the front end of a Subaru station wagon.

"Good eyes, kid," Joel says.

"I didn't even see that one before," Rick says.

Michael can't determine the age or sex of this body; it's too far away. But he thinks it's a small one. Its head has also clearly pulled away from the bark of its tree, almost as if dazed. Michael darts his glance between the two bodies, and he comes to the realization that the movements these things are making are nearly mirror images of one another.

He voices this to the room, and as he does, the bodies begin moving slowly, almost cautiously, away from the trees.

Several survivors draw in breath sharply.

Joel says, "If those things are gearing up for attack again, we need to be arming up."

There's a general sense of frantic movement in the lobby, away from the windows, but then –

"Wait, wait!" Rachel yells.

The bodies have become more mobile, finding their balance on their bent limbs. But the body across the street is moving *away* from the library, southeast toward the other body. And that body is also beginning to amble south down Peterson.

"Where are they going?" Kayla whispers.

"I don't know," Rachel breathes.

The lobby is frozen in a state of nervous uncertainty. Michael is suddenly aware of the knife's edge on which they're teetering: At the whim of these bizarre things that used to be human beings – or at the whim of whatever controls them – this glass-walled library could at any moment be facing an assault by things that can melt glass with something inside them... something that the bodies are using quite consciously as weapons. Despite the relative thickness of the glass, Michael is not at all sure that they're safe in here. If thousands of these things were to coordinate and throw themselves at the windows ... well, then that would spell the end for this motley band of survivors. Michael doesn't care *how* well stocked they might be with O-negative blood.

"Okay," Joel says, his voice full of edgy wariness, "we got lucky there, but Jesus, we gotta get moving."

"Michael's right, we need to start taking blood from everyone," Ron says, stepping up. "Start loading those tranq darts with blood and anticoagulant, have them ready."

"Before we do that, though, we need to test it," Kevin says. "Right? Like how much do we need to put into each dart canister? Will just a drop work? If it does, then we don't have to be sucking whole pints out of people and making them all woozy and shit, just as those goddamn things are attacking."

"All right, I agree with all this," Scott says, "but our potential test subjects just went south. Literally."

"He's right," Michael says. "What are we gonna test it on?"

After a moment of indecision, "Okay," Joel says, "regardless, we need to start with something on hand. Let's use the blood we have first, and then test it if the opportunity comes up. So come on, come on, let's get moving, we can't afford to rest yet."

And now everyone is moving again.

"Everyone strong enough, I want blocking windows," Joel says. "Get those bookcases moving, but obviously be careful not to crash them *through* the windows. Pair up and take off."

With that, nearly all the men in the lobby take off in all the directions of the compass, pairing off with one another. Michael is about to grab Scott and find an opportunity when Kevin stops him.

"Give me a hand with the tranq guns?"

"Sure."

The guards at the door have switched with the twins, Chloe and Zoe, and as Mai and Liam hurry off toward the north side of the library, the two girls collapse onto the haphazardly placed benches, as if they're about to fall unconscious. Michael notices an elaborate tattoo on Zoe's lower back as she leans forward – another remnant of another life.

"Don't you dare fall asleep, ladies," Kevin says. "I need you to watch for those things – if you see one come close, we need to test this stuff."

"Yes boss," Chloe mutters, sitting back up.

"And I need help with the blood," Bonnie says to Rachel and Kayla. "Let's get it in order."

The trio of women, three generations, branch off toward the main checkout desk, where the blood-soaked cardboard box sits, along with the six tranq rifles that Kevin and the girls managed to grab from the wildlife office.

As the small group hurries over, Joel stops Chrissy.

"Hey, can you go through this whole place and gather whatever food you can find? We can defend ourselves till we're blue in the face, but if we don't have food and water, it's all for naught."

Chrissy's eyes are so exhausted that they seem cadaverous. "Sure."

Joel grabs her shoulders. "Keep it together, okay? You're doing great."

She just stares at Joel.

Michael remembers what Chrissy said moments ago about the Rapture. It was the first time he saw her clear-eyed and passionate about something. He spares a quick thought about how her worldview is affecting her mindset in the face of this disaster. Because right now, in the wake of that particular discussion fizzling out, her expression has returned to hopelessness. Michael realizes he's in the midst of an all-too-real sociological and psychological experiment.

"Every door is unlocked in this place, so that shouldn't be a problem," Joel says to her. "Bring everything you find right here, okay?"

Throughout the lobby, there's a feeling of running-on-empty desperation. Chrissy trudges away blearily, and the rest of them drag their feet and swallow dryly, on the verge of dehydration, he's sure, and starting to feel the effects of prolonged hunger. From all corners of the library come the sounds of large things scraping across carpet and tile, some grunting, and very little conversation. Something is going to have to give – soon.

Joel is actually about to partner with Scott to help with the bookcases when Michael takes hold of his arm.

"You know these folks are running on fumes, Joel. If they're going to be any good to us at all, they'll need not only food but also sleep."

"As soon as we get a minute to catch our breath, we'll start arranging shifts."

"And they'll need ... something to hope for."

Joel looks at him. "I don't know what that could be. Maybe above my pay grade."

"Yeah."

"Isn't survival enough?"

"It is in my book," Kevin says, looming next to them. "Come on, dude. Let's figure this out. These tranq darts could be the answer to everything."

He leads Michael to the tranq rifles, and together they lay out the components of the arsenal. The slim, lightweight rifles themselves have a straightforward loading mechanism; it's the darts that take some figuring out. There are several needle types, and two varieties of syringes. One is clearly meant for delivering the payload into the canister, which is a long projectile that ends with a bright blue, feathery stabilizer; there are two ends to the canister: a liquid chamber for loading and an air chamber to be pressurized. The other syringe is the pressurizing syringe that, once the dart hits the target, will plunge the blood into the flesh.

The darts are uniformly 5cc capacity, and the two men can only guess what kind of pressurization they'll require in practice – just as they can only guess how much blood each dart will need to have the desired effect.

"I want to test this bad boy immediately," Kevin says.

"We only have six rifles," Michael says. "Even if these things work, how much good are they going to do us against – " He lowers his voice. " – against an army of those bodies?"

"You never know," Kevin shrugs. "They could make all the difference."

"Fair enough."

At that moment, Chrissy calls weakly from the room adjacent to the one where Michael and Rachel found Kayla. "There's a Deep Rock water cooler here, and two extra bottles!"

Joel's voice comes from somewhere a few rooms away. "Excellent, keep it up!"

Michael takes a sighing moment to sit on a bench next to the checkout counter, and his eyes fall on his daughter, who is working industriously with the blood units, under Bonnie's tutelage. But what catches his eye is the way Rachel is guiding Kayla's actions. Rachel reminds Michael so profoundly of Cassie at that moment that he mouths a *wow* – the same set jaw, the same patience, the same light touch, even under stress.

"Body!" Chloe cries from the doorway. "We got a body!"

Kevin grabs a tranq rifle from the counter – it's not loaded with anything yet – and he and Michael race through the lobby, maneuvering around large tables covered with books, and peer out the windows.

"There!" Chloe says.

A naked, bloodied body is practically galloping across the library lawn, directly south and past them. It's gone, out of sight, before the men even have a chance to lock on to its features.

"Look at how it moves!" Rachel says, a weight of appalled resignation in her voice. "How is it even – ?"

"They've grown accustomed to their new bodies," Joel breathes.

And then there's commotion and shouting from the south end of the library as the survivors there watch the same galloping body pass.

"Aw shit, man," Kevin says. "Where the hell are they going?"

"Let's assume they're up to no good," Rachel says.

"Sounds like a safe assumption," Kayla says in her small voice.

"And we'll assume they're doing it close by."

"Let's get a few of these things ready, in case another opportunity comes up," Kevin says.

"Another one!" Chloe says, pointing.

This body is much farther away, not unlike a dark red insect in the distance, east on Oak, but scurrying between houses – again in a southerly direction.

Bonnie surges forward. "Okay, we have *two units* of O-neg blood left." She lets that sink in. *"Two units.* We had at least thirty units when all this started. We've been filling those squirt guns with it, and that's worked a little bit, but I'm really hoping those tranquilizer guns will work better, because we need to be a lot more effective. More efficient. I'm just afraid we wasted so *much."*

"What about drawing blood from our bodies?" Michael asks. "You said you had the equipment."

"I have the equipment, but I don't have a sterile environment – no gloves, bandages, and like I said, not even any alcohol."

"And if anyone gets an infection from a blood draw," Kevin says, "well, that person is essentially a goner."

"Theoretically, we could go back to the hospital to treat someone, if it came to that, but ..." She shakes her head doubtfully. "... I don't think we should count on that being a viable option."

Kayla brightens. "Wait, there's alcohol in that room I was in! Rubbing alcohol. Would that work?"

Bonnie regards Kayla hopefully. "Yes! How much?"

"Just a small bottle, I think. Maybe a little bit gone. I noticed it because I thought it was water at first."

"Can you go get it?" Rachel asks.

"Sure!" Kayla trots away helpfully.

Rachel smiles. "I like that kid," she says, catching Michael's eye. "Reminds me of me."

"You were never that cute," Michael teases.

Rachel punches his shoulder.

Bonnie turns back. "So, it's not just having the equipment and making sure it's clean. It's also – well, if this goes on for a long time, and we're attacked relentlessly ... it's not like we have gallons of blood at our disposal at any moment – or gallons of Heparin. Drawing blood takes time, treating it takes time. It takes a toll."

"Which is why testing these darts is imperative," Kevin finishes.

Bonnie agrees. "And we have only so much storage space, too. We have that little fridge running off the generator, and it's holding what we've got, but I can see running out of space."

Michael has been watching Kevin hefting one of the two remaining blood units. In his other hand, he's holding a payload syringe for a tranq rifle. He seems unsure of himself.

"You ready?" Michael asks him.

"What do you guys think? Try a capsule with just 1cc of blood?"

"That's about, oh, a quarter teaspoon," Bonnie says, unable to suppress a huge yawn. "Is it enough?"

"Seems a good start anyway," Kevin shrugs. "Can I just – poke the bag?"

Bonnie walks him through the process of drawing blood from its plastic enclosure, and Rachel volunteers to use her geometry skills to organize the refrigerator and maximize the space they have for the blood.

"Don't take any blood out of the fridge for too long," Bonnie reminds her. "It needs to stay cold."

"Okay."

Michael takes the opportunity to share a few words with his daughter as they walk the open hallway and into the room that holds the fridge. The space still shows evidence of Kayla's makeshift occupation.

"You hangin' in there?"

Rachel, kneeling next to the half-height fridge – which has been transformed into the survivors' personal blood bank – considers the question but appears to come up blank.

"I don't know." Her eyes are red, and there are dark rings around them. She's clearly drained, but Michael has no answer to offer for that. "Daddy, I miss Tony."

"I know."

"I even miss Susanna."

Michael cocks his head at that.

"I wish everything would go back to how it was."

He touches her shoulder. "Me too."

"So many people are dying. I can't stop it."

Michael watches the movement of her hands as she carefully organizes the premade tranq darts, the filled syringes, and the anticoagulant, almost effortlessly bringing a sense of order to the collection.

"Who told you *you* were the one responsible for that?" he says, placing a hand on her shoulder.

She stares into the fridge. "*I* did! I mean, we're all responsible for that, aren't we? We have to save as many people as we can! And I'm not doing my part! I felt like I was, before. I felt like I had the answer! I *wanted* to have the answer. But it's not working."

He lowers his head, thinking.

"You're right," he says. "We need to do whatever we can to save lives – and we have. *You* have. The difference is that you can't hold yourself responsible for every death that you can't prevent."

She sniffles, sighs, closes the fridge door. She shakes her head minutely.

"Rach, I think you may have saved more lives than anyone left on this planet."

... anyone left on this planet ...

As the words leave his mouth, they stun him. His teeth clack shut as he ponders them. Are they really facing the end of the world? What lies ahead? How will they survive, assuming they can withstand the ridiculous fact and ferocity of these formerly human monsters?

He manages to continue: "But saving a life is very different from preventing a death."

Rachel gives him a look, about to object, but –

"Another one!" Zoe yells.

Just beyond the door, Kevin shifts into high gear. He has the pressurizing plunger in one hand, about to ready the rifle. Rachel hops up and follows Michael out into the lobby.

"How close?" Kevin is saying.

"You got some time with this one, it's moving slow," Zoe says.

Kevin swallows audibly, inserting the plunger. He settles in at the front doors, between the twins, who are ready to slide open one of the doors at his word. Michael approaches him, just in time to watch the pressure build in the canister sufficiently to move the small air stopper into position. The tranq dart is now primed for its strike.

Kevin takes up the rifle and carefully inserts the dart.

"I guess that's it," he says.

"Looks right to me," Chloe says from the right side of the door. "Ready for the door?"

"Sure."

She pulls the door along its track, leaving a foot-wide gap.

The small clutch of survivors moves to the doorway. As they do so, Kayla returns from her scavenging with a three-quarters-full bottle of rubbing alcohol.

"What's happening?" she says.

"Watch," Rachel says, grabbing Kayla's hand.

There's movement in the expansive yard to the northwest, perhaps thirty yards from them. Something blue. It's moving in lunging bursts, behind a clutch of shrubs and trees.

"I think it's injured," Michael says.

The body scurries into view, one arm dragging. It's a young man, dressed in a tattered Denver Broncos jersey that only barely covers its torso; boxer shorts are also barely holding on, twisted at the knees. Its mouth is open at an unnatural angle, and the upclenched jaw appears cranked to the left, as if dislocated. The upper face is slathered with sap. Its eyes are gummed over, but the body seems drawn inexorably south. Yes, it's obviously injured, but its single-minded purpose won't let it pause in its journey. A broken, involuntary wheeze rhythmically escapes its mouth.

"Ready?" Chloe breathes, turning to watch Kevin heft the rifle.

"Yep." He takes aim, steadying himself against the metal edge of the door. "Here we go."

"Wait ... wait ..."

The body limps out into the open, away from any foliage, and it's in clear view.

"Okay," Chloe says, "whenever you're ready."

Kevin's breath stops, there's a moment of complete stillness, and then he fires the tranq rifle. The dart flies straight and true, attaching itself to the thing's hamstring.

Kevin's breath lets loose. "Whew!"

He pulls the tranq rifle up and away.

All eyes are on the body, which has barely missed a single dragging step. But now it judders to a stop on the concrete path and seems to consider something. A raspy cough escapes its mouth, and that sound ratchets up to a screech of distress.

"Here we go," Rachel breathes, grabbing Michael's arm.

The thing seems to be scratching at itself, in a state of painful confusion. In a moment it has dropped straight down, flat on its back, writhing like a pinned bug. Bonnie turns away from the sight, but even more so from the sound – that flat bray of sound, that hoarse screech.

Michael can't see what its inner light is doing, but if what Rachel told him is true, the illumination is now sparking out.

"It's taking longer," his daughter says now in a voice laced with distress. "It's in pain. Can you shoot it again with more blood?"

Kevin's eyes are locked on the body.

"Wait for it ..." he says.

The body continues to jerk on the pavement.

"Kevin!" Rachel calls miserably.

"It would take too long to prepare another dart, anyway – but look, it's happening." He gestures out the door.

The body's jerky movements are becoming more random, less rhythmic. The sound it's making goes from inhuman bleat to something more guttural, something like a human response from that ravaged throat.

The thing is screaming now.

"Oh, I can't listen!" Bonnie cries, moving away from the door. She jogs back into the gloom between bookcases.

"What do we do?" Zoe asks.

"Can we treat it?" Michael asks.

"Treat it how?" Chloe says.

"Nice to hear we were all prepared for this," Scott says.

"What is that?!" Joel says, arriving in the lobby and rushing toward the door.

No one answers.

They're all staring outside, at the broken thing on the concrete. At the man on the sun-baked pathway who is turning on his side and staring at them with sap-slathered eyes, attempting to wipe at them furiously, screaming in red-faced pain under the weight of countless injuries.

Whatever force is overtaking these human beings is contorting them into an impossible posture: back-breaking, limb-cracking, joint-popping. But there's more than that. *Much* more than that. There's the teeth-shattering business these bodies have been consumed with for the past few days. The constant gnawing of tree bark in pursuit of ... whatever they need inside the cellular structures of those pines. The resulting ravaging of their mouths and throats and digestive tracts. All of that would be enough, but Michael – eyeing the blunt horror on the sidewalk – is pondering less obvious repercussions.

What of the inhabitation itself? The radiation at the center of the head? What is that doing to the host skull, considering the havoc it has wreaked on its targeted victims, or anyone who has gotten too close? Rachel spoke of malleable flesh in the affected bodies – a *give* in the skin, perhaps allowing the freedom of movement necessary for that incomprehensible crablike posture. Given all that, is the return to humanity in fact a more horrific fate than death? Beyond all the obvious damage this possession has caused, there's the very real possibility that something cellular is at the center of it, and that's what spells disaster to Michael.

He's glancing worriedly at his daughter, who has placed so much faith in the fact that they can turn these people back from their horrific fate.

A strangled sound is coming from the body on the sidewalk.

A sound that becomes a word: *"Huuuurts."*

CHAPTER 21

Rachel is grasping at Michael's shirt.

"Daddy!"

"It's talking?" Kayla asks in a horrified whisper.

Bonnie glances at Kayla worriedly, and Michael knows that in any other reality, the older woman would be jumping up and shielding the little girl from this atrocity.

"Is he normal again?" Kayla is asking.

"Shhh," Bonnie says, now moving her body as if to protect the girl, and then realizing the absurdity of that impulse.

"There's another one!" Zoe says, her head turned north.

Sure enough, another bent-back body is scurrying south, seemingly emerging from the yard of a home just across the street – a young woman with the tattered remains of a nightie hanging off her body. The body hops up onto the library lawn, heading toward the concrete walkway in front of the library. It will pass directly in front of them.

But the screams of the man on the sidewalk demand their attention. The man is in intense pain, his body jerking spastically, as if on fire. The limbs flail, unmoored from their sockets. Michael cringes at the sight, trying not to imagine what's happening inside that body.

Most of the man's sounds are animalistic, just gargled shrieks of pain. But here, as if echoing Michael's thoughts, comes that unmistakable word again:

"*Huuuuuurts!*"

"Did you bring any pain killers?" Michael says.

Bonnie appears hesitant. "I have a good supply – not much, but enough."

"What did you bring?"

"Well, the remaining morphine." Bonnie glances furtively at Scott.

"Very nice," Scott mumbles.

Rachel seems in tune with Bonnie, giving the man a dirty look.

Michael can't guess the meaning behind that exchange.

Bonnie's voice is still pitched low. "I'm sorry Scott. But we need to be mindful of what we might need. What if one of us gets hurt?"

"Can we spare a little to treat him?" Rachel asks, gesturing anxiously to the man on the ground.

"Not with those things just roaming around," Kevin said.

"Can we bring him in here?" Rachel's voice is on the edge of hysteria, counterpoint to the continuing savage cries from outside. "We have to do something!"

"Are you volunteering?" Kevin asks rhetorically. He's watching the female body come closer, moving inexorably south. "I'm not setting foot out there, not for one of those things."

There are tears in Rachel's eyes.

Then Michael notices something.

"Look at that," he says.

"What?" Kevin says.

"It's moving straight south."

"So?"

Everyone watches the female in the midst of its single-minded route. She's thirty-ish, and her skin appears bleached-white under the remains of the blue nightie. There's no deviation in her crab-like motion, no pause, no random gesture. The eyes don't deviate from their straight-ahead gaze.

"So, that man on the ground is now ... human ... right?"

Kevin thinks about that. "Technically. In a manner of speaking."

"So that thing out there is passing by a human being, and it doesn't care. It's not attacking."

"You're thinking ... because that thing isn't attacking him, that we're safe." Kevin wipes sweat off his forehead. "Right? I think that might be a dangerous assumption."

"I'd agree with that," Scott says, pacing behind them.

The survivors are mostly quiet, watching, considering. Rachel is squirming, listening to the strangled cries. The female is perhaps twenty feet beyond the young man now, paying no attention to him. The body simply crawls past, her limbs moving fluidly despite the horrible stance, looking utterly alien in its human skin.

"Passing him now," Michael breathes.

"So she is," Kevin says.

"So we can go get him," Rachel says, "we can go get him and help him!"

"You *are* volunteering!" Kevin says.

"I guess I am."

But before anyone can react, Michael is slipping between the roughly slid-open doors, nearly tripping but breaking free into the smoky sunlight.

"Daddy!" Rachel calls hoarsely, grabbing at him – too late.

"Get the morphine ready!" he calls back. "Not a lot – we need to keep him awake!"

He tries to tune out Rachel's hissing cries as he steps out into the open. He takes a moment to gather himself, glances around to gauge the threat. The female body continues its inexorable scuttle south.

He turns back and calls softly to Rachel and the others, "It's okay."

The sun is stabbing down with increased heat, despite the layer of smoke and other atmospheric phenomena. He feels instant sweat prickle his skin as he jogs toward the squirming body – farther away than he thought! He feels an immediate regret for this course of action.

And now his eyes lock on yet another cranked-over body, scurrying south in the far distance, east of Peterson, crossing Oak. He lets out a cough. His vision stings from the lingering smoke.

Multiple voices rise in conflict behind him, but he can't make sense of them as he aims directly for the body on the concrete. Twenty feet, fifteen. He latches on to the man's ragged screeches, and they are terrible. Ten feet away, Michael gets a full look at the body, and he realizes he has underestimated the horror. Blood is flowing in bright rivulets from the man's gullet, and he's making a desperate gargling sound.

"Huuurts!" the man gasps again, focusing his watery eyes on Michael.

"I'm here to help," he replies.

Michael takes a look around, makes sure the female is continuing its southward lurch. Yes, the pale body is almost out of sight, beyond some shrubbery at the edge of the library property. The streets are baking under an alien sun now, and there's a strange anticipation in the air. As if more bodies might flow from any direction at any moment. He feels reckless. Too reckless. But for now, beyond the ravaged cries of the man in front of him, everything is preternaturally quiet.

He gets his bearings, and leans over cautiously. His first instinct is to grasp the man's arms, but he's wary of touching him. He saw firsthand what happened to Danny. Michael is almost sure that this man is no longer a threat, but there's still a seed of doubt. He wants to hurry, but he's unsure...cautious. On the heels of that thought, he hears someone – Bonnie? – shout from the library doors:

"Careful!"

He gestures behind himself with a hand, shushing them, and

then focuses on the young man. The eyes are peeled painfully wide, imploring. He's trying to lift his arms toward Michael, but it seems none of his limbs will cooperate. Blood pulses out of his nose, runs in a thick stream, staining the concrete. Michael knows time is short for this man.

He tentatively reaches toward the man's face, as if tempting a flame. He feels nothing. There's no radiation, no heat. He's not entirely sure what he's supposed to sense, but nothing is happening.

Throwing caution to the wind, Michael takes the man by the forearms and begins to drag.

The man screams like an animal – a bleating, horrific screech, new blood erupting from his mouth in an obscene bubble, eyes bugging out of his skull, muscles out of control, flailing – and then he deflates, unconscious.

"Good God!" Michael says to the empty streets, and keeps pulling. The arms feel loose in their sockets, and for a queasy moment, Michael has the sensation of dragging a broken corpse.

He's alive, he thinks. For Rachel's sake, let him be alive.

Michael is about fifty feet from the front doors, and he already feels as if he's out of strength. He can hear the voices behind him raised in either encouragement or alarm. He can't make sense of them; he's breathing too heavily. His eyes flit left and right as he pulls the body without pause. He can feel the smoke deep in his lungs as he heaves in oxygen. The man's deadweight is a slog.

He doesn't see any more bodies. The street remains eerily silent.

Thirty feet.

The voices behind him are a chorus of hysteria. He singles out Rachel's voice, repeating *"Daddy!"* like some frenzied mantra, and now he sees the reason for their alarm: The body of a child has crab-walked out of its yard, on the other side of Oak, and is crossing the street, a hundred yards to the northeast. It's a young boy, perhaps seven years old, and its blond hair is dark with sap and splinters. Michael watches it as he drags the unconscious man. The boy doesn't seem to notice him at all, just climbs the curb onto the library lawn and then scurries away from him, toward Peterson.

"It's fine!" he yells over his shoulder.

Pulling, pulling.

But the voices seem to rise an octave, and that's when Michael bumps into something.

"Shit!" he bellows, inadvertently relinquishing his hold on the man's right arm, thinking he must have hit a small tree, but there's a raspy grunt of seeming surprise – right at his left ear – and Michael knows he's in serious trouble.

He pivots away from the man on the ground, letting the other arm drop, and he stares at the very mobile body that stands there, poised like an obscenely fleshy spider, its inverted head pointing at him like an accusation.

Michael swallows heavily as a black pit of fear opens in the precise center of his chest. He sees all the faces in the window beyond the body, how they've all gone silent now, motionless with fear.

The body is that of a large, grizzled man, perhaps early sixties, his skin sun-leathered, his muscles lean from hard work. He might have been a late-in-the-years mechanic, or a farmer. The tobacco-stained but mostly gray goatee on his chin looks like an arrowhead directed at Michael's heart. He's wearing a stained white tee shirt and jeans, which are torn at the joints and falling away. The body is mostly still, staring, considering, but it's ever-so-slightly angling toward Michael, and its wide nostrils are flaring. Blood is leaking out of them, down into the unblinking, deadened eyes and into the ragged hair.

A throaty growl issues from its cranked-open and massacred mouth. Michael freezes.

A long moment passes as the thing in front of him seems to gauge Michael's level of threat. Then the thing's flat eyes shift to the right, away from Michael. Then they move back. The body is still swiveling in his direction, but now in fits and starts. It appears ready to launch – either toward Michael or away from him – and Michael positions himself to jump in the opposite direction of wherever this thing chooses to go.

The mouth lets loose with a gravelly bark, spraying Michael with flecks of bloody wood mulch. There's anger in its face, if not the dead eyes – he can see it in the brow and the cheeks, an undeniably human expression of rage even in the clutches of what is quite possibly an alien intelligence.

In the midst of his terror, Michael tries to gather something, anything, from that expression. Tries to find motive there, tries to find reason. But all he can see is a cold unreason, a wholly inexplicable monster in bent-over human form.

It barks at him again, as much a clearing of a savaged throat as an angry expulsion of sound, and Michael doesn't dare move a muscle. He can only watch as the old man's head does a slow jab at him. Michael can imagine the radiation inside the skull, promising harm, but he can't actually see it under the bright sun. He knows it's there, waiting to hurt him. And now the head lunges at him more sharply, like the snout of an aggressive dog. The snarl becomes more pronounced.

Michael feels that any move he makes will be the wrong one.

But Kevin makes the decision for him.

A tiny flash of blue, and the body in front of Michael twitches. Its attention wavers. And then its face twists in confusion. The body thrashes once – a full-body spasm – and its growl becomes a yowl of pain. It wobbles to the left, and Michael can plainly see the blue tranq dart embedded in the right side of its upthrust abdomen.

The grizzled man falls to the ground and flails. Michael can see Kevin in the distance, at the doorway, the rifle still aimed in his direction. The big man brings the weapon down, watching.

Michael does a quick survey of the area, sees no further bodies. Emboldened, he creeps closer to the old man and studies his face. The features are clenched, every muscle vibrating, and a choking gasp is hissing involuntarily from the mouth. It's a heart-breaking sight, to see humanity return in the grip of mortal anguish. But Michael has no doubt that human consciousness *is* flooding back into this body: The eyes flicker and brighten, from corpse-flat to livid, from dead to very much alive, brimming with awareness of a sudden and absolute agony.

The eyes lock on him.

Blood gurgles forth from the mouth, as if given release.

"Come on, old man," Michael says, and reaches down to grab hold of his arms. He starts to drag him, trying to ignore the helpless screams of protest. Unlike the younger man behind him, the old-timer doesn't lose consciousness, but Michael senses the same dislocation of joints, the same looseness of limbs. He grits his teeth, blotting out the screams, not caring to imagine the suffering, but that's impossible. This man's only hope is inside that library.

Michael pulls him the rest of the way to the library doors and gets him over the threshold, and the voices are a cacophony, Bonnie urging everyone out of the way so that she can administer morphine, several others helping her cause, and Rachel yelling at him for taking the risk. As he lets go of the arms and puts the man in Bonnie's care, Rachel bats at him angrily.

" – can't believe you went *out there!*"

"Okay, thirty milligrams of morphine, here we go."

"Is that enough?" Chloe is sobbing at the sight of the wretched man on the floor.

"That's plenty. Any more than that, and his respiratory system will explode."

"From the looks of him, that's already happened," Joel says from somewhere behind them.

"Can we stop that bleeding?" someone asks.

"I don't know," Bonnie says miserably.

Someone shoves Michael brusquely in the back, and he peers over his shoulder to see Kevin squeeze through the doors and make his way toward the Broncos fan's body.

"Guys!" Joel says, too late to stop Kevin. "You can't be this impulsive! It's dangerous out there. We gotta use our heads."

Michael, watching Kevin retrieve the body, abruptly realizes that he's still breathing far too quickly. He can't seem to get hold of his respiration, and adrenaline is spiking through him with each breath. He glances around wildly, reaches for Rachel's arm.

"Daddy?" she says, seeing the expression on his face. "Daddy! Are you okay?"

Michael can only shake his head, which is threatening to throb with pain again. It is fear that has bloomed inside him, belatedly, and even as he recognizes that he's in the grip of a panic attack, a sort of delayed reaction to what just happened outside, he can't stop it. Black spots begin to appear in his vision.

"Sit down!" Bonnie yelps. "Rachel, sit him down there," she directs, and his daughter guides him to the bench just to their left, and shooing Zoe aside.

"Put your head down."

Michael sits and follows her instructions – gentle even amidst chaos – feeling instant relief under her touch. He focuses on slowing his breathing, sucking in long, slow, deep inhalations. He closes his eyes, trying to think of something else. His first thought is the money in his closet back home, and the meaninglessness of it all, and he shakes away that thought. Shakes his head, embarrassed with himself more than anything.

Kevin has arrived with the other body. The Broncos jersey that had been barely hanging off this young man now flags the spot on the concrete where he became human again.

Voices are sounding all around him. When Michael regains his composure, he sees that Bonnie is attending to both bodies to the left of the doors, checking for egregious wounds. She's using wetted towels and tape to stop bleeding. People are running back and forth at her bidding. Men are returning from their window-buttressing duties, and the lobby is suddenly a riotous scene. Liam and Brian, breathing heavily, are popping dislocated shoulders back into place, much to the consternation of the younger women in the lobby. Kayla is curled up against the far wall, unable to look away, but an expression of disgusted alarm is etched across her features. Michael has to admit that the sight makes even him feel vaguely nauseated.

He turns away, realizes Rachel is speaking.

"... don't have to be such a hero!"

"What?"

She sighs dramatically, right in his face. "In case I wasn't clear when I saved your life – *twice!* – I'd like you to live, okay?"

"Someone had to get him."

"It didn't have to be you."

"I think it did," he says.

"What are you *talking* about?"

He shakes his head, which is beginning, again, to feel as if his brain is dislodged from the linings of his skull. The sloshing pain makes him gasp.

"I don't know."

"Ugh," Rachel moans, rolling her eyes as only she can. "Dad!"

Bonnie has the grizzled man's mouth propped wide open, and she's examining it with repulsion. Every once in a while, she's reaching in and yanking out a bloody splinter or a mound of sodden, red mulch. She's directing Chrissy to do the same with the younger man's mouth, and Chrissy is surprisingly composed as she does so.

In the middle of all this, Kevin speaks up over the general chaos of voices.

"Well, we learned that the blood darts work – and at really low levels."

"How low?" Joel says.

"Basically the smallest amount I could put into a dart – 1cc."

Michael speaks up. "I think the body was slower to turn than it might have with a larger amount, though. Turn back human, I mean."

"Yeah," says Rachel, "like it took longer for the blood to flow through it."

"No point wasting any blood if the end result is the same," Joel says.

"I guess so."

Michael notices Scott fidgeting against the same wall where Kayla is cowering. He appears to be chewing the insides of his cheeks again. He's watching Bonnie tend to the bodies.

Scott is the kind of perpetually pissed-off guy who will never find satisfaction in any situation. Michael knows the type. Steven at work is – was – that kind of character: pessimistic, sarcastic, entitled. As if the world has wronged him, and from now on he's in it just for himself. *Fuck everyone else. Give me what's mine.*

Scott meets his gaze, and Michael breaks the contact.

His thoughts drift back to the notion of Steven in the past tense. He visualizes the large man unconscious, splayed back in his office chair, the way he was the last time Michael saw him. Except he knows, now, that Steven is probably no longer in that building but rather wandering the streets – perhaps even searching for Michael, among all other survivors, searching, searching, wanting to end him. Carol, too. They're just like these two bodies were, ravaged by an insane presence, probably beyond help. He imagines his colleagues in this state, and he shudders. He wouldn't wish this "cure" on them.

Now Scott is at his side.

"I hope you all know what you're doing," Scott says. "This is fucked up, I hope you understand."

Michael feels a stab of irritation. He opens his mouth, then closes it.

"I'll ask again: Do you have any other ideas?" Rachel says.

"Yeah, sure, I have an idea: How about we leave them alone?"

"And just sit here and twiddle our thumbs?"

"Yes!" Scott sees he has an audience again. "Look, if those things out there can sense us, why not just let them have what they want? Who cares about a bunch of goddamn trees, anyway?"

"Hell yes," Mai says, watching the proceedings from afar, over by the counters. "This shit is freaking me out."

"Let them suck on the things, get everything they need, and then leave us alone," Scott says. "If we just let them do whatever the fuck they want, we'd probably be safe! Did anyone think of that?"

The room is silently frenetic for a few moments, working on the bodies in the doorway, and Michael can sense everyone forming responses. He decides to break that silence.

"Because that's not what we're about." He shuts one eye against the pain that results from his speaking loudly. "I'm not really into letting those things make the rules. I don't want them to just take what they want. And who knows what they really want? Right? This could be just the beginning. We have a solid chance at putting the hurt on these things, and at the same time saving a lot of people. Why wouldn't we take that chance?"

Michael can feel Rachel's gaze, but he opts not to meet it.

"He's right," Kevin says, glancing over at Scott. "How do you keep turning up, anyway?"

"I'm not the only one thinking this." Scott gestures to Mai, who's nodding emphatically. "Okay, let's say you're right. It's an alien invasion. Whatever's up there is sending down directives to all these former humans, telling them to eat these trees and, oh, attack us if we get to smart for our own good, and, well, then back off for whatever reason." He shakes his head. "So, okay, given all that, what if the *aliens* can sense that you just did *that*?" He points at the bodies. "The truth is out there, right? And the truth is, they know exactly what you're doing, and they're gonna send down another directive, and they're gonna wipe us out! When, all along, we could've just waited till they were done and gone."

"That's the thing, Scott," Joel says in a reasonable voice. "We don't *know* that after everything, they'll be done and gone. We have to assume they'll be coming after us until we're all dead. Or on the run."

"We shouldn't assume anything," Scott says pointedly. "There's not one person in here that knows what's going on. Yes, theories are flying wild, but no one really knows. Why are we messing with them? Are we trying to piss them off? I'd rather make the choice that keeps us alive. And maybe that's just to be quiet and survive another day."

Mai has been watching him. "Gotta admit, that's the side I'm on."

"Scott, Mai, I don't want to just scavenge for the rest of my life," Joel says, "while they make the rules. I want to live again."

Scott puts his hands up in surrender. "Fine, fine. I'm done."

"As a human."

"I said *fine*."

"All right, can I ask a favor, then?"

Scott glares into space.

"You and Bonnie are the only hospital personnel we have left here, and I need you two to head up this whole effort with the blood. We need to be armed for a full-on assault. I'm talking about defense, okay? I think we can all agree on that. We need to be ready for every single one of those things attacking this library. I want you two taking blood from every survivor. Bonnie, can we draw blood straight into the tranq darts?"

She considers that.

"And how many tranq canisters do we have, anyway?" Joel looks around for an answer.

"We scrounged up maybe two hundred in that box," Kevin says. "They're reusable ... not that we'll be able to retrieve many ..."

Bonnie says, "To maintain a sterile environment, we really need to keep the blood draws and the weaponry separate. And there's the question of the anticoagulant. It's not like I have a jug of it. It'll only take us so far."

"Fair enough, well, I'm relying on you two to find the most efficient way to make this work. Bottom line is that we need all those darts filled and ready."

Bonnie and a reluctant, almost petulant Scott join at the edge of the messy scene, along with Kevin, while at least ten survivors have crowded around the two unconscious bodies at the doorway. Everyone is in a state of nervous inactivity now, glancing around uselessly. The ground is spattered with deep-red wads of mulch, which has caused several survivors to back away from the scene, nauseated. But Michael notices that all three of the young women, Chrissy and the twins, are still dialed in to the situation, showing teary, red-eyed calm in the face of the horror.

The bodies are gray and devastated. Worst off is the young man, the Broncos fan. Someone has kindly pulled his boxer shorts back up, in a desperate reach for modesty, but it looks to Michael like a cruel joke. The rest of his body is scraped up, at least a dozen contusions cleaned and covered with tape. The body has obviously lost a lot of blood, and the vast majority of that has been internal. Outside the hospital, there's very little they can do for that, but Bonnie has done her best to instruct Chrissy and Chloe how to apply a compress on the throat without obstructing air flow.

But there's a constant trickle from the young man's mouth that Chrissy can't stop, and Michael can see the desperation in her eyes.

The Broncos fan will probably be dead within the hour.

Michael believes it's the grizzled old-timer who will give them their best chance. His body is also gray-tinted and bloodied, and Chloe has taken up the task of administering pressure to the throat, but the body looks heartier. In his case, the devastation of the ... possession ... seems more survivable.

But, as Michael surveys the scene, he comes to a slow realization of why everyone is standing around, mostly silent. Why the increasingly humid air is filled with a hopelessness engendered by the sheer fact of these bodies' desolation. The lobby has the feel of tragedy, of miserable dread. The bodies look like corpses at the end of a reprehensibly violent act – broken, blasted, beaten. And Michael feels that the shared consciousness of the room is understanding the wider truth: These bodies are representative of every other one out there. Beyond help. In the grip of inconceivable pain. Unable to be saved.

It's under this fog of despair that the old man convulses once, as if in slow motion, and belches out a gout of blood. His eyes open, and he squelches out a single new word.

"Need."

CHAPTER 22

It's that single word again – *need*.

It seems to clarify everything. It echoes what Michael himself heard at the hospital, in the midst of that prisoner's screams. Hearing it for the second time, he feels its significance like a blow to the solar plexus.

Whatever they're dealing with, it has the sweaty aura of desperation, and somehow that fills the survivors with a tentative hope. If what they're dealing with is essentially a despairing species, then might the upper hand belong to the survivors, no matter how outnumbered they are? It's probably flimsy reasoning, considering the hundreds of thousands – possibly millions – of possessed bodies out there, but it provides a spark of hope.

The body of the old man continues to writhe in misery, with increasing fervency as the pain medication wears off, and it continues to speak that single word, the sound of it warbling and trailing off. The eyes rolling, the body spasming, as if it is in the grip of the most delirious fever. Even after Bonnie administers another dose of morphine, and the body relaxes toward unconsciousness again, that word mumbles from its broken mouth.

"It's like an addict," she whispers.

Night falls before anyone realizes it, and by full dark, half the survivors have drifted to sleep among piles of fallen books, in the various anterooms of the library. Michael, still feeling that jarred-loose vulnerability in his skull, welcomes a sleep shift around 9 p.m., settling into a quiet nook near the Mystery section. He drifts away immediately but wakes in fits and starts through about four hours of slumber.

At one point, he wakes to the murmured sounds of lovemaking nearby, feels captivated by it, the fact of it happening in the middle of the apocalypse. He glances around a tower of paperback mysteries to see Mai moving her body rhythmically atop someone – he thinks it might be Liam – then leaves them to their privacy and falls away into unconsciousness again.

Before he knows it, Ron is shaking him gently awake. Michael checks his watch.

3:00 a.m.

He's gotten a total of nearly six hours, and although his eyes are gummy and gritty, and he feels as though he could sleep six more, he feels grateful for the lack of pain in his head. Even before his concussion, sleep has always been the most effective balm.

"Trade ya," Ron whispers.

"Sure."

And now Michael is at the library's front doors, one of three early-morning sentries positioned at the building's perimeter so that the rest of the survivors can get some much-needed sleep. Including Rachel. On his way toward his lookout point, he found his daughter curled up on a blanket with Kayla spooned against her, Rachel's arm thrown over the girl's midsection protectively. He stood there and watched them sleep for long moments, feeling something like sadness in the midst of hope.

Michael can see no movement outside except the slow wheel of stars, partially obscured by smoke from the foothills. With no electricity out there, the city is pitch black, save for the illumination from the heavens – the star field is unprecedentedly bright, especially to the southeast, where no smoke obscures it – and a quarter moon drifting across the southern hemisphere. He knows that to the west, the scene remains breathtaking: columns of fire and the atmospheric horror that seems to instruct whatever is happening to the bulk of humanity.

He's glad he's guarding the front doors instead of the delivery doors on the west side of the building. The relative peace is a relief – despite the fact that the blood-turned bodies are in the next room, occasionally groaning and sending chills down his spine. That room once held dutiful librarians quietly processing returned books, and now it holds this impossible deathscape.

Otherwise, Michael can hear very little sound. There's only the distant thrum of the generator on the roof, which is mainly powering the break-room refrigerator now, full of blood units and tranq canisters. All the canisters have been prepared with 1cc of O-negative blood each, with its attendant drops of Heparin. Joel made sure each survivor had a chance to check out the refrigerator and learn how to prepare and fire one of the six tranq rifles.

Joel also made everyone drank their share of water, and root out some kind of inor sustenance from the break-room cabinets, which were stocked here and there with an assortment of crackers and an occasional peanut butter jar, some cookies. Michael knows the food will, if necessary, last a couple days, but a trip to a local grocery store or at least the 7-11 will have to be on the horizon if they have any hope of surviving.

But those considerations will wait for another few hours. Michael's belly is reasonably satisfied, the early morning is quiet and black, and it's all he can do to keep from falling into unconsciousness again on this bench.

His thoughts keep veering into disconnected memory: the recent image of Rachel and Kayla overlaid with pictures of Cassie with a young Rachel curled in a motherly embrace ... an image of Susanna alive and resisting the thing that would inevitably overtake her, struggling in their bed while he was across town stealing more useless cash ... an image of Earth embattled and imprisoned ... and jagged imaginings of enraptured souls drifting skyward, red and gleaming.

He can't sleep. His body is practically buzzing. And yet his eyes keep gritting toward slumber, his mind pulling him down a dark hole, only to release him, then grab at him again.

"Hey," comes a whispered voice.

Michael starts violently, turns to see Bonnie approaching.

"Sorry," she says, placing a hand on his thigh as she sits next to him. "I know it's my turn to sleep, but it ain't happenin'. Thought I'd keep you company a bit."

He gives her a smile. "Til I bore you, anyway."

"Right, then I might just fall asleep against your shoulder."

He wipes at his eyes, gets some grit out of there. "How's it going with those two?"

Bonnie voices a weary sigh. She glances in the direction of the two men lying unconscious on the floor in the book-return area. Bonnie and Scott have been attending to them.

"Not good. I haven't been able to decrease the amount of morphine I'm treating them with, and I'm going to run out some time in the next week on just these two bodies. It's not sustainable." She shakes her head sadly. "The cure works, I mean Rachel nailed it and has every right to put all her hopes on it, but the internal problems are so severe." She releases a little whimper. "Dislocated shoulders and hips ... popped joints ... hyperextension ... broken jaws ... all the internal bleeding and the pain."

"Can't stop the bleeding, outside the hospital?"

"Exactly." She considers that. "And even if I *had* a working hospital at my disposal, I'm not sure I could even figure out what to do. There's probably some kind of heat probe that would fix them up, some kind of laser machine ... chemicals ... but let's face it, their entire digestive tracts are compromised." She shakes her head. "I don't know."

"Have they said anything else?"

"There are periods of lucidity just before I administer the injections, but they're in a lot of pain. Close to delirious. It's almost like ... like their consciousness is still gone, you know? Like whatever was inside them has left something there. The humanity might be back, but they still feel the impulse of whatever took them over."

"But what else have they said?"

"Not much, and it's really just the older man. I think ..." Her voice goes lower. "I think he actually said, 'Help'."

"Oh my god."

"Yeah, so there's that to deal with."

"What I keep thinking about is ... well, what's happening inside their heads?" He can't prevent a grimace from taking hold of his mouth. "Whatever inhabited their skulls – that light, that radiation – what effect is it having on the surrounding tissues?"

Bonnie is nodding sorrowfully.

"It obviously isn't catastrophic, or they'd die immediately after turning back. But it's got to have lingering effects. Right?"

"I've thought of that, too," Bonnie whispers. "You remember I was telling you about the motorcyclist back at the hospital? His head was broken open, and we could look directly at that thing. That ... sphere. It's not like I got too close to it, but I got the feeling, almost ... that it was protecting the tissues around it. Not damaging them, but using them. A kind of symbiosis, maybe."

She hasn't lifted her hand from his thigh, and Michael glances down at it. "Oh," she says, noticing his glance and removing her hand.

"No, that's okay."

She manages a smile and looks away.

Bonnie is obviously exhausted, and torn apart by grief and stress, but she reminds him of Cassie quite powerfully. It's not so much physical characteristics that remind him of his late wife – his *first* late wife, he reminds himself dismally – but the essence of her in this woman's expressions. The kindness, the earnestness. The comfortable, natural, lived-in beauty.

"Michael, will you do me a favor?"

"Sure."

"I know we're practically strangers, but I could really use a hug."

"Gladly," he replies, and turns in her direction, takes her into a tight embrace.

For long moments they clutch at each other, and in a moment Bonnie is weeping into his neck. There's a basic animalism to the embrace, all sweat and heat, and Michael loses himself in it. But beyond the physical, it has the effect of grounding him inside his head, of calming the chaos there, of bringing back to him something elemental that was lost since he woke. Humanity?

"I just … keep waiting for the next thing," she whispers in his ear. "The next ridiculous thing. The next attack. The next death."

"I know."

"Do you think we're going to be okay?"

Even though she's speaking almost directly into his ear, he can barely hear the words. He lets a few beats of silence hang there as he thinks of the best way to answer. Is she asking about the two of them personally, or humanity in general? And in either case, should he go for honesty or deflection or a kind lie? He goes for the latter.

"I do," he says.

She makes a grateful sound. "I hope so."

"All we can do is take it one moment at a time. We've made it this far."

"You're right."

She finally pulls away, and there's a moment when she's staring at him, inches from his face, and they nearly kiss, but the moment passes, and they separate.

"I'll try to get some sleep," she says. "Thanks Michael."

She disappears into the shadows, and Michael is left alone. He's not surprised to find that he is aroused. And wide awake now. He repositions himself and takes a long look outside, squinting to find any threats in the darkness. There's nothing.

For the next two hours, Michael strains his eyes mostly for naught, catching glimpses of only two bodies in the distance, dragging themselves south on uncooperative limbs. But he does see something else. To the southeast, in the approximate direction the bodies are heading, he thinks he sees a column of red luminescence drifting skyward. He can't be sure if it's a tangible thing or some kind of residual glow from what's happening to the west. He can see it best when he doesn't look directly at it but rather looks at it in his peripheral vision. He decides not to inform anyone about it, as it doesn't constitute any kind of threat.

Over the course of those two hours, he also hears several faraway explosions, and he wonders about their origins. Surely no aircraft can still be falling from the sky. These must be structure blasts in the spreading fires in the foothills.

Around 5:30 a.m., the sun peeks over the suburban horizon, backlighting everything in his line of vision, revealing a spare, quiet neighborhood, peaceful and yet full of foreboding.

Fifteen minutes later, Joel walks into the lobby.

"Yeah, I really stink now," he announces.

"I think we all do."

"Listen, Michael, I'm thinking I need to take the chance, get over to the precinct and grab some weapons."

Michael considers that. "You want to leave?"

Joel pauses. "Yes, going to the precinct would require leaving."

Michael swallows. "Sure it's safe?"

"Maybe as safe as it's gonna get. You proved yourself that those things don't really have eyes for us right now. Early morning, get in, get out, before those things even realize it."

"How far is that from here?"

"Other side of College, off Howes."

"Hmm," Michael says, "can I make a suggestion?"

"Of course."

"A shorter trip first. Test the waters. And at the same time, get something even more vital than weapons."

"You're talking about food. Where are you thinking?"

"The Safeway. See what we can forage."

"That's south. Right where they're headed."

"True. How about the Food Co-Op? Straight up Matthews, left on Mountain. All of a quarter mile from here. I used to go there all the time with Rachel, actually."

"Okay, fair enough. A quick trip. See how the land lays. And that's the right store. Especially since you know it so well. What do you say? Want to just get it done?"

Michael stares at him. "Now?"

"Let's go."

"We'll let everyone know, right? Arm up as well as we can?"

"Goes without saying."

Michael takes a breath. "Okay. Let's do it."

Joel looks contemplative. There are sounds of others stirring around the library, quiet voices coming from other areas. Michael stands up and stretches, yawns expansively, watching the policeman.

"Listen, Mike ..." Joel says, searching for words as he steps closer. "This situation ... I don't have to tell you things are out of control. It's basically been chaos for four straight days. Nothing has been predictable." He glances around, makes sure they're alone. "We're backed up against a wall here. I've just been counting everything off in my head, and it's not looking good. We are unarmed. *Un. Armed.* If we can get to the store successfully, then I might try to get to the precinct immediately and arm up, but that's thinking two steps ahead. I mean, these things are *aggressive*. And there are *thousands* of them. Hell, hundreds of thousands."

"What are you trying to say?"

"Christ, I don't know – maybe I just want to make sure you've got my back." He laughs mirthlessly. "I never had an assigned partner, well, except for when I was a rookie. I just had a one-man car for street duty, but I never really needed a partner, right? I mean, it's Fort Collins. Nothing ever happens here. But … the fucking apocalypse? That's a different matter."

"I guess it is."

"So can I count on you?"

"I'm your man. I mean, I'm also watching Rachel's back. My little girl. But I'll do what I can."

"All right, let's get this thing going."

Within twenty minutes, the entire crew is assembled in the lobby, and their collective reaction to Joel's idea is a study in conflict. It's undeniably true that the level of hunger among the survivors is tilting toward a crisis point. For days, most of them have failed to consume decent food – most recently, they've persisted on pilfered crackers, spoons of peanut butter, half-consumed Pringles cans, the occasionally discovered apple, and quickly spoiling hospital food.

During the conversation in the lobby, Michael comes to the realization that he didn't eat anything at all yesterday. He chooses not to share that fact with anyone, least of all Rachel or Bonnie, who would definitely get on his case about the oversight. The upshot is that there's a noticeable decrease in the level of energy among them, and that's unsustainable.

However …

"Daddy, you can't go out there!" Rachel already has tears in her eyes.

"It's too dangerous, isn't it?" Bonnie puts in, glancing around. "Right?"

"That's the thing – I don't think it is," Joel says. "Not at the moment."

"Um, did you see what happened yesterday, when he went out there?" Rachel asks. "That thing was *barking* at him."

"It wouldn't have been if I hadn't stumbled right into it, like a moron."

"That's right," Joel says. "These things are programmed now to just drift south. They're going somewhere, and it ain't here."

"But that could change at any moment, couldn't it?" Rachel asks. "In an instant!"

"She's right," Ron offers. "From what we've seen, their instincts – for lack of a better word – can change at any moment, determined by that sound we've all heard more than once."

"We go in quick and fast, armed with tranq guns and water rifles," Joel counts off with his fingers, "barricade ourselves inside, leave the Hummer idling. In and out within five minutes, fill bags with food and first aid, whatever else. Back here within twenty minutes."

"And if those things suddenly turn on you?" Rachel asks, near hysteria.

"The moment we hear that noise, we sprint back."

Rachel is shaking her head worriedly, and Michael notices Kayla comforting her, placing a hand on her shoulder. He finds the gesture deeply affecting, and he can't take his eyes off it. It's a small movement, but it speaks emotional volumes. He contrasts the moment with what he knows he's about to do – the danger he knows he'll face – and it brings him an unexpected sense of calm.

"Well, I'm all for it," Kevin says. "I could use a goddamn Ding Dong."

"Don't think it's that kind of store," Joel says, "but we'll do our best."

"You want company?"

"I think Michael and I can handle it. Easy in, easy out. I want a full crew barricaded here in case something happens."

Bonnie is reluctant about the whole endeavor, but she ends up taking tallies of anyone who might need medicine or supplements, in addition to a first-aid list that she scribbles out for general purpose. Soon, most of the survivors are knotted around Joel and Michael, adding their needs to the community list until the idiosyncratic requests become too much to bear.

"Whoa, whoa, people," Joel says, "all I can promise is that we'll focus on protein and try to find all the fresh food that's still viable, okay? We gotta be smart."

"And we gotta get moving," Michael adds. "I want to get this done."

At that moment, he catches Rachel's eye. At the edge of the group with Kayla, she's watching him sadly. He gives her a wink, trying to effect an unworried air, but he's pretty sure he has failed at that.

By 6:30 a.m., they're armed and at the front doors, poised to break for the Hummer. Joel has the weapons – two tranq rifles and a single Super Soaker filled with O-negative – slung over his shoulder, and Michael has the vehicle's key in his fist. Not a single body has been spotted in the vicinity of the library in the past hour. In fact, nothing of any consequence has been seen for perhaps seven hours.

"Clear?" Joel calls behind him.

Mai's voice comes from the north side of the library. "All clear!"

Jason Bovberg

"Scott?" Joel yells after a moment.

"I don't see anything!" Scott says from the south.

"Ready?" Joel whispers to Michael.

"As I'll ever be."

Michael takes a last look behind him at the clutch of survivors who are watching them, nods, then pushes his way outside. Joel falls into step right behind him. As they make directly for the Hummer, a thin layer of ash breaks from Michael's footfalls in rhythmic drifts. He wonders – in a sickening moment of clarity – whether there are human remains in there. He's sure there are.

The morning is comparatively cool, but the sun already has a thin hardness, streaming through the high smoke. He reaches the vehicle and pulls the front door open, climbs up. In a few seconds, Joel is seated next to him, the tranq rifles secured at his feet and the Super Soaker cradled in his arms.

"Let's do it," he says. "Still clear."

The Hummer rumbles to life, and he shivers violently for a split-second. He's looking in all directions, anticipating a rush of bodies from all corners. The demise of young Danny, through the window directly behind him, is far too fresh. The shattered remains of that safety window are still scattered across the back seat. But the entire area surrounding the library is deserted now.

Michael maneuvers the Hummer to the street. In a few moments, they're out of sight of the library's front entrance, moving toward Matthews, and their collective breath is taken away by the sight on the western horizon – a view unattainable from inside the library.

The burning continues unabated and appears to be at the edge of the city limits, at the foot of Horsetooth Reservoir. Michael wonders seriously now if a fire like that could actually jump into town and begin crawling through subdivisions. Depends on the wind, he guesses, and thankfully there's none of that. But the fire is the less remarkable phenomenon. All along the Front Range, wide columns of throbbing luminescence reach from the ground into the sky, and beyond. The crimson light is clear even in the bright of day.

"Fuck me," Joel whispers.

"Yeah. It's stronger. It's everywhere."

Michael watches the columns, horrified but curious. It's as if light is stabbing through the smoke – well, not light, but a physical manifestation of light: solid things in the midst of the ephemeral smoke. They don't look like anything he's ever seen in his previous life.

"What the hell is it, man?" Joel says, voicing Michael's own confusion. "What are they doing?"

Michael can only shake his head. He tears his gaze from the skies and makes the turn onto Matthews.

"Hate to think of what happened to those damn Thompsons," Joel breathes.

"Those are the brothers? The hunters?"

"Right – up there in the foothills, last I talked to them. Couple of assholes armed to the teeth, even before this fucking thing happened. They probably started most of those fires. And believe it or not, they're on our side."

Matthews is deserted. There's still white, smoldering smoke coming from College, but no active flames. Joel watches the area with regret slashed across his features.

"Goddamn jet crash," he mumbles.

"No kidding? My god. Right into Old Town?"

"A FedEx cargo plane. Took out a few blocks before we commandeered a firetruck from the station on Remington. I only knew some basics, but we got the water flowing." He sighs. "Where it all started for me."

"Yeah?"

"Met your daughter right over there."

Eyes darting left and right for any sign of danger, Joel tells Michael his story: from when the world stopped in the middle of his early-morning shift, through the crash of the cargo jet and the fruitless attempts to save the businesses there, to the hospital, where it seemed they'd make their final stand – only to discover that nothing was as it seemed. The bodies wanted something very different than human flesh.

"We thought they were zombies, you know, like in the movies – fuckin' zombies, man. It's like, that's what we were programmed to expect, somehow, by TV shows, movies. Hell, I've even read a few zombie books in my time, although I'm more of a sci-fi guy. I don't know, maybe *anyone* who saw those bodies twitching back to life would jump straight to 'Braaaaains.'"

Halfway up Matthews, on the east side of the street, they come upon a VW bus. A body is trapped inside it.

"Look, look," Michael whispers, slowing the Hummer.

He and Joel watch it curiously. The vast majority of the bodies that were stricken in their vehicles or in their bedrooms were able to maneuver themselves out of those spaces, to somehow manipulate door handles and escape. To disengage from seatbelts, even. But this one, for whatever reason, never did.

Its limbs claw at the driver's side window, feebly, and it's clear to Michael that it has very little energy left. It's gaunt, and its features are slack, expressionless. The body is that of an older woman, long gray hair like a crooked curtain, mouth open and dry, cheeks hollow and sunken.

"Why's it stuck?" Joel asks.

"That's what I was wondering." Michael watches, feeling a combination of resentment and pity. "Maybe its foot is caught ... maybe the door is stuck. Hell if I know."

It barely acknowledges them as they slowly pass, staring momentarily with its dead, flat eyes.

"Gives me the friggin' creeps."

CHAPTER 23

Michael makes the turn onto Mountain Avenue, and the two men hold their breath, not sure what to expect along this major downtown artery. There's no movement, only abandoned vehicles and an unnatural silence under the light of the new day. Smoke drifts from the storefronts directly to the west, heaviest midway up the block to the northwest, in the separate block of buildings where the FedEx jet crashed.

The Fort Collins Co-Op, unassuming with its quaint and colorful storefront shade, appears on the right, and Michael pulls up and shuts off the engine. Fortunately, this section of Old Town has been spared, although just a block away the facades of businesses are crumpled and black.

They sit in their seats, in breathless silence, listening. Ahead of them, reaching into the sky, the red luminescence throbs. White smoke drifts northeast. Ash continues to drift like light snow, some of it touching the window with an audible click. At least twenty cars and trucks in the near distance sit abandoned in the street, most of them jammed against the gutters. One of them is wedged straight into the Coopersmith's dining patio.

"Too quiet," Michael says.

"Let's do it, huh, before it's not so quiet anymore?" Joel takes a Super Soaker in his grip and slings one of the tranq rifles over his shoulder. "I'm leaving the other rifle here. You're gonna be the primary shopper, okay? We get in there, you grab some bags or boxes and we'll both start filling 'em up, but I'm also gonna be on lookout. I got your back. Clear?"

"Yep."

They open their doors simultaneously and hop to the ground. Michael lets Joel take care of all surveillance and goes straight for the glass doors. Expecting to push right through, he finds them locked.

"Shit."

"Great. Okay, let's break the glass."

"You sure?"

"Do it."

"With what?" Michael searches the area for something heavy, a rock or a piece of metal – there's nothing in the immediate vicinity.

"Use your heel."

Michael looks around superfluously, guiltily, feeling like some vandalizing asshole, and backs up against the door. He kicks backward with the heel of his shoe, but the rubber just bounces off. He tries again, much harder – nothing.

"Oh Jesus," Joel says, backing against the other door.

He gives it a good whack with the heel of his boot, and the glass shatters clangingly, falling to the ground in great shards and fragmenting. The shrill echo seems to blast across all of northern Fort Collins.

"Go, go!"

Michael ducks through the broken door, watching for any dangerous hanging glass, and enters the dimly lit store. It's cool inside but smells vaguely sour. In another day or two, it will smell like full-on rot. He peers down the length of the three aisles, seeing nothing but cold shadows. He hears nothing. He goes straight for the counter and grabs a small pile of paper bags with sturdy handles, calls out to Joel that he's ready to start loading up. Joel ducks through the door, keeps an eye on the street.

"Are we clear in here?"

"No movement."

Satisfied, the cop hurries to the counter and grabs his own bag, both weapons slung over his shoulder.

The store is almost ludicrously small, a local grocery specializing in herbal supplements and remedies, all-natural fare, but it has most of what they'll need, and the size will spare them from running the lengths of long aisles at a supermarket. Michael goes straight for the tiny produce area on the left. It has been five days since the electricity failed, and most of the items look wilted and on their way to spoilage, but Michael fills two entire bags with apples, oranges, peppers, bananas, berries, peaches, melons, and whatever else looks edible. The bags fill quickly, and he hustles back to the counter with the heavy bags, grabs two more empties.

The store is small enough that it's lit by ambient window light better than a supermarket would be, but still, the aisles toward the back, in particular, are cloaked in darkness and shadow. Michael glances back there again and feels a small spurt of fear in his chest.

Beyond the produce, Michael starts shoveling cheeses and some select precooked meats into the next bag, then he turns around to more shelves and finds crackers and some cookies. He knows the store almost intimately, having shopped here for years with both wives and Rachel. He even remembers the clerks cooing over Rachel when she was a baby. Now he's essentially stealing from the shelves, and no one left in the world would care.

Michael notices Joel dropping items into a bag closer to the front of the store.

"You find the first-aid stuff? It's next to the – "

"Just found it," Joel says. "Vitamins … bandages … pain stuff."

"Grab any ointments you can – "

Something clanks in the rear of the store, and both men freeze. Joel drops his bag to the floor, grips and aims his Super Soaker. Then with his left hand he grabs at the flashlight in his belt, frees it, and directs a cone of light in the direction of the noise. Michael watches the shadows jerk around. There's nothing back there.

A few minutes pass.

Finally a great shudder sounds outside, rattling the windows, followed by a booming crash that Michael feels in his ribcage.

"Aw shit!" Joel yells, running for the front door. He expertly raises the Super Soaker while holstering the flashlight.

Michael's heart is in his throat.

Joel darts his gaze west toward College.

"Nothing … nothing," he's breathing. "Wait, wait, here we go!"

"What?!"

"Something collapsed." The cop hurries back toward Michael.

A cloud of smoke and ash rushes past the front windows then, some of it wafting through the shattered door. It sounds like a patter of dry rain. Michael experiences a dark rush of September 11 memories as the debris casts the entire store in further darkness.

"I think it was the restaurant on the corner, where BeauJo's used to be," Joel says. "That building. The FedEx plane might've clipped it. It's probably been smoldering all this time."

"We gotta get out of here, right? Like, now?"

"I still don't see any bodies. Let's just get what we need."

Joel hurries back, slinging the Super Soaker and getting busy with his bags.

"Got bread," he shouts, hacking out a cough as the debris begins to fill the store. "Okay, you're right, we gotta split. Wrap it up and let's go."

"Just want to get some liquid." Michael jogs to the cooler on the east side of the store and fills a new bag with water bottles and cans of soda and juice. The smoke and ash reach him, acrid and thick, and he sneezes violently several times, each one turning into a cough. "Damn!"

Joel, just to his left, is checking the final shelves, swiping items into his open bag, moving down the aisle.

A bright green door, just beyond the baked goods, leads into a store room or office, perhaps. Michael spots it just as Joel turns toward it. The cop reaches for the knob, twists it but finds the door stuck in the jamb. He yanks hard, and it flies open.

"Hey!" the cop blurts.

A possessed body flings itself out of the small room, crumpling Joel to the vinyl-tiled floor. It's a young woman, not much older than Rachel, her casual work outfit torn at the seams, and there's a nametag on her breast, partially loosened from its blue fabric mooring. Joel kicks at the body randomly, viciously, a string of curses flowing from his mouth. His bags of groceries go crashing across the floor, and he reaches for his weapons, but he can't find leverage. The thing on top of him has little strength – it has that same look on its upturned face as the thing in the VW bus, perhaps because it hasn't eaten, but it still manages to lunge its head at Joel's body, attempting to inflict harm.

Michael throws himself at the body and shoves it off Joel, sending it colliding with shelves full of health products.

"Why'd you open that door?!"

Joel grunts and swivels on the floor, getting a handle on the tranq rifle, as the body moves almost lethargically back at him. The slow movements give Joel time to right the rifle and send a tranq dart into the body's exposed flank with a solid *thunk.*

The woman twists and trips, and begins gasping. Her eyes are blinking spastically, her mouth contorting. In the small confines of the store, the sound is ghastly. Joel scrambles backward, away from her, and Michael helps him up.

The debris and ash are clearing at the door, but the two men continue to cough as they breathe heavily. Michael hears a cough from the woman, too, hacking, and then morphing into a helpless scream of what sounds like pain.

"Nooo-ooo! Noo! Neeeeee – "

Joel is venturing back, collecting the items on the floor back into their bag. "Let's go, for Chrissakes."

Michael steps backward, watching the body as it thumps onto its back, no longer arcing backward. It twists and writhes, one shoulder obviously dislocated.

"Huuuuuurts!"

Joel clambers past him. "Come on!" He stops at the door and searches the street.

"We're just gonna leave her?"

"Damn right."

Michael turns for the groceries on the counter. He gathers all six bags by the handles and goes for the door. He keeps casting glances at the woman, who is still twisting and screaming on the floor. Her foot catches some boxed merchandise on the shelf, knocking a stack to the floor.

It's at that moment that he recognizes her. Her name is Felicia. She has probably helped Michael with his groceries a dozen times, joked with him and Rachel. Perhaps even with Susanna. However casual, he has a history with this poor woman. He's not sure if it's the lingering effects of the concussion or just the stress of the situation, but the memories come sluggishly: bits of conversation, her demeanor at checkout, her genuine smile at seeing him and his family, occasional shared pieces of her personal life. Something about school. Some kinship with Rachel that they exchanged words about. Changing majors. From English to business, wasn't it? She wanted to own a store like this.

Joel ducks out into the street with his bags, hurrying to the passenger side and tossing everything in. Michael, casting glances back at Felicia, is right behind him, curling around to the driver's side, stepping up onto the running board, and dropping his bags through the broken rear window, onto the floorboards. His lips curl at the dried blood on the jagged glass.

Joel is climbing in when Michael pauses, looking east and west on Mountain. There are no bodies on the street, just the still-diminishing cloud of dust at College, where that entire corner seems to have exploded. It's like a war zone.

Michael can hear Felicia crying in distress inside the store.

"We have to bring her back," he says.

Joel glares at him.

Michael doesn't wait. "I know her, I can't leave her." He breaks for the store again. He takes a moment to kick out a couple of larger shards of glass from the broken door, to give him room to carry her out. Then he's through and going for the woman.

Her eyes lock on him. She's still blinking exaggeratedly, as if trying desperately to focus.

"Helllppp!!" she cries.

Felicia's body reminds him only marginally of the bodies outside the library. Without the damage to the mouth, and therefore the throat and stomach, she seems simply human ... not as grossly injured, and probably a more likely candidate for turning back. She has a pretty face – wide-set eyes and a pert nose, a mouth that he remembers as happy. Short blond hair.

He takes hold of her flailing arms and begins to pull her toward the entrance, trying his best to ignore her wails. She's trying to make words, but the pain makes her incomprehensible. Michael wishes she'd just fall unconscious.

"All right, all right!" Joel shouts behind him, coughing. He comes around to her feet, takes them up. "Christ, you and your daughter, man! Cut from the same cloth!"

"Actually, I think I got it from her."

The woman is beside herself with pain, her eyes bugged, turned up in their sockets, the jaw locked open and soundless now. The body is rigid. Michael and Joel carry her through the door and toward the Hummer. The street remains deserted.

"Let's get her up into the back," Michael says.

"Yep."

The body writhes once, fish-like, in their grasp, the sweaty skin difficult to hold on to. Felicia finds her voice and brays a hitching, incoherent gasp. Finally, the two men settle the body onto the rear seats and close the doors. Michael bends over, planting his hands on his knees, and coughs smoky phlegm for twenty seconds while Joel scans the street. The woman continues to screech, threatening to reignite the pain of Michael's concussion.

"You all right?" he asks when Michael goes quiet.

"Yeah, let's move."

The return to the library is uneventful. The woman in the VW bus is still weakly batting at the window, but otherwise they encounter no bodies. Michael is convinced that even if they had, the things wouldn't have been aggressive. Felicia in the grocery office merely wanted out – perhaps at this point her body was desperate for any kind of sustenance, as it hadn't consumed anything in days. Michael wonders fleetingly how long a human body might persist under possession without nourishment from food and water – or trees. Either way, Felicia merely wanted to escape after days of captivity, and search out whatever the thing inside needed for the body to remain workable. Joel and Michael were just in the way. It reminds him of what Rachel and Bonnie told him of their stand at the hospital – how the reanimated bodies simply leapt past them, out into the night.

They didn't expect any survivors.

This thought fires through his damaged synapses, and Michael ponders it as he steers the Hummer onto the library lawn and drives toward the front entrance. Joel hangs on in the passenger seat, his weapons between his knees. The Hummer is filled with Felicia's anguished gasping.

If this whole thing actually has an otherworldly source – if, to put it bluntly, this is an alien attack – and it was a partial failure because it didn't affect every living soul ... in fact, left five or six percent of the population alive ... then that *must* give the survivors some kind of opening. An opportunity to exploit a vulnerability. And perhaps they're already seeing that play out. Does the fact that all those bodies have suddenly disappeared mean that the things possessing them recognize a weakness? That they understand that the survivors have found a way to hurt them, even turn them back? Are they afraid?

Michael comes to a bouncing stop near the doors, and the men climb down out of the huge vehicle. The faces at the front doors appear celebratory, but Michael can't hear what they're saying. He surveys the empty land around the library, in all directions, and finds nothing. He beckons someone to join them and help with the groceries ... and the body.

Ron, Kevin, Rachel, and the twins burst out the doors, and Rachel crashes into her father, embracing him tightly.

"We heard some kind of explosion up that way," she says. "Thought you were done for."

"Still alive," he says. "I keep dodging bullets, huh? We have a passenger. Where's Bonnie?"

"She's with the – "

"Bonnie!"

In his peripheral vision, Michael sees Kevin and the twins already taking bags of food from the Hummer's rear seats, but he goes to the door on the opposite side of the vehicle, where Joel and Ron are about to maneuver out Felicia. The young woman has fallen mercifully unconscious, and Michael only hopes she's still alive.

Bonnie appears at the doors.

"Prep a morphine shot!"

"Okay," she answers, "what did you find?"

"Someone at the store – go ahead and get that shot going."

"Right." Bonnie jogs back.

"Ready?" he says.

Joel has his finger at the woman's carotid artery. "She's alive," he mutters, reading Michael's mind. "Probably dehydrated and starving ... multiple dislocations ... other internal traumas we have no idea about ... you know, the usual! But hey, at least she wasn't chewing on trees!"

There's a tinge of worry beneath the sarcasm – the notion that the only hope these turned human beings have of survival is if they haven't been doing exactly what they've been somehow programmed to do. If they've had the bizarre luck to be stuck in a storeroom or trapped in a car. And what are the survivors supposed to do? Search the city for such oddities? All the while assuming they're safe from the other bodies that might at any moment turn aggressive again?

As the men hurry Felicia inside to Bonnie's care, those thoughts are underscored by the discovery that the young Broncos fan has died of his internal injuries. His corpse is in the corner, covered by flattened cardboard boxes.

"He had a pulse this morning, but then ... nothing," Chrissy says. "The old man hasn't really improved either."

Mai pokes her head into the room. "We need to get that body out of here."

Scott pipes in behind her, "What if those things come looking for these bodies? You guys keep bringing them in!"

"Bill and Brian offered to wrap him up and take him out the back entrance to some shade there," Chrissy says, ignoring Scott. "On the northeast side there. They're looking for bags."

Bonnie is examining Felicia and administering the morphine.

"We don't have much of this left!" She takes advantage of the woman's unconsciousness to have Ron and Joel help her pop her left shoulder and hip, right knee, three fingers, and jaw back into place.

"No wonder she was in pain," Joel says.

"So lucky to be trapped in there," Bonnie says. "No injury to the digestive system, obviously, but also no injury to the mouth and teeth, and no scrapes and cuts from running around out there."

Rachel is staring at the woman, who now looks practically peaceful. "Dad, we know her, right?"

Michael nods thoughtfully.

"Felicia," Rachel whispers, seeing the nametag. "Oh my God, I remember her. I talked to her about her classes."

"How we doin' out there, Liam?" Joel calls.

Liam is poised at the front doors, twenty yards away. "Nothing, no change."

Joel claps Michael back. "Gotta say that went pretty well."

"Did you see any – " Kevin starts.

"Just her," Michael says, "and one other, trapped in a car. Nothing aggressive."

"So where the hell are the rest? Where'd they go?"

No one has an answer to that question.

Bonnie says, "Okay, she'll be out for a while. But she looks good.

Cross your fingers, but she might be our best bet for bringing someone back. Better than that poor man."

The group stands indecisive for a moment, then files out.

Chrissy and the twins have taken to laying out the food atop a large table at the edge of the lobby, categorizing and itemizing it. Scott is there, too, and he's the first to speak.

"The cop is back in my good graces. He brought soda."

"You guys did good," Chrissy says. "Lots of good protein and some fun stuff, too. Thank you."

Joel appears frustrated, watching everyone standing around. Michael already knows that the cop is a no-nonsense leader, but he's also gathering that Joel has no patience for inaction. Even immediately after completing a risky trip, he's obviously thinking about the next move – and exasperated that not everybody else is thinking that way.

"God dammit, I wish I had a radio." He's pacing. "We need to know what's going on. Whether those things are gathering somewhere, or if they're up to something new and we're hiding in here while they couldn't care less. We should be talking with those damn brothers. The Thompsons. I betcha anything they know what's going down. I mean what if we're strongholding here, putting up a defense for no reason?"

"Better safe than sorry, right?" Scott says, twisting open a soda bottle. "Are you really suggesting that we not protect ourselves?"

"Hey," Chloe says, "we should be rationing this stuff, shouldn't we?"

"She's right," Kevin says.

"There's plenty," Scott says, tilting up the bottle for a long pull.

"Chloe," Joel says, offhanded, "you're in charge of rationing. Can you put together a schedule with portion control and all that? Assume we're gonna be here a few days, at least."

"Um ... sure."

Kevin shakes his shaggy head, watching Scott finish off his soda. "Anyway, Joel, who says those brothers are still alive?"

"They're alive. Those guys are survivors."

"They're up in the foothills, surrounded by those things. They were right up there in the thick of it, when the bodies became aggressive. Hell, man, you saw what happened to that kid, that Danny, out on the street – and he was protected by the equivalent of an armored truck."

"Well," says Michael, still standing with Rachel, watching Felicia through the open door of the book-return area, "do you think we're safe enough to go get a radio? And weapons? How far is the precinct?"

"Farther than the store."

Bonnie speaks up. "If we're just making trips willy nilly now, we really ought to be getting supplies from the hospital."

"We're not making trips 'willy nilly,' Bonnie," Joel responds, perturbed.

"You realize," Scott says, "that this is exactly the conversation those little green men *hope* we're having in here."

"What are you talking about?" Rachel says, exasperation in her voice.

"Okay, if it's true that those things can sense what we're up to – like you said earlier – then don't you think they might just be waiting for us to lower our defenses? They're just itching for us to fuck ourselves over. Hell, maybe you've unknowingly brought in a couple of spies there." Pointing at Felicia and the old man, who is on the verge of expiring.

"Plus," Mai puts in, "we're not the only survivors, you know. We've all seen others out there. There are probably a bunch of other groups just like us, doing what we're doing. Maybe they're the ones getting attacked."

"And next time is our turn," Scott finishes.

This is met with silence.

"Since when did Scott start making sense?" Kevin says.

Rachel looks at Scott with an expression that isn't quite as exasperated as before. "I think he's been working through some things."

"I'm hungry," Scott says, ignoring their comments. "Chloe, what can I eat?"

"Yeah, let's eat." Joel takes a deep breath, stops pacing. "I think we'll all feel better after we get some food in us."

Michael watches from a distance as the survivors descend on the table, already deferring to Chloe, who has found some paper and a pencil and is marking down items on-the-fly. Zoe and Chrissy, under Chloe's direction, use knives found in the library break room to divvy up the larger foods.

"You got beef jerky?" Bill asks Michael as he approaches the table. "I love you, man."

"Okay, I'm taking on the role of den mother," Bonnie says, and in her expression is the relief of being able to talk easily. "Balanced meals for all. Everybody get your protein along with the carbs."

Rachel leaves Michael's side and joins Bonnie at the edge of the table. After looking over all the food, she tosses her dad a grateful smile. Then she takes half an apple from Chloe, savors it.

In a moment, there's actually laughter coming from the general area, and the sound of it fills Michael with uneasiness. This light moment doesn't feel right. Not yet. He can see it in Joel's face too; the cop has also kept his distance.

Someone takes his hand, halting his thoughts. It's Kayla, looking up at him. She's chewing something.

"Thank you for going to get the food," she says. "You should have some."

And Michael's misgivings soften under a flood of warmth. He kneels in front of her and embraces her.

"You're more than welcome. I'm just glad you're okay."

After a while, she leads him to the food, after everyone else has moved away into small groups. Rachel joins them, as does Bonnie, and the four of them feel the healing energy of nourishment in their bellies.

CHAPTER 24

The rest of the day finds a strange indecision settling over the survivors. A feeling of safety behind barricaded walls, freshly satisfied hunger, an aura of restfulness following the first real sleep that the group has enjoyed in days – it all adds up to a general sense of health but a nagging feeling that they could be doing more. That they *should* be doing more. That, essentially, they're spinning their wheels.

Despite all that, the entire group convinces Joel to put off an immediate trip to the precinct, which is significantly farther away than the store. There's still plenty to do in their effort to barricade this place, and one more day might bring more information.

Joel agrees with only some reluctance, but a few times during the afternoon, Michael spots the cop gazing out on the empty world with jaw-clenched anxiety.

A few feet away from Felicia, Bonnie has created a station where she collects blood from the survivors, storing it in the small refrigerator there. Every once in a while, Bonnie calls out a name, and that person responds dutifully, rolling up his or her sleeve. This goes on for a few hours in the afternoon, giving a certain rhythm to the uneasy day. In the middle of it all, the old man finally passes, never having regained consciousness.

Later, Michael looks out on a quiet, motionless night for the second time. He can't argue with Joel – or his own feeling that something vital is happening beyond this library. Something that they should be paying attention to. Somehow.

The homes along Peterson are all lightless, seemingly dead in their lots – brick-and-mortar corpses in the center of well-tended landscapes. The lawns haven't even had time to overgrow, although some are starting to brown under the heat. Lifelessness pervades, and yet the fingerprint of humanity remains vivid on everything. Michael wonders what this street will look like next month. Next year.

What will Fort Collins look like in ten years?

He glances up at the sky, sees the same vague ribbons of light coming from the southeast, sees the haze of smoke drifting under starlight. Nothing new.

If the people gathered here can get beyond this, a whole new life awaits them, he knows. A survivalist's life. He's not well-versed in such things, always preferred the creature comforts of modern technology to the rugged outdoors. And yet his thoughts flit toward the first thoughts of a new, makeshift family ... Bonnie and Kayla, fellow survivors he has known for mere days and hours, are a part of this flashing foreshadow – even Joel, a brother he never had, and Scott, the asshole cousin. He frowns, feeling grief and bewilderment but also an anticipatory comfort at the thought. A new beginning, in some sense.

It's too soon to be thinking this way, isn't it? Why are these thoughts even occurring to him?

Ah, Suze. He bows his head. *I wasn't there. I should've been there.*

It's nearly 4 a.m. when Michael hears a small cry from the book-return area where Felicia is recovering. Bonnie has charged him with administering pain medication in the event Felicia requires it – preferably in pill form if she wakes with manageable pain. Thanks to Joel's efforts at the Co-Op, they now have several boxes of ibuprofen.

He scans the lawn and street one more time, then moves silently into the book-return room, where he sees Felicia moving sluggishly on her crude pad assembled from cardboard boxes. She's in the center of the room, possibly exactly where Kayla slept when she was all alone here.

Felicia's eyes are open and appear to register confusion. Her head moves back and forth, taking in the foreign surroundings. As he gets closer, he can see tears leaking down the sides of her face. She's uttering a stream of whimpers, even though she's obviously still somewhat lulled by morphine. Her expression is a mask of dull fright.

"You're okay," he whispers, coming to her.

Her head lolls in his direction.

"I'm Michael," he says softly.

"I ... I ..." she manages, and confusion clouds her expression again. "Who ...?

"Are you in pain?"

She nods, trying to form words.

"Can you swallow a pill?"

Another nod, and another whimper.

"Wait here."

Michael takes a moment to check the front door again, survey the area, then he goes for a cup of water and six ibuprofen capsules. He carefully helps the young woman down all six pills. She even reaches up weakly with one shaking arm – an arm that had to be roughly twisted back into its socket following its dislocation – to help guide the cup. Quiet sobs of pain issue helplessly from her throat.

"Let me know if that doesn't help."

"Huuuurts." She cringes. "F – feels wr – wro – wrong."

Michael is stunned to hear so many full words come out of her.

"What feels wrong?"

She brings up a wobbly hand and touches her head, grits her teeth.

"You've been through a lot," he says. "Just keep as still as you can, let yourself heal."

She gives him a long, wet look. "Wh ... what h – h – h – "

"Uh," he says, quieting her and trying to determine the best way to answer her inevitable question. He decides not to upset her further – yet. "You've had an accident."

She struggles with something. Her mouth moves, but no sound comes out.

"Do you need morphine?" he asks, knowing that Bonnie has already warned him not to use any, if at all possible.

She frowns, shakes her head sluggishly but reluctantly, as if drifting toward unconsciousness but needing to say something crucial. She looks at him very seriously.

"What is it?" he whispers.

"They – they – they – " She shows frustration, and her mouth moves in fits and starts, painfully. "They c – c ..."

The room feels abruptly very small, claustrophobic, and Michael can smell Felicia's sweat. She's dripping with perspiration, not just from the humidity of the room but from her internal struggle. He wipes at her brow with a towel.

"They ..." Michael urges.

Felicia closes her eyes, concentrating.

"C – c – c – c – "

She's struggling mightily with her speech, and Michael leans toward her, lifting a hand as if to coax the word out of her.

"They ..." he repeats. "They what?"

Her eyes begin to unfocus.

"No, no!" he pleads.

And then she's out.

"Damn it!" he hisses.

He checks her pulse, and finds it strong. She has a low-grade fever

– to be expected. He sets her head gently to the floor and studies her face. She's still wearing makeup that she probably applied the morning of her shift at the Co-Op. Her life before this moment means very little anymore, but he's proud that he's been able to return it to her, for whatever that's worth.

What was she trying to say?

"Everything okay?"

Michael jumps a little.

Bonnie is leaning against the doorjamb, watching him. She's sleepy-eyed and drawn.

"She was awake. Talking." He stands, frowning, keeping his eyes on Felicia. "She tried to tell me something. And I think it was important."

"What did she say?"

"She's scared. Doesn't know where she is. And I think … I think she wanted to talk about 'them'."

"Them?"

"I mean, she called something 'they.' Like she was talking about those things … whatever was inside her."

Bonnie watches her. "But she fell asleep again?"

"Yeah."

Bonnie approaches Felicia and kneels. She touches the young woman's flesh, gauges the temperature, checks her pulse and her pupillary response.

"A lot of moisture coming from her eyes," she says, concerned. "I'll give her a small dose of morphine in case that's pain. We're running on morphine fumes, though."

She sets to work, and Michael excuses himself to the front doors, where he scans the area almost superfluously. There's no activity at all.

After a while, Bonnie joins him at the doors, yawning and stretching, and Michael studies her.

"Couldn't sleep, huh?"

"I've never been a great sleeper," she says. "And now? Forget it."

"Still …"

"Can I get you anything?" she asks, ever the caregiver. "Water?"

He shows her the bottle he's been nursing. "I'm okay."

She pulls up a folding chair and sits right next to him, looking out onto the early morning. She takes a deep breath, lets it out slowly.

"Not much to look at," she whispers.

"I know, it's so … so blank. And yet so menacing."

A pause.

"I can see now where Rachel gets her bravery."

"What do you mean?"

"The way you ran out to help those men earlier ... the trip to the store ..."

Michael stays quiet, acknowledging her words with just a small smile.

"Listen, Michael, I'm sorry about your wife. And I'm sorry I'm only saying that now. It's just – I don't know. It's so difficult."

He shakes his head, formulating a response, and emotion surges up, startling him. He finds he can't speak for a moment. He feels Bonnie's arm at his shoulder, and he nods gratefully.

After a few silent minutes, he composes himself.

"Did you lose someone?" he asks.

She only nods.

"Do you want to talk about it?"

"Mmm, not really."

"Okay."

"I mean, yes, eventually I'll need to talk about it, but I feel like I can't yet. It's all so surreal. You know. I can't process it." She smiles humorlessly. "I feel like I've been crying about everything *except* that."

"I haven't had a chance to thank you for taking care of me, back there at the hospital. I probably owe you more than I realize."

"You don't owe me anything, Michael."

"Except maybe my life."

"No, *that* you owe to your daughter." This time, her smile is genuine. "You would probably have woken up in that building, disoriented. Confused. Walked out onto the streets, wobbly, dizzy. Crying for help." She's teasing him now. "And sooner or later, you would have fallen in with the wrong crowd. I'm sure of it."

There's a long moment of silence while they watch dawn gradually paint the horizon with the first hints of tarnished gold.

"She really did save me," Michael breathes. "And I think you did, too."

She accepts the compliment wordlessly and just sits with him. After a while, her head leans toward his shoulder, and he accepts the weight of it. It's not long before she's breathing in deep, even breaths, and he's afraid to move a muscle, just wanting her to sleep.

CHAPTER 25

"So ... any thoughts?" Joel stares down at the unconscious Felicia. "They *can't?* They *come* ... they *could* ... it could be anything ..."

"That's all she said. So far anyway. *'They c-c-c'.'*"

"How about 'They *cook'*?" Scott says, almost laughing. His unkempt red hair complements his bloodshot eyes. "Remember that *Twilight Zone* episode? *To Serve Man?* Come on. Even if she could speak lucidly, I don't think we want to base our strategy on the ravings of one of those goddamn things."

Joel just glares at Scott.

"That's just it," Michael says. "I don't think she's one of those 'goddamn things' anymore. She's one of us – or at least the closest we've seen."

"Joel's right, though," Bonnie says. "It could mean anything."

"Look, all I'm saying," Michael says, palms up, "is that she was scared, way scared, and she was trying to say something. Something about 'them.' Whoever that is."

"Maybe something's still poking around inside her head, did you think of that?" Scott says. "That would scare me more than anything. Worming around in there. And it's one more reason she probably shouldn't be in here with us."

Michael folds his arms. "She's staying."

Joel and Rachel and Ron stand to his left, Scott and Mai to his right. They're all crowded into the book-return area, watching Felicia sleep. The woman's head is turned away from them, but they can see her minutely jerking in unconsciousness, as if under the sway of a nightmare. She appears to be gradually coming out of the morphine slumber.

"So ... what? You think ... she could be communicating some kind of retained memory? That's the question, right?" Joel says. "Something left over from what she became?"

"That's what I'm *hoping*, I guess." Michael glances around.

Bonnie has a worried look on her face. "What's she going to say?"

Scott makes a disgusted sound. "This is how it starts, I'm telling you. This is how you guys work. You get all riled up about something that's really just an interpretation. What about the facts?"

Michael observes the slightest nervous twitch at the edge of Scott's mouth. "Okay, facts," he says. "We have a number of observable phenomena here, so what are the facts as you see them?"

"Well, I wasn't here when she apparently woke up, but what I've heard so far has been stuttering and raving. Fevered nonsense. There's no way to know what's going on in that head."

"All right, so you prefer to observe a situation and dismiss it for what it's not, rather than speculate about what it could be? Not really into the 'theory' aspect of science?"

Scott is struck silent for a moment. Then, "Oh, okay, so I see where Rachel gets that sense of humor."

"I'm with Scott, though," Mai says, playing with a few strands of her hair, absently braiding them. "Feels wrong having these bodies in here. We don't know what they're capable of."

Joel scratches his chin thoughtfully. He turns away from the group and makes his way to the front doors, where Liam and Chrissy are perched on high alert. Liam glances around at Joel's approach.

"I don't see shit," he says. "It's a graveyard out there."

"No movement all night."

"I hate this," the cop whispers. "This waiting. This paranoia."

It's still not long after sunrise, and the sun is searing in from the east, right into their eyes. Michael lets the light laser into him, feels the grittiness in his own gaze. By all rights, he should be asleep right now. His shift is over. But with Felicia approaching potential lucidity again, there's no way sleep would take him.

Joel is well rested and as cleaned up as he can manage. When he woke, he said he was ready to make a run for more traditional weapons at the precinct west of Old Town, find some new radios, and even send a team to the hospital for supplies and stronger meds. And hell, assuming they could get mobile enough, who's to say they couldn't relocate at the Marriott and suffer through the apocalypse in style? Or at least assemble at a grocery store.

But now there's indecision in the air, and Michael doesn't see any of that happening in the near future. He thinks Joel has reluctantly come around to the same thinking, despite Scott's typical objections. Felicia's damaged words, her repetition of that one word, *they* –

sounding for all the world like a repeated warning – have sent shivers through the group.

"God dammit," Joel says.

Michael knows he's frustrated by the need to stay holed up despite the ghost-town quality of the immediate vicinity.

The twins walk sleepily into the lobby, notice everyone milling about uncertainly.

"Oh no," Chloe says. "What's going on?"

Rachel very quickly fills her in.

Joel turns to Bonnie. "What's the situation with the blood?"

"I've drawn from everyone except Michael. Obviously he was recently concussed, so I held off. It's probably safe now, though. We have tranquilizer canisters filled and ready to use in the little fridge. We also have the two units we came in with. To really store more, I'd need more supplies."

"How many canisters again?"

"One hundred sixty-seven."

"I'm brimming with optimism," Mai says.

"Yeah, supposing we have to face forty thousand bodies out there?" Scott says.

"Then maybe we'll throw you out to 'em first," Rachel says, not without a small smile.

There's laughter all around, and even Scott cracks a smile.

"I'll tell you another option," Kevin says. "We get the holy fuck out of here."

"Damn right," Scott says.

"Is there any kind of tower around here? I'm thinking we get somewhere way high up, see what we can see. Fort Collins isn't famous for tall buildings, but we've got some high spots, right? Let's go, man. This doesn't feel right."

Ron chimes in. "We just spent two days barricading this joint."

"Plus, there's so much to read!" Mai says with a grin.

Kevin presses on: "Look, I've got a bad feeling about this. I've had it ever since we got here, and those damn things stopped chasing us. I just know they're up to something, and God knows it won't be any good. I'm serious. I say we load up the trucks and go."

"But after we get a view high up, where then?" Bonnie says, forlorn.

"Well, maybe that's what we'll find out. I don't know – east?"

"You think we'd find any scenario out there that's better than this one?"

"No," he says frankly. "Maybe. But that's what we all said about the hospital. At least we'd be moving."

"And what's the benefit of that?" Rachel asks.

"We'd be searching, right? Finding answers. Finding other survivors. I don't know."

"Sure," Joel says, "I think that's the ultimate goal, at least it's mine, but things have been so unpredictable that we can't just take a leisurely stroll out there and see what answers we can find. Have you forgotten what happened on the drive over here?"

"Of course I haven't forgotten that," Kevin says, "but maybe we should be remembering that your more recent trip to the store was pretty damned uneventful."

The conversation continues to revolve around itself, and tempers continue to teeter on the brink of flare-up. Michael removes himself from the knot of survivors and finds some of the rationed food. He practically inhales some beef jerky, feeling a quick protein surge. He follows that up with a small portion of water. When he's done, he leans against a doorjamb and watches Felicia. She continues to suffer in unconsciousness, and he wonders not for the first time whether whatever has happened to her inside is irreversible.

Chances are good that she will never again be a fully functioning human being.

The thought worms its way to his center and clenches like a fist.

As he pulls away from the door, he catches a glimpse of Rachel and Kayla settling into a nook near the elevator. They speak quietly with each other, shoulder to shoulder, and Rachel holds Kayla's hand in a loose grip. Occasionally one of them even utters a soft giggle. Michael is not ignorant to the selflessness that is allowing Rachel to appear calm and friendly to this young girl, all in the interest of helping Kayla cope. At the thought, Rachel glances his way, giving him what appears to be a grateful smile. Michael might even call it a peaceful smile. He winks back at her.

Somehow he finds his way to one of the cushioned benches along the south hallway and sits down, yawning.

And he's almost instantly asleep, sprawled across the bench.

No one disturbs him.

When he wakes from a thick, dreamless sleep some four hours later, the neighborhood surrounding the library is still deathly quiet, simmering under the summer heat.

Michael uses the restroom, which is already beginning to stink, and then he hurries to Felicia, who still hasn't achieved consciousness. Bonnie assures him that she would have woken him if the young woman had stirred.

Then Michael wanders to the front doors, his eyes roaming the rows of homes across the streets to the north and east. He remembers those first hours after they arrived, the bodies that scurried south. Where in the hell did they go? What was their purpose? Why that direction, when it had already been established that most of the ambulatory bodies had scrambled off in the direction of the foothills, into the forests of conifers? He remembers the vague glow coming from the south, wonders if it means anything.

It's becoming warm inside the library, and an impatience is spreading from Joel to the others. As Michael stands there, some heated argument breaks out among Ron's crew about one of their former members. Michael tunes it out, but tempers are flaring, and it's Mai who calms everyone. "He wandered out on his own, you know. I'm not some temptress. Everybody makes their own decisions. I liked him. I wish he was still here. Jesus."

Mai strikes Michael as a pleasing combination of no-nonsense and sensual – certainly all the males among these survivors pay her special attention. She's sharp and flinty, opinioned, but also playful. Combine all that with a lean, athletic body and a sweet face – not to mention the subtle blue dye streak in her hair – and you have something lethal. Michael's glad she's on their side. He wonders how long she'll be able to use her charm to defuse volatile situations. Because it's only going to get worse in here.

Michael turns from the door and wanders over to the table where Rachel and Kayla have been playing a card game. They found a number of games and decks of cards in a small room off the children's area. Kayla is laughing as Michael approaches, and not for the first time, he marvels at this girl's resiliency. It also seems to be contagious: Rachel is more relaxed and – yes – happier than Michael has seen in ...

My god, he thinks. *Years. It's been years.*

As he arrives at the table, Rachel glances up and says, "Hey Daddy."

"You two having fun?" he says, placing his hand on Rachel's head, letting it drift down through her hair.

"Kayla was just showing me a card trick."

"My daddy knows a lot of them. He's good at cards."

As Michael catches the present tense, Rachel notices his expression and nods.

"Kayla's good at the games, too. She's taught me a few."

Bonnie walks up. "I think she might be waking up." She gestures toward the book-return area, to which they have a clear line of sight.

Michael turns, sees Chrissy in there, attending to something.

"Let's go."

At the threshold to the room, Chrissy notices him. "Michael! Come in. I was labeling those canisters when she cried out a minute ago. She opened her eyes, but then she fell back to sleep. But she's stirring again. You might want to stick around."

Michael steps in, takes quick note of the blood canisters at the counter. They'd agreed to a simple categorization by donor initials and date, noted by red Sharpie on the canisters.

"As soon as she's conscious, I want to get some of this ibuprofen in her." Bonnie joins Michael, squatting near Felicia's supine body, which rests atop the makeshift bedding made of blankets found in Kayla's office. "I examined her this morning, and ... without sounding too optimistic, she seems to be in good shape. No fever ... the swelling is going down at the joints. Of course, that's external ... but I think if there were anything major happening internally, we'd be seeing evidence of it. There's nothing noteworthy." She lowers her voice. "There's a good possibility she might be okay. Thanks to you."

Bonnie lets her hand rest briefly on Michael's shoulder.

He shrugs, tries not to show how important it has become to him that Felicia survive. In whatever condition.

"I couldn't leave her there to suffer."

Bonnie joins Chrissy, calling back, "Michael, I still think she'll be a while waking up. It's about time you donated some blood to the cause. You ready?"

"Of course."

Midway through the draw, Felicia opens her eyes. They remain wet and streaming, and new tears seem to flood out of them upon waking. She turns her head left and right as if searching for something, and Michael can see her jaw working in some kind of convulsive motion that confuses him – not quite gagging but an intake, a sucking.

"Almost done?" Michael asks Bonnie.

"Yep," she says, finishing his eighth small draw and slipping the needle out. "Pressure here," she instructs, holding an alcohol-soaked paper towel at the entry site, and letting him go.

Kneeling next to Felicia, he notices the woman trying to focus. It reminds him of what he spoke to Bonnie about earlier – about the lingering effects of the radiation inside the skull. The survivors have seen firsthand that the glowing orb can wreak hideous damage outside the skull it inhabits, but it appears that it's protective of its host body. It wouldn't do much good to those bastards if the flesh surrounding the inhabitant suddenly started melting at the moment of possession. But had the orb displaced tissue? Had it moved anything roughly out of its way? Or was it purely energy?

Possession? Inhabitation? Michael shakes his head.

Felicia's eyes settle on his, and she looks at him pleadingly.

"I – I – I ...." Her mouth contorts.

"Do you need pain relievers?"

She shakes her head quickly despite obvious discomfort. Her hand snakes out and grabs his – the grip is sweaty and desperate. She closes her streaming eyes and concentrates, dealing with inner turmoil.

"They ..." she says quietly. "... life."

"Life?"

"D – d – dying."

Michael is listening intently, and he's gradually aware of a great commotion coming from the south section of the library, some shouting. He tries to tune it out, but then Ron is bounding into the lobby.

"Truck!" he calls. "Coming fast!"

There's a flurry of movement around him, and Chrissy bumps him roughly on the shoulder on the way out, but he stays rooted to the spot. He squeezes her hand gently. "Life, death ... which one?"

Felicia shakes her head in agonized frustration.

"Inside," she warbles, eyes shut tight. "D – d – dying."

He says, "And the trees have what they need?"

Michael can hear the horn of a vehicle now, coming in aggressive bursts.

Felicia opens her wet eyes. She looks scared out of her mind. "Neeeeed."

"Pain relievers now?" Michael whispers.

Her head moves in a trembling nod.

He searches behind himself, finds the cup of liquid ibuprofen, and manages to get it down her throat, and Felicia turns away, still in apparent pain.

"Neeeed."

Michael still has the shouting in the lobby tuned out, hoping Felicia will turn back to him and tell him the answers he wants, but she won't. He feels a hot frustration, deep inside, and he isn't even sure why he needs these answers. He wants to help this unfortunate young woman, of course, but there's something else. It's maybe as simple as wanting to belong to this group, to which a part of him still feels like an outsider. He woke up too late, he defied them early with his trip home, and he's been on the periphery for too long. They've accepted him, yes, and yet a small part of him feels like a fraud.

But now Felicia is unconscious again, and the shouting at the front doors has become too loud to ignore.

CHAPTER 26

There's a throng of survivors at the front doors, watching a big American truck hop the curb, bounce loudly, and come tearing across the grass.

Michael arrives next to Joel in time to hear him say, "Jesus, man, we are vulnerable here. We have plenty of weapons for those things, but nothing against, you know, assholes."

The truck fishtails briefly on the grass, then rights itself on the wide concrete path leading toward the front doors. It slows to a halt next to the Hummer, and it's at that point that Joel breathes out a ragged sigh of relief.

"Holy shit, it's the Thompsons." The cop actually has a smile in his voice, his tension easing away. "Never thought I'd be so happy to see those good ol' boys."

"The Thompsons?" Scott says skeptically, arriving behind them.

Joel is already on his way out the front doors, striding toward the big steel-gray truck. It's a battered behemoth. A huge man descends quickly, awkwardly from the cab – then what appears to be his twin exits the passenger side. The Thompson brothers are wearing matching blood-spattered camouflage that's almost hilariously large, and big black boots. They're wobbling a little on the path, looking stunned but purposeful, and they're glancing around the entire property, paranoid.

"Hey Jeff ... Pete ..." Joel calls.

"What the hell happened to your radio, Officer?" the out-of-breath driver, Jeff, says. "We've been trying to get you on the horn."

"Lost it with my cruiser – things got crazy back there."

"We saw that for sure. Been keeping tabs on you from the ridge."

"You got that goddamn whole crew in there?" Pete says. He reaches Joel and pauses with his brother, wheezing, peering into the library.

"Yeah, that's the hospital group you saw before, plus the group from the college."

"Well, listen up," Jeff says, "you gotta get the bejeezus outta here."

Joel's jaw clenches. "What do you mean?"

"Those things are gunnin' for you, man. Y'all are in their sights." He gestures southeast. "They're all crowded up over there for something, and you are *too* close. Too close. Pete didn't even want to come over here, he said we should – "

"What the fuck, Jeff, you're talking outta your goddamn ass!"

"Wait!" Joel holds up a hand in a halt gesture. "What are you talking about?"

"Like I said," Jeff says, "we've been trying to get your attention, right Bro?"

"Uh huh." Pete is keeping an eye out across the acreage.

"Couple days ago, those assholes got all aggressive, right? That's the last time we talked to you before you went radio-silent. You were goin' out to search for someone – " Michael knows immediately that Pete is talking about him " – and we were gonna hightail it out of Masonville, which was pretty much flattened by fire anyway. But would you believe those things kept coming at us, even on fire? I mean, in full flame, the fuckers!"

"Craziest shit I ever saw in my life," Pete says. "And I've been seeing some crazy shit."

"I don't know, been a lot of crazy shit."

"Point taken."

Survivors have been streaming tentatively out of the library as they perceive that the large men pose no harm. Kayla clutches Bonnie's arm as they approach, and the girl's eyes squint against the sunbeams streaming through the smoke. Pete nods to the survivors as they appear. He's huge and fragrant. Kayla half-hides herself behind Bonnie as Pete takes off his hunting cap to wave at his sweaty face.

"You said there's a bunch of those things south of us?" Joel says.

"We've been watching those goddamn things for days – for some reason, they're assembling at that Udall nature area, you know, west of the Wal-Mart? Thousands of 'em. They're just squatting there."

"That's where they were going!" Kevin says.

"Those bastards are a mile away, massing there just like in the foothills. One difference, though."

"No trees," Joel says. "No pine trees, anyway."

"Bingo. They're just … sitting there. No, they're there for something else – and it might be you."

"What?!" Bonnie yelps.

"They had us on our heels before, why would they – " Joel begins.

"Strength in numbers?" Michael says, and the group considers that.

"So I told you about Mike Richards up there at the Rod and Gun Club, didn't I?" Pete says, turning to Joel.

"Yep."

"Well, he croaked. They just swarmed over him. We barely got out of there ourselves, but we did manage to take half his arsenal. And we'd already cleared out Active Arms. I've got a crapload of AR-15 hardware in the truck for you."

Joel is taken aback. "Hell yes!"

"And then we're leaving, no offense. I know you need the hardware. I got boxes and boxes of 30- and 50-round magazines. You either gotta get the fuck outta here – sorry, young lady – or there's a very real possibility you're gonna have to defend this place like the fuckin' Alamo."

A wave of disquiet crashes across the open concrete, quiet cries of distress and gestures of alarm.

"Well, that settles it, let's get out of here!" Mai says, pushing away from the exterior wall she was leaning against. "Screw this place!"

"This library is barricaded better now than any other place I can think of," Ron says.

"Yeah, but there's plenty of other places where there aren't a thousand of those things nearby!"

"You're assuming they're going to attack?" Kevin says.

"Why shouldn't I?!"

"Have you heard anything from Buck?" Joel asks Pete.

"He's the cop south of town? Yes sir! He's looking for you too. He's managed to stay put down at the Harmony hospital somehow. He's doing okay, he's got a small group there, holed up."

Ron says, "Good to hear. He's a standup guy." Michael remembers Joel mentioning the CB communication among all of them, before everything started getting worse – and worse.

"Well," Joel says, "whatever we do, we can sure use the weapons. We have some defense here, but nothing metal, if you get me."

"You're talking about the blood, right?"

"Yeah, we've rigged up some tranq rifles with it, and it's been effective but ... a little weird."

Rachel gives him a look.

"Tranq rifles?" Pete says. "Man, who was the genius thought of that?" He glances around, notices Zoe raising her hand in a modest salute, Chloe right next to her hugging herself in a state of alarm. "Anyway, Buck was talkin' about the same thing, the blood, using it as a weapon. I don't think he got as far with it, though. He's still a Second

Amendment dude through and through."

Kevin, peering into the back of the Thompsons' truck, says, "I'd guess the Constitution doesn't much matter anymore."

"Constitution will transcend this," Pete says solemnly.

"Not if there's no one left," Scott calls, combing his hair back with his fingers. He's exiting the library cautiously, glancing up repeatedly into the heavens.

And then Rachel speaks up.

"Right, yay for guns!" Her voice isn't exactly dripping sarcasm, but Michael can hear it, being a practiced soundboard for her sarcasm. "We need more out-and-out killing as opposed to efforts to help these people."

"People?" Pete echoes. "Those things stopped being people a few days ago."

"A point of contention around here," Joel says.

"All I'm saying," Rachel says, "is that I don't think of the blood so much as a weapon as ... well it's the reason we're alive. And it could be our best protection."

"You might be right, young lady," Pete says, "but there's really no time to debate it. You use what you got, is what I say."

"Anyway," Joel says. "Thanks."

"We're all in this shitstorm together, right?"

"Maybe I had you guys pegged wrong the whole time."

"Which is what we kept telling you all those years." Pete winks broadly. "Right."

"All right, now listen," Pete says. "I ain't stayin' here, and I don't think you ought to either. You did us a solid a few days ago, and I'm just payin' you back now."

Michael follows them out just as commotion erupts behind him. Mai and some of the others – Liam and Scott among them – are already racing back to the library to gear up for an escape. Michael hears Mai ask, "Who's going?" Bonnie is trying to reason with her. Most of the others are just standing around, indecisive.

As Joel, Pete, and Kevin stride ahead of him toward the truck, Michael observes the neighborhood again. It's so quiet that there's almost a *negative* energy to it. It's as if he can feel it in his ears, like they're on the verge of popping. He flexes his jaw, and in fact his ears do pop.

Probably the concussion still having its way with me.

He walks farther out onto the concrete path, Ron jogging past him to help Joel. When Michael has a view of the sky to the west, he cranes his neck to search the horizon. It's still pulsating with a sickly crimson, the columns seeming at once to be flowing down and reaching up.

Wait. Sickly?

Is that how he would characterize this phenomenon, or is that just the suggestion of Felicia's words coming back to him? He's reminded of that old H.G. Wells story, *War of the Worlds*, probably the most famous alien-invasion book ever. In that story, a very healthy and aggressive alien species means to conquer Earth, but what they didn't count on was that a foreign atmosphere would not sustain them. From the moment they arrived, they were doomed. Michael isn't sure if he's remembering the book or the movies. Either way, they arrived healthy and were undone by Earth itself.

If what the survivors are dealing with is indeed alien in origin, then it strikes Michael as the opposite of Wells' vision. Perhaps what they're dealing with is a dying species, somehow – remotely? – feeding off a very particular resource on Earth, and in the act of doing so, becoming slowly healthy again. And it's using Earth's own inhabitants to do its bidding. Anger burns inside him now, watching the skies.

He wonders again whether these things ever expected the likes of him to survive. If they did, what purpose was he serving in their ghastly plan? He forces the pessimistic thought away from him.

Michael turns back to the small clutch of survivors grabbing weapons out of the truck. They're twenty feet ahead of him, apart from him. The library group is behind him, behind glass and stone.

He feels abruptly separate from all of them.

There's that sensation again, that feeling of remove. If it's true that the survivors have an obligation to fight back, to reclaim the world, how is Michael part of that crew? Maybe he should have died back at home, or at his office. That's when the world ended, and that's when *he* should have ended. He doesn't blame his daughter for saving him from that fate, but it *was* his fate.

Maybe it should have been his punishment.

A small, bitter laugh escapes his lips, and he feels a weight of self-loathing overtake him.

He wonders if these people would have taken him in so easily had they known he was a fraud. Imagine Bonnie learning what he'd been involved in when these things struck!

He feels a pulse of that negative energy again, his ears popping.

At the same moment, Bonnie says from the library doors, "Do you feel that?"

The group stops, its members glancing around at one another.

Yes, they all feel it.

And that's when the sky opens up with a roar so massive that it knocks the survivors to the ground.

CHAPTER 27

Michael trembles under the weight of the sound, covering his ears. He curls on the ground, protectively, but then he angles his head to try to spot Rachel. There she is, right at the library entrance, in front of the propped-open glass doors. Father and daughter make eye contact for the briefest of moments, and then she shuts her eyes tight, burying her chin in her chest to wait out the deafening sound.

The roar seems to last for a full minute, and then it slices off cleanly, leaving the world shaking. He hears glass shattering in the distance, and Michael, filled with dread, twists to scan the library windows across the length of the building. They're wobbling minutely in their frames, but miraculously they're holding strong. He can see the trees rustling not from any breeze but from the energy of the roar. And in the absence of the otherworldly sound, he can now hear car alarms wailing.

"Oh no," Bonnie is saying, positioned above Kayla protectively. "What now!"

Michael catches sight of Chrissy and the twins, sprawled on the ground, glancing up and around blearily. Just visible through the doors of the library, Rick and Mai are on the floor, dazed. Rachel is shaking her head.

"Can't be good," Pete says, on one knee, anchored against an exterior book-return kiosk near the front doors. "That never means anything good."

Joel, already recovered, is rushing two boxes of ammo from the truck toward a library entrance. His footfalls on the warm concrete sound hollow, echoing off low stone walls. "Everyone get ready! It could mean anything, but expect the worst."

"Let's go, let's go!" Kevin calls, also back on his feet, hauling his own armfuls of ammo.

"Don't get too worked up, now," Ron warns, looking over at Pete, but his gaze looks worried. "Sometimes it doesn't mean a goddamn thing."

"Probably not this time, though." Scott has crept out of the library and clings to the glass door, watching the skies.

Michael gets back to his feet, listening intently to everything. He's frozen on the concrete path. There are no new bodies rushing onto the streets, no further noises from the sky. In the wake of the alien thunder, all is calm. But there's an electricity hanging in the air, seething, crackling. Survivors are now hustling all around him. Someone hands him two AR-15s, and he awkwardly takes them in both fists.

"C'mon, c'mon!" someone yells.

A throbbing void seems to have settled around the library. Something is definitely different. He pops his ears, turns. The sky above the library is smoky and red, as it has been, but is it more intense? Straight above them, the drifting smoke seems to swirl under some kind of atmospheric influence. The smoke moves unnaturally, in shifting fits and starts.

"Something's happening," he breathes uneasily.

Bonnie is also staring skyward. "Oh God."

Behind her, Chrissy and the twins are trembling with an awed fear, Chrissy clutching a charm at her breast. Michael is sure it must be a cross.

A chirping noise sounds from the cab of the Thompson brothers' truck almost immediately. Jeff is already struggling with his bulk toward the truck, and the chirp lights a fire under his hefty ass. He hefts himself up to the cab and grabs a squawking walkie talkie off the driver's seat.

" – read, do you read?!" a voice crackles.

"Jeff here."

"Jeff! Get the fuck out of there!" The voice comes through full of static and panic. "They're coming – fast – go – get the fuck – "

Several screams echo across the square.

"Holy shit!" Pete yells, and pushes himself away from the wall. He jostles into an unwieldy jog.

Jeff keys the walkie talkie. "How long, over?"

"Now, now, they're coming fast, leave now – !"

"What's going on?" Kevin is asking, using the truck to stand. "What? Who is that talking?"

"That's Trevor on the ridge," Pete calls over his shoulder, his voice high and tight. "He's watching our back. Bastards are coming, and they're coming fast. Are you coming or going? We gotta go!"

"Trevor?"

"We're leaving! I suggest you do the same! Follow us. We'll go for high ground!"

"Where?" Ron says, uncertain.

Jeff is already firing up the truck.

"What's happening?" Scott calls from the doors.

"Where are they coming from?" Joel says, looking around wildly. "I don't see anything!"

"There's nothing out there!" Kevin says.

"They're a mile away, though, aren't they?" Michael says, not sure what to do. "Right?"

"I don't – " Joel is staring around wildly, from the faces at the library entrance to the trucks sitting idle just yards away. "*Shit!*"

Michael hears them first, the mad scramble of thousands of bodies scraping across asphalt, tumbling over one another, gasping in seeming anticipation. Inadvertently, he raises his arm in that direction – due east – pointing, but he's unsure what's happening. The incomprehensibility of the sound roots him to the spot, unable to form words. He glares back at Rachel, finds her poised at the entrance between Joel and Kevin, staring at him and beyond him. Her eyes are bulging with fear but show a grim determination.

Everything is stuttering into slow motion.

And then there they are, pouring down Elm Street, heading straight at them. The bodies form a great wall of flesh, like an organic thing, choreographed and synchronized, a mass of giant teeming spiders. Limbs clutch limbs for leverage, for balance, fluidly, in concert, all in service of propelling this impossible conglomeration forward. There are housewives and businesswomen, morning joggers and bicyclists, shop owners and cops, couch potatoes and senior citizens. There are ninety-year-olds, and there are three-year-olds. There are representatives of every race and religion, every body type, every age – all manner of human beings – their eyes enraged, their inverted mouths stretched wide, crooked and gasping.

They're leaping and sprinting, their collective, roiling breadth filling the entire street, from porch to porch.

A chorus of screams erupts from the library's interior, and the thought that bursts through his own mind is –

This is happening.

"Aw *fuck!*" Jeff yells from the truck, and revs the engine brutally. The horn blares. "Let's go! Let's go!"

Pete is stunned motionless for a moment, holding his rifle in his hand like some useless stick, watching the flood of bodies flow down Elm like a rushing tide.

"Pete!" Jeff screams, honking in mad, staccato bursts. The truck lurches forward and stalls. Jeff lets loose with a barrage of profanity that Michael can barely hear under the alien cacophony.

Right next to him, Pete very clearly says, "Fuckers were just waiting."

"What?!" Joel yells.

"They were waiting for us to come here," Pete says unsteadily, managing only to take one lurching step backward, away from the sight. "They were watching."

Michael understands somewhere inside himself that he can't move his feet. He's as planted to the spot as Pete. Standing ten feet from Jeff's truck, he's torn between leaping into the relative safety of the cab and making a dash up the concrete toward Rachel, toward the questionable safety of the library, and the indecision has frozen him.

Everything is chaos.

Rachel is screaming his name, and then Joel is grabbing his shoulder.

"We have to get inside!"

Wordlessly, he lets Joel yank him backward, away from the truck, but despair clutches at him.

The two men sprint toward the library, and as they race across the last few yards of hot cement, Michael sees the tide of bodies reflected in the window glass. It's a huge, teeming flood of distorted humanity. It has reached the corner of the library commons and is about to crest over onto the concrete. In seconds it will swallow the trucks.

Joel is yelling as soon as they cross the threshold.

"Go! Go! Take the rifles! Bonnie, I don't know what good the blood can do, but get it out here! Get those tranq rifles ready, and be ready to get them where we need 'em! Now! Go!"

Most of the survivors are already stumbling around in disarray, but now a measure of focus takes hold. Bonnie rushes toward the refrigerator in the book-return area, closely followed by Mai and Zoe, screaming nervously about collecting the blood canisters. Kevin shouts over her about the more traditional weapons at the front doors, and Michael flows in that direction with Joel and Ron and Liam and Scott.

Chrissy and Chloe remain at the front doors, backed away from the men, their hands cupped at their mouths, screaming for Pete. *"Get in here! Get in here!"*

Michael looks at the two brand-new AR-15s in his grip, remembering that he's holding them, and at that moment, Joel takes one from him, frantically helping him load a magazine into the remaining one, thumbing off the safety and shoving him hard on the shoulder.

"Get ready to barricade these front doors! You too, Kev!"

Outside, Pete is shambling toward the front doors, spinning to judge the distance of the threat. Seeing Pete launch himself toward the library, Jeff has fired up the truck again and leaps the big vehicle forward, turning sharply away from the entrance just as forty bodies seem to envelop the truck bed, slamming it down with their collective weight. Other bodies career underneath the tires, jerking the vehicle to a shuddering stop. The wheels spin uselessly atop flesh that goes instantly pulpy, spraying the concrete with red mud.

As Pete rushes through the doors, the truck is completely swarmed, invisible beneath the bodies.

"Jeff!" Pete wails, and then the doors are shut, and Bill and Rick are locking them, moving large tables against them.

"*No way those will hold!*" Scott yells. "*For fuck's sake!*"

"Move back!" Michael yells, grabbing Scott's shoulder. "Get away from the window!"

The horde sweeps up the path, a mass of gasping anger and hyperactive limbs. Michael holds his breath, staggering backward with the rest of the group, holding Rachel and Kayla to him – and then the bodies crush against the thick windows, battering, darkening the lobby. The scrabbling things are all panting and thumping, their dead eyes staring in, their mouths open, their red glows perilous and bright and flashing from their throats.

"It held!" Chloe cries from Michael's left. "It's holding!"

"*Shit, shit, shit …*" Kevin is repeating endlessly, but he responds to Chloe: "Yeah, but for how long?" He's backing away from the doors, unsure what to do.

Michael tries to get a glimpse through the throng to determine Jeff's fate, but it's impossible – it's body on top of body on top of body. The lobby darkens further, and now the collective luminescence from the things' throats is like an evil red fog surrounding them, swallowing the lobby, a poisonous radiation that promises to consume them at the slightest wrong move. The things' heads are stabbing at the windows, mercilessly, and the library is filled with a discordance of knocks and thuds. Their collective gasping is like a sustained, gravelly hum. At the lobby doors, the glass is already fogging, smearing under the radiation, but it's remaining resilient.

"Listen for breaking glass!" Joel calls. "Everyone!"

Chloe is staring at the front doors, beyond the makeshift barricade. "The glass here isn't as thick. This glass at the doors." She has surprised Michael, keeping her cool in the face of unimaginable horror, but she's just a kid thrown into a warzone. "If it's gonna break, it's gonna break right there." She gestures with her heavy rifle at the entrance.

Joel is right next to her, aiming. "I think you're right."

"Those bastards!" Pete is shouting, fiddling with his rifle. *"Bastards!"*

"How many of them are there?" Kayla says meekly from under Michael's right arm.

"Thousands?" Rachel says, a hard swallow cutting the word in half. She glances up at him as she pushes away.

Michael can see tears in her eyes. He can sense his daughter's conflict – the weight of responsibility she feels to save as many human beings as she can, and the realization, even as she cradles her own rifle, that that responsibility is about to be dealt a massive blow.

The bodies continue to press against the side of the building. Michael can hear shouting from the south and north wings: The things are swarming on all sides of the library, blotting out the world, their limbs scratching at the walls and windows, searching for entrance. The thumping becomes an oppressive and unnerving racket. Michael is waiting for one of those thumps to become a crash of broken glass.

Bonnie and three others emerge from the north end, carrying boxes full of blood-filled canisters. "Here! Here!" she's calling. "This is our best defense."

"Yeah, from what? A hundred of these things?" Scott says, sweaty and visibly shaking. "What about the ten thousand after those? He backs up against the drinking fountains by the stairwell and grasps at it for balance. "We gotta be ready to lock ourselves in the bathrooms or something! I'm just saying we need to be ready!"

"What are they doing?" Bonnie cries, really seeing the bodies against the glass for the first time now. "Why are they – "

But her words are cut off by the crack of Pete's rifle and the crash of shattered glass at the left door. There's a collective gasp from the survivors, the loudest of which come from Liam and Chloe flanking the door.

"What the hell are you doing?" Joel yells at the large man.

Pete can only mumble. "It was about to give."

Bodies are immediately surging in through the hole, their upside-down, angular movement seeming more than ever like a throng of agitated spiders. Joel, Michael, Kevin, and Ron raise their AR-15s simultaneously and fire. The bodies squeal as the bullets hit them, tearing through their flesh, but they continue toward them inexorably. They scream and flinch but keep coming. Michael stares at them, appalled, unconsciously bringing down his weapon.

"God!" Rachel yells from somewhere.

"The heads!" Joel calls. "Aim for the heads!"

Michael aims and misses. He screams his annoyance. He focuses, aims again, and delivers a headshot to the closest body, whose luminescence immediately sparks out as the skull explodes out behind it in a red mess. The body falls limp at the vestibule. The others follow suit, and more bodies fall, but they're climbing through with increasing rapidity.

"Need help in the lobby!" Ron calls loudly. "Now!"

"Like fucking immediately!" Kevin yells.

Pete seems to snap out of his daze, and begins firing into the churning tumble of flesh.

The lobby is soon a maelstrom of lead, rifles firing ceaselessly at the bodies squeezing through the gap. Bodies crash to the floor, extinguished in a messy, red tangle, piling up, and yet more bodies keep pushing through. Muzzles strobe in the claustrophobic dimness of the lobby, and the sound of gunfire is like an endless string of deadly firecrackers.

Scott screams incoherently, backing away toward the bathrooms.

"Hold the line!" Joel calls. "They're slowing down!"

Michael can't believe it, but it's true: The pile of bodies across the front entrance is growing, becoming more and more of a roadblock against easy entry. The things are slipping on blood, fumbling as they climb atop the mountain of corpses. They're hissing and leaping, straight into rifle fire. But they're not mindless. In fact, most of them are disturbing in their intelligence and ferocity. One of them, a lean young woman in ripped jeans and a white tee shirt, rises over the pile, eyes Michael with a vicious sneer, and prepares to leap, angling her body strategically, but before he can even take aim, her head is obliterated by Ron's weapon. The body goes tumbling backward toward the door, partially blocking it.

"Thanks," Michael coughs.

He sees only a look of terror on Ron's face – a quick flick of *Not doin' this for you, pal* – and then he's reloading and firing once more.

Michael hears Joel yell something, but he can't make it out over the gunfire. Someone grabs his shoulder. It's Joel at his ear.

"Be efficient! We've already gone through a lot of ammo!" The cop shows him a new magazine, sets it at Michael's feet.

Within minutes, the pile of bodies is so great that the influx has slowed significantly, and Michael backs off, listening for other cries of alarm from other sections of the library. The bulk of the survivors are right here in the lobby, breathless with amazement at what has just taken place, and eager to pitch in if the wall of bodies breaks and more of them flood in. But it seems to be holding, and only the occasional boom of gunfire breaks the creepy, shifting silence.

"Watch your fire!" Joels yells in the relative silence. "Conserve your ammo!"

"Can they get in?" Bonnie asks from the back of the room, trying and failing to push back on her panic. "Are we safe? Are we safe? Joel? Michael?"

"Take it easy," Joel says, breathing heavily.

"What are they doing?" Scott's voice is near hysteria.

"Obviously they're trying to get in," Kevin says. "Finish us off."

"Christ, man!" Scott yells. Eyeing an unused AR-15, he strides across the lobby, grabs it, and finds a full magazine. With some uncertain effort, he shoves it in place. "Why am I even here? I shouldn't be here. And now I'm buried beneath a million of those fuckers!"

Michael watches the pile of bodies at the entrance, aiming his rifle, waiting for movement. The rear of the pile seems to have effectively crammed the shattered door – or at least the pile in combination with the bodies' weird compressing motion from the outside.

He feels Rachel join him, grasping his forearm. He glances down. One hand covers her mouth in dismay. She's staring at the pile of bodies. He matches her gaze, and whereas before he saw them as monsters, it takes her expression to see what she sees: broken and bleeding human beings, destroyed victims of this horror show.

"Oh Daddy," she whispers.

"I know."

An oppressive quiet returns to the library. The survivors are panting, jogging from room to room with their weapons, double-checking their ammo, their eyes large with fear. The library is utterly surrounded, packed in by thousands of those monstrosities. At every window, Michael glimpses upside-down faces and twisting limbs, torsos and hands and feet, squirming minutely, caught under the weight of the bodies on top of them, and the bodies on top of those bodies, all vying for entrance.

He doesn't dare get too close to any of those windows, but he does watch them. He remembers all too clearly the way that red luminescence softened that glass of the Hummer's window, allowing one of the things to steal that boy. Danny.

Michael isn't exactly relieved to see some fogging of the glass, but at least there are no signs of softening, of the glass giving way.

"What are they trying to do?" Mai says, striding in from the north annex, red-faced. "They can't just push in like that. They can't even move, the way they're pressed up against the windows. I mean, look at them."

"I don't want to look," Kayla says.

But it's mesmerizing. In the absence of the generator lighting –

nobody has made a move to turn anything on – the only luminescence is coming from the rare gap between the compressed bodies or the multitude of glowing orbs in the throats of the bodies themselves. The heads continue to stab at the windows, all around the library, lending a rhythmic thumping to the red throb of the glow itself. In the claustrophobic heat of the late afternoon, the library feels like the pit of Perdition.

"We need light!" Michael calls to whoever will listen. He can hardly see anybody. "That generator's on, right?"

No one answers at first, but then Brian speaks up from the south hall. "Not a whole lot of fuel up there, but should be okay."

"Someone flip a switch, for Chrissakes!" someone says. Michael doesn't recognize the voice.

"Where?" Mai says.

"Anywhere!"

Just as Michael starts searching the lobby, he notices the overhead lights flickering softly as if struggling, and then finally turning on. "Got 'em," Chrissy calls from somewhere.

A measure of relief filters through the lobby, but it is short-lived. Both Pete and Ron utter exhalations of surprise and lift their weapons. One of them fires, Michael isn't sure which.

"What?!" Joel yells, twirling.

Michael doesn't see it at first. But a gasping noise reveals it: Three bodies have managed to squeeze through the gap and are poised at the top of the corpse pile, staring down at them.

Someone else fires, and the top of one of the bodies' skulls jerks in a red mist. The remaining two bodies are abruptly rushing down this side of the pile. They're both thin, nimble bodies, and in the midst of his horror – fixated on their angry, intelligent, focused gazes – Michael understands that these cursed things have achieved an awareness of the human body, a sense of athleticism, a strategic notion of which kinds of human bodies are best suited to certain kinds of attacks.

"Look out!" he yells.

One of them lands directly atop Pete, crumpling the big man to the floor, and the other clambers into Mai, sending her sprawling. It's the seasoned hunter who lets out a whimpering yell, though, panicking as he falls and using his rifle to batter the body on top of him. Joel and Kevin leap into action, kicking at the body – that of a young man in gym shorts and a roughed-up tee shirt – but it holds firm, wrapping its arms backward around Pete's upper torso, the head stabbing mercilessly at Pete's face while simultaneously snarling at the two combatants above it. The rifle clatters to the ground.

"It's strong!" Kevin screams.

Pete emits a long string of muffled syllables, and Michael quails at the sight of the thing's head stabbing repeatedly at his face.

"Watch the door for more!" Joel yells, kicking and battering with his own rifle.

Michael and Rachel have descended on the second of the bodies, which has bounced off Mai and landed in a wreck against a book display. It attempts to scramble back up, but Michael delivers a vicious strike to the bridge of its upturned nose, and a geyser of blood sprays his forearm. A throaty screech escapes the thing's mouth, and it locks its flat eyes on Rachel, whom it perceives as the lesser threat. It makes a leaping move for her, and Michael kicks savagely at the body, knocking it off course, but it clutches at her lower leg, behind itself, blindly but with preternatural assurance.

"No!" Michael roars, kicking again, but the head nearly catches his foot in its open mouth.

A rifle fires once, then a second time, and there's a screech, but Michael isn't sure where it came from. All he sees is his daughter in peril, and he screams at the body, hammering at it repeatedly with the butt of his own rifle.

Then the body spasms, a gaspy grunt launching from its throat. It falls to its back and squirms for a moment, then stops thrashing. Rachel kicks away from it, panting, leaving it there on the floor. The thing whips its head around three times, and the eyes begin blinking rapidly, almost violently, and it occurs to him what has happened.

Bonnie is standing apprehensively above the body, an empty syringe in her fist, the other hand steadying herself against the book display to her left. Behind her, a rifle has ended the threat of the other body, and Joel and Kevin are tending to Pete. But Michael only has eyes for Bonnie.

"Nice work," he wheezes, gulping air.

"It's the blood," she says, shrugging but breathing heavily. "Like Rachel says – it's our best defense."

CHAPTER 28

Kevin, Ron, and Bill – who looks once again on the verge of a heart attack – have heaved the two new bodies on the pile at the entrance, effectively sealing the gaping hole in the glass door. Pete, for his part, has regained his clumsy feet, although he has sustained obvious injuries. He's gasping, almost choking, working his jaw. He stands proudly, though, his big trembling fists checking his rifle. He's monitoring the area with eagle eyes, occasionally shaking his head – presumably at his own stupidity. He's murmuring to himself, sweating profusely, pacing. There's no further movement at the doors, except for a slow twitching among the bodies; it doesn't appear alarming.

The twins are tending to an apparently unharmed Mai, and Michael kneels next to Rachel, making sure she's unharmed.

"I'm fine," she keeps repeating, shrugging him off. "Dad!"

Michael backs off, noticing that her hands are shaking with near-spastic tremors, and despite her toughness he sees a despairing fear behind his daughter's eyes.

She softens a bit, letting him help her up.

"All right," Joel says, taking advantage of the stunned lull. "We are seriously low on ammo. But we've got six tranq guns. I need six good shooters to take those and spread out with – " He glances around, then, his eyes red-rimmed and twitching. He's seeing the doubtful, sullen glances that everyone is exchanging. "What?"

It's Scott – backed up against the drinking fountains again, clutching his rifle, aimed low – who speaks up.

"There's a thousand of those things out there," he says. "And no matter how many of them we blow away, there'll be another thousand right behind them. Just waiting. Do you honestly see a way out of this with six tranquilizer rifles and a few more boxes of ammo?" He glares around. "Does anyone?"

In the center of a lobby strewn with the bleeding dead, claustrophobically shut in by countless reanimated corpses, not one of the exhausted survivors says a word for a long moment. The silence intensifies the sense of doom. The library pulses with crimson light, and Michael notices almost subconsciously that it's rhythmic. He can feel it in his chest. He imagines the collective red luminescence drifting, throbbing, in columns toward the sky, toward whatever influence guides these things' motives.

Under everything is the sound of weeping – Michael thinks it's one of the twins – and now, in the silence, Michael can hear only occasional thumping … the things' heads attempting to gain entry at any point possible. But that has subsided, and in its wake is that turgid and still rhythmic pulse. There is an inevitability to it – the overwhelming sense that the survivors never really had a chance. Michael feels it like an almost tangible weight.

"*Are* they doing something to the glass?" Chrissy says. "Are they melting it?" She's watching a pane closely. Faces are mashed against it, upside-down, furious, their mouths moving around an impossible crimson glow.

Kevin is glaring at the same pane of glass with contempt.

"So what do we do?" Mai says. Her voice has a defiant kind of sturdiness, but Michael can tell she's having trouble keeping it that way. "What *can* we do?"

More silence.

"Can we go to the roof?" Mai asks.

"Maybe," Kevin says, "but for what purpose?"

"Time?" Ron says miserably. "Last stand?"

"Just … shut up, okay?" Scott says, doing his own pacing. He looks gaunt and defeated.

Michael catches a glimpse of Liam in the south hall. The sweaty young man has one hand planted on a bookcase behind him, and his right hand is placing his AR-15 on the ground, gently, as if any sudden movement might cause the things at the window to thrash about more wildly and break the thick glass. He makes a gesture that tells Michael he's out of ammunition. Kevin looks Michael's way from his left, shaking his head in stark, red-tinted disbelief, and the two men share the briefest of glances until Kevin looks down, for some reason unable to maintain the human connection.

"Christ!" Joel barks abruptly. "Don't let this asshole get to you! Scott has been ready to give up from the start! Get off your sad-sack asses! It's the only way we're gonna survive this thing!"

Scott's voice is reasonable, receded in red shadows. "No one is under any obligation to follow my lead, cop. They can do whatever the hell they want. But you can have this rifle." He makes a show of leaning the AR-15 against the drinking fountain. "I won't be in the line of fire anymore. I'm going upstairs."

"Bastard's gonna lock every door, barricade himself up there," Kevin says.

"You can't do that, asshole," Joel says. "You can't lock us down here."

"Christ, I never said I *would*! What is with you people?!"

Michael grits his teeth and tunes the voices out. He has latched his attention on his daughter, who is standing wearily next to Bonnie at the main checkout area. Kayla is buried into her side, not crying but in a kind of denial, and Rachel is petting her dark hair. For a reason that Michael can't quite pinpoint – or perhaps for many reasons – he feels a fat lump develop in his throat. His eyes blur.

Rachel eventually meets his gaze, and after a moment she beckons him toward her. As men shout behind him, he makes his way to his daughter, and Bonnie, and before he knows it, he's engulfed in an embrace. Arms fold around him, and he's not even sure who they belong to. He can smell his daughter's scent, and he can feel Bonnie's warmth, and he can sense Kayla's innocence – a reminder of Rachel in childhood, a remembrance of a very different time – and he tries consciously to lose himself in it, closing his eyes tightly against everyone and everything outside this circle.

It's not the loud voices that finally pull him away. It's not the sound of rifles reloading, or the clamor of survivors hustling back and forth, or the roar of something atmospheric spelling their demise.

It's the silence.

The racket of those bodies' heads against the glass. Earlier, he thought that the sound had subsided. It has. In fact, it has subsided dramatically.

Michael is in the act of opening his eyes and glancing toward a window for a closer look, but then Ron hurries in from the south hall.

"They're coming through the windows."

"What?!" Joel says, moving immediately.

"Oh God," Bonnie breathes.

"What do we do?!" Chloe says, seemingly ready for anything. "What do we do?"

"What do you mean they're coming through the windows?!"

Michael hurries past Chrissy to the closest window, hopping over two sprawled bodies, nearly slipping in a large splatter of blood. He comes to an uneasy stop next to the massive pile of bodies at the front doors. Outside, several of the things' heads are pressed firmly against the smeared glass, and now all the dead eyes swivel almost lazily and lock on his. The red pulse in the things' heads is only too apparent, and it seems to be working at something: It seems to be the utter focus of the otherwise still bodies.

And then he sees that the glass is fogged not by breath – as he originally, unconsciously assumed – but by whatever weird radiation is being emitted from that glow. It *is* working on the library window glass. Despite the thickness and strength, it *is* working.

Michael's first instinct is to touch the glass with his fingers, but he snatches his hand back, wary. Instead, he lifts his rifle and –

"Wait, don't!" Pete cries, beginning to maneuver his bulk toward him. "I'm just – "

With the muzzle at the end of the AR-15's barrel, Michael nudges at the glass, and it gives sickeningly, like half-molten plastic.

"He's right," Michael calls over his shoulder. "They're coming through. They're coming through all the windows."

The effect of Michael's words is instant, galvanizing the group back into action.

"Shit!" Joel shouts. "Okay, this is it, people, spread out! Arm up! If you don't have a rifle, try a tranq gun! If nothing else, use the end of the rifle to batter the head. Extinguish that fucking light! Get ready! Be smart!"

Michael backs away from the window, watching it, watching every window in the vicinity, every window that will at any moment fall away and allow the entrance of countless things intent on ending the lives of all the survivors. Commotion reigns behind him, voices shouting, feet pounding in all directions.

Wait, Michael thinks, the word repeating into an inner echo.

"Here they come!" someone shouts from the north end of the library, and Michael flinches at the sound of gunfire.

"Go, go, go!" Joel is yelling.

Kevin and Ron sprint in that direction, but Michael stays put. He's staring at the canisters of blood that Bonnie hauled out to the book-return area. Chloe is fidgeting a few feet away from it, considering it, not understanding how it can help her. She's grabbing at Zoe's forearm while her sister is in the midst of dissolving into horrified tears.

Michael finally breaks from his paralysis and goes stumbling toward them. The unassuming box is loaded with the small pressurized canisters, each with a small protective cork on its end, waiting to be loaded into one of the six tranq guns scattered around the library.

Something deep inside him clicks.

Coordination.

Just like them.

In his mind's eye, he sees the bodies sweeping up the street toward the library – the synchronization of movement, the horrifically fluid choreography of limbs, all working in concert toward one objective. He doesn't need to glance behind him to see them working toward a different common objective now, all their heads stabbing in unison against the glass to achieve entrance.

The lobby is in chaos, but Michael grabs Chloe's shoulders. "Who knows how to fire these tranq rifles?" he yells loud enough for everyone in the lobby to hear.

Eyes wild, he acknowledges the twins, and Rachel and Kayla, and Bonnie, who is enduring a full-body tremble, on the verge of collapsing into shivering sobs. Chrissy has backed against a wall, her weapon empty, and can only watch as the window glass fogs. Her eyes are unblinking, her mouth slack. Liam is running toward them, seeking the safety of a group at the center of the lobby, giving up on his station.

No one answers at first. They're succumbing to horror.

"Hey!" he screams. "We're not done yet! Bonnie!"

Bonnie, her face a ruined mess of tears, manages to meet his gaze.

"This is our last shot. And it's not about the guns. I don't think the guns matter anymore. It's about this blood right here."

All eyes move to the unassuming box at Michael's feet, weighing its balance against the awesome, gasping threat literally pushing in at the library windows.

This? Against that?

"We gotta hit 'em with this blood all at once!" he yells. "We have to be coordinated! Just like they are! We need to grab everything! All the blood! *Everything* with blood in it. I'll take care of the tranqs, but get everything else. Bonnie!"

Bonnie pushes herself away from Rachel and Kayla, still sobbing, but determined. She rushes toward the book-return area.

"Chloe," he says, looking straight into the girl's eyes. "And you too, Zoe. Get the tranq guns. All of them. Bring 'em here. Chrissy, you too, we need all six! *GO!*"

Chloe, haunted yet willing, and Zoe, dazed and barely hearing him, follow his orders without question, immediately locating two of the four tranq rifles leaning against the main counter. Chrissy is unable to hold back gasping sobs as she joins in, constantly wiping at her eyes, so Mai – dry-eyed – takes charge, yanking the woman toward the main checkout area.

"Liam!" Michael calls. "Get ready to fire. Take some canisters here."

Bonnie crashes into Michael.

"Here!"

It's another box, labeled INGRAM, and it's full of various hospital supplies, including the final unit of O-negative blood, and about two dozen syringes fat and dark with cold blood. She has cleared out the little fridge. It's everything. At the realization, Michael looks into her eyes, and there is a bottomless fear there.

"If we get out of this," Michael says, forming a strategy while staring into the box, "you're gonna be the hero, you know."

Bonnie can't take her eyes away from the front windows, to the right of the pile of destroyed human beings. One of the bodies outside is reaching a knobby forearm through the glass, which is half-stretching and half-breaking around the limb. The hand is scrabbling around, intermittently reaching out toward them as if independent of its body. The glass is pushing inward like tempered-glass taffy, close to falling away.

"I don't want to be a hero," Bonnie says. "I just want to be alive."

Against every instinct to flee – up the stairs, into inner rooms, even into the non-functional elevator – the small band of survivors surges forward into an inner circle, surrounding the new blood. They're mostly women, as the rest are at the windows in other parts of the library, expending the last of the metal ammunition or using the rifles themselves as last-ditch blunt instruments. Michael and Mai take two of the tranq rifles and hand the remaining four to Liam, Chloe, Chrissy, and Rachel.

The boy and the wet-eyed women, reluctantly lurching forward, take the rifles into their hands and study them with varying degree of hopelessness. Michael hurriedly gives them a primer on loading the canisters into the chambers, and then the shooters are ready, their pockets filled with small payload darts.

"Those are gonna save our lives," Bonnie says, "so shoot straight. Right, Michael?"

"Could be." He gestures to the box. "Kayla, are you fast?"

"Yeah."

"You'll run darts to anyone who needs them, okay?"

"Okay."

"Whoever runs out, okay? They'll call your name."

Kayla nods.

"We'll back up the tranq guns with these syringes," Michael says. "I need Bonnie, Zoe, and – Rick, here take these! – I need anyone who doesn't have a rifle to grab these syringes. Get over here!"

Michael searches for Scott and fails. But now there are louder voices coming their way. Ron sprints in from the north end of the library, where rifle blasts are diminishing and a fleshy commotion foreshadows the man's words:

"They're inside."

"Oh God," Bonnie cries.

"We should get to the roof."

"I've got one more idea," Michael says. "Here, help us out." He shouts the plan to Ron, hands him two syringes. "Remember, each body needs only a small amount. Get it in, plunge, get it out, and go on to the next one."

In the distance, Brian and Bill are in the act of falling back. Michael can see them swinging their rifles in the dim distance. Gunfire has dwindled away under the alien throb, and now even Joel is backing away from his windows, letting his rifle clatter to the floor. "That's it! I'm out!"

"This has to be coordinated," Michael shouts. "We'll start shooting at the same time, all at once, on my mark. And once we start, we give them all we have until we're out of blood. Clear?"

"Aw, fuck, let's do this!" Mai cries.

"Okay, go, spread out! Tranq guns first, syringes backing them up! Go! Wait for my word!"

Michael takes the windows near the front doors, and the survivors spread out in a loose line. Chloe is ten feet from Michael, just beyond Rachel, and Liam is beyond her. Chloe brings her tranq rifle to her shoulder, aiming at windows just south. "I've seen so many officers firing these," she says brusquely. "Never thought I'd be doing it."

"You'll do fine," Michael says. "Here they come."

Chloe takes aim at the body pushing through her window. It's an older woman in a shredded nightgown, scowling directly at the survivors as it climbs forward, pushing through the glass as if through a birth canal. Chloe casts fearful glances at Michael, and he nods frantically, continuing to encourage her.

"Wait," he says to her. "Wait for it to come through a little more."

On the north side of the lobby, several bodies – having gained entrance through windows in that annex – have given the men chase, and now, as Joel and Bill and the others clamber into the lobby, those come to a halt, regarding the survivors assembled there. Their skin is bloodied from squeezing through the glass; one is literally dripping in syrupy rivulets. Their throaty gasps rise and fall, wary.

The survivors are surrounded.

"Everyone ready?!" Michael calls. "Find a target!"

There's a long moment of held-breath silence, during which both the survivors and the reanimated bodies have paused in a state of uncertainty. Michael catches the briefest glimpse at his window of an upside-down face – a young woman, her otherwise beautiful features cranked into villainy – her dead eyes regarding him, taking his measure, along with the other survivors around him. He sees something in her expression that he can't place, but it boosts him.

"FIRE!" Michael screams. "Keep firing!"

His tranq gun *thunks*, sending a dart into the young woman's strained neck, and in his peripheral vision, he can see Chloe reacting backward, having fired her own rifle. The body at Michael's window is already flailing, gasping, stuck in the window frame, landing on its back on the hard, jagged metal. Michael is watching it, watching for the next body, and yes, the next body is there immediately – another older woman, this one larger, uglier, meaner. Blood and sap is smeared down the forehead, and the black hair is twisted in all directions, Medusa-like.

"Reload!" Michael calls, laboriously inserting a new dart into his own rifle.

"Trying!" Chloe shouts.

"Bonnie!" Michael says.

Lip curling, Bonnie leaps forward with her syringe before the body can get fully into the window frame. She plunges the needle into the woman's face just as the body skitters across the floor, swiping at Michael and smacking him straight in the balls. Michael falls back helplessly, his rifle nearly falling from his grasp. Through squinted eyes, he sees Bonnie flailing backward too, the syringe apparently undepressed.

They know our weaknesses! The thought whisks through his head.

"I got it!" Chloe says, sending another tranq dart flying. It embeds itself below the young woman's left eye, and immediately the head begins to whip into a frenzy. The body partially blocks the window frame, but here comes another – a young man in sleep shorts – twisting around the metal frame to gain partial entrance. His inverted face peers at them with red malevolence.

Michael grits his teeth against the pain and clambers back up.

"Reload!" he manages, loud enough for everyone to hear. "Reload!"

"I'm trying!" comes Liam's voice from somewhere.

Now Bonnie steps forward again. She jabs the needle into the new thing's shoulder, and before the body can react, she has injected a squirt of blood and yanked the syringe back violently, nearly breaking it off in the flesh. The young man pauses, as if shocked, and then begins to gasp and writhe. His top half crumples atop the now-screaming young woman below him.

Another body – a raven-haired woman, dead eyes flashing – surges through the glass, its head stabbing at Bonnie's arms as if to knock the syringes from her grip. Bonnie lets out a helpless scream as the radiation throbs against her arms.

"Bonnie!" Rachel cries.

Somewhere, Kayla is crying.

Michael reaches out to yank Bonnie away from the threat, and out of nowhere, Scott is battering the new body down with the butt of an empty AR-15. Some kind of growl is coming out of his throat. The body is gasping at him, strategic with its lunges. It's attempting to launch full-bodied at this new red-haired threat, but Scott is ruthlessly crushing the skull, and after a few moments, the inner light sparks out from sheer violence, the head bleeding out. Scott is left breathing heavily, watching the gap.

He releases a savage bark of triumph.

The moment he tears his gaze away, yet another body is squeezing through, a gangly man, obscene in his crabwalk. The thing uses its spindly legs to launch itself against Scott, whose next brutal swing with the rifle whiffs over the body. The thing clutches onto Scott with its long limbs, elbows and knees moving frantically, and Scott relinquishes the rifle and begins punching at the thing's gut and its inverted, raging face.

"No!" Bonnie cries from Michael's grasp.

"*Keep firing!*" Michael calls to anyone who's listening.

And then Bonnie has wrenched free of Michael's grip and is diving into the fray with her syringes.

"Scott!"

She plunges one needle straight into the gangly-limbed thing's abdomen, yanks it free, and then starts shoving her foot at the head, which is twitching and gasping deep in its throat. It collapses shortly, straight atop Scott, who is already crawling backward on his elbows, scurrying away. He kicks at the sparking head with desperate fury and loathing, and the body goes reeling backward and up, colliding with Bonnie, who yelps in surprise.

Before Michael realizes what's happening, Bonnie has fallen straight toward the open window, directly into the cranked-back grasp of a new crawling body. Her syringes fall uselessly to the floor.

He reaches for her, but it's too late.

The thing glares at Michael as it stabs at Bonnie's face in a series of livid, strobing bursts.

Both Rachel and Scott screech raggedly, a chorus of despair.

Michael sends a dart into the thing's gullet, and it bleats like a shocked animal, twisting away from Bonnie's slack face.

Oh Jesus.

Michael numbly reloads. All around him, the corpses are closing in.

"BONNIE!" Rachel screams.

"Keep firing!" Michael shouts, finding strength in a reserve that he's unaware he had.

He can't look at Bonnie's body, which twists and writhes like a ragdoll underneath the approach of further monstrosities. He half-sees Scott, emotion coughing out of him, pulling at Bonnie's body, dragging her out of the maelstrom.

Another one of the things – a lanky, hairy, nearly naked man – squeezes through the gap shoulders first, snarling, trampling over the struggling bodies, and a tranq dart suddenly appears at his shoulder. Michael didn't even hear the gun, doesn't know who sent it flying. The body slumps, jerking.

Gasps are turning to screams throughout the lobby, which seems to be shrinking to the size of a tiny dot, and Michael can't tell if it's the survivors making the sound or the increasing number of turned bodies, but he has no time to even consider it.

But darts continue to fly, syringes continue to be depressed, and as Michael's shocked gaze swirls in chaos, he sees all the survivors delivering their payloads. Ron and Kevin are tirelessly pummeling corpses flowing in from the north end of the library. Joel has taken one of the tranq rifles and is hurriedly shooting into a gap just north of the front doors. Michael catches only a glimpse of young Liam, now holding a syringe in his fist, stabbing it into the exposed heart of a wildly thrashing female, her long hair whipping. Even Kayla is leaping over newly humanized bodies, racing new tranq darts to Chloe and Chrissy. Through it all, the knot of the survivors is closing in, and Michael feels at the center of it all, stunned and yet filled with resolve.

Another body is trying to squeeze through at his window, pressing at the remaining glass, which spiderwebs almost wetly and bends out of the way. The body reveals itself to be that of a young girl, Girl Scout age, twisting through the gap, her sap-hardened hair molded to her small skull. Chloe is reloading, so Michael hurries his own dart prep, steps forward, and jabs at his trigger, but the girl is quick, her little arm snaking upwards and deflecting the barrel. The dart goes wide, clattering off the window. The girl is suddenly right at him, stabbing her head at his hand, and he feels it go tingly, partially numb.

"Fucking hell!" he yells, losing his balance.

And that gives the Girl Scout just enough time to fully squeeze her legs through the broken glass. She falls upon Michael as he stumbles backward. Another tranq dart ricochets harmlessly off the wall to the right of the window, and he hears Chloe curse.

"No!" Rachel shouts, suddenly there, kicking at the diminutive body.

"Stay at the window!" Michael yells, warding off the gasping head with the rifle, but he can't fully manipulate the trigger with his numb right hand. "God dammit!"

The piercing dead eyes are like lasers boring into him. The small head stabs at his neck, at his face, at his chest, and finally Rachel, screaming, makes solid contact with her foot at the girl's chest, sending the little body clattering across the floor. The body comes to a jarring stop against the display, then is back up in its crab stance, scrabbling back toward them.

Michael twists on the floor, feeling something wrong at the skin of his face, but he manages to switch hands with the rifle – just in time to send a dart at short range into the Girl Scout's upper arm. She goes sprawling beyond him, almost instantly braying in a very different voice, and collapsing on her back, the blue dart embedding further. She twists and screams and coughs, and her eyes fill with moisture, the pupils miraculously regaining human life. The girl blinks spasmodically, her mouth still wrenched open.

"Daddy, are you okay?!" Rachel's voice warbles at him. Her eyes are blasted with emotion.

In the corner of his vision, he sees Chloe fire a tranq dart at point-blank range into a body at the window.

There's shouting everywhere. Michael flops his head over on his buzzing neck, in time to see Ron firing at a window, and a body falls twitching to the library carpet. He hears screams from the north side of the lobby – more bodies retaining a semblance of human life.

Michael feels consciously on the brink of being overwhelmed by the situation. He kicks against the sensation, using the leverage of Rachel's arm to haul himself back up. His chest and neck are tingle and spasm, and when he brushes his arm past his cheek and nose, he feels an alarming disassociation with his own flesh. He feels a sick dizziness and nearly falls over again, and then quite abruptly he feels vomit erupting from his mouth.

The vomit is filled with blood.

He's done for.

In a flash of memory, he remembers home, he remembers Susanna peaceful and cold in death, he remembers his bloody nose …

Rachel staggers back, her hands to her mouth, and she sees something in his expression. She knows. She knows perhaps before he does.

"NOOOO!!" she cries.

At that moment, father and daughter share a glance at the center of hell.

In the space of perhaps a full second, everything in their shared life hangs in the humid air: every mistake, every joy, every laugh, every tear. The image of Rachel in his hands, tiny and fragile at the hospital, surges forward, pressing at his eyes – washing over him and through him. Holding his hand at the mall, giggling like crazy at some shared game at the arcade. Jumping into his lap at Christmas and hugging him hard. Twirling with him in the back yard under the evening sun, as Cassie watches from her chair on the porch. Eyeing him mischievously over a game of chess. Proudly sharing a graded essay. Crying with him, her head at his shoulder, at the hospital while Cassie lies dying. And yes, the yelling, the defiance. Waking to find her hefting that shotgun, there with him at the end. At the beginning.

And shrinking now to a tiny dot, behind all this, is his crime. His betrayals. He was never destined to survive this thing. His punishment was preordained.

Michael feels a peaceful warmth overtake him. He finds the courage to smile at his daughter one last time.

He bends to the INGRAM box, pulls out two full syringes, and rushes the window, climbing over the wildly twisting bodies. He thrusts his head into the gap, coughing and vomiting out whatever is inside him, spraying it into a claustrophobic chaos. He thrashes his whole upper body about, raging into the spindly, jumbled mass, feeling another rush of blood jet away from him. The bodies around him gasp and scatter. Bodies writhe beneath him, facing him in their thrust-back poses, and to these he delivers short stabs of blood, pumping bursts of it into every body he can reach, and the air fills with screams.

They squeal horridly around him, as his hands find their targets, stabbing, pumping, stabbing, pumping. They lunge and recoil, they gasp and screech, their dead eyes blinking, streaming, retaining agonized life as if reluctant to receive it. He climbs farther out, vomiting again, using his lips to fan out a fine mist, and the cries of tortured animals fill his ears. He buries the syringes in body after body, using them to creep forward now into the teeming mass, and finally they're emptied of blood. The bodies envelop him then, stabbing with their heads, and he vomits again, sending them screaming again.

The sky boils with an angry crimson, and as Michael stares upward, he feels he's at the eye of an alien tornado.

He doesn't know how long he's been angled out of the window, but it seems an eternity. He can feel his life literally rushing out of him, and the world begins to halt and stammer around him, like film jerking from its sprockets.

There are bodies everywhere. The sight astounds him.

But he can also see something else.

Even before an alien thunder rips open the sky, he can see fear.

He can see it in their expressions. The inexplicable, relentless anger in their collective faces, seeming just a moment ago to seethe and burn from behind their human features, is faltering into distress.

Fear.

CHAPTER 29

The sky bursts.

Michael feels himself falling to the ground as the bodies beneath him dissemble. He watches the sky shift and stutter. The alien thunder crashes upon him like an endless wave.

He can sense a multitude of bodies scrambling over him, shifting underneath him, away from the library, wounded, frightened, trembling under the din. Disorganized. Others – those struck by blood dart, and those stabbed with the syringes still in his hands – wail and twist on the ground, their noises obliterated under the roar.

The bodies climbing over him watch him warily with their flung-back gazes, their eyes flat and dark, their expressions intense. They stab at him still, tentatively, defensively, the energy of their inner light straining somehow. He can feel fear in the light, even as their radiation clutches at him.

Have I done this? Have I caused this fear?

Because it is definitely fear he senses.

And something else there.

An image, flickering in the viscera. He grasps at it, fumbling slowly. He can't focus.

His breath moves in and out of him raggedly. There's no pain. He can barely move his uncooperative, damaged limbs. Everything is muffled chaos in his peripheral vision.

He tries to form Rachel's name on his lips. He can't feel his mouth, although now a new torrent of blood comes gurgling up his throat, erupting out of him and pouring down the sides of his face. He coughs involuntarily, barely able to breathe in the aftermath. He feels impossibly weak.

More bodies shift past him, their breath like vinegar in his nostrils.

One of them stabs at his right ear, buffeting him, and the radiation feels like sharp cold.

The image again.

What is that?

His consciousness feels sluggish, and the question occurs to him one syllable at a time, stretching out to infinity.

At some point, he's aware that the sound from the sky has ended, but he can still hear only a deep, claustrophobic rumble, as if he's underwater.

To his right, he sees the great piles of bodies at the library's perimeter, a war zone of injured humans leading up to the blasted entrance and bruised and shattered windows. Framed in one of those windows, Mai is staring out at the retreating bodies, a tranq rifle still at her shoulder, a tentatively triumphant look on her pretty face.

There's another figure, a hunched figure at an adjacent window, glaring out at the departing bodies as they race onto the streets in all directions. A figure he doesn't recognize at first.

In a numb daze, focusing as best he can, Michael locks onto this figure, trying with his lethargic consciousness to read her expression. Bodies scurry away from her, like a breaking wave.

Felicia.

She's the one they're afraid of.

He sees it now.

He understands.

She's angled at an unnatural lurch in the broken-out window, but it's clear to Michael that she will not only live, not only survive, but make all the difference.

Then Rachel is in his line of vision – *Rachel!* – and she's screaming at him, tears in her eyes, splashing onto his face. She's grabbing his shoulders and pulling at him, and he can feel the movement of his body but can't make it work under his own power. She's wiping at his face, clearing it of blood.

"Daddy, no, please no, you can't go!"

He's aware of a body scurrying past her, and she gives it a furious kick. He catches fleeting glimpses of bodies retreating from the library, spidering away in random paths. They're no longer a collective mass. That thought, solid and reassuring, surges through him.

His blurred vision locks on his daughter, and he feels tears flood his eyes.

Rachel.

My little girl.

He knows she's going to be safe now. She's going to survive. A feeling of heat spreads through him. She's going to live on. He reaches up a trembling hand, finds her cheek. She grabs his hand, sobbing. Her sound warbles away, down a tunnel.

He should never have been surprised by her tenacity, by her bravery. Even here at the end. He knew that strength was inside her. It didn't come out of thin air. It didn't come from nowhere. It came from him. He instilled that in her.

Rachel is his daughter.

His flesh.

His blood.

"Please don't leave me, Daddy, please!"

The words are so far away.

"I love you, Daddy, I love you so much, please don't leave!"

Rachel is cupping his face with her trembling hands, turning it toward her, but he can't seem to focus on her. Now she's hugging him fiercely, but he can barely feel her. And Kayla is joining her, her little face anguished. The two young women appear in his dimming vision larger than life, hovering there as if they're the whole world.

Someone is pounding at his chest, trying to bring life back to him – Michael can feel it as if from a distance – but he knows it's too late. The faces move in a flurry.

He feels the warmth of Rachel's touch, trying to help him, even as his body relaxes into death.

He focuses on a final thought.

I saved you.

Acknowledgments

Back in 1998, with the help of Robert Devereaux and Darin Sanders, I started a small press called Dark Highway Press. We published a beautiful limited-edition hardcover of Robert's wonderfully naughty *Santa Steps Out*, and we achieved a small measure of industry acclaim. In 2000, bringing on Kirk Whitham, I edited/published the weird western anthology *Skull Full of Spurs*, to further positive recognition. Those were great times. It felt like the sky was the limit. But … then it was time to raise a family, and my little publishing house moved to the back burner.

Cut to 2014.

My first published novel, *Blood Red* (the first book in this trilogy), was accepted by Jacob Kier at Permuted Press, a small house devoted to apocalyptic horror. Definitely a highlight of my writing career. The lead-up to *Blood Red's* publication – and the debut – consisted of some of my proudest moments as a writer. Unfortunately, those great times were short-lived as well, and ultimately I dissolved my contracts with Permuted for *Draw Blood* and the concluding novel, *Blood Dawn*. One broken heart later, I realized that now, 15 years later, was the perfect opportunity to rev up Dark Highway Press again. Which is why you see that new logo on the spine.

This is an exciting, precarious time for the *Blood* trilogy. I feel as if my child has now left its nest, on shaky wings, still full of pride but a little unsteady. Trying to find its way in the world. It will need the support of family and friends and early fans to nudge it confidently into the open, and in that respect, this second book is already on its way toward a bright future.

Big thanks to my family, as always: to my first-reader wife Barb and my daughters, Harper and Sophie, who are my models for strong young women in this series. To my uber-supportive sister, Missy, who continues to be my most fervent cheerleader on the left coast. My mom, to whom this volume is affectionately dedicated, is proving to be my most effective salesperson and biggest fan. And again to my late father, John Bovberg, whose shadow falls long and proud over every word I write. Even the naughty words.

Huge shout-outs to James W. Powell and Kirk Whitham for help getting this book into shape. And to all my other early readers, Darin and Sally Sanders, Corey Edwards, Justin Bzdek, Alli Oswandel, Dawn Cyr, Bob Kretschman, Dan Kaufman, Lavon Peters, Jeff James, Mike Parish, and my tech advisor, Michael Dragone.

On the publishing side, thanks to Lisa Péré for her exceedingly sharp proofing skills, and to Christopher Nowell for the cover art and design. And finally, big thanks to the authors who took precious time from their own writing schedules to read these first two books and provide generous cover blurbs for *Draw Blood*: Jonathan Maberry, Joshua Gaylord, Grant Jerkins, Craig DiLouie, Robert Devereaux, David Dunwoody, and Robert Beveridge. You're all my heroes.

About the Author

Jason Bovberg is the author of *Blood Red*, the sequel *Draw Blood*, and the forthcoming concluding volume in the *Blood* trilogy, *Blood Dawn*. He is also the author of *The Naked Dame*, a pulp noir novel. He lives in Fort Collins, Colorado, with his wife Barb, his daughters Harper and Sophie, and his rabid canine, Cujo. You can find him online at www.jasonbovberg.com.